PENGUIN BOOKS

THE SEA LADY

'Truly wonderful . . . simply beautiful' *Daily Telegraph*

'Uplifting' *Psychologies*

'A potent tribute to lost dreams and harsh realities' *Independent*

'Oceanically ambitious' *Sunday Times*

'Demonstrates the considerable scope of Drabble's talent'
The Times Literary Supplement

'Excellent' *Harper's Bazaar*

By the same author

The Sea Lady

A Late Romance

MARGARET DRABBLE

PENGUIN BOOKS

PENGUIN BOOKS

Published by the Penguin Group
Penguin Books Ltd, 80 Strand, London WC2R 0RL, England
Penguin Group (USA) Inc., 375 Hudson Street, New York, New York 10014, USA
Penguin Group (Canada), 90 Eglinton Avenue East, Suite 700, Toronto, Ontario, Canada M4P 2Y3
(a division of Pearson Penguin Canada Inc.)
Penguin Ireland, 25 St Stephen's Green, Dublin 2, Ireland (a division of Penguin Books Ltd)
Penguin Group (Australia), 250 Camberwell Road, Camberwell, Victoria 3124, Australia
(a division of Pearson Australia Group Pty Ltd)
Penguin Books India Pvt Ltd, 11 Community Centre, Panchsheel Park, New Delhi – 110 017, India
Penguin Group (NZ), 67 Apollo Drive, Rosedale, North Shore 0632, New Zealand
(a division of Pearson New Zealand Ltd)
Penguin Books (South Africa) (Pty) Ltd, 24 Sturdee Avenue, Rosebank, Johannesburg 2196, South Africa

Penguin Books Ltd, Registered Offices: 80 Strand, London WC2R 0RL, England

www.penguin.com

First published by Fig Tree 2006
Published in Penguin Books 2007

1

Typeset by Palimpsest Book Production Limited, Grangemouth, Stirlingshire
Printed in England by Clays Ltd, St Ives plc

UK PAPERBACK
ISBN: 978-0-141-02745-6

OPEN MARKET EDITION
ISBN: 978-0-141-03303-7

You'll not forget these rocks and what I told you?
You'll not forget me – ever, ever, ever?

'Dialogue on the Headland'
Robert Graves

The Presentation

The winning book was about fish, and to present it, she appeared to have dressed herself as a mermaid, in silver sequinned scales. Her bodice was close-fitting, and the metallic skirt clung to her solid hips before it flared out below the knees, concealing what might once have been her tail. Her bared brown shoulders and womanly bosom rose powerfully, as she drew in her breath and gazed across the heads of the seated diners at the distant autocue. She gleamed and rippled with smooth muscle, like a fish. She was boldly dressed, for a woman in her sixties, but she came of a bold generation, and she seemed confident that the shadowy shoals of her cohort were gathered around her in massed support as she flaunted herself upon the podium. She felt the dominion. It pumped through her, filling her with the adrenalin of exposure. She was ready for her leap.

The silver dress must have been a happy accident, for until a few hours earlier in the day nobody knew which book had carried off the trophy. The five judges had met for their final deliberations over a sandwich lunch in a dark anachronistic wood-panelled room off an ill-lit nineteenth-century corridor. The result of their conclave was about to be announced. Most of the guests, including the authors, were as yet ignorant of the judges' choice.

Ailsa Kelman's wardrobe could hardly have been extensive enough to accommodate all six of the works upon the short-list, a list which included topics such as genetically modified crops, foetal sentience and eubacteria: subjects which did not easily suggest an elegant theme for a couturier. Would it be suspected that she, as chair of the judges for the shortlist, had favoured a winner to match her sequinned gown, and had pressed for its triumph? Surely not. For although she was derided in sections of the press as an ardent self-publicist, she was also known to be incorruptible. The sea-green, silvery, incorruptible Ailsa. And her fellow-judges were not of a calibre to submit to bullying or to manipulation.

The venue of the dinner might also shortly be observed to be something of a happy accident. The diners were seated at elegantly laid little round tables beneath a large grey-blue fibreglass model of a manta ray, which hung suspended above them like a primeval spaceship or an ultra-modern mass-people-carrier. They could look nervously up at its grey-white underbelly, at its wide wings, at its long whip-like tail, as though they were dining on the ocean floor. Like the costume of Ailsa Kelman, this matching of winner and venue could not have been planned. The museum was a suitable venue for a prize for a general science book with a vaguely defined ecological or environmental message, but the diners could as easily have been seated in some other hall of the huge yellow-and-blue-brick Victorian necropolis, surrounded by ferns or beetles or minerals or the poignant bones of dinosaurs. The dominant theme of fish had prevailed by chance.

The programme was going out live, and noses had been discreetly powdered, hair adjusted, and shreds of green salad picked from teeth. Now the assembly fell silent for Ailsa's declaration. Although the winner did not yet know the result, the cameramen and women did, and some of the more media-wise of the guests were able to read the imminent outcome from their disposition. Great sea snakes of thick cable twisted across the floor and under the tables, and thinner ropes of wire clambered up like strangling weeds on to the platform and connected themselves to microphones and control buttons. The technology was at once primitive and modern, cumbersome and smart. The platform on which Ailsa stood was temporary and precarious, and the fake grass matting that covered it concealed a hazardous crack.

Posture, Ailsa, posture, said Ailsa Kelman to herself, as she straightened her shoulders, drew in another deep breath, and, upon cue, began to speak. Her strong, hoarse and husky voice, magnified to a trembling and intimate timbre of vibration by the microphone, loudly addressed the gathering. The audience relaxed, in comfortable (if in some quarters condescending) familiarity: they knew where they were going when they were led onwards by this siren-speaker. They felt safe with her expertise. She took them alphabetically through the shortlist, travelling rapidly through the cosmos and the biosphere, sampling dangerous fruits, appraising the developing human embryo, interrogating the harmless yellow-beige dormouse, swimming with dwindling schools of cod and of herring, burrowing into the permafrost, and plunging down to the black smokers of the ocean floor. She summoned up bacteria and eubacteria and ancient filaments from the Archaean age, and presented her audience with the accelerating intersexuality of fish.

Behind her, around her, above her, in the wantonly and wastefully vast spaces of the Marine Hall, swam old-fashioned tubby three-dimensional life-size models of sharks and dolphins, like giant bath toys, and the more futurist magnified presences of plankton and barnacles and sea squirts and sea slugs. Ailsa Kelman shimmered and glittered as she approached her watery climax. And suddenly, all the foreplay of the foreshore was over: Ailsa Kelman declared that the intersexuality of fish had won! The hermaphrodite had triumphed!

Hermaphrodite: Sea Change and Sex Change was the winning title. The winning author was Professor Paul Burden, from the EuroBay Oceanographic Institute in Brittany and the University of California at San Diego.

Applause, applause, as a tall bearded marine biologist picked his way over the seabed of Marconi cables towards the platform to receive his cheque and present his weathered outdoor face to the bright unnatural lights. A television person conducted the applause, encouraging a crescendo, insisting on a diminuendo, attempting, not wholly successfully, to impose a silence. Some members of the captive audience were by now quite drunk, and, deprived of the false concentration of suspense, were growing restless.

The hermaphrodite had won!

'This is a brilliantly written survey of gender and sex in marine species . . . prefaced by a poetic evocation of a distant and placid asexual past . . . covering bold hypotheses about the evolutionary origins of sexual reproduction, followed by startling revelations about current female hormone levels, current male infertility, and rising sexual instability caused by POPs and other forms of chemical hazards . . .

Few were listening to the formal citation. However, because of the cameras and the controlling conductor, nobody could yet move. They had to sit and pretend to follow Ailsa Kelman's eulogy.

The jaws of sharks, fixed in the gape of their everlasting grins, displayed their triple rows of teeth above the diners.

Now the prize-winner was saying his few words. Oddly, he pronounced the main word of his title with an extra syllable, an unusual fifth syllable. 'Herm-Aphrodite,' he said, conjuring forth an intersexed Venus-Apollo from the waves, a goddess or a god of change. He spoke of intersexed males and females, of transitionals. '*When I was young,* he was saying, *hermaphrodites*

4

were more common in the invertebrate world. My first published paper
was on the life cycle of the marine shrimp . . .'

Ailsa Kelman stood on the platform, back straight, breathing evenly and listening hard. She smiled rigidly outwards and onwards as the marine biologist spoke. Professor Burden was speaking very well. He was a proper scientist, a hard scientist, but he was also a literary man, and keen to prove it. Now he had moved on to Ovid and his *Metamorphoses* and why they had become so fashionable at the beginning of the third millennium. He mentioned the nymph Salmacis and Hermaphrodite, joined together in one body in the fountain of life. The question of the mutability of gender which had so intrigued the ancients, he was saying, had now become a serious item on the very different agenda of evolutionary biology . . .

Ailsa found it hard to concentrate on the content of his speech, elevated and displayed to the public view as she was, as she so often was. But she tried. She was dutiful, in her fashion. She was a professional.

Public occasions enthralled Ailsa Kelman. She loved their special effects, their choreography, their managed glamour, their moments of panic, their humiliations, their heterogeneity, their ephemeral and cynical extravagance. She rose to these occasions and blossomed in the surf of them. She was in her element here.

The marine biologist mentioned the escalating incidence of uterine cannibalism in certain species. Fish siblings, it seems, increasingly tend to devour one another in the womb. The womb is a surprisingly dangerous environment, he was telling the obligatorily attentive diners.

Ailsa swept the cavern of the darkened room with the searchlight of her gaze, looking for predators and prey, for the faces she wished and feared to see. Her wicked brother

5

Tommy was not here tonight, although he would probably have been invited. He was invited to everything. He would be at the Guildhall, or at the palace, or at the embassy, tickling or devouring other fish. She could do with a drink now, having prudently abstained during dinner. Soon she would be handed briefly back to her place at table, where she could receive the thanks of the president and the sponsors, and retrieve her evening bag and her refilled glass, and set off to cruise the room.

Her evening bag was a sensuous little folly made of a kind of fine dull pewter-coloured chain mail. Its texture of soft silky metallic links was a joy to her fingers. It was a fetish bag. She had bought it in Scarborough, and she had owned it for thirty-odd years. She had never possessed a dress that became it as well as the dress she wore this night. Her little bag was a comfort to her, in her peacefully celibate late incarnation.

Would she dare to wear her mermaid dress at the dinner near the northern borders after the degree ceremony at the end of the week? Or was it too metropolitan?

This was the summer season of prizes and of honours.

The television programme director was making frantic circular wind-down gestures at the marine biologist. The biologist was paying no attention to them, carried away as he was by his brief victory and by his important message about the shifting sands of sex. The director started to signal for assistance to Ailsa Kelman: they had to be off air in a minute and they urgently needed an exit line. Ailsa, seasoned though she was to such small presentational crises, was not quite sure how best to intervene. She had admired the book, and did not want to offend its large lean penguin-suited author. She did not wish to show him disrespect. But a camera lens was zooming in upon her glowing face, and she found herself brutally interrupting him by saying, 'And so, goodbye to you all from the Marine Hall and the Plunkett Prize ceremony, and our congratulations, once more, to the winner, Professor Paul Burden. Remember that fish are not always what they seem!'

A more meaningless sentence have I never uttered, said Ailsa Kelman to herself as the director cued applause, as the cameras panned out to the pillars, as the silenced marine biologist bowed a little ironically beneath the looming belly of the manta ray, as jewelled and wrinkled and spotted and eager young white hands reached for wine bottles, as talk and laughter began to spread and splutter and wash from table to table. It was over, it was done, and now she could get down, carefully avoiding the dangerous creek in the rostrum, to join the fray. It could have been worse, it could have been far worse. The sponsors could not complain. She had worked hard, and earned her fee.

Circling the room, glass in hand and little metal lucky bag dangling from her shoulder, she spoke to friends and foes in short bursts, moving on in mid-sentence, her eyes restlessly darting around the further reaches of the murky cavern. The face that she most keenly sought and avoided and hoped and feared to see was not here. He had not come, although this might be thought to be his natural habitat. It had not occurred to her, when she first took on this job so many months ago, that it might precipitate a meeting with him, after so much time, after so many years passed. But then she had begun to think he might be here after all, and that a confrontation might be even more imminent than she had more recently anticipated. Had he stayed away this night because of her? Did he think of her as often, as punishingly, as painfully, as she thought of him? Was he too perplexed by what had passed? Or had the heavy years silted over the memories of damage and distress and buried them beyond pain and beyond recall?

Fossilized, petrified, mummified, oxidized, mineralized, entombed.

Had he forgotten that he ever knew her? No, that could not be.

She had made sure of that.

She had not seen him in the flesh for decades. She had seen his photograph, as he must have seen hers, but they had not met. He had moved in different circles, and he had taken care to avoid her, as she had taken care to avoid him. They were both public figures, but their glittering spheres had been separate, discrete and crystalline.

But at times, over recent months, she had felt that they must be coming together, like the iceberg and the *Titanic*. She had suffered, for a good year now, a superstitious sense of <u>convergence</u>. This week, next week, sometime . . . Perhaps she had taken on this science book business *in order* to meet him again, and now was disappointed that he was not here. (This had been put to her as a possibility by the only other person who knew the whole hidden story: her confessor, her confidante, her lady from Rio.) It was time. It was time to face him again. But he was not here. He should have been here. He was a Fellow of the Society, and he had worked for many years with fish, but he was not here. She would have to wait for a reunion.

But she would not have to wait for long. Although this night had failed as a rehearsal, the catastrophic event was at last imminent. He too, wherever he was this night, must by now surely know that they were about to meet again. He had sent Paul Burden to her as his <u>herald,</u> as his <u>harbinger</u>, to warn her. Do all marine biologists know one another? How large was the pool in which they swam, the big fishes of the underwater trade?

Although he was well tanned, Paul Burden was not much of a diver. He was more of a laboratory man. Diving was out of fashion. Making that kind of a splash was out of fashion. It was all DNA and genes and chromosomes and microbiology and eubacteria these days. Or so all those books had taught her.

The lofty space had seemed at first even murkier when the harsh glare of the television lights was dimmed, but now her eyes and her expectations had adjusted, and she surged on cheerfully, consigning her sense of his absence to the lower depths of consciousness. She enjoyed these public post-prandial promenades, she enjoyed the attention, she enjoyed the slinky rub of her skirt on her firm thighs. Her feet were divinely comfortable in their little flat gold net slippers. In earlier days, at such events, she had vainly walked on high heels, on high knife heels, like Hans Andersen's poor Little Mermaid, but now she knew better.

She had all at her command. She liked the random, promiscuous mingling, the screeches of false laughter, the dull murmur of platitude, the conviviality of strangers, the sparkle of bracelet and necklace, the clean flicker and colour and sheen of the female fabric, the dull heated faint nicotine odour of the male. She spoke briefly to congratulate Paul Burden, she spoke to the woman from Bristol who had written about extremophiles and black smokers, and she paused to compare notes with fellow-judge and distinguished gravel-voiced physiologist Professor Hilary Gravely, who was still uncompromisingly clothed in the workmanlike grey suit she had worn for the sandwich lunch, and whose feet were comfortably and conspicuously encased in brand-new white and pale blue Nike trainers. (She suffered, as she had told Ailsa over one of the judges' meetings, from bunions.) Ailsa was cornered by a radio interviewer, she produced a sound bite for a journalist, she presented her cheek to a one-time publisher. She kept moving.

Most greeted her with a flattering friendliness, pleased to share her ephemeral circle of light, although one elderly gentleman went out of his way to accost her to tell her that the first three chapters of the prize-winning book were what he said 'could only be described as metaphysical tosh'. It was not clear whether he was an old buffer or a Nobel Prize-winner or both, but she listened, then smiled, then moved on. He no doubt thought she was a celebrity simpleton: why bother to protest and try to prove otherwise? She seemed to have learned, at last, to be less confrontational. It had been a hard lesson, but she hoped she had learned it. She was appeased by a more flattering brief encounter with an old flame, with whom she had once, decades ago, shared for a couple of nights an improbable bed in Adelaide: they greeted each other with cries of public delight, and he complimented her upon her speech.

'Was that wonderful phrase about the placid asexual past from you or from Burden's book?' he wanted to know, as he stared intrusively, with the claims of an old intimacy, right into her eyes.

The whites of his slightly protuberant brown eyes were jaundiced, and his polished forehead looked steep and bleak and confrontational beneath his streaked receding hair.

'I think it was me,' said Ailsa. 'But it could have been him.'

'Does he tell you, in his book, when sexual reproduction began?'

'Nineteen sixty-three?' guessed Ailsa.

'No, no, that was sexual intercourse. Sexual reproduction began in the Precambrian. Or the Silurian or the Devonian. Or some place and time like that. Didn't he tell you?'

'If he did, I've forgotten. There was a lot to digest.'

'And now it's back to parthenogenesis and asexual reproduction. The sexual imperative is over. Pity, in a way.'

'It lasted our time,' said Ailsa.

'It certainly did,' said the old flame, with a smirk of conspiratorial gallantry.

'Brave days,' said Ailsa, distracted by thoughts of her only daughter Marina, both of whose children were the offspring of sperm donors.

'But now we have Viagra,' he said, 'to keep placidity and asexuality at bay.'

'We're probably better off with the placid asexual future,' said Ailsa.

He agreed, too promptly.

'Yes,' he said, 'sex causes nothing but distress. We're better off without it.'

'You conceded that very quickly,' said Ailsa.

'What else should I do?' he challenged.

'I was in love with a marine biologist once,' said Ailsa impulsively.

She continued, rashly, 'I was madly in love.'

'Was that before or after our little fling in Adelaide?' asked her ageing and extinguished suitor.

'Oh, long, long before. In the Precambrian, or the Silurian.'

'Was he as handsome as Paul Burden?'

'Of course.'

'You're looking very well yourself,' he said.

She stared at him appraisingly, in a detailed manner that implicated his vain attempt to disguise his thinning hair.

'Women last longer than they used to,' she said. 'They're full of preservatives.'

'So are we all,' he said: but he had lost her, and she was once more on her way.

After a rolling tour of the tables she came to rest for a moment of refuge by a grouping of sea squirts set into a solid glassy display panel. The sea squirts (creatures labelled as *Stolonica socialis* and *Polycarpa pomaria*, of the Ascidian class) were tastefully placed against a frozen flowering bouquet of seaweed fronds of coral-pink and lettuce-green. A caption read, confusingly, that 'these solitary sea squirts often occur in dense aggregations'. Ailsa took this apparent paradox in, instantly, but knew she did not have time to worry about it now. She filed it, and moved on.

The coral reefs were absorbing carbon dioxide at an alarming rate, the book on neurology and environmental pollution had argued. Or was it Paul Burden who had said that? She had read so many books on so many unfamiliar subjects in the past months that they had all merged and converged in her memory. Her brain was too full.

But she did not fail to recognize troublemaker P. B. Wilton, the poison pen of the quality press, with his tight smooth pale-fleshed face and his high-set narrow eyes and his pale thin sandy eyebrows, who now advanced upon her refuge. She had known Phoebe, as he was known to his many enemies, for years. Had he had a face lift? If he were a woman, one would guess so. Or was it the tautness of malice, the perpetual strain of maintained mischief that so distorted his childlike ageing features? His skin seemed darker than usual, it had a hard pinkish finish, as though he had been on holiday in the sun, but the veneer was only skin deep. Beneath the burnish, he was a pale man still, an indoor man of obsequious spite. He had blood on his conscience, if not on his hands. He was a wanton killer. Broken marriages, ruined reputations, even a putative suicide or two had been laid to his charge.

Poor Effie Fitzroy, she'd jumped off the roof of a multistorey car park.

P. B. had taken a stab or two at Ailsa, but unlike some of his victims, she had warded off his attacks.

You wouldn't catch Ailsa jumping off a roof. She'd been near the edge, but she hadn't jumped.

P. B. greeted her as an old friend, as an accomplice.

'Ailsa, treasure,' he said floridly, advancing to brush his face against her cheek.

'Peter,' said Ailsa, inclining, but avoiding his touch.

'A triumph,' said P. B.

'So,' said P. B., 'this was a bold move on your part.'

'What was?' asked Ailsa, with instant suspicion.

'Reading all those books. Did you understand any of them?'

'Of course.'

'*I* haven't read any of them, of course. I know my limitations.'

'I didn't understand them all, but I understood enough.'

'Enough to make a judgement?'

'Yes, enough to make a judgement.'

They stared at each other, old adversaries, old rivals, both of them long-term inhabitants and survivors of the killing pool of the media. They knew each other's weaknesses, each other's strengths. P. B. knew that Ailsa Kelman could not resist any publicity, any exposure, however hostile. You trailed the bait, and she came snapping. She courted attacks, taunts, embarrassments, for the sake of the product, which in his view was the product of herself. She needed notice. She needed attention. She would never be satisfied. Indifference was death to her. Celebrity was the breath of life to her. She had invented herself, and reinvented herself, and reinvented herself yet again. Showgirl, academic, trophy wife, media star, media whore, and, in sum, a clever, clever girl.

So he placed her, so he judged her, so he attempted to dismiss her.

And he, what was he? Ambiguous, slippery, inconstant, treacherous, witty, poisonous, ingratiating, unmotivated. It was not clear to Ailsa that he was homosexual, as he was now generally supposed to be. He had had a wife at some point, it was rumoured, and now he had no known partner. If he was gay, he hadn't come out. If he was straight, he hadn't come out. A bisexual, hermaphrodite, neuter, androgynous, dissimulating covert heterosexual. A man of unmotivated malignity.

Neither fish, flesh nor fowl.

So she saw him.

'So what next? What else?' asked Peter Wilton, in that harmless, sincere, companionable, curious way of his that had elicited so much indiscreet and interesting gossip from her and from others in the past.

'Any journeys, any adventures, any holidays planned?' he pressed. 'Where are you spending the summer? Your daughter Marina says you're not a very good granny. I saw her the other day, going in to do her shift at Burlington House as I was going into the RA. Did you see the Soutine? Ghastly, ghastly. She says that her girlfriend's mother is much more reliable as a babysitter. She says that even the sperm donor sometimes babysits.'

His hard unnaturally polished skin gleamed with an almost phosphorescent glow. There was no sign of wrinkles, of the natural forgiving fullness of age. She could see him, in a sudden perception, as an embryo, as a baby, as a neonate. She could see him as though reverted to a small child, with its innocent apprehension, its trusting vulnerability. Did he apply lubricants and ointments each night to preserve and polish this unpleasingly tight texture?

She did not welcome these mean-spirited reflections, and she tried to shake them off. If women can fill themselves with preservatives, why shouldn't men?

She did not believe that the sperm donor babysat, but if he did, it was good of him. She had the grace to think this thought, in passing, but she did not deliver it as a hostage to

P. B. Wilton. She did not know who the sperm donor was. Her daughter Marina did not tell her mother everything. Marina kept her secrets. Ailsa did not like to think that she told these secrets to P. B. Wilton.

She stared at her old friend Peter. They had known each other for thirty years. How had they become their savage selves? It was a mystery. They had mutated. They had evolved into hard-jawed monsters of the deep, sexless, battle-scarred, smooth with defensive plating, enclosed in ageless shell.

'In a couple of days,' she said, throwing him a sprat, 'I'm going up north to get an honorary degree, at the University of Ornemouth. That's the next excitement.'

'Congratulations,' said P. B., opening his lashless eyes mockingly. He hesitated, and then he continued, with carefully offensive timing, 'Whatever for?'

One had to laugh, and so she did.

'Do you mean why am I going, or do you mean why am I getting the honorary degree?'

'Whichever. Both.'

'I'm going because we used to spend our summer holidays near there, and the degree is for my contributions to culture.'

'Culture?'

He let the word float questioningly in the air between them. A little sadly, it floated: waterlogged, submerging, a small paper boat too fragile to carry any cargo.

'Culture,' she repeated.

'There's a word,' he said, with a sigh that might have been of nostalgia.

'Yes,' said Ailsa.

'There *was* a word,' he said. His tone was ambiguous, as usual, but it bore a taint or tinge of respect or regret.

'Yes,' she repeated.

He rallied.

'But surely it's a very *nouveau* little university? And a tin-pot little place? I'm not sure if it deserves you. It's not worthy of you. You are an Edinburgh-educated girl, aren't you? Or was it the University of Sussex that you graced? You've got some kind of a Sussex connection, haven't you? Didn't you spend a year digging around in the archives in Falmer?'

'Ornemouth is a very beautiful place,' said Ailsa reprovingly, her voice modulating into its let's-be-serious-for-a-moment mode. 'It's a historic city. With a bell tower, and all that kind of thing. Cobbles and ramparts and salt baths and an estuary and an esplanade. There's nothing tin-pot about it.'

'*Is* it a city?'

'The queen turned it into a city two years ago. She elevated it. It wasn't a city then, when I knew it, but it is now.'

'So you are being honoured as a local girl made good?'

'I shall be pleased to see it again. I haven't been up there for years. It's a beautiful coastline. It's very unspoilt.'

A flicker of incipient boredom and dismissal moved over his face like a high thin floating cirrus cloud. His concentration span, like his weekly column, was short. He did not want to be told dull and harmless stories about unspoilt seaside resorts and Ailsa Kelman's girlhood. They were no use to him. He was about to drift away, looking for stronger meat, when he thought of a new tack.

'Did you holiday there with your brother Tommy? Did you play together like Eustace and Hilda? Was it Shrimp and Anemone territory?'

'How did you guess?'

One should not underestimate Peter. He was very clever, and he had read a lot of books, although he spent so much of his time trying to pretend that he had not.

She held out her glass to a passing waiter for a refill, and continued riskily, teasingly, 'Except that Tommy was older than me, and nastier. He bullied me, I didn't bully him. In *The Shrimp and the Anemone*, it's the other way round. Big sister bullies little brother. It wasn't like that with us. Tommy was horrid to me, most of the time. He still is. If we had been twins, he would have devoured me in the womb. Like those uterine cannibals that Paul Burden has just described.'

P. B. considered this.

She had sailed into dangerous waters.

Thin ice, near the wind, perilous reefs.

'How did he bully you?'

'Once he tied me to the hook behind the waterfall in the cave and said he was going to leave me there till the tide came in and drowned me.'

'Like Andromeda?'

'Not really. There wasn't a dragon. It was just the tide. And I was rescued by this other boy. It was part of the game. We were only children. It was more Enid Blyton than Perseus and Andromeda, really. I used to love Enid Blyton.'

'And how is Tommy? Is he getting an honorary degree too?'

'I trust not. Not this year, anyway.'

'I don't suppose there will be many photo opportunities in Ornemouth? Or scandals? Or stories?'

Ailsa seemed to hesitate, as though on the brink of an indiscretion, but contented herself with, 'Oh, I'm sure shocking things could happen, even in Ornemouth. Mary McTaggart is going to sing for us. Do you know Dame Mary?'

'Of course,' said P. B., who claimed to know everybody who was anybody.

'She's lost weight,' he continued, after a pause, in a modulated tone, of not patently insincere regret.

'I've met her,' said Ailsa with a degree of caution, 'and I've heard her, but I can't say I know her. Do you know her well?'

'Not *very* well,' said P. B., this time with a note of such uneasy and uncharacteristic disavowal that Ailsa swerved away.

Dame Mary was not a liability, was she? Nor had P. B. implied that she was. She sensed that P. B. could have scored there, with some insider knowledge, but had chosen not to do so. P. B. seemed almost protective about Dame Mary: she could not think why. Chivalry was hardly in his line.

Would Ornemouth prove to be a mistake on every level?

'You've already been on holiday,' accused Ailsa. 'You look quite brown. Somebody told me you were in France with the Beckmans. Was it nice? Was it very grand? Was it a chateau? Did it have turrets?'

'So Tommy bullied you by the seaside,' pursued Peter Wilton evasively. 'I can't see you putting up with being bullied. I bet you got your own back. I bet you were a proper little tyke.'

She noted this interesting and unexpected dialect word, chosen perhaps for what he might wrongly have thought to be its local flavour, but continued, undeterred, 'It wasn't quite like that.'

'What was it like?'

'Ah,' said Ailsa Kelman. 'If only I could remember. That's really why I'm going back. To see if I can remember. To try to find out what happened, so very long ago.'

At midnight, or thereabouts, Ailsa Kelman shed both her sex and her species. She drew her dark red bedroom curtains, and hung her silvery dress in the closet, and unhooked her white boned armour from her full soft breasts, and gave a last caress to her loving little pewter purse, and combed her thick short crop of stylishly ashen hair before the oval mirror.

When she climbed into her bed, she ceased to be a woman. She swam back, through the metamorphoses of time, to the undecided embryo in the amniotic sac. This was a technique she had been taught by the lady from Rio. Under self-hypnosis, the bones dissolve, the flesh melts away, the body dwindles, and the past liquefies. She travelled back, through the ridged red tunnels, to the dark sustaining waters of the womb, where she floated, unmade, unformed, uncommitted, forgiven, and free.

She hopes she may learn to swim freely once again, in the three dimensions she was born for, not live as if trapped in a flat and frozen plane of glass. It is possible, it can be done. We can go back to the source, if we can find the true source, and immerse and suspend ourselves in it. It is the source, it is the fountain, but how may we find it again, after so many temptations and compromises, after so many wrong turnings and mistakes?

When she was a child, she had read about the hermit crab. The boy had shown her a book of seaside wonders, one memorable afternoon, and later he had shown her hermit crabs upon the shore. The hermit crab changes its abode, when it grows too large for its borrowed lodging. The lobster sheds its shell. During the period of homelessness, the soft-bodied creatures are tender and vulnerable. They hide away, until their defences grow once more. In Paul Burden's book she had learned, to her astonishment, that some of the creatures of the sea are ageless, in their endless cycle of self-renewal. It is almost impossible, even with the new technologies of modern microbiology, to tell the precise age of some of the creatures of the sea. Time leaves no marks upon them, they evade our human knowledge. They are dateless, and therefore they are free.

She had also learned that it is fanciful to suppose that the sexuality of the embryo is undecided. The fertilized egg knows its sexual destiny at inception, and long before its ensoulment.

But it may change its destiny later in life, according to Paul Burden's book. A fish may change, so why not men and women? Sex is no longer destiny, as once it was.

The book on foetal sentience had been disturbing. Ailsa had once been involved in a foetus scandal. She had worn a plasticated foetus on a chain around her neck. It had been in a good cause, but she had long repented of this foolish act of bravado. As a publicity stunt, it had been all too successful. She had never been allowed to forget it. It hadn't been her own foetus, from her own womb, but she had lied about it, and defiantly claimed it as her own.

A sac of water, a drop of brine, a curved teardrop, a cell with a permeable membrane, a glass embryo. Her mind and her dreams are full of the imagery of all the books she has been reading. The images of the laboratory have penetrated her soul. She looks to them for a new ensoulment.

She drifts into sleep, and dreams. Dreams come to her generously, offering her their forgiveness, their vast possibilities. Her dream creates the image of a drop of water. Her dream creates the point of a needle, pressing tenderly, insistently, against the delicate sphere of the soft egg of the teardrop. The needle of memory prods and attempts to pierce; it is about to penetrate. Will it suck out the heart of the egg, or is it about to implant other cells and other memories within the egg? The cell is a teardrop, convex, vulnerable, with a thin surface that can barely hold its shape. But it holds.

Prince Rupert's tears of hard yet brittle glass.

Prince Rupert's tears, St Cuthbert's beads.

In her sleep, she feels the hot tears grow and well and swell. The divisions between the cell walls dissolve. The impenetrable will become permeable. The glass will melt without shattering. Something will dissolve, something will merge. She is unborn, and free to begin again.

She will wake with salt tears in her eyes, thinking of her imminent journey back to the beautiful city by the northern sea. For a moment, as she wakes, this deep knowledge will be with her.

The knowledge of the depths will be with her when she wakes, but then it will be lost with the light of the morning. And then she will rise, and leave behind the whispering shell of the pool of the night, and resume her sex and species, and become once more her busy selfish self. She will prepare for the journey.

The silver dress, the hired robe, the scarlet hood, the green silk, the bell tower, the summer season.

Old Man Travelling

He too after a manner was now travelling backwards. He was sitting in his window seat, in G16, in the mobile phone-free compartment, and although he was looking forwards, facing the direction of travel, he was travelling backwards in time as he journeyed north to his childhood. He was, inevitably, thinking of the past, and wondering whether he had been wise to embark on this journey, to accept this invitation. It had seemed innocent, at the time. It could not have been intended to cause distress. He could not have suspected a hidden hook.

He was old enough to remember that this was the route of the train that was proudly called the *Flying Scotsman*, and that this line, when he was a boy, had been known by its initials as the 'LNER'. His mother and his aunt had often muttered those monosyllables. The 'London North Eastern Region': that was what those large separate mantric letters had signified, although he had known the letters by heart long before he had known their meaning.

The trains of his boyhood had been driven by steam. They had grunted and snorted and hissed and hooted like living beasts. They had frightened him, although he had tried not to show his fear. He had stepped backwards on the platform, involuntarily, as they approached. They had made him flinch. Now all that boiling power had been tamed and calmed by diesel or electricity, and the names of the companies that ran the trains had changed so often in recent years that he no longer knew who was in practice and in law responsible for his safe transit. Nationalization had been followed by privatization, and privatization by various hybrid forms of ownership, and now it seemed that some form of nationalization was proposed once more. He did not envy those who ran or tried to run the railways. He did not envy the Minister of Transport. Running the laboratory and organizing the marine research unit and setting up its public interface had been enough and at times too much for him. The money men had got him down. They had <u>worsted</u> him.

The train, gathering speed as it travelled northwards from King's Cross, trembled and shuddered slightly on its track. There had been accidents of late.

He had studied the new Emergency Procedure pamphlet, with its icons representing an External Door, a Disabled Call for Aid, a Window Hammer, an Emergency Ladder, a Fire Blanket and a Light Stick. He had been too lazy and too fatalistic to attempt to locate any of these objects. The <u>icons</u> and the names would suffice. /sə'fais/   /ˈaikən/

He sat back, and tried to calm the agitation that was troubling him.

The approach to King's Cross had been unsettling. The neighbourhood was a building site of concrete slabs and abandoned traffic cones and soaring cranes and drunkenly leaning traffic lights stuck casually into sand-bagged oilcans. The taxi driver had dropped him off on the gridlocked north side of the Euston Road, just outside the calm forecourt of the British Library, and he had made his way with his wheeled suitcase past St Pancras along a much distressed pavement, and eventually down through what was clearly a temporary underpass to the mainline station. Above ground, the road heaved and buckled and bent on makeshift struts and ramps, and below ground, dead-end tunnels and contradictory signs and ramshackle Dickensian wooden steps and blocked entrances offered a vision of <u>indecipherable</u> confusion. Loudly inaudible announcements had tried to direct and to redirect the struggling mass of baffled short-distance commuters and burdened long-distance travellers. He was instructed not to leave his luggage unattended, and informed that there was a signal failure at Baker Street, and delays on the Piccadilly Line because of a person on the track at Arnos Grove.

The train was a refuge. He preferred the train to the aeroplane. Trains were soothing and rhythmic, they lulled and they rocked on a journey of regression.

His seat had been waiting for him. Mrs Hornby had fixed it all for him, with her usual competence. She had prepared an information pack for him, with details about his accommodation, his hosts, the timing of events. She had established, well in advance, his dietary requirements. (These days, he preferred when possible to avoid both fish and meat.) She had provided him with a map of the town, now a city, and marked the location of his hotel on the once familiar seafront. She had measured his head, with some mirth, and ordered his ceremonial robes.

He was a lucky man, to be so carefully minded. He had led, of recent years, a protected life. He had retreated into his shell. So why had he taken what might be considered a risk?

He had been free to decline this invitation, or so it had seemed. It had arrived last October. It was now July. His first impulse had been to refuse. These days, he declined many of the requests that came his way. Some asked too much of him, some too little, and he was suspicious of them all. But this letter, open on his desk, with Mrs Hornby's neutral query pencilled in the top right-hand corner, had made him hesitate. Indecisively, he had let it lie, which was against his custom. It had lingered on, presenting its flattering phrases and its courteous appeal. He could think of no elegant way of refusing the honour that was offered to him, and the more time passed, the harder it became to find an appropriate excuse. After a suitable period of delay, Mrs Hornby appeared discreetly at his elbow to prompt him. Should she draft a reply, she asked him, in that carefully neutral tone that made no assumptions about the nature of that reply. No, he had said, he should write this one himself.

When she had left the room, he forced himself to pick up the innocently threatening document. The paper was of a thick rich cream weave, with a wavy line like a watermark in it, and the handsome crest and dour motto were heavily embossed in a deep oxblood-red. The text was laser-printed, but the large signature was handwritten with a flourish in bright blue ink, an ink which declared its authenticity. The date proposed for the ceremony was then several months away.

Beneath the bell tower, robed in scarlet and bottle-green and black. In July, on the north-east coast, overlooking the North Sea.

Hic labor, hoc opus est.

As he looked at the date, and at the crest with its leaping salmon, an alarming wave of longing had risen in him. Suddenly, he longed to go back. The curves of the three bridges and the sublimely repeating arches of the viaduct appeared before him with hallucinatory clarity. He was not aware that he had consciously thought of them for years. Too much troubled water had flowed beneath those bridges, too many decades of his life. But back they came now, the majestic arches, the long summer nights, the thin high blue of the sky, the town of slate and sandstone, the great estuary. He sat there, at his desk in London, on a dark, enclosed late-October day, and saw the heavenly light flooding the enormous plain of salt water. He ached with desire. His throat felt swollen with desire and grief. As he watched the composite image of his memory, a perfect rainbow began to rise irresistibly above it, and superimpose itself upon the childhood scene. The rainbow echoed the curve of the Old Bridge over the river.

A spectacular, a holy landscape.

A mirage, a delusion.

As though one could get back, behind the back of time, behind the heavy leather curtain, behind the thick membrane, to the place before time was, to the innocent soul.

Sitting on the train, months later, in July, travelling northwards, he tried to swallow. His mouth was dry, and the glands in his neck felt tender. Perhaps he was harbouring a cold. Or was this nostalgia? If so, he admonished himself, it was unwarranted, for his connections with this place towards which he journeyed were tangential, insubstantial. As a small child he had lived there, intensely, in a few years of war and end-of-wartime exile, but it was neither his birthplace nor his natural home, and he had not kept up with what might have been his contacts. Those whom he had known there, most of them, had also moved away. Some who had not moved had died. He had never been back. He had perhaps almost gone so far as to avoid going back. So why, now, did the memory of it sweep through him like a sickness? Was this yet another manifestation of the sentimentality of encroaching age?

His eyes filled with water more easily these days.

Not many animals weep.

He wanted, once more, to see the bridges and the arches and the viaduct and the sea. He wanted to see the northern light of Ornemouth and of Finsterness.

Dolerite and whinstone, dolerite and whinstone. Granite and sandstone, granite and sandstone.

The Great Whin Sill.

A black ledge of rock, a bedrock of memory.

He had waited one more day before he sent his acceptance.

During that day, the strange yearning kept flowing and swelling towards him, from a distant source. That night, he dreamed of the bell tower. He dreamed that he was climbing up, towards the belfry, on a crumbling and ever-extending and ever-steepening and ever-narrowing spiral stone staircase. He woke before he reached the summit.

In the morning, he had written in his own firm hand to thank the Vice Chancellor for her generous offer, and to say that he would be honoured and delighted to accept. He looked forward greatly, he had said, to revisiting the town, and to meeting the Vice Chancellor.

He had no idea who the Vice Chancellor was. The name and the credentials meant nothing to him. He meant to look the Vice Chancellor up in *Who's Who*, but had forgotten to do so. The Vice Chancellor was a woman, and she was Vice Chancellor of a new-fangled, jumped-up institution. It was a recent foundation in an ancient and historic border borough. In his boyhood, this university had not been born. There had been an ancient Grammar School, and a few secondary schools, and a teachers' training college, and a small marine biology institute attached in some administratively problematic manner to the University of St Andrews over the border. And several infants' schools, including the one on the north bank of the river where his aunt had taught, where he had been for a while her pupil. But there had been no university. The university had been part of the great expansion of higher education in the 1960s, following the Robbins Report of 1963. It was much welcomed. The location was hailed as ideal.

Its Department of Marine Biology would be, it proclaimed, world-class.

The new university, to judge by its notepaper and its motto, had gone in for an old model. It had gone for the archaic hocus pocus of honorary degrees and anthems and crests and

Latin mottoes and arcane appointments and instant traditions, to shore up its rawness, to shelter it from the bleak wind howling over the dark sea.

He had hesitated, but then he had accepted. The place itself had called to him. It had not let him rest.

And so the months had passed, and July had come, and here he was, on his way to the north.

One evening last year Mrs Hornby had had to squeeze him into the collar of his starched hired white-tie outfit: they occasionally referred to this intimate moment of mutual horror and hilarity. Her fingers had pressed against his windpipe. The collar had seemed to be half a size too small, although it was the size that he had worn without too much discomfort two years before. This was the closest they had ever been to each other. These days, he avoided any form of physical proximity. He did not like to be touched.

He gazed at the smeared window of the compartment, and at the passing landscape. He could choose to stay his eye on the glass pane of the train window, and to see the reflection of his own good-looking, pleasant, good-humoured, generous face. Or he could look through the pane to watch the familiar fields and canals and scruffy skewbald ponies of England as they travelled past him. Is there another world, beyond the mirrored self, and beyond the visible world beyond the self? He had once imagined that there might be. He had believed it might be there perpetually.

The glass ceiling, the glass wall of the aquarium. He had once studied the optics of fish.

One could spend one of many lifetimes studying the optics of fish. Happily studying the optics of fish. Or the limbs of lobsters. Or the spawning of lampreys. Or the sex changes of wrasse. Or the cleaning symbioses of sharks.

Some species are not aware of the glass. Some of them

nose against the glass. Some of them attach themselves to the glass, with grey lips and sucking mouths. They suck and suck, for safety, for attachment, maybe for pleasure. It is in their nature to attach themselves to the glass.

But others dash themselves against the glass. It is in their nature to do that.

What if there were to be a way out, even now? He is not a brave man, but neither is he a man to surrender without an effort, to go under without a struggle. Perhaps even now he can hack his way out of his imprisoning self with a stick or a hammer or an axe? One last heroic gesture, and, like a character in a thriller, he could be free. One more _ingenious_ thought, one more divining leap, and he could free himself, and climb out of the wreckage. A new beginning, a new endeavour, a new element. Forgiveness, _remission,_ a new dimension. It cannot be that one is stuck for ever in the _mire_ and the _silt_ of all that one has ever been. It cannot be.

And yet the dull nose rubs, the blunt wall snubs.

A man must choose. It is necessary to choose. The road narrows, the choices diminish. One presses one's ugly nose against the glass. There is no longer any way through, there is no way out, there is no way back. Time has solidified. What had once seemed fluid has become resistant. It is not yet opaque, but it may soon become so. The cataract may form, the vision may turn to milk. Choices made long ago will blind him. His eyes grow thick as milk and dim as horn.

The fish nudge and nose against the invisible wall. They circle and they cruise. The water of time lacks oxygen. It grows murky, it dims and thickens, it fills with particles of dead and decomposing matter, it suffocates.

Two newspapers lay unread on the table before him: one he had purchased at the station, the other was the complimentary copy provided by the _rail company._ They would be full of things he did not need to know and things he did not want to know. There would be names that he preferred to avoid, photographs of faces that he preferred to avoid. Sometimes, when Mrs Hornby arrived early, she discreetly removed items from the newspapers before offering them to him. She was acquainted with his professional paranoia, his personal phobias. But these two broadsheets were undoctored, and might well harbour offensive material.

He had not yet examined the names of all those whom he was due to meet. He knew he would only forget them. He was bad at names, and his short-term memory was already overstocked. Why try to squeeze in the Chancellor, the Vice Chancellor, the High Steward, the Speaker, the Visitor, the Public Orator, the Dean, the heads of the various departments? Why study the roll-call of local landowners, of local industrialists and manufacturers, of sponsors and benefactors? The new university had gone to town with its lengthy list of ancient and modern appointments, with its newly forged traditions. These were the names that stitched the expanding community together. These names remained in the folder. He would look at them later, as he approached his journey's end.

So the Vice Chancellor was a woman. That at least was modern. He did not know her field.

He knew the name of the local duke. He had met him, once or twice, at functions in London. He remembered little of the anachronistic duke. He was called Gerry, and he was prematurely bald. He was quite a new duke, a young duke. He had never met the father. His family had not been on familiar terms with the aristocracy or the gentry.

Mrs Hornby would have supplied the university with an up-to-date version of his curriculum vitae, his paper life. She would have disguised the lacunae and smoothed out the graph of his past. And she would have supplied him with shorthand reminders of issues he ought to mention, anecdotes that he might like to tell, people he ought to remember to thank. Unlike some of his contemporaries, he had not descended to the level of the after-dinner-joke book, and usually he managed to sound spontaneous, but Mrs Hornby's notes were a safety net, in case his mind went blank.

He had prepared an outline of his short speech, to be delivered towards the end of the graduation ceremony. He did not much care for making speeches, and increasingly disliked the sound of his own public voice. He could hear himself repeating himself, but what was one to do, at his age? He would do his best. Others did not seem to notice his repetitions, or, come to that, their own.

He had a reputation for wit and fluency. He had the gift of the gab. He did not know how he had acquired it. Most of the time, these days, he felt like a fraud, waiting to be exposed. This was not wholly paranoia, for he had been attacked. His reputation had been threatened, his achievements mocked, his discipline and faith downgraded. But he could put on a good face, for the public. He did not sound or look bitter. Did he?

His throat was slightly sore. He swallowed, to test it, and his brain received a message of ominous but possibly imaginary discomfort. Was he developing a summer cold? Would he find himself speechless at the ceremony, and if so, what would that portend? People have been known to lose their voices, in an instant, in moments of stress or denial. Or was this an early indication of something more deadly, like the onset of cancer of the oesophagus? He had smoked heavily as a young man, in his buccaneering days, as young men did in the fifties and sixties. For how many years had he steadily filled his lungs with nicotine and tar – seven years, eight years, nine years? Should he recalculate once more? He had tried to work it out so often. He had even tried to work it out while attending the memorial service of the man who had finally established, beyond all reasonable doubt, the link between smoking and lung cancer. He had stood there, in the solemnly suited congregation, mouthing the words of 'Immortal, Invisible, God Only Wise' while trying yet again to remember how old he had been when he had first started to buy packets of twenty, regularly, to smoke on his own.

He recalled his trips to the corner newsagent's in Cambridge, and the heavy consumption on the coral island in the Indian Ocean. Not many people had thought it very dangerous to smoke, in those days. They had thought it dangerous, but not very dangerous. People didn't know about nicotine, or low-level radiation, or asbestos, or DDT, or aluminium, or lead poisoning, or the perils of bedside toys painted with luminous paint. Or they said they didn't.

The career of the woman who had established the dangers of low-level radiation had been undermined by the efforts of the man who had established the dangers of smoking. They had been rivals, enemies, intent on public good and private glory, and both had met much resistance. Both had lived long lives in science, into their nineties. The man who had tried to thwart the woman had attended her funeral, shortly before dying himself. What had been that stubborn, vain old man's thoughts, as he mouthed the words of the hymns? Had he repented of his attempts to block the woman's research, or had he attended the funeral in a spirit of triumph? In order, finally, to see her off, and to make sure that she had gone to earth for good?

Rivalry endures until death and after. The man had hated the woman, or so it was said. This story had tormented Professor Humphrey Clark, with good reason.

Darwin had tried to behave well towards the ill-fated Alfred Russel Wallace, but despite Darwin's good intentions, Wallace was doomed to be labelled and remembered as 'forgotten' – a paradoxical afterlife.

Darwin had died at the age of seventy-three, Wallace at the age of ninety. Wallace had been a pall-bearer at Darwin's funeral.

Funerals, memorials, ceremonies. The tea-parties of the dead. He attended many of these now, even though he was only in his sixties. And he worried more, now, about his own life after death. The worry demeaned him.

Again, delicately, he swallowed. He ran his fingers over the back of his neck and down the sides of his throat. He swallowed again. The fingers felt no swelling, but there was a sensitivity of the mucous membrane. Not quite a soreness, but a sensitivity.

He had so many ways of cheating himself in his smoking audit. He would cheat in his calculations, shaving off six months, reducing the recollection of his intake. Not that any of these sums mattered. Of course he did not have cancer of the oesophagus. He had been pronounced healthy at his last annual medical check-up. A slight problem with cholesterol, despite his largely vegetarian diet, but nothing to worry about. His chances of dying of a stroke or heart failure in the next ten years were moderately low, according to the instant multiple calculations on the Private Healthcare Policy computer.

Whenever he had thought, over the past few months, of the transcendent landscape of bridges and arches and estuary, his throat had begun to ache. He could induce, at will, a sense of inflammation in his throat and neck, and a pain in what would have been his tonsils, had not his tonsils been surgically removed half a century ago. Just as some lines of poetry, some phrases of music, some painful childhood memories never failed to elicit a Pavlovian prickle of imminent but invisible tears, so the prospect of this journey seemed to have animated a physical and by now predictable response. He had lowered his guard, and an infection had entered him. An infection not of the body, though it seemed to have this bodily manifestation, but of the spirit. An infection of a missing, disembodied, severed, long-ago incinerated organ.

Less than nine years of nicotine inhalation, but probably more than seven and a half. That was less than a tenth of his life. Considerably less than a tenth of his life. He had in his college days affected untipped French Gauloises, because they were fashionable and he had wanted to be one of the boys, but as a postgraduate he had moved on to a brand with lower tar. Now, like most of his contemporaries, he never smoked.

As a child, he had been enchanted by the Diophantus riddle about time, by the notion of the pie chart of a lifespan.

Though they did not talk about pie charts then. It was a recent coinage.

Hippocampus, Diophantus.

The memory trick.

A cup of tea or coffee might help. Should he go in search of the buffet car, or would the young woman pass with her trolley? Tea, like the tabloid-sized broadsheet paper, was free, thrown in with the high price of his first-class ticket. He would wait for her. Glancing now out of the window, he saw a neat new red-brick housing estate, all hipped roofs and economy conservatories, then swans floating serenely in a small semi-industrial brick pond, fringed by sedge. He knew this southern stretch of the northern track well. It was the end of term now, the beginning of the long summer holidays. Children would be looking forward to the freedom. And there, on cue, in a rural housing estate back garden, was a child, a small child in a floppy white canvas hat, waving at the train, as in a storybook of long ago.

He could hear the trolley's approach. It seemed to advance

with extraordinary slowness and innumerable delays, as the young woman dispensed coffee and tea and bottled water and small cellophane-wrapped packets of biscuits to the left of her and to the right of her. He could see her clearly now, a pallid-faced, small-featured girl in her twenties. She was dressed in a dark blue monogrammed tabard, and her dull fair hair was tied back in a pale blue headscarf-bandeau with the rail company's name written upon it. Her cool manner suggested that she considered she was putting much effort into being patient with her clients, and wished them to know this. He prepared himself to be polite or even pleasant, to try to alleviate the ill-borne dullness of her task. Politeness, as his mother often used to say, costs you nothing.

When she paused by him, bringing her vehicle to an irritable halt, he waited for her to repeat the phrase he had heard advancing with her along the compartment. 'Would you like any refreshments, sir?' she asked. He smiled, and opened his mouth to say, 'I'd like some tea' but when he tried to speak, no sound issued.

She repeated her request, a little less graciously.

He tried again, with the same result. He seemed to have been struck dumb. He swallowed, and massaged his throat with his fingers, and tried again.

By now, she had understood that he was in some difficulty, and her indifference melted into concern.

'You'd like a drink?' she suggested helpfully.

He nodded humbly, and made a gesture towards the teabags.

'Tea?' she hazarded.

He nodded, and mouthed the word 'Yes'. And in the same manner, they negotiated the milk. He declined, with a shake of the head, the sugar and the biscuits.

She had transformed herself in an instant into a pleasant,

caring person, nurse-like in her attentions. As though he were an invalid, as perhaps he was, she arranged before him his hot water, his teabag, his impotent little plastic stirring implement. She prodded his teabag for him, and gazed at him in anxious interrogation to see if she had prodded it enough. Mutely, he assented, and she fished out the bag and returned it to a waste bin attached to her trolley. This was not a courtesy she extended to everyone. She tried to insist on helping him with the top of his little carton of milk substitute, but he felt he had been coddled enough, and waved her away. She must pursue her ward duties, he indicated. He could manage on his own.

'Thank you,' he mouthed in his distinguished, public way. She smiled at him, with intimacy, with familiarity, and said, in a slightly louder voice than was necessary, that she would soon be returning for lunch orders. And then she moved on.

He had difficulty removing the foil top of the milk substitute. He had never been very dexterous, and with age was becoming less so. His fingers were clumsy now. A little spurt of white liquid escaped on to the table. He dabbed at it with the paper napkin she had left with him.

After his first sip of too-hot tea, he tried, surreptitiously, secretly, to speak. To produce a sound, any sound. He could swallow, and he could cough, but something seemed to have paralysed his vocal chords or his larynx. Again he fingered his throat and his Adam's apple, once gawkily prominent and vulnerable, now comfortably shrouded in friendly folds. He was not a fat man, but he was not a scraggy man. He was a well-built man, with a reassuring physical presence. Or so he liked to think that others thought.

The trachea, the larynx, the adenoids, the uvula. The hyoid bone at the root of the tongue, the horseshoe bone that gave man speech, the bone that differentiated man from ape. He would not like to have to label any of these on an anatomical model. It was a long time since he had thought of anything as grossly human as the parts of his own speaking apparatus. The human was not his subject.

Mrs Hornby's fingers had been forced to try to compress the folds and wrinkles of his throat into the stiff cardboard of the white dress-shirt front. This act was beyond and beneath and above her professional duties, and both of them had been in a state of shock at the unprecedented contact, but if she had not helped him, he would have been late for the dinner at Lincoln's Inn. It was lucky that she had been working late that evening. He had had to summon her from his study to the bedroom door. She had not crossed the threshold of the bedroom. She had wrestled with the recalcitrant little gold studs under the dim bulb of the corridor wall-light fitting, before asking him to move into the brighter light by the window that looked over the garden.

As a child, he had been thin and sickly and scraggy.

He sipped his slowly cooling tea.

The light weight and false texture of the polystyrene beaker were unpleasant to him.

Had he been struck dumb by God, for his sins? Had he been struck dumb to prevent him from speaking out? He did not consider these possibilities very seriously, but of course he considered them. He had been brought up to do so. He considered his sins of omission and commission daily, as the Book of Common Prayer had taught him to do, and he held himself responsible for them, even though he did not know what they were, and no longer believed in the God who had watched over him, the God who might lead him to a godly, righteous and sober life. He had a fertile imagination and could hardly begin to process the multiplicity of explanations and associations that rushed into his consciousness. His sins

37

were many and his burden heavy. He deserved to lose his voice, because he had abused his voice.

'*It serves you right.*'

That was a phrase which came back to him, from his childhood. But they could not have used it to him then, could they? They were not unkind, unreasonable people. They could not have blamed him for his illness.

He tried, discreetly, to hum, but did not seem to achieve much resonance. He could not get his soft palate to connect properly. His throat vibrated, but no sound issued. A motor difficulty, or a swift-onset virus? Aphasia, aphonia? The problem seemed very local, so he reassured himself that he was not having a stroke. Everything below the collarbones and above the jawline felt fine.

This disconcerting sensation must, he concluded, be connected with his return to the landscape of his boyhood.

For it was during his sojourn in the northern outpost on the outskirts of the beautiful town of slate and sandstone that his tonsils had been removed. This much he could remember clearly. He had been taken to the infirmary, and his tonsils had been cut out, and then he had been taken home to convalesce. He had lain speechless, bedridden, shocked by the indignity of the pain. They had told him in a kindly, worried, grown-up, deceitful way that it would not hurt much. But it did. They had given him a little brass bell, a brass cow bell from Benares, to keep by his bedside. He was to ring it if he needed attention. But he did not dare to ring it very often, because of the steepness of the stairs, and when he did ring it, they did not always come. His grandmother came more often than his mother and his aunt, but even she did not come very often.

They had said he could keep his tonsils pickled in a jar, but they forgot. They threw them away. He never saw them. He was not sure whether he would have wanted to see them or not. They told him that tonsils were not useful organs. You could do well without them, they said. Like the appendix, they weren't much use.

His baby sister had not been allowed to come upstairs to see him because, independently, she was suffering from measles. Most of the children of the neighbourhood had measles that summer. He must not catch the measles, and he must understand that Lizzie required a lot of attention.

The cat had not been allowed to visit him either. He missed the cat more than he missed his sister.

But they had brought him books to read.

Books were allowed.

Oh yes, they had brought him books.

How old had he been, when he first read these books? He could not be sure. If asked (and he was occasionally asked) he would give approximate answers. Nine? Ten? Eleven? What did it matter? Nobody now alive knew the answer to that question. It would have taken some research to establish the date of the operation on his tonsils. It had a date, but nobody would know it. Would the infirmary have kept records for so minor an event? He could still remember by heart his National Health Service number, although he was never asked for it these days. He could recite it to himself, as he sat here in carriage G16 of what was once the *Flying Scotsman*. He had been made to learn this number by his aunt. But perhaps he hadn't yet had a number, when he went into the infirmary? The National Health Service was in its infancy, in those immediate post-war days, in those lost unnumbered days. Maybe his tonsillectomy had preceded the birth of the NHS. The NHS had been conceived during the war, but it had not been born until two or three years later.

The removal of the tonsils did not appear on his distinguished academic record.

His memory of those days had dried out into fixed moments, into little, hard, dry, screwed-up paper pellets. The richer details, the broad expanses, had drifted beyond recall. They would never blossom and unfold again, not even in the swelling tide of tears that flooded towards him from the enormous main.

The Public Orator pauses here, to take stock of what has happened so far. The Orator, a withdrawn, black-gowned, hooded, neuter, neutral and faceless figure, confronts choice. The Orator, at this point, is presented with too many choices.

The theme of public and private behaviour has been introduced. Two of the principal characters have been presented, in some detail, and we suspect that they are soon to meet. They are much of an age, although the woman, as so far presented, seems to believe herself to be in her prime, whereas the man, in so far as we have observed him, seems to fear that he is past his prime. Times have changed, notes the Orator. Over the past hundred years, over the past fifty years, gender expectations have altered. Both sexes live longer, and women still live longer than men, but women live longer and in better shape than they used to do. They do not give up so easily.

We know that we are on a journey backwards in time, towards some form of welcome or unwelcome reunion. We know that surprises may be sprung. Betrayal, envy and ambition have played their part. The denouement has not yet been decided, and not even the Orator knows the shape of the end of the story. Will the story be tragic or comic, open or closed? We cannot tell. But the nature of the denouement is not the Orator's present problem. The Orator's problem lies in the selection of memories, of anecdotes, of telling moments. In the selection lies the meaning. From the selection, for better or for worse, will unfold the sequence and the ending.

The Orator disdains the primary vulgarity of plot, in favour of an ambitious attempt at meaning. Telling stories is telling lies. But the meaning is not clear. Perhaps there is no meaning. Perhaps, at this late stage in the lives of the protagonists, there is nothing but a dying buzz, a dull echoing boom, a confusing sequence of increasingly disconnected events, an involuted series of diminishing circles. Maybe nothing will emerge from the endeavour towards meaning.

The Orator is not a puppet master, and on principle dislikes artificial arrangements, narrative devices, false dawns and false epiphanies. The Orator disdains short cuts and paper resolutions. The Orator is stubborn and fastidious. If there is no meaning, then meaning will be withheld, renounced. It is all too easy to impose a semblance of meaning. It is all too easy to play tricks, to conjure up fantastic reconciliations, where Jack shall have Jill and nought shall go ill. Most fall back wearily on these devices. On words, words, words. The weariness they betray is a manifestation of despair. To find a true resolution, that is the hard thing. But the Orator has got this far with the narration, and cannot honourably retreat.

How far back can we go? The past is dry and may never flower for us. It is not a question of memory, and it is not a question of effort. It is a question of good faith. Only for the pure of heart will the past revive. To the impure, it remains dead and lost, lost and dead.

Hic labor, hoc opus est.

It is hard, it is hard.

When the heart is corrupt, the enterprise is doomed.

Too late, too late, booms the foghorn over the grey fog and the invisible water.

Try again, try again, tolls the bell from the bell tower over the steep slates of the roofs of the city.

Turn again, turn again, tolls the bell.

To fail is to fall is to die.

To move forward, we must move back, back to the plain land of bread and butter, when we were as little children, with few temptations, in a carefully rationed world.

The Bedroom Weeks

He must be brave, they said, because the baby was ill.

She was not really a baby, but she was too little to be brave, whereas Humphrey was a big boy now. So he went into the infirmary meekly. He felt miserable but noble. It is easy to persuade a child that it must be noble. Even at that age, he was aware of having been managed and manipulated into good behaviour. But for many months afterwards, he could not get out of his mind the horror of coming back to his senses in the infirmary ward. When he regained consciousness, his throat was so sore that he could not swallow, and yet he had to keep trying to swallow, in order to experience, again and again, the pain. He felt as though saw-edged knives had scored raw patterns across the back of his gullet. Deep nausea had seized him, and he had vomited up a deep brown stinking clotted fluid, with streaks of blood in it. It came up his throat and down his nose. He had tried to find a bowl or a potty to be sick into, but he could see nothing in reach, and he could not cry out, so he had been sick on the chequered linoleum of the floor.

The bed had an iron bar, like a baby's cot. He had to lean over the bar to vomit. He was ashamed.

He had thought the nurses would be angry with him, when they came to wipe it up.

He found that he was wearing threadbare over-laundered flannel hospital pyjamas, with pearly buttons worn to thin discs. The cord of the trousers was frayed at the ends. And the ward was full of old men. He had thought at first that he was delirious, when he saw the old men. Had he been sent into a war zone? Were these the wounded, evacuated from the front line? But no, they were too old, and anyway the war was over now. They were very ancient and very ugly. He saw pallid withered faces, bald heads covered in dark splattered stain marks, heads with grey hairy tufts sticking out at angles, stubbled chins with whiskers and warts and blebs and growths, and clouded watery eyes. Gnarled hands and thin wrists protruded from shrunken sleeves. One old man sat on the edge of his bed with his stick legs dangling. He was wearing a nightshirt, and the boy could see high up along his indecent withered thighs, and into the cave of shadows between them. He could hear painful coughing, from all around him, from deep throats of rasping phlegm. His own throat was a torment to him. The sound of the coughing of the old men was a torment to him.

They had brought him into the infirmary, and taken away his clothes, and put him into a girlish green pinafore, and made him lie down on a trolley bed. Then they wheeled him into another room, where he lay on his back beneath a battery of bright lights. They had covered his face with a large suffocating white pad, and told him to breathe deeply. The smell of the ether had been thick and semi-sweet and nauseating, but he had tried to do what he was told. He had tried to be good. Coloured swathes and spirals and hideous galaxies of purple and bruised yellow-green and brown had swirled into his face and up his nostrils and into his head. He could see these spirals even with his eyes shut. They were inside his eyelids, beating in his eyes. He had been told not to struggle, so he tried very hard to lie still. And when he woke, he was in this long ward, in this humiliating iron infant's crib, in these unfamiliar pyjamas that other sick boys had worn before him.

When he vomited, the sick came down his nose as well as

up his throat. He had not known that there was a pathway down the nose that was connected with the throat. It was disgusting.

When the nurse came to wipe up the sick, she was not cross with him. She had smiled at him, and then turned away her head as she applied her mop, and she had said to herself, not to him, 'It's a shame. That's what it is, it's a shame.'

One of the old men had cried out to the nurse, in a thin angry wail. 'Nurse, nurse,' he had moaned. And she had said, again to herself, as she wrung out the mop in the bucket, 'Oh, shut up, Grandpa.' She had said it without malice, patiently. As though the old man were the child. Was it her real grandpa? The boy thought not.

His grandpa was dead. He had been in the Merchant Navy. He had been a famous swimmer. Humphrey could not really remember him.

When the nurse left, she patted his hand, and said, 'Cheer up, son.' She patted him with the hand that had held the mop that had wiped up the curdled mess. He tried not to shrink away from her, because he knew she meant to be kind.

When she left, he inspected more closely the borrowed garments that he was wearing. What had they done with his short grey trousers and his blue shirt and his socks and his shoes and his jacket? They would be very angry if he had lost them. And his mother would not like the buttons on this pale striped pyjama jacket. They did not match, and the top one was missing. She was pernickety about things matching. The war had made orderliness difficult for her, but she sometimes said she enjoyed 'pitting her wits' against the disorder. She knew how to 'make do and mend'. But she would not have approved of the odd buttons. Two were of a faintly iridescent shell-like substance, but one of them had two holes, and the other had four holes. They were not even a pair. And the third

45

and lowest button, above his navel, was a small grey-cream fabric-covered disc, of an unpleasantly rough texture. It had no holes, and the stitching pierced crudely right through its centre. He felt at it with his fingers. Perhaps it had a little metal rim, under the fabric? He picked at it and picked at it. His fingers did not like it, but they could not leave it alone.

And he could not resist the temptation to try to swallow. Back it came, again and again, the pain, the insult.

How long would he have to lie there, helpless, with the old ones? Nobody had told him. He did not dare to ask. And anyway, he could not speak.

The shell button with four holes was the nicest.

The seashore was a treasure trove of shells. Pale pink and oval ones, like a baby's fingernails. Slate-grey, mussel-blue-black, greenish-bronze, russet-pink and pearly-silver. Little delicate cusps and slivers and moon-like crescents, worn by the tides, and stonier snail-like shells, with spiral helical ridges. They lay washed up on a bed of sand, on a fine grit of shell and sand, of shells and rocks and stones ground to grains of yellow and red and white. His mother liked to collect the best of the shells, and she stuck them pointlessly and thriftily with glue on to little cardboard boxes. Her masterpiece, her treasure, was an encrusted shoebox. She kept it on her bedroom window sill.

St Cuthbert's beads she gathered from the beach, and hoarded in her box. They were little crinoids of the lord: the fossils of sea lilies, from which the saint of Lindisfarne had made his rosary. She did not know what they were, but she knew the legend, and she collected them because they were ancient and curious.

Whinstone and dolerite, dolerite and sandstone.

The Great Whin Sill.

The Great Black Ledge.

The Great Chalk Shelf.

The topography of the region was written in the child's heart and laid down and embedded in the chalky history of his bones.

During the war, parts of the beach had been out of bounds, cut off behind barbed wire and cement blocks, but now they were allowed to walk on the shore and play on the sands, on their own. He had played there with his friend Sandy Clegg, weeks ago, long ago, in the spring, before the tonsils and the measles. They had played at submarines and battleships, at explorers and shipwrecks, at pirates and at walking the plank.

Would anyone have told Sandy where he was? He did not trust them to explain things properly. The little north-of-the-river village school of Finsterness was closed now, because of the epidemic. The summer term had ended early. His aunt had made the decision. He had heard them discussing it. 'I think we'd better close down,' she had said. 'There are so many off sick, it's not worth trying to keep going.' His mother had seemed to agree. She did not always agree with his aunt, but in school matters, she tended to defer to her older sister. So if Sandy did not go to school, who would tell him where Humpy had gone? He sensed that his mother did not quite like Sandy's mother. She had some objection to Sandy's home and family, but he had no clue as to its nature. It was an adult mystery. She permitted Sandy to come to play, but she never addressed him as Sandy, although she was happy to call her son by his baby name of 'Humpy', which was a much sillier name than Sandy. Sandy Clegg was always 'Alistair' to her.

His mother did not like many people in the village or the town. She was in exile there, on sufferance. She wished she were back home, in the industrial Midlands, amidst the bomb wreckage, not stranded on this far shore with her sister and her mother. But Humphrey did not really remember his first

47

home, the house that his mother called home. He knew that this was not his home, and that he would have to leave it soon. But he could remember little else, however hard he tried. Sometimes his mother said to him, 'You do remember your daddy, don't you?' and he would pretend that he did. Had Daddy been that man who had arrived late at night, 'on leave', in a heavy coat, exhausted from a long train journey in the blackout, smelling of coal dust and sweat? He had not stayed long. Perhaps that had been Daddy. But even if he was Daddy, Humphrey did not really remember him. He could tell that his mother was unhappy and anxious and angry when she spoke of his father. He could not tell why she was unhappy, and he did not know whether she was angry with him, or with his unknown father, or with Auntie Vera, or with Grandma, or with the war that was now over.

Daddy was abroad, in a region called the Far East. He would be home soon. He was doing important work, with the Navy, but he would be home soon.

The war had driven Humphrey and his sister and their mother north, to this town at the mouth of the wide river. It was home to his grandmother and his aunt, but he and his mother and the baby were lodgers. They had pooled their points and coupons, and taken refuge from the bombs, and the temporary shelter had become his home, and his friends here were his friends for life.

He fingered the cloth button, and waited for rescue from his iron bedstead. And hours later, his auntie came, carrying a bulging shopping bag. He could see her from far off, as she walked down the long ward with its high windows. She was smiling, but a little nervously. She was a schoolmistress, but not a very authoritarian schoolmistress, and she was out of her element here. In the school, in the village, everybody addressed her deferentially as 'Miss Neil', but here, over the river, she was not so important. Like him, she was frightened of the doctors and the nurses, although she did her best to conceal it. Miss Neil walked proudly and stiffly, on her best behaviour, in her best dark green suit, and on top of the coils of her reddish plaited hair sat her green felt hat with the lucky pheasant's feather stuck in its gamboge twill hatband. Her scrubbed face shone and her cheeks were hawthorn red and weathered by the north wind from the North Sea. She was smiling, but she was in a slight huff, which she explained as she sat down by his bedside.

'They ought not to,' she said. 'They've put you in with the geriatrics.'

He looked his bewilderment. It was not a word he knew, though he learned it at that instant, and did not forget it.

'The old men,' she explained in an undertone. 'They've put you in the geriatric ward. I know they're full, but they ought to have found you a children's bed.'

She did not kiss him, or touch him. She was not a demonstrative woman. But she smiled at him.

'Well, Humphrey,' she said in a deliberately and unconvincingly cheerful voice, 'and how are we now? How are we feeling?'

He could not speak. It was just as well, as he wanted to say that it hurt, and she would not want to hear that.

'Well,' she said, 'you're coming home tomorrow. They haven't got room for you here, so you're coming home tomorrow. But I've brought you a present or two. Just to keep you going, overnight.'

Even in his reduced state, he was pleased. Presents had been rare in those days of austerity. She took the objects from her bag, and laid them on the threadbare cream blanket with its pale blue frayed satin binding. A book, and a bobbin for making French knitting. Four nails, stuck in a painted wooden

49

cotton bobbin, and a big blunt needle with a large long eye, and some coloured wools. She said she would start him off with it, and she did. The thin tube of knitting began to extrude and excrete itself through the hole in the bobbin, as her fingers worked busily. You have a go now, she said, and he had a go. You looped the wool over the nails, and you kept pulling at the tube as it grew. Very good, said Auntie Vera, very good. You're doing very nicely.

He liked the praise, though the product was disturbing.

The book was a paperback picture book called *Monsters of the Deep*. It was a different shape from most books he knew. It was oblong, but it was wider than it was tall. It had illustrations of fish and squid and whales and sharks and other sea creatures, and in the middle of the book there was a double spread that opened up into the longest sea serpent ever known. There was a picture of a phosphorescent fish that glowed, five miles beneath the surface of the ocean. And another one with great jaws and a light set in its head on the end of a long dangling stalk, like a fisherman. And one strange underwater creature that no man had ever seen. How could they draw it, when no man had ever seen it?

You can read that later, she said.

His aunt disapproved of the old men. When one of them got out of his bed and started to stagger across the floor, she looked appalled. Humphrey knew that she could see too much of the old man's legs, and his legs were a monstrous sight. The woman and the boy tried to look away, as the old man lurched from bed end to bed end, muttering to himself under his breath. His feet were bare and blue and buckled, and the joints of his big toes protruded at a grotesque angle. His toenails were ridged and yellow and thick as horn and they curled over like the toenails of an animal. His toenails had become claws. He was menacing but frail, as he stumbled along. He was menacing because he was frail. Where were his slippers? Why didn't somebody make him put his slippers on?

His aunt didn't stay long. She had to be getting back, she said, to hold the fort back home. He hadn't asked after his little sister, he hadn't thought to, and she hadn't been mentioned. Maybe she was dead? Probably not, or Auntie Vera would have said so. She wasn't even ill enough to be in the infirmary. He was the really ill one in the family. He wanted to ask after the cat Blackie, but Auntie Vera said he must try not to talk.

His auntie said she'd be back in the morning, to collect him in the ambulance. It would be fun, wouldn't it, riding in the ambulance, over the bridge from the old town and over the river to Finsterness, their northern fishing-village-outpost by the sea? She didn't think they would use the siren, because he wasn't an emergency. But they had promised the ambulance. He wasn't well enough to go on the bus. And he'd have to stay in bed when he got home, and be good. How long? She didn't know how long. Till he was better. Grandma would make him a nice junket. It would slip down very easily, she promised. He wasn't to chew anything for a while. He must rest his throat till it was better.

When she had gone, he did a little bit of his French knitting, and read his book. The marine monsters were exciting.

Once he had seen a strange long waving thing in a rock pool, one of those deep rock pools that you could see only at the very lowest tide. The thing was yards long, and thick as a man's arm. An eel-like thing. A conger eel. He had liked to think it was a conger eel.

Along the coast, to the north, there was what had once, before the war, been a famous tourist attraction. It was a pool called the Pool of Brochan. Humphrey had never seen it, but he had seen grey-and-white postcards of it, and he yearned for it. It was a deep round natural rock pool, a natural inlet from the sea. In this pool of emerald water lived tame codfish. They came to the hand to be fed, like chickens, the guide-book said. He longed to see the tame and friendly fish, but how would he ever get there? It was nearly ten miles away, unimaginably distant, over the border, in another country. Who would take him?

A trolley came round with the old men's tea, but he wasn't expected to eat any, which was just as well, as it looked and smelt horrible, of cabbage and gravy. He hated gravy. He liked dry food better. They gave him a glass of water and a pill. He managed to swallow it. It went down, scraping its way over the raw ravine of his gullet.

The beastly old men ate noisily and clattered and coughed. He wanted to kill them all. It would be easy to kill them. They were hardly alive. They were at death's door. He wanted to kick their skinny legs and batter their splotched blotched thin egg-like skulls. He wanted them dead. They were ugly and useless and offensive. He wanted to go home, to the home that wasn't really his home.

When he got there, he spent a long time in the little attic bedroom at the top of the house. Days and then weeks, it seemed. He didn't get better as quickly as they said he was going to, but maybe they had been lying all the time.

Tonsillitis with complications, he heard his mother say to his aunt, in an important tone.

The curtains were the old blackout curtains. They were very familiar to him. They were nigger-brown, with a repeat-ing woven pattern in a lighter gold-yellow thread, and they had a thick black bunchy ill-stitched lining, that was meant to keep out the Germans. The pattern looked to him like demons with curved horns and curly forelocks, though his grandmother said that it was just a design. He had not told her about the demons, because that would have made him feel foolish, but he had at one point dared to ask her what the pattern meant. She said that it meant nothing. She said it was 'just a design'. He found it hard to pull the curtains back, because he was not tall enough to get a proper purchase on them, and the curtain hooks snagged and caught on the rail. The view from his window, unlike the views from the front of the house, was constricted, for his little high window looked across the alleyway to the brick wall of the house next door. In the house next door lived Mr Fell, who was a widower, and who spoke to nobody. Mr Fell was a recluse, and rarely ventured out.

He liked the dignity of the words 'widower' and 'recluse', but in the street, in those earlier days when he had been allowed out to play outdoors, he took pains to avoid any close sighting of Mr Fell.

His bedroom had a sharply sloping ceiling, for it was under the roof and next to the water cistern. The ceiling was white-washed, and he had begun to scratch faint marks on it to measure his advancing height. The last year or two of his progress were scratched, at monthly intervals, into the incline. Nobody had noticed the scratches yet. They would be cross with him if they saw them. The whitewash flaked and its harsh alkaline unevenness set his teeth and his nails on edge. But he had to make the scratches, to mark his growth and the passage of time.

Chalk, lime, bitten fingernails, the school blackboard. The blackboard rubber, dense, packed with dead chalk, dead numbers. The irritability, the sensitivity, the alien particles of matter. He hated the oblong of the blackboard rubber with its rough and matted surface. His aunt wielded it without fear, but he hated it.

He liked the cistern, though, which jutted out in a wooden box into the corner of his room that was furthest from the door. It made companionable, watery noises, which reassured him that there was ongoing life below, and that he was not alone in the house. The sound of water was pleasing to him.

He lay up there, alone, with his tender throat, and wondered about Sandy Clegg. He was told that Sandy had measles, like his sister, but was this true? He knew his sister wasn't dead, because he could hear her whining and crying downstairs. He could hear their mother rocking her in the rocking chair, and singing 'Ten Green Bottles' and 'One Man Went to Mow', although she was really too old for that kind of comfort now. Rock, rock, backwards and forwards, an insistent rhythmic grinding that soothed and excited at the same time. One man went to mow, *went* to Mower Meadow. Two men, one man and his dog, *went* to Mower Meadow. He understood that his sister Lizzie couldn't come up to see him. He didn't really want to see her much. But he couldn't understand why Blackie wasn't allowed up, because cats don't get measles or tonsillitis. They get cat flu, but that was different. Nor could he understand how Blackie had managed to allow herself to be confined to the downstairs. She wasn't always an obedient cat, and she liked to be in his bedroom. She liked his bedroom best.

He shared a guilty secret with Blackie. She liked to get into his bed and suck at his pyjamas. She would nestle in his bed, hidden under the covers, and suck, rhythmically, at the crook of his elbow. He liked it when she did this, although he knew it was probably wrong. He couldn't see why, but he suspected that it was wrong. She would suck and purr, and purr and suck. It was very comforting to him. But she didn't come up any more. She had forgotten him.

In bed, he read his way through book after book. He quickly

exhausted the two new books that had been given to him as treats – a *Just William* story and a book on aircraft spotting. He studied his aunt's gift of *Monsters of the Deep* closely, admiring the fish with telescopic eyes and the gulper and the black vampire squid. He wondered at the hideous female angler fish, who dangled a luminous lure before her wherever she went, and devoured her husband and reduced him to a sac of sperm. Then he moved on to the old books that were part of the house's furniture. Robert Louis Stevenson, R. M. Ballantyne, Walter de la Mare, Charles Kingsley, Jules Verne. Some of these books had belonged to his grandparents. They had embossed bindings and coloured illustrations. He was a precocious reader and he made his way through volumes which were in part incomprehensible to him. He liked *The Water Babies*, even in its lengthy unexpurgated Darwinian version, and he read Jules Verne's *Twenty Thousand Leagues Under the Sea* with rapture. He enjoyed Ballantyne's *The Lifeboat*, convinced at first that it was set on his own northern coastline, and that it would at some point in the narrative turn out to be connected with the local heroine Grace Darling, daughter of the lighthouse keeper. But it wasn't. This was disappointing, but he enjoyed the melodrama nevertheless, and read again and again the lengthy footnote on the Royal Humane Society's rules for the recovery 'of those who are apparently drowned'.

That phrase, 'apparently drowned', was magical to him, and he longed to be able to revive a dead man. Again and again, he read the instructions about how to clear the dead man's throat, and how to excite his breathing. 'If there be no success, lose not a moment, but instantly, TO IMITATE BREATHING, replace the patient on the face, raising and supporting the chest well on a folded coat or other article of dress. Turn the body very gently on the side and a little beyond, and then briskly on the face, back again; repeating these measures cautiously, efficiently, and perseveringly about fifteen times in the minute . . .' Page after page of advice followed, ending, 'The above treatment should be persevered in for some hours, as it is an erroneous opinion that persons are irrecoverable because life does not soon make its appearance, persons having been restored after persevering for many hours.'

So the apparently drowned might be recovered, and he himself might learn how to recover them. He vowed to practise this useful art, as soon as he was allowed to swim again. He was a good swimmer. His grandmother, teasingly, sometimes called him 'Captain Webb', after the first man to swim the English Channel. This was silly, but although it was silly, it pleased him.

Ballantyne's *The Dog Crusoe* also entranced him. This was a tale of a young man and his dog, and of their adventures on the prairie, with Indians and scalping knives and grizzly bears and wild mustangs and stampedes. The prairie was oceanic and endless, like the sea that swelled towards the northern horizon. The hero rejoiced in the swell, the undulation, the wide circle of space. Here, too, men were recovered from apparent death, and were dug out alive from the shallow grave where the red varmints had buried them. The remote and distant violence delighted and soothed him. The redskins roasted dogs alive and ate the raw liver of the buffalo. They were cruel and treacherous and they would cut off your scalp. They were evil and glorious.

What was a scalp? He was not sure. Was it the top of your head? Was it skin, or was it part of the skull too? He did not like to ask anyone, because he was ashamed of his interest in scalps. They would have needed a very sharp knife to cut off the skin and the hair. Did it kill you, being scalped, or were you only 'apparently dead'? Could you survive without your scalp? Could you walk around with your skull sliced and your brains open to the prairie sky?

When he had read *The Dog Crusoe* for the third time, he turned to the random volumes of *The Children's Encyclopedia* that his aunt brought back from the little school library, closed now for the summer, and he made his way through those too. They were full of nuggets. At one moment he saw himself as an astronomer, at another moment he explored the oceans, and then he became a specialist in the songbirds of Britain, or in the hummingbirds and hornbills of America and Africa. He pondered 'the immensity of the universe' in Volume 5, and read about the 'little thyroid gland that makes us wise or stupid'. (Were the tonsils glands? He thought they might be, but he couldn't find any articles about tonsils. Perhaps he could be a surgeon when he grew up?) In Volume 8 he discovered an extraordinarily puzzling and challenging article called 'Mysteries of the Border Line', in the Group 4 series on Animal Life. It was about Portia's caskets, and cellular growth, and how simple organisms develop, and how the present of the child is in its past. The article featured sea squirts, which he knew. He learned that they were degenerate creatures, because the sea squirt begins its life with a spinal cord, but loses it as it grows older, to become 'the most helpless and immobile creature in the seven seas'. It regresses, and evolves backwards. He learned that sea squirts are really called ascidians, and that in Greek this word means 'little skin bags'.

The old men on the ward were helpless.

Was the sea squirt simply lazy, asked the enquiring article. Had it abandoned its ambitions with its backbone, and sunk to the seabed in despondency? It could have been an evolutionary miracle, and speeded progress by millennia, if it had made more of an effort. But it had lost heart and given up.

It had been a dead end. The struggle had been too much for it.

This was one solution proposed by the author, but the article conceded that there might be others.

Sea squirts had no will power and no ambition, that much was clear.

Perhaps he would become a scientist, and solve these mysteries.

He also read in *The Children's Encyclopedia* that some members of the animal kingdom change sex during the course of their life cycle. These changes seemed particularly frequent with marine species. There was much yet to be discovered about these mysterious evolutionary processes, said the *Encyclopedia*.

'*Little is known*' was a phrase that often caught his attention.

The richness of the unknown world was almost unbearable to him. Mighty, altruistic visions of sacrifice and glory and discovery swelled in him as he lay alone, up in his attic room. The books were full of such promise, such large questions, such wild hope. He knew that he would try to solve the mysteries. It was his destiny.

His throat was feeling a little better by now, and one day he plucked up courage to ask after Sandy. He was told he had to be patient, Sandy was still in quarantine. He longed to go with Sandy to find sea squirts, and to examine their backbones, or lack of backbones.

Emboldened, he asked after Blackie. They evaded the question. Was Blackie in quarantine too? Well, sort of, they said. They were truthful people, from church-going stock, brought up to let their yea be yea and their nay be nay, and they were not practised in deliberate deception.

To throw him off the scent, they brought upstairs to him

a new-old puzzle book, a school prize that had once belonged to his late grandpa. This was called *Mathematical Riddles of the Ages*, and they said he might like the early puzzles, which wouldn't be too hard for him.

His grandpa had been big and burly. He was famed for having swum, once, to the island, which was dangerous, because of the currents. Humphrey could not remember him very well, but he admired the memory of this exploit.

He could get up the next day, or the day after, they said. Dr Dunbar had said he could get up soon.

Dr Dunbar was a tweedy man, moustached and fierce and yellow as nicotine. He stank of tobacco. Even the fraying flex of his stethoscope stank of tobacco.

So, on Humphrey's last evening in bed, while he ate his special orange jelly with real tinned mandarin segments in it and real sweet evaporated milk poured over it, he studied the mathematical riddles of the ages. How did the Egyptians build their pyramids? How did the ancient Babylonians learn to predict the eclipses of the sun? What did Archimedes discover in his bath? Who designed Stonehenge? Can we measure how fast light travels?

Deep into the book, towards the end, he came across the wonderful riddle of Diophantus. Once upon a time, the book told him, in Ancient Greece, there was a great mathematician called Diophantus whose works revealed some of the eternal secrets of the world of numbers. And Diophantus loved mathematics so much that he caused a mathematical riddle to be engraved upon his tombstone, as an epitaph, for later generations to wonder at. And the riddle went like this.

God granted Diophantus to be a boy for the sixth part of his life, and, adding a twelfth part to this, God clothed his cheeks with down. God lit him the light of wedlock after a seventh part of his life, and five years after his marriage He granted him a son. Alas! Poor late-born wretched child; after attaining the measure of half his father's full life, chill Fate took him. After consoling his grief by this science of numbers for four years the bereaved father Diophantus ended his life.

The question was, '*How old was Diophantus when he died?*'

The boy had no idea, and could not begin to think how to discover an answer, but the question entranced him. When he sneaked a look at the solutions at the back, he was told that Diophantus died at the age of eighty-four, but he could not work backwards from that answer to the method by which the answer was achieved, as he knew he was meant to be able to do. He was too young. His brain strained and yearned to understand, but it failed. It nudged against its limits, and it failed. But there was as yet no shame in the failure. On the contrary, there was a sense of thrill and glory and expectation. One day, he resolved, he would get his mind around these matters, and know *how* to know *why* we know that Diophantus lived to be eighty-four. Scooping up the last melting blebs of jelly with the special silver Coronation teaspoon, he was filled with expectation, hope and happiness.

The book had a line drawing of Diophantus, looking sad and wise and Greek and dignified. Diophantus did not look like the coughing, hawking, spitting old stooges in the infirmary ward, although he had lived to be eighty-four. Poor Diophantus, who lost his only son. Did Diophantus end his *own* life, because of grief, or did he just die of old age? The message wasn't clear, but it was haunting. And the poor son of Diophantus, the poor 'late-born wretched child'! Humphrey was moved by the chill fate of the father and of the son, who had lived and died so many thousands of years ago.

Perhaps a life of numbers would be best, in the long run. The boy resolved to be a mathematician when he left school. He would devote himself to the science of numbers. He vowed that he would recite his tables to himself every night, when he couldn't get to sleep, and practise his mental arithmetic every morning, and then, when he was older, he would be able to answer all the riddles. He swore to himself, as he rocked himself to sleep, that he would master the riddles.

Though maybe it would be better to be an astronomer, or a deep-sea diver, or the captain of a lifeboat?

He rocked and rocked, and fingered his pyjama button, and wished that Blackie would come.

When he was allowed up, the next day, and came downstairs for the first time, there was no sign of Blackie. He could not see her anywhere. He found her abandoned basket, its blanket dusted white with DDT, stuck shamefully at the back of the cupboard under the stairs. They told him at first that she had gone to live with Auntie Janie in Newcastle, but he did not believe them. Their hesitations gave them away. He never saw Blackie again. He held it against them for the rest of their lives.

His sister was still there, but she did not seem at all pleased to see him. She screamed at the very sight of him. Her red, square, yelling face and her wet rubbery pink lips and her runny nose and her lank fair wispy curls made him very unwelcome. In response, he started to cry for Blackie, although he was such a big boy now. He had forgotten what it was like, downstairs. It wasn't as nice as he had remembered. The familiar terrain of the front room and the dining room and the kitchen seemed unfriendly, as though bedimmed and bewitched. His legs felt shaky and they looked thin and white and wasted. He almost wanted to go back to bed, where he had felt, for a while, both hopeful and powerful. When he stopped crying, he said he wanted to see Sandy Clegg. Tomorrow, his mother said. She always said tomorrow. Everything would be tomorrow. Nothing would ever be now. He sat curled up in the deep lumpy armchair in the front room, picking at his toes, and restlessly turning the pages of the *Monsters of the Deep*. You could feel the coiled metal springs of the armchair through the worn loose cover. The black vampire squid looked like an underwater bat. Would Sandy like it? Would it *terrify* Sandy? Would it *bore* Sandy? Would Sandy ever again be allowed to come to play? Had Sandy Clegg forgotten him?

For endless hours he sat in the chair and pined, in an agony of self-pity and an enjoyable loathing of his hostile baby sister. She hated him, he hated her. It was not an important hatred.

But tomorrow did come, and with it came Sandy, who appeared at teatime, just as he used to do before the illnesses. Sandy confirmed, in few words, that he had had the measles and had felt fairly awful. Rotten. He'd felt rotten. (He was always uncharacteristically tongue-tied when within earshot of Humphrey's family.) When encouraged, he boasted a little about his high temperature. The pale boys compared notes. Fresh air, it was decided, would be good for both of them. Provided they didn't stray too far or get into trouble. Could they go to the beach? Yes, tomorrow, they could go to the beach.

Sandy's house was much older and much nearer to the sea than Humphrey's grandmother's Edwardian semi-detached in Burnside Avenue. The Cleggs' house was called Number 8, Turkey Bank. Nobody knew why Turkey Bank was called Turkey Bank. Turkey Bank was a terrace of old cottages, at the edge of the northern village-outpost of the town, and Number 8 was the last house in the row. It had a sea view, looking south towards Ornemouth Bay, and in the distance you could see the headland of the cove hiding the cold forbidden fenced-off rough-hewn seawater Victorian bathing pool. The house next door to Sandy's was a boarding house, which used to take in summer visitors, though the war had dried up the supply of guests. The war had filled the sea with fish, and emptied the resort of custom.

The Cleggs did not take summer visitors.

They were superior.

The small, remote and silent Mr Clegg worked in an office in the town, for the council, or the government, or something official like that. He had not been called up because he was official. The boys had no notion of how he spent his time, or how he earned his living. Mrs Clegg was an eccentric. She read library books during the afternoons, omnivorously – detective stories, romances, thrillers, children's adventures, memoirs, politics, history – and in the evenings she made notes in school exercise books. She even wrote, intermittently, during the day. She wrote in pencil, laboriously, methodically, with a slight frown on her face. Had she been a spy for England, watching the coastline for enemy attack during the war, and noting the movements of shipping and aircraft?

Like Humphrey's mother and aunt, Mrs Clegg seemed to approve of reading, though she never talked about it.

The next day of his convalescent downstairs life, Humphrey was told he could go out to play. Having been confined to his room for some immeasurable time, and comforted with books, it now seemed to Humphrey that he was being forced outdoors, whether he felt like it or not. Having been shut up with his books, he was now being told to stop frowsting over them and to get out. The inconsistencies of adults were nothing new to Humpy and Sandy. Philosophically, they took their chance, and, the next day, they scarpered. The books would wait for their return. The tides and the sands beckoned.

And so began the endless weeks of summer.

What had Mrs Clegg been noting in her notebooks? Prices, temperatures, news items, plot summaries of her library books, food availability and points and coupons, hobbies, wireless programmes, cinema showings, gossip in the queue at the fish shop. She had been requested to include notes on sex, but, like so many of the project's volunteer diarists, she found this problematic, and for the most part she avoided the subject, though she managed to include a token comment on the noise made by a tomcat on the prowl.

She liked listening to Town and Country *programmes on the Home Service with A. G. Street and Professor Joad. She never went to the cinema in Ornemouth, but she conscientiously noted the titles of some of the programmes.*

It was a summer without a horizon. Day after day of limitless sunshine rose for Humpy and Sandy, day after day of space opened for them. It was the finest summer of the century. Wave followed wave along the curving shore. The leash that had held them to their homes grew longer and longer, and eventually they were allowed to run wild. The adults in Humphrey's house were preoccupied with other matters, discussed in lowered womanly voices at the kitchen table, or after bedtime, in the evenings, over knitting or mending. He thought he heard the words 'troop ship' and 'decontamination' and 'radiation' – or did he later imagine that he had heard them? They were heavy words, words beyond his knowledge. (Did that mean he could not have heard them?) Plans were being made, worries were being voiced and debated, but Humphrey did not listen. When he heard his father's name, he shut his ears. He did not want to hear about the man called

Philip who would soon be on his way home. He buried his head under the bedclothes, and wished that Blackie were still alive.

The nights were sometimes bad, but the days were good.

The two boys explored to the edge of their known world, and beyond it. They extended their territory inland to the west through the town and up the estuary and the brackish river, and northwards along the beach and the coast path. They were provided with sandwiches and apples for their outings. Sandwiches of white bread, filled with beef dripping, with salty white crumbly fat and dark reddish-brown gravy jelly. Jam sandwiches, of homemade raspberry and gooseberry jam, jam made from the berries from the weatherbeaten bushes in the back garden.

Their long absences were condoned. Nobody followed them, nobody spied on them, and after a while nobody bothered to nag them not to go near the edge and not to swim out of their depth. They swam, and scrambled together along the cliffs, and waded in the river, and fished, and dug holes in the mud, and stared at the degenerate sea squirts, and collected buckets full of mermaid's purses, and captured razorfish and cockles. At the northern limits of their terrain, they found the secret drip of a waterfall in a cave, and behind it, a heavy rusting iron ring set into the living face of the rock. Who had been there before them? Smugglers, castaways, fishermen? It was a secret place that marked the limits of their daring.

They broke their way through the barbed wire into the abandoned wooden shack of the tearoom by the lighthouse, and they set up a lookout post amongst the dusty crockery and the triangular ashtrays and the spider-webbed shiny red-lipped advertisements for Craven A cigarettes. They surveyed the horizon through a pair of binoculars with a cracked lens that had belonged to Humpy's dead seafaring grandpa. They watched the intermittently marooned sheep graze on Barbed Wire Island, half a mile off shore. The new games were more thrilling than their pre-measles child's play at pirates and submarines. They had entered a new stage of their lives.

Did they quarrel? Later, when he was expelled from paradise, Humphrey could not remember that they had ever quarrelled. They were united. Occasionally they joined gangs from Finsterness or from the town, or merged with formations of school friends. But mostly they kept themselves to themselves, a closed twosome. Sometimes they were obliged to mind Humpy's little sister Lizzie or Sandy's little brother Andrew, or to go on errands, but they endured with good nature these small infringements of their freedom. Humpy Clark and Sandy Clegg, the terrible twins, inseparable, blood brothers. Humpy's mother said, once or twice, 'You ought to go and play with the Carpenter boys sometimes, they're always asking for you.' But he didn't hear her. He didn't listen. He didn't believe her.

They were called the terrible twins, but it was only a joke. They were the same age and much the same size, and they were both skinny, but otherwise they didn't look alike. Humpy had thick fairish-brown hair, and brown eyes, and his skin turned very brown in the sun. Sandy had silky fine red hair, and blue eyes with fair lashes, and freckles, and his skin was milky-pale and blue-veined under its thin wash of seaside tan. His body looked white in the trembling water.

Sandy had two little brothers, but the smaller was only a baby and didn't count. Andrew didn't count much either, though he would sometimes whine that he wanted to play with them. Humpy and Sandy were the oldest, and they had the power.

The days were long, and in the evenings the summer light lingered.

The terraced house next door to the Cleggs belonged to stout Mrs Binns in her flowered pinny, whose fisherman husband had been drowned long before the war. Nobody remembered him. She used to take in summer lodgers, and this year, for the first time since the war, a holiday family arrived for the whole of the month of August. Mrs Binns did their breakfast and their fish tea. The quiet holidaymakers were from Sunderland. The Robinsons had come for the sea air. Mr and Mrs Robinson, and their daughter Heather. Mr and Mrs Robinson looked too old to have a daughter as young as Heather. Like the son of Diophantus, she was a late-born only child. Sandy said he could hear her at night, crying in her bedroom, through the party wall. In the mornings she would kneel on the settee in the front room, leaning over the hand-embroidered antimacassar on its back, and gaze out of the little square-paned window after the boys as they set off on their expeditions. They never thought to ask her to join them. They had no pity on her. Perhaps they enjoyed her envy. Her loneliness fortified their friendship. She had thin fair flossy thistledown hair cut straight round the edges, with a side parting. The floppy longer side of her hair was held back by a large brown hair slide which sometimes had a crumpled bow of limp blue-and-white checked ribbon attached to it. Her mouth was too wide and her nostrils were too wide and her shoulders were too high. She looked peaky and poorly, and her breathing was shallow in her chest.

Of an evening, after tea, Heather Robinson played ball, alone, endlessly, persistently, by herself, on the end wall of the cottages. One, *two*, buckle my *shoe*. Under leg and over leg and *turn*, under leg and over leg and *turn*. Twizzle and *catch*, twizzle and *catch*. Clap your handles, twizzle and catch and *turn*. Monotonously, on and on she went. Making the games more and more difficult for herself, so that she always lost.

She made it so that she could never win. She could never reach her goal. She played hopscotch by herself, against herself, with a little chipped triangle of slate, throwing it from scratched square to scratched square on the dead-end pavement at the end of the terrace outside Number 8, and hopping and jumping. *One, two, three, four/five, six, seven/eight and* turn. *Eight/seven, six, five/four, three, two, one.* All by herself, alone. Sometimes she chanted to herself, quietly, under her breath.

Sandy Clegg and Humpy Clark saw Heather Robinson and they heard Heather Robinson and they were, after a fashion, introduced to Heather Robinson, but they did not speak to her.

She was excommunicate. They gave her no hope. She expected no quarter.

Humpy was enraptured by the company of Sandy. Why did nobody warn him against rapture? Did they warn him, and did he not hear them?

The sea was full of fish, and the rock pools were teeming. British trawlers and British fishermen had been requisitioned for the war effort, and the dwindling cod stocks had replenished themselves with wanton millions of eggs. During the war the brave fishermen of Finsterness had been busy on anti-submarine patrol and mine-sweeping. They had protected convoys and carried secret supplies through the dangerous waters to the Resistance in Norway, or so the locals liked to boast. The fields of the sea had lain fallow for five years, but now they were ready to be harvested again. The fish were so thick you could walk on them. The fishermen at the little harbour claimed that when they went out, they had only to drop a line over the edge of the boat and they could catch enough codling in an hour to feed a multitude. Like Jesus and the miracle of the loaves and fishes. The codling and the haddock were waiting to be pulled up out of the bay. The

Scottish haddock had the thumbprint of St Peter on its flank, for this was the very fish that had fed the five thousand.

Sandy and Humpy were taken out with the fishermen several times, and it was exciting: feeling the tug on the tarred line, and hauling, and seeing the struggling creatures surface nose-up through the clear brine, with their lips pierced by the hooks. Up from their living element they came, swirling blue-green-white and belly-silver through the water, up to the killing air. Mercilessly the boys watched as the men wrenched the mussel-baited hooks from the throats of the fish, mercilessly they watched as the fish gasped and flopped and jerked and died on the curved wooden planks at the wet bottom of the coble. The boys would take one or two gutted fish home in a canvas bucket for tea. Codling and haddock were the favourites. They didn't bother with mackerel. Mackerel were a waste of petrol, said the fishermen. They despised mackerel. Mackerel were dirty fish and fed on sewage and dead men's flesh.

The petrol from the boat's motor spread streaked and oily flowers of iridescent blue and mauve and green upon the waters of the bay.

Nobody ate mussels in those days. Mussels were cheap bait for fat white fish. The British were conservative about fish. In the south of England they preferred cod, and in the north they liked cod and haddock. And that was that, for generations yet to come.

Nobody liked the cod liver oil the government made you swallow, but you had to swallow it, just the same. It was the law. The oil came from the cod of Iceland. Iceland did well on the war.

But the boys' private fishing expeditions, with net and bucket, were more exciting than the adult boat trips in the bay. More innocent, less lethal, but more thrilling. The teeming pleasures of the foreshore were more satisfying than the capturing of the homely, edible, slab-familiar codling. The creatures of the foreshore were as exotic as the fabled monsters of the deep. The boys hunted the saltwater fish in the rock pools and the sandy low-tide shallows. They discovered small flat greeny-yellow dabs disguised in the sand on the shoreline, and transparent shrimps with delicate joints and whiskers, with egg-eyes and egg-roe. They found crabs of many species, and the many-coloured fish of the rock pools. There were fish with spines, and fish with sucker mouths, and fish with spots and stripes: an endless variety of creatures. Their uselessness was their glory. The boys knew the humble gobies and the blennies, and the vertical bony-bodied quaint pipefish that swam so proud, so thin and so erect.

And they pursued the freshwater fish in the deep quarry pond in Maybrick Field, enticing them with maggots and sliced worms. They caught minnows and stickleback. They became experts at the fish watch. They knew they would both be champion salmon fishermen when they grew up.

Neither they nor the stickleback knew that the stickleback was the classical animal of ethology. They did not know that Niko Tinbergen, the sage of stickleback scholarship, had written the words 'Study Nature Not Books' over his study door. But they followed his advice, unknowingly.

Maggots were easy to come by. If you left a piece of old bacon in the garden shed, it would soon begin to heave and seethe. Nobody had a refrigerator in those days. Maggots and blow flies were familiar to housewives and to schoolboys.

They tried to take the tide-pool fish home and to keep them as pets. But at first they couldn't manage to keep them alive for long enough to make the experiment satisfactory. They tried jam jars, and Kilner pickling jars, and tin buckets, but the fish continued, disappointingly, to perish, and to float reproachfully to the surface, their underwater colours fading rapidly. Even the hermit crabs died, extruding themselves from their protective shells and growing queerly larger in death. (How could so large a creature have curled itself up into so small a space?) The boys felt sad when they saw the dead fish and the dead crabs, but they persevered, scientifically, mercilessly, and one day they spotted their aquarium, covered in dust and cobwebs, standing on a shelf above a workbench, in the ramshackle Crossways Garage on the corner by the crossroads.

Jock, the garage mechanic, was nice to the boys, though their mothers seemed not to care for him. Jock was dark and leathery and melancholy, with a gaunt, handsome face and brooding eyes set in deep sockets. His hair was black like a foreigner's, like a gypsy's. Jock gave them hard round white peppermints from his sweet ration. The mints were called Mint Imperials. Sometimes he gave them a drink of highly coloured and poisonously delicious Cherryade, a drink that stained their tongues and lips a sharp synthetic wicked pink.

Jock smelled of oil and grease. He was a loner. He was of a different stock.

Jock sold them the tank for a shilling.

The tank had something to do with motorcars or perhaps motorbikes, but they didn't know what, and didn't care. They weren't interested in cars and motorbikes. They weren't very interested in pushbikes. Humphrey's Auntie Vera had a pushbike, with a big basket, on which she used to ride to school, but the children didn't have bikes. That summer they went barefoot.

It was a square tank of solid thick greenish glass, and, unlike a real aquarium, it was as tall as it was wide. It looked spacious and romantic. Surely fish would like to live in it? Surely they would live happily within its swirling wavy watermarked walls? The thickness and patterning of its green glass were strange and mysterious.

The boys carried the tank home to Turkey Bank. They scrubbed it clean and polished it, and rinsed off the soap several times, and set it up on a platform of bricks in the small paved backyard between the outside WC and the coal shed. They brought sand and small pebbles and uninhabited shells from the beach to make a bottom layer, a seabed, and in it they planted little fronds and trees of green and crimson and brown seaweed. They weighted the seaweed with twists of lead and little metal washers. One or two larger stones served as rocks: these stones were already supplied with a living shrubbery of algae and with encrustations of pimpled barnacles and domed limpets. The boys made an arch, of two leaning stones, to make a landscape for their fish. They knew they needed weeds, for oxygenation and aeration. It was lack of oxygen that had killed their first little prisoners. Impatiently, they waited two whole days for their tank of seawater to establish its balance before they went fishing again.

Heather Robinson next door watched them as they set off with their canvas bucket.

She watched them as they came home with their catch.

They released their trawl of fish into the tank with a feeling of omnipotent magnanimity, and the dazed fish, after the first shock of arrival, seemed grateful. They began to dart about, exploring the vitreous green space of their new residence. They swam through the arch and nuzzled the barnacles.

Would there be enough air for them? It was Humphrey who thought of the rubber dropper. He stole it from the bathroom cabinet at Burnside Avenue. It was one of those little glass tubes with a rubber squeezer on the end. Humpy's mother used it for putting olive oil down your ears when you had earache. If you squeezed the air out of it, under water, it acted just like those little automatic electrical aeration pumps they had seen in the solitary showpiece tropical fish tank in the pet shop in town. You had to be patient, you had to sit there and squeeze the little lung, lifting it in and out, and in and out, to refill with air and then with water. This was boring. But it was worth it, if it kept the fish going.

And the fish did keep going. The tank was a success.

It was easier to study fish in a tank than in a rock pool.

Sandy was good at the names of the fish. He remembered names and words better than Humpy. Sandy liked words for their own sake. But Humpy watched to see how the fish behaved. He watched their patterns of fighting and hiding, of grouping and darting and nuzzling. He watched their little gulping mouths and their beating fins. Some of them could swim backwards.

It was a small and complete world, and they were proud of it. The adults also approved of it as a worthy educational project, but the boys did not let that discourage them. Adults were not always wrong. The boys would spend minutes at a time squatting on their haunches by it and peering into its miniature marine garden. On their explorations on the beach and foreshore, they would collect new treasures for its decor – a red snail, a green snail, an empty shell worn smooth to spirals of mother-of-pearl. A frond of luminous sea lettuce, a pebble with a streak of glittering fool's gold, a periwinkle. Auntie Vera was so impressed by their dedication to the tank that she bought them a little book called *Treasures of the Sea-Shore*, with pictures of fishes and mermaid's purses and dead men's fingers and sea squirts and scallops and bladder wrack. '*For Humpy and Sandy, 17 August*', she wrote on its flyleaf, in her big clear round schoolmistress's script. The book had a stiff dark blue cover with the title picked out in gold, rather like a Bible. It was a slim dark blue Bible of the seashore.

They were pleased with the book, and with the respect that it showed to their hobby.

One evening, Humphrey, lingering on the stairs on his way up to bed, overheard them in the kitchen. 'It's a shame,' his aunt was saying. 'But I know it's got to be.'

He could hear the resigned click of his grandmother's wooden knitting needles.

'It's been quite long enough,' his mother then said in a weary tone. 'We've been quite long enough.'

'It's a shame for the boy,' said Auntie Vera. 'He's picked up so well.'

The end of the summer was approaching, and they would have to leave soon. He knew this, and he did not know it. There had been unexpected delays. He had thought that perhaps they might stay here for ever, in this headland outpost of women and children. But of course that could not be.

The last days of August and the first days of September were calm and mild and warm. The sea was flat and smooth, and in the evenings the small waves curled and broke without force. The low sun slanted, the fields were yellow, the wind-carved hedges were dotted with scarlet hips and berries, the garden was full of mauve and golden autumn flowers. The yellow sea poppies turned a silky withering orange, and the weatherbeaten leaning trees changed to russet and to red. Bitter purple sloes hid themselves among the thorns.

The grown-ups did not speak to him much, directly, of the removal. His mother, when she referred to it, spoke of 'going home'. But the place to which they were going was not and would not be his home. It was not even the same house. The old pre-war house had been demolished. They were going to a new house, and a new school, and a new life.

The boys never discussed Humphrey's imminent departure. They had no way of speaking about it, so they behaved as though it would not happen.

Nobody spoke. That was the way it was.

It was the crisis over the fish that made them speak.

On one of their last days, they caught a new fish, a dazzling new greenish-bronze and rose and tawny fish, of a species they had not seen before. It was large, by rock-pool standards, a good three inches long, and bristling with spines and bravery. They netted it, and carried it home in the sun-faded pale blue-green canvas bucket, and released it into the aquarium where it dashed around angrily. Neither of them liked the way it hurtled about. They watched it uneasily. It's too big, Humphrey said, and Sandy agreed, it was too big. Sandy said it was a sea scorpion, but Humphrey said it wasn't. It didn't look very like the picture of the sea scorpion in Auntie Vera's book. But then, none of the creatures looked exactly like the pictures in Auntie Vera's book, except for the limpets and the mussels, and even they were more complicated and more various than they seemed at first sight.

The handsome fish dashed angrily.

Sandy liked the name, 'sea scorpion'. He liked the words. We'll let it go in the morning, he said.

But when Humphrey went round to Turkey Bank in the morning, the new fish had vanished. There was the tank, and all its smaller, duller inhabitants, but the fine stranger had disappeared. Sandy was in despair. 'Someone stole our new fish,' he kept repeating. They would have blamed poor innocent Heather next door at Mrs Binns's, but the Robinsons had unobtrusively packed up and left on Saturday. Humphrey thought of suggesting that Mrs Clegg had done it, but he didn't dare. Who could it have been? They crouched down, interrogating the tank for its secrets. Where was their fish? Had some envious thief taken it in the night?

It was Humphrey who found it dead, tail up, wedged between two bricks by the wall, a good yard away from the aquarium.

At first they went on trying to think of someone else to blame, but they knew it was useless. They had only themselves to blame. The fish had committed suicide. It had jumped out of its confines, like a salmon up the falls, and opted for death. The salmon leap up the falls in hope of life, but their fish had abandoned hope. The sea was beyond its reach and beyond its hoping. They had murdered it.

The boys felt rotten. They did not like to touch the stiffened corpse. They wished they had left the fish in its pool, where it had been at home and happy. They did not need to say this to each other, because they were in accord, they were thinking with one mind. Nevertheless, Humphrey spoke.

'You look after those,' he said, gesturing at the remaining fish and weeds and little water scuttlers.

He said it without reproach, and Sandy took it without offence.

'I'll look after them,' pledged Sandy solemnly.

They did not look at each other, but the agreement was sealed. Humphrey would leave, and Sandy would stay. That was how it would be. That was how it had to be. They had no choice in the matter.

They never mentioned their imminent parting again and did not say goodbye. They went on playing together, in the last days, as though the summer would have no end. Humphrey observed the packing and the parcelling, and was even drawn in to do a little sorting and discarding himself. 'You can't take *that* with you,' his mother would say of important and valued objects. Her adult views seemed arbitrary to him, for they were not based wholly on size. Some of the objects he hid, others he relinquished. Trunks were made up and sent in advance by rail, hand luggage was kept separate. Humphrey made a final mark on his bedroom ceiling. He would be back soon, of course he would be back. And on the last morning, he got into the taxi, and off they went to the railway station, without a backward glance. Not looking back was bravado. Not saying goodbye was bravado. It was better not to say goodbye. It would be bad luck to admit that this was the end.

The last day of the holidays. The last day of summer. The end of an initiation.

Dumb with his aching throat, Professor Humphrey Clark listened to the rhythm of the train, which had acquired a soothing and even monotony as it had picked up speed beyond Peterborough. You could still see the cathedral of Peterborough from the railway, if you remembered to look: it was not yet totally obscured by the shopping mall and the carpet warehouse and Pets at Home and the multi-storey car park.

Whinstone and dolerite, dolerite and whinstone. G16, G16. One man went to mow, went to mow a meadow.

Why had that jingling lullaby come into his head? When he was little he had thought that the men in the song went to a place called Mower Meadow. In his boy's imagination, it had been a golden field, full of ripe ears of wheat and scarlet corn poppies and white-petalled yellow-centred marguerites. Flowers waist-high grew wild in Mower Meadow.

His mother in the rocking chair, with his sister on her knee. He was too big to sit on his mother's knee.

Out of the cradle, endlessly rocking.

Hippocampus, Diophantus.

Hippocampus hippocampus is a sea horse. It is also the name of the seat of memory in the brain.

The latest news from the sea horse breeding programme at the Green Grotto had not been promising. Sea horses are fashionable, but they need more than money to survive. They are occasionally fished up from the wild, off the cold coast of Britain, where their cousins the pipefish breed, but they are rare now, and around the world they are endangered. They are too quaintly attractive, too unthreatening for their own good. Their magical properties have put them at risk.

The cold coast of north-eastern Britain is not as cold as it was. Global warming has warmed it up, and species are migrating northwards.

Humphrey Clark looked at the menu. Crayfish sandwiches with mayo were on offer. Should he order a Brie and rocket baguette? None of those three words had existed when he was a boy, or not in their present configuration. Should he risk some wine? The menu offered him House Red Vin Pay [sic] D'Oc for £10.95. It said it was specially blended of ripe, rich fruit with firm body and a smooth finish. The Chilean red boasted great depth of colour and vibrancy. Or he could have a Chablis Premier Cru with depth of fruit, freshness and concentration.

He was on his way to what was supposed to be a celebration.

He looked out of the window for guidance, and met again his own image on the lightly rain-spotted glass. Was he now as ugly to small children as those old men in the ward had once been to him?

The hermaphrodite crayfish. He remembered the whole sentence from *The Children's Encyclopedia*: 'Hermaphrodites are more common in the invertebrate world.' A microbiologist called Paul Burden from San Diego had recently published a popular science book called *Hermaphrodite*. It seemed to have been well received. Not his kind of thing, probably, but he ought to overcome his resistance and have a look at it one day. It had been shortlisted for the Society's Plunkett Prize. He had been invited to the prize dinner, but Mrs Hornby had told him he wouldn't have been able to accept even if he had wanted to go, because he had a dinner engagement at the Athenaeum, and so she had declined on his behalf. The Plunkett Prize ceremony had been a black-tie do, last night, or perhaps a couple of nights ago. He hadn't even seen the invitation: Mrs Hornby had taken possession of it, declined it, and disposed of it. He wondered if Burden's book had won. He had not seen anything in the press, but then he hadn't looked, had he? He'd won the prize himself, long ago, in the days when he had been more in fashion.

The railway tea had been free, but the baguette would cost him £3.95.

He tried to remember what it was like, being a boy. He could not remember what a cup of tea and a slice of bread and butter might have cost when he was a boy.

The Public Orator has been able to fill in some of the gaps in Humphrey Clark's memories of Finsterness and Ornemouth. The Public Orator knows things that Humphrey Clark has forgotten, and, unusually, has had access to a form of audit. He knows the price of a bottle of milk and a loaf of bread in post-war Ornemouth. Twopence halfpenny, in old money, in 1947, for a large white loaf: that had been the going rate. It is hard to credit this now. These handwritten notes are useful as a guide to inflation, and they also record the dates of events. But there are gaps of time and shifts of attitude that they do not cover. The records are incomplete. They tell one side of the story only. The records do not follow

Humphrey Clark back to the Midlands and to Covington. Schoolboy Humphrey escapes surveillance there.

It is part of the Orator's job to retrieve the telling anecdote, the personal foible.

The Public Orator diverts his attention from Humphrey Clark in Coach G, and glances anxiously towards the material figure of Ailsa Kelman. The Public Orator must keep track of Ailsa Kelman too. She, like Humphrey Clark, is on her way towards the past. The timing of her meeting with the past is a worry to the Public Orator.

Ailsa Kelman is not on the East Coast train to Newcastle and Ornemouth and Edinburgh, although she might have been. She had at one point thought of booking herself a seat on it. But she changed her mind. She is on an aeroplane.

Ailsa does not have a Mrs Hornby in her life, to squeeze her into whalebone corsets and to dress her hair and to hook up the back of her dress and to answer her letters and to make her bookings and to prepare her folders and her schedules and her timetables. She has an agent, but she does not have a personal assistant. She likes her privacy and her freedom too much. At times, when her engagements become complicated and her double bookings confusing, she will go into an overdrive feminist mode and blame the male culture of servant dependency that makes women like herself such martyrs to the very concept of independence. She has at times spoken forcefully and angrily and even persuasively about this, for Ailsa can find an ideological excuse for anything.

She can explain that she has missed out on being able to receive help of any kind, through being from the wrong class, in the wrong era, and of the wrong sex. But in her heart she knows that it is largely a highly personal selfishness rather than a generic female weakness that prevents her from employing a personal assistant. She has tried once or twice over the years, and it has never worked. Ailsa is too proud and too capricious and too inconsistent and too sudden in her whims to be able to employ anybody. She is a nightmare. Yes, Ailsa will nod enthusiastically, when challenged: a nightmare!

So here she is, pressing her nose against a small thick unreflective slab of aeroplane window, wondering if she will be able to see Durham Cathedral from the air. Or any other landmark that she recognizes from the old days. She is flying to Newcastle, and there she will pick up a hire car to drive herself north to Ornemouth.

She wants to be free to explore, to examine those old seaside memories of long ago, when they had been children playing on the shore.

Ailsa likes to be airborne. She likes aeroplanes. They are modern and charged with adrenalin, stress and promises. They lack the old-fashioned lull and lullaby of the train. They carry no childhood baggage. Ailsa cannot get on an aeroplane without feeling a spurious sense of importance, however short or dull the flight. Hers is the first generation fully to enjoy this freedom, this unnatural stimulus, this defiantly extravagant consumption of diminishing resources.

Like a child, Ailsa Kelman still expects something new to happen every time she approaches the departure gate. She knows that the story is not over.

That could have been a fatal seaside summer, says Ailsa to herself. She is lucky to have escaped its protracted consequences. She is lucky to be alive and well, and remarkably fit for her age. And game, she hopes, to confront it all once more.

Somewhere down there is the town of her birth, and the ruined industrial coastline that nobody has ever visited for its sea air. You could walk for seven leagues under the sea in the old mine workings, but you couldn't play on the sullied shore.

You could scrabble for nuggets of coal and slack on the beaches, but you couldn't play.

She had told P. B. she was going to Ornemouth, but he hadn't been very interested. The day would soon come when no secret would shock, no revelation would intrigue. She would soon be yesterday's news. Even if she rode naked on a white horse down Whitehall, nobody would notice.

Well, she would make them notice.

The attendant on board this cheap flight is respectful and addresses her as 'Ms Kelman' with appropriate deference and a conspiratorial smile of apparent recognition. But Ailsa isn't a fool, and she knows they're trained to address everybody by name, to be obsequious to everybody. Everybody is somebody. It's hard to keep your head above water, these days. It's hard to stand out from the crowd. It's a tricky business, status.

A living dog is better than a dead lion. So said the Preacher, in Ecclesiastes. *Vanity, vanity, all is vanity.* So said the Preacher.

Ailsa Kelman remembers the price of a loaf and a herring. She knows the records well, for she has studied them closely, but they constitute only a small fraction of her extravagant action-packed history. The Public Orator fears that she may deny them, she may refuse them, and leap over them into some other and less relevant reality. She may decide to inhabit some other story, to privilege another section of her life. The Public Orator hopes for coherence and conjunction. He does not wish to be obliged to force the plot. He wishes it to unfold itself as a plant unfurls its fronds towards the light, according to its nature. But for this unfolding, he needs the help of Ailsa Kelman.

Humphrey Clark studies the menu. He does not remember post-war prices very well, but he remembers leaving Finsterness and arriving in Covington, where he was never to feel at home. As a boy he did not like the new house. He did not like the new city. He did not like his new school. He did not like the bland taste of the water that came from the taps. He did not like the sooty smell of the air. He did not like his father, who reappeared in his life as an unwelcome stranger, contaminated by war.

His father was a tall, lean, shy, bespectacled, serious man, who seemed nervous in the company of his two children. He tried to make overtures to Lizzie, but she fought to get off his knee and ran away at his approach. Humphrey tried to hold his ground, politely, but it was hard.

He did not settle easily after the uprooting. He pined for his bedroom by the water cistern. He could not adjust. At school in Goldthorpe Road, he was behind with his lessons, although, in the little school at Finsterness, he had been ahead. He could not understand why this was so. His teacher said he was making what she called 'slow but steady progress', but he knew better. He knew he was not making progress. He was growing more stupid. His learning capacity was on hold, in abeyance. He did not yet know the words 'abeyance' and 'regression', but he felt the meaning of them in his spirit.

At school, he was teased. When his mother called 'Humpy' to him across the asphalt playground, the other boys sniggered, as though his nickname had a bad meaning. He did not like his school uniform of maroon and grey. It made him look silly.

He worried silently, inwardly, about the aquarium in Sandy's backyard in Turkey Bank in Finsterness. Were the fish and the hermit crabs and the anemones surviving? What would happen to them in the winter?

Sometimes he thought of the death leap of the sea scorpion. He and Sandy had murdered the sea scorpion. It had been a wicked act. His mother and his aunt and his grandmother had murdered docile Blackie, who had sucked at his pyjamas for comfort like a baby, and he and Sandy between them had murdered the fighting fish.

He never thought of writing to Sandy. He had no stamps, and no paper to write on. He had to be brave, until the next summer, when he might be allowed to go back.

Was the word 'stoic' familiar to him at that age?

Professor Humphrey Clark, travelling north through the Midlands, and looking out at a flowing landscape of cooling towers and poplar trees, could not remember what words he had then known, and how he had articulated his feelings to himself. But he could remember the feelings. And he knew that he had known the story about the little Spartan boy gnawed to death by the fox he hid under his cloak. He had read it in *The Children's Encyclopedia*. He had never quite understood what the little boy intended to do with the fox, or why he was hiding it in the first place, but he remembered the message of the story very well: *Don't show that it hurts*.

He had been stoic. He had stuck at his lessons, he had settled down, he was tolerated. He did well in his maths and got good marks. Gold stars, occasionally, were stuck upon his homework. He still thought he would work harder and harder and solve all the riddles. He had not forgotten about Diophantus. Diophantus was his secret well of promised knowledge. He would say the name to himself, for comfort. He wasn't sure if he was pronouncing it right, in his head, but he thought that he was.

Nobody else knew about Diophantus.

He still couldn't work out the age of Diophantus correctly. Did he die aged eighty-three, or aged eighty-four? There was something wrong with his adding up, but he couldn't quite work out what it was. Algebra was the answer, but they didn't do proper algebra yet.

Covington had its consolations. Humphrey liked the nature table, where the fruits of the suburbs were laid out on a bed of brilliantly green moss. Acorns and conkers and prickly sweet chestnuts and beechnuts, red and yellow palmate and pinnate autumn leaves, black and blue and copper and scarlet berries, hips and haws, winged seeds, and elf-cup mushrooms growing on wrinkled silver bark.

The days in Covington filled in, and he started to live a trivial, superficial, bare-kneed, short-trousered boyish life. He began to present a fair outward imitation of a schoolboy. Nobody, seeing him, could have told that he was a fraud. Christmas came, and with it came Auntie Vera and Grandma. Auntie Vera and Grandma brought suitcases, and presents wrapped up in wrinkled red and green coloured crêpe paper, and news of Finsterness. Humphrey found the meeting of the two worlds disconcerting. His Midlands world was shallow and fragile, badly damaged and newly painted, full of danger and false steps. It was built precariously, on rubble. The summer past and the winter present did not fit together. They were of two different orders of reality. His memory world was deep, but Auntie Vera and Grandma could not fully restore it to him. It had been sealed off.

Auntie Vera spoke of Sandy Clegg. She reported that he was getting on well in class, but gave no details. Soon Sandy would be going to the big school, the Grammar School, in the old stone building across the bridge. If he passed the Common Entrance, which of course he would. Auntie Vera did not mention the backyard aquarium, although she had once taken such an interest in it, and Humphrey thought it would be bad luck to ask her about it now. He was deeply puzzled by the knowledge that even then, *even at that instant*, as he sat there watching Grandma dozing and toasting her legs into mottled blotches by the gas fire in 38 Greenside Close,

Covington, *even at that instant* Sandy Clegg continued to exist, and continued to pursue a life in time. He would have preferred to have believed that the other life had stood still, suspended in his absence, arrested from the moment of his departure.

They went on a family outing to the pantomime, dressed up in their best, and Lizzie cried when the stout, gruff-voiced Pantomime Dame shouted personal remarks at a child in the second-to-front row of the audience. The child was wearing a red velvet frock, and she was fidgeting and jumping about a lot. The Dame asked the red velvet child if she wanted to go to the Ladies, which was embarrassing, and not at all funny. Lizzie was afraid the Dame might pick on her next. Lizzie was wearing a blue woollen dress with a white lace collar that had been handed down from somebody called Cousin Joan whom they had never seen. In those days, most people wore second-hand clothes.

The Clarks were timid children. They did not like to be conspicuous. It was inconceivable to them that a person could wish to be noticed, could wish to attract attention or to stand upon a public stage.

While they were looking anxiously through the front-room window for the taxi to take Auntie Vera and Grandma to the station for their homeward journey north, Humphrey heard Grandma say to his mother, 'Well, think about the summer, won't you? See what he says.'

Humphrey heard this, and remembered it, but he said nothing.

When Grandma's birthday approached, in June, his mother told him to write Grandma a birthday letter. He sat there dutifully at the kitchen table, but he could not think of anything to say. He asked his mother what to put in his letter.

'Just wish her a happy birthday, and tell her about something that happened at school. She'd like that.'

That is what his mother said.

Why would she like it?

Because she would, affirmed his mother.

Dear Grandma, Happy Birthday, he wrote dutifully.

Tell her about how your class went to the swimming pool at Moorhead, prompted his mother. Your grandpa was a great swimmer, she said.

We went swimming at Moorhead Baths, he wrote dutifully.

Humphrey was a good swimmer. Some of the boys in his class couldn't swim at all. The pool smelled of chlorine, and the green-and-white tiles were slippery, and the lockers stank of wet wool and other people's socks, but he had enjoyed the outing. He had jumped off the top springboard, and tried a somersault. Nobody else had dared, and Mr Lester had said well done. Humphrey had told his friend Alan Burns about Lifesaving, and about how to bring drowned men back from the dead even when all hope had gone. Alan Burns had been interested, and had allowed Humphrey to practise Lifesaving on him. Humphrey had told Alan about Grace Darling and the rescue of the survivors from the wreck of the *Forfarshire*. He had written a composition about 'Grace Darling, Daughter of the Lighthouse Keeper', and Miss Matthews had given it a gold star and asked him to read it aloud in class. It had not been very good, but she had liked it.

In those days, Grace Darling had not been appropriated. Boys were allowed to be interested in Grace Darling, and nobody warned them off. Miss Matthews had not tried to grab Grace Darling back from him.

He did not think Grandma would be interested in any of that, at her age, so he did not write any of it down. He could not think of anything else to write to her. Words deserted him. He gazed with deep dissatisfaction at his childish handwriting and its boring message. He hoped for better from himself.

'Is that enough?' he asked his mother.

'Tell her you look forward to seeing her in the summer,' she said.

Humphrey tried not to betray pleasure or surprise.

Did his mother mean it?

Humphrey stared at his sheet of notepaper. Then he wrote, in one reckless burst of fluency,

> *I look forward to seeing you in the summer. Please tell Auntie*
> *Vera to tell Sandy I am coming.*
>> *With love*
>> *from*
>> *Humphrey*

Would they all be going? He could not imagine that his father would go with them to Finsterness. His father was always at work, at the office in Corporation Street. Did his father ever have a holiday? Sometimes he went away to London, but that was not going on holiday. His father went to meetings in London, work meetings about town planning and reinforced concrete and reconstruction and zones. And if his father did want to go to Grandma's, there would be nowhere for him to sleep, would there?

Humphrey did not often venture into the new double bedroom where his parents slept. It had a new double bed, and a new dressing table with an oval mirror, and a new wardrobe. It was called a Utility Suite.

Mrs Clegg noted in her little book that divans were for sale at Bewick's with metal base, mattress and headboard for £8 7s. 6d.

The only piece of old furniture in his parents' bedroom was something they called an ottoman, which was crammed full of hoarded papers and letters and old school exercise books. He knew, without being told, that he must never look at anything in the ottoman.

The room was not forbidden, but it was unfamiliar, unhomely, unwelcoming. He knew they did not want him in there.

Humphrey tried to piece the summer's plans together from hints and suggestions. He was afraid to ask a direct question, though he did not know why he was afraid. An uneasiness possessed him. He wanted so much to go to Finsterness that he was sure that something would prevent him. He anticipated disappointment. He muttered charms and incantations, to ward off unknown disasters. Superstitiously, he touched every lime tree in the avenue on the way home from the bus stop. He never missed one. He knew that if he missed one, he would never see the northern sea again. He would be condemned for ever to the inland Midlands. When other boys discussed their summer holidays, he tried to keep quiet, though sometimes he said defensively, for conformity's sake, for pride's sake, that he too would be going to the seaside. The word 'seaside' was a decoy, for it suggested buckets and spades and French cricket and sandcastles with paper flags on sticks. Finsterness was not like that. It was not a bucket-and-spade place.

He wondered if he would ever see the Pool of Brochan.

Alan's family was going to the Isle of Man.

The Isle of Man was posh, Blackpool was vulgar.

These distinctions meant nothing to Humphrey Clark.

As the end of the summer term approached, Humphrey's forebodings intensified. He could tell that something bad was happening. Sometimes he overheard phrases like 'it might not be sensible to take the risk' or 'just in case anything happens'. There was even talk about hospitals. His mother said once, out of the blue over breakfast, in a falsely cheerful tone, 'Well, the infirmary at Ornemouth isn't all that bad, is it, Humpy? They did a good job on your tonsils, didn't they?'

Were they planning to send him back to the infirmary, to the ward full of beastly old men?

His mother seemed even more anxious and preoccupied than usual, and took to lying down on her bed in the afternoons.

One Saturday morning, they told him that their plans had altered. Mummy wasn't very well, so they wouldn't be going to Grandma's for the summer after all.

At the time, he said nothing. He put his spoon back in his cereal bowl, and said nothing. He said nothing at dinner. He said nothing at tea. He said nothing all day, and he went to bed in silence. When he said his routine prayers at night, he prayed that they might change their minds.

This approach produced results. The next morning, his father asked him if he was feeling all right. Humphrey answered, 'Yes,' but did not amplify.

'You've gone very quiet,' said his mother.

They knew quite well what was the matter with him. There was no need for anybody to speak about it.

After three or four days, when his father came back from work, he came straight into the kitchen, where Lizzie and Humphrey were having supper, and sat down on one of the bentwood kitchen chairs by the Rayburn. He very rarely did this. Humphrey and Lizzie carried on eating their cauliflower cheese. Humphrey had saved the brown crispy bits until last. His father waited until Humphrey had finished, and then he said, 'I've been thinking about the summer, Humpy, and we think you would like to go to your grandma's, wouldn't you?'

Humphrey nodded.

'Would you mind going on your own?' asked his father.

It was the first time he had ever been asked an adult question, expecting an adult answer. Was it a trick question?

He took the risk. Again, he nodded.

'We think you're a bit young to go on the train by yourself,' said his father, 'but when the term's over, Auntie Vera can come to fetch you.' He paused, took his glasses off, and polished them on his blue spotted handkerchief. 'The sea air will be good for you,' he said almost apologetically, as though ashamed of this concession to his son's hidden desires.

'What about me?' asked Lizzie.

But it seemed that Lizzie was too little to go without her mother. She'd be too much for Grandma and Auntie Vera. She had to stay with Mummy. Lizzie didn't know whether to be cross or pleased. But Humphrey knew what he felt. He felt relief at this reprieve, an overwhelming relief. He didn't care whether Lizzie went or not. Lizzie was irrelevant. He was happy to go on his own. This meant that he could return to the places. He and Sandy could return to the places. His powers would be restored to him. He would shed the carapace of the uniformed subjugated Covington schoolboy from Greenside Close and Goldthorpe Road Junior School, and become once more a free spirit.

The sea air would be good for him.

That's what they all said, as they anxiously justified their kindly decision.

The sea air would be good for him.

The whinstone and sandstone would be good for him.

The arches of the three bridges would be good for him.

The sea air would be good for him.

Professor Clark mouthed an order for a gin and tonic and a Brie and rocket and marmalade baguette, and the young woman brought them to him.

Abeyance, latency, regression, recession. He had not known these words when he was a boy, and they were not wholly present in his conscious mind now, but somewhere the notions of them swam, in the creeks and inlets, amidst the green and crimson infusoria of wordless memory. The cold sharp fluid flowed down his stiff sore throat, as he journeyed onwards and backwards towards the places that were his childhood.

Sandy Clegg had been the one for words. And where was Sandy now?

The barman in the *Flying Scotsman*'s galley had been generous with the gin, as well as with the ice and lemon. The drink had a kick.

Beastly, rotten, mean, barmy, batty, awful. Spiffing, scrummy. Gosh, corks, blimey, golly.

These had been some of the words of his uncontaminated boyhood; these had been the counters and the coinage. And these words swam up busily now into his active recollection, as he tackled the small-format section of one of the broadsheet newspapers. The pages seemed happily empty of those names that lurked like cowards in the caverns of his mind, ready to dart and strike, but nevertheless here was much that tended and intended, on a more general front, to provoke and to distress. Here, for example, was an article about a new exhibition of contemporary art that had aroused some controversy. The exhibition included artefacts that were decorated with words that in his childhood had been unknown to him. Rude words, forbidden words. When had he first come across these words that now appeared so freely for women, servants and children to read? (He was old enough to remember the *Lady Chatterley* trial, although servants had not been a feature of his home life.) Had he first encountered them at school in suburban Covington? At Goldthorpe Road Junior School, or at King Edward's Grammar School? Surely he had not known them in the innocent outpost of Finsterness, or in the quiet solemn strait-laced handsome town of Ornemouth?

Bum and *tit*. Those words he had known as a schoolboy. But these words, here on the page before him? Did his serious black-haired Japanese-American grandson know these words?

Of course he did. All children knew them now, even in rural England.

He had been protected, at the school in Finsterness, because Miss Neil was his auntie. A circle of discretion had surrounded him.

His grandma's black cat in Finsterness had been called Blackie, but the black cat next door but one was called Smuts, and nobody in Finsterness had sniggered at that. 'Humpy,' his mother had called to him, across the arena of the playground in Covington. He had not known till then that it was a lewd and silly name.

Simple days, simple times.

Now he knew it all. He had lived through the austere fifties, and the liberating sixties, and the shifty seventies, and the mercenary eighties, and the power-driven, value-free nineties. He had become worldly, and at home in the world. He had grown leathery with age, invulnerable, thick of skin, and idly, imperviously pleasant. He had worked hard at this transformation.

His throat, however, had remained tender, vulnerable, and easy to infect. And now he was speechless, on his way back to his childhood.

The tonic cooled and soothed his throat, the gin sparked his neurones and flickered through his synapses. He could feel the gin at work somewhere in the back of his head.

The hippocampus stores new memories. The old memories live on, already deposited, in some other part of the brain.

If the hippocampus fails, you can still move backwards in time, to those earlier days (to Blackie, to the ether and the infirmary, to Mrs Binns and her lodgers, to Jock's aquarium and to the Spartan boy), but you cannot increase the memory store with new impressions and carry them on with you into the future. And so time itself changes shape and is distorted. The past swells like a tumour and displaces the present.

Should he try to find time to revisit his grandmother's old house, or the village school in Finsterness, or the little row of cottages at Turkey Bank? He was booked into the hotel for two nights, for Mrs Hornby had persuaded him that it would be too tiring for him to take the afternoon train back the next day. He had the time, the university term was well over, and his minimal teaching and administrative duties were in abeyance. So he would have a free evening, unless other events had been arranged to fill it in.

He had enjoyed teaching, once.

Did those once familiar buildings yet stand? Turkey Bank would still be there, for it was picturesque and old and the whole row must by now be listed as a grouping of architectural importance, but the village school had been an undistinguished structure, built in the 1920s. The Grammar School over the bridge, which Sandy Clegg had in due course attended, was an historic building, with a fine academic record, and it stood where it had always stood.

Mrs Hornby's helpful notes had informed him of this.

The plain slices and solid pudding of the past, were they still there? And would the shining sea of hope and of discovery renew its invitation, so late, so late, so late in the day? Or was he condemned to nudge for ever with his ugly nose against the smeared glass?

Did the tame codfish in the rock pool still come to the hand to be fed?

What had happened to Sandy Clegg? He did not often think of the inevitable end of his friendship with Sandy Clegg. It was hard to think of Sandy Clegg growing older, in real time. Maybe he still lived in the north-east. Maybe he had moved on, decades ago. Had Sandy followed the story of the successful career of his old boyhood playmate, Humphrey Clark? Or had he forgotten that he had ever existed? Humphrey's memories of Sandy Clegg were sharp, discrete, fixed, but the emotion that surrounded them was fluid and murky. Had Sandy prospered in life, as he himself had done?

He had forgotten most of the children at his aunt's school. Only a few names lingered. He remembered the lonely little holiday girl, who had played her solitary games so persistently next door, during that long hot summer, but he had forgotten her name. The memory of her stubborn, stoic misery stayed with him, but her name had gone. He would know it if he heard it, but he could not summon it back without a prompt. He hoped that she had escaped from the loneliness of Finsterness, and had enjoyed a rich and happy life, with friends and family, with children and grandchildren. He would never know what had happened to her, and he did not like to consider why he remembered her so well.

At the end of his compartment he could now see a family party, which had joined the train at Grantham – a young mother with three young children. They were not a first-class family, but they had been found seats in first class as the rest of the train was full. He had overheard the little drama of this, conducted with great friendliness and laughter on all sides. And now the young mother was being very attentive to her offspring, in a textbook manner, and keeping them quiet with a selection of magazines and games. She wore her sunglasses on top of her head, perched on a jaunty little knot of baby-pink ribbon surmounting her sun-fair hair, which was tied up in what might once have been called a ponytail. Her trousers were a deep bright shocking pink, and round her throat she wore a necklace of sparkling iridescent green-blue-silver beads. (Were artificial pearls still coloured by a coating of fish-scale brew of guanine crystals? The brew that, magically, was known as 'essence of Orient'? He had been in love all his life with the glitter of fish.) The children wore blue baseball caps and highly coloured shirts emblazoned with various slogans and studded with medallions and glittering insets of reflective glass. The smallest child had a toy helicopter. The two older children had a magazine each, and a pen each. He heard the mother say to them, 'You see, you just have to join the dots, and you'll see the picture come.'

They applied themselves earnestly, as children used to do. No bickering, no bad language, just the earnest quiet application of pencil and crayon.

Were they setting off on their summer holidays?

Mrs Binns at Turkey Bank had had a jam jar full of glass beads, for threading and unthreading. Humphrey had wanted to have a go with them, but beads were for girls. She also had some Prince Rupert's tears, in a separate pot in a cabinet. Nobody was allowed to play with those, they were too special, they might shatter if you held them in the wrong way.

They looked lighter, less solemn, these children, than the children of his childhood. They looked much happier than – and now the name came back to him, surfacing unexpectedly – they looked happier than that girl called Heather Robinson. Their colours were brighter, more playful, more eclectic, and their mother was bright and girlish. This family had never known rationing, austerity, prohibition. They had lived all their lives in a world of baguettes and burgers, of chocolates and Coca Cola. Not in a world of dripping and jam sandwiches and Cherryade and compulsory cod liver oil.

Shipham's paste. There had once been a treat called Shipham's paste. These children would not know about Shipham's paste.

But some things do not change. The children still liked to join the dots, and to see the picture come.

The Public Orator waits to see the picture come. He sees the faces rising in the broken mirror of the water. Like dead fish, like drowned men, they rise from the depths, and quiver, and reassemble.

Ailsa Kelman, as a child, had played the old childhood games. She had joined the dots, and found the hidden shapes and faces. She had played Fives and Conkers and Battleships and Hangman. A combative child, she had liked competitive cut-throat games, and she liked to win. She had tried to beat her brother Tommy for years, and occasionally she had succeeded. But she had also played girlish games, silly soppy shameful giggling girlish games. She had peeled the hard green cooking apple, and thrown the peel over her shoulder to see if it formed the initial letter of a sweetheart's name. She had played counting games with the stones of sour and shrivelled stewed plums: Rich man, poor man, beggar man, thief. She had gazed into the wishing well, and asked the Witches of Bonsett or the Fairy Folk of Finsterness to show her the features of her betrothed-to-be.

She had pretended to see the faces of men, the faces of sweethearts, before she invented feminism. But what she had seen had been unknown shapes rising towards her from the depths.

On the surface her own clear features gazed back at her seductively, dangerously, obstructively, from the glassy mirror of the water, but the future had lurked in the depths of the well, beneath the reflection.

★

Humphrey Clark was experiencing the physical sensations of memory retrieval. The prickling of the gin, the throbbing of the throat and the comforting cradle pulse of the train were bringing back to him the image of his forty-year-old Auntie Vera. There she sat, in the empty seat opposite him, in her neat ivory rayon blouse with its little round collar and its self-coloured embroidered chain stitching on the pocket over her flat left breast. Her tailored jacket was a heathery blend of colours, a mix of lavender and mauve and green. She wore a modest little gold chain round her neck and a golden pheasant brooch upon her lapel. The sprightly pheasant had an eye of ruby-red. He had loved that brooch when he was a boy.

On the train to Ornemouth, all those years ago, Auntie Vera had given him some puzzle books, with crosswords, and join-the-dots, and anagrams, and spot-the-hidden-faces. She apologized because they were a bit childish for him.

Spot the hidden faces.

She said she had a nice book waiting for him in Burnside Avenue in Finsterness. 'You'll really like it, I know,' she said. 'It's your summer holiday present.'

He asked her what it was, but she wouldn't tell him. It was a surprise.

Then she retreated into her reading of her Boots library book, with the little metal membership tag that marked her place. It was a historical novel called *The Proud Servant* by Margaret Irwin. It was about somebody called Montrose. Humphrey didn't know who Montrose was, and Auntie Vera didn't seem to want to tell him. He knew the story was set in Scotland, because he had seen the map, hand-drawn like an old manuscript, just inside the front cover of the book, on the end pages.

At Doncaster, they had to change trains. This was the bit that he could never have managed by himself, she said, though maybe, next time, if he paid attention, he would be able to come on his own.

On the next train, she told him about the holiday family that was staying with Mrs Binns in Turkey Bank, next door to the Cleggs. They were called Kelman, and they were from Bonsett, in County Durham. There was a Mr and a Mrs Kelman, and two children, and a West Highland terrier. Mr Kelman was a chemist and he worked for a big company. Something to do with creosote and coal tar, said Auntie Vera vaguely. She thought the boy's name was Tommy. The dog was in disgrace because it had misbehaved in the porch, but Auntie Vera's view was, better the porch than the parlour. 'The children will be nice company for you and Sandy,' said Auntie Vera, before returning to the adventures of Montrose. 'Sandy's got quite friendly with them both.'

The thought of the two strange Kelman children filled Humphrey with a guilty apprehension. He and Sandy had been mean to Heather Robinson, poor lonely late-born child. They had ignored her. But Sandy had made friends already with these two strangers. Humphrey did not want interlopers.

Nothing much had changed in Burnside Avenue in Finsterness. His attic bedroom had the same old blackout curtains. The water cistern made the same companionable noises. He had grown an inch and a half. There was a new young neutered ginger tomcat called Orlando, after the cat in the picture books by Kathleen Hale that Lizzie liked so much. Mr Fell's house was still silent, its upper windows shrouded with grief. Grandma gave him a boiled egg for tea, with Marmite toast fingers. She timed the egg for him very carefully, just as he liked it, five minutes exactly, with the wooden egg timer. The egg timer hung from a brass hook on the wall by the gas cooker, and the orange sand trickled slowly from one end to the other, through the narrow glass waist, just as it always had done. It was a five-minute timer: if you wanted your egg hard-boiled, you had to turn the timer over and begin again. The numbers were written on the yellow wood in ancient silvery paint.

The sands of time, the sands of life.

The surprise book from Auntie Vera was called *The Fresh and Salt-Water Aquarium*, by the Rev. P. W. Twigg. So it wasn't that much of a surprise. It was a second-hand Victorian book, but Auntie Vera said it was a classic work and would teach him a lot. She had bought it in the town's antiquarian bookshop. It announced, in Gothic script, that it had Eleven Coloured Illustrations. It had a bookplate stuck inside its cover, which showed a woodcut of a boy on a dolphin. It was *Ex Libris* Charles Ruthven, 1868. Being second-hand made it more valuable, not less, Auntie Vera explained a little anxiously.

'It's quite a valuable book,' she said, as she watched him inspect the illustrations of shells and crabs and anemones and fish and insects. 'You must try to take care of it. You can show it to Sandy tomorrow. But I'd keep it indoors, if I were you. Better not let it get wet.'

And she smiled, to show that was a joke.

It was too late to see Sandy tonight, even though the sky was still light.

As he set off to Turkey Bank the next morning, he was still sure that Sandy would be expecting him, would be looking forward to seeing him. But, as he walked along the familiar streets, his confidence waned. He knew every stone, every tree, every garden wall and hedge, every manhole, every pavement slab upon the way, and one by one they marked the ebbing of his faith. It was a bright cool morning, with great white cumulus clouds sailing overhead like towers and castles in a blue sky. The sea shone in the level bay. By the time he turned the last corner, and saw the picturesque row of cottages of Turkey Bank ahead of him, he had lost hope. Why on earth should Sandy want to see him again? Nearly a whole year had passed. A tenth of their whole life had gone by since last summer. It had been foolish, childish, to expect Sandy to want him to come back. He should have stayed in exile, in suspension, and avoided this encounter, this rejection.

Mrs Binns's house had been repainted, in a kind of yellowy ochre wash. He couldn't remember what colour it had been before, but he saw that this was new. The Clegg house was off-white, as it had always been.

He would be so angry with Sandy if all the fish had died. But he would never be able to say so. He was not good at anger.

His heart was pounding with anxiety, and he wondered whether to turn round and retreat. Maybe Sandy would already have gone out for the day. Maybe Humphrey wished that Sandy had gone out, so that he could delay the moment of shock and disappointment.

Sandy's mother spotted him as he made his way along the side passage to the back door. She was standing at the sink, rinsing out a well-worn thin aluminium pan, and she knocked on the open kitchen window at him, and spoke to him through it. 'Hello, Humphrey,' she said. 'So you're back, are you?' She seemed quite pleased to see him, though not very surprised. She had always seemed well disposed to him, in her accepting and unemphatic way.

'Sandy's expecting you,' she said. 'He said to tell you they've gone down to the harbour. They've got Andrew with them.'

Open, face-up, on the wooden draining board was Mrs Clegg's exercise book of notes. She had been looking at it while cleaning the pan. He could see watery spots on her pencilled markings.

'Thanks,' said Humphrey. He tried to peer down the passage, into the backyard, to see if he could see the aquarium. He didn't like to go and look. It would have felt like trespassing. He couldn't see the tank, but that didn't mean it wasn't there. He couldn't quite see round the corner. She had meant to dismiss him to the harbour. He'd better do what he was told.

At least they had left him a message.

So on he went, and there they were, sitting on the edge of the harbour wall. It was nearly high tide, and they were dangling their feet over the rising water. Sandy and Andrew Clegg, and the two new Kelman children, sitting in a row, with their backs to the ramp of grounded fishing boats, and with their backs to him as he approached them down the cobbles of the landing.

Should he shout?

He would have to get up on the wall and walk along the top of it to reach them. He felt exposed, although he had walked along that seawall a hundred times.

Sandy turned as he approached. All four of them turned as he approached. Their eight eyes turned on him.

Sandy said, 'Hello, Hump,' in a deadpan, neutral tone.

Humphrey sat down at the end of the row, next to the girl. There was nowhere else to sit.

The girl was looking angry.

Humphrey Clark did not want to be lumbered with a left-over younger sister.

The girl looked away as soon as he sat down next to her, and stared at the horizon with an expression of what he took to be scorn upon her face.

Tommy and Ailsa Kelman, from Bonsett in County Durham. They had had a week's start on him, and they had made good use of it.

Tommy Kelman and Ailsa Kelman. They had ruined his life.

Tommy was a year older than Humphrey. Ailsa was younger, but not much younger.

He would never escape from either of them. He knew they would haunt him for ever, until the day he died. They would intertwine their destinies with his. They would never let him go. Friends and enemies, snakes and ladders.

They sat there in a row, the five children, while Humphrey came to terms with what had so horribly and irreversibly happened. Tommy Kelman had co-opted Sandy, and his sister Ailsa Kelman had somehow got in there too. That was the kind of people they were, the kind of people they would continue to be. Humphrey liked to think, later, that he had recognized their fatality in that instant, as the lapping water of the harbour slowly rose. He liked to think that he had bravely bitten the bullet, like all those young heroes in R. M. Ballantyne and Captain Marryat. But he knew that he had almost certainly betrayed signs of confusion and distress. He had almost certainly sued for peace and pity. He had probably not been very brave. He had been craven, and weak, and pathetic. 'Pathetic' – 'Don't be so pathetic' – that was a schoolboy word they used and misused a lot, in those days. He had been pathetic. He had suffered, and he had been pathetic, and they had spotted his weakness, and they had gone for the kill.

Though they did not act in unison. Not even then.

Tommy and Ailsa Kelman did not look like world-conquerors. Who could have guessed then that they had such talents, such ambitions? Tommy Kelman, gadfly and by-line and sycophant and financier and multi-millionaire. Ailsa Kelman, headline-seeker, exhibitionist and *agitateuse*. They did not know themselves what they would be. They knew they were going somewhere, but how could even they have known where it was? Their destination did not yet exist. It was waiting for them to help to create it. They were to ride towards it on the heaving swell of the times they lived in. They came from nowhere, out of nowhere, and there they were, perched on the seawall in distant Finsterness, dangling their feet above the rising water, as though they owned the ocean and all that they surveyed. Was this a pretence of confidence? How could the child Humphrey tell?

They were both pale-skinned, urban pale, unhealthy, off-white. They both had broad faces, with wide brows and wide-set grey-brown eyes. Tommy had reddish slicked-down hair, and his large ears stuck out conspicuously, as boys' ears do. His eyes were small and bright, and with age were to grow smaller and duller. He was nondescript, pasty, sly and knowing. He was unformed, ugly, embryonic. But he was as clever as two monkeys, and as quick as a weasel. He was watchful and patient and tricky. Tommy knew things that Sandy Clegg and Humphrey Clark did not know. Words, gestures, and what he mockingly called 'the facts of life'. Over the long weeks of summer, innuendoes and secrets slowly and deliberately leaked out from him. Poisonous secrets, poisonous innuendoes. He released them, for the sight of the pleasure of the damage they would do. Humphrey admired him, despised him, envied him, feared him. Humphrey was fascinated by him.

Humphrey was slavish with the desire to please this interloper, who knew so much.

Was it all scripted, as they sat there in that row? Surely Tommy Kelman cannot have intended to turn into Tommy Kelman?

Tinker, tailor, soldier, sailor, rich man, poor man, beggar man, thief. Journalist, presenter, anchorman, courtier, thief. Insider dealer, entrepreneur, speculator, rich man, risk man, gambler, con man, thief.

Tommy's sister Ailsa Kelman was nervous, tenacious and fierce. Her hair was wavy and wiry, and it was darker and thicker than her brother's. It was strongly coloured, a dark metallic copper like beech leaves. It stood out from her head, although her mother tried to make her tether it above her ears with kirby grips. Her strange-shaped face was broader across the cheekbones than her brother's, and her chin was more pointed. Her face was pointed like a python's. She licked her pale lips like a snake. Her arms were freckled. Her hazel eyes were large, and with age and attention were to grow larger. She was not a pretty child.

Tommy was a toad, Ailsa was a cobra.

Mrs Binns had a cupboard full of cards and defective jigsaws and battered board games, for visitors on rainy days. Snakes and ladders, Monopoly, Halma, Chinese chequers. She had a jam jar full of glass beads, red and green and turquoise and pearly, for little girls to thread and unthread in different patterns. You weren't allowed to take them away, when you'd made them into a necklace or a bracelet. You had to put them back in the jar for the next little girl.

Heather Robinson had spent a lot of time with those beads. Ailsa briskly unthreaded her last year's efforts, and began to remake the beads into new patterns, but she hadn't the patience to finish anything properly.

The jigsaws were frustrating. You got so far, but there were always pieces missing.

Ailsa Kelman, Tommy Kelman and Sandy Clegg. Three red-headed Nordic children, sporting a recessive gene, a minor mutation.

Ailsa was not content to be a left-over younger sister, which was the status that destiny had allotted to her. She resented her role. She did not like being a girl among boys, a goose-berry, an extra. She could not accept it. She insisted on tagging along. She whined and nagged and loitered and refused to leave. The local girls of Finsterness were traditionally more docile, more willing to segregate, more willing to go off on their own to play their girlish games. Ailsa stuck to her brother, stuck along with Sandy and Humphrey, even when they made it clear that they didn't want her. At first Humphrey wondered how she got away with it – did she have some secret hold over Tommy? When they tried to leave her behind, or told her to go off and play by herself, her face would turn grim with misery, but she didn't cry, or not that he could see, and she didn't give in. After a few days, when she'd got the hang of the mild-mannered Humphrey and the reflective Sandy, she began to show another side of herself. When pushed, she could lose her temper in a spectacular manner. Over a lost ball, a lost game of cards, an insufficient portion of a Mars Bar, or a taunt and tease too far.

Ailsa hated discrimination, because she was always on the wrong side of it.

Ailsa hated to lose at Snakes and Ladders. She did not cheat, because it was hard to cheat at that simple and overt game, but once, when luck was against her, she knocked the whole board over, accidentally on purpose, and once she threw the dice so violently that it got lost for some time behind the settee.

'Ailsa's having one of her tantrums,' Tommy would snigger, but even he was afraid of her tantrums. She could kick and bite like a pony. She was as brave as a scorpion. And in some ways she was bolder than her brother. She was a fearsomely brave swimmer. She wasn't a good swimmer – Humphrey was much the best swimmer of the quartet – but she was a headstrong swimmer. She would head out through the rearing breaking waves, fearless and determined, first into the icy water, as the boys shivered and hesitated in the shallows, with cold knees and shrivelling willies and cold bottoms. She wore a dark blue seersucker bathing costume and a turquoise bathing hat with a raised pattern of big white daisies on it. Sometimes her costume slipped and exposed her nipples. She swam until her skin puckered and pimpled and turned a dull mortuary grey. She was full of pluck. She was skinny and weedy and girlish and she wasn't very strong, but she was brave. She stood her ground when they played danger-ously, jumping on and off the seawall, dodging the waves as they came swirling up the sluice and the concrete slipway.

She wanted to swim in the Victorian saltwater bathing pool, but its little cove was still fenced off and the pathway and steps that led down to it were out of bounds. She tried to climb over the wire, but old Mr Bristow caught her at it and shouted at her.

She listened to the story of how Jackie Hexham had been drowned in the sluice, and she laughed, and she said she didn't care.

Mrs Clegg: July 12, 1946. Jackie Hexham washed over sluice.
July 18. Jackie Hexham's funeral. Mrs Hexham did not attend.

The terrible twins were twins no longer. Humphrey was marshalled into a corner of a foursome. It was better than being left out. It was better than the lonely fate of Heather Robinson. Humphrey could not put Heather Robinson out of his mind. But it was too late to feel sorry for her now.

Tommy, Ailsa, Sandy Clegg. Sitting in a row, making mock.

Tommy undermined and poured scorn on everything. On *The Children's Encyclopedia*, on Humphrey's favourite comic *Rainbow* and on the worthy *Children's Newspaper*, on lonely Mr Fell, on the Reverend Twigg's precious *Fresh and Salt-Water Aquarium*, on the sad fat man with a broad flat nose and a stammer who sold the delicious vegetable-fat ice-cream cones and wafers on the seafront. Humphrey did not dare to mention the fish tank that he had entrusted to Sandy's care, and which now stood empty in the backyard, because he did not want Tommy to make fun of it. Sandy offered no explanation for the abandoning of the aquarium project, and Humphrey did not dare to ask. The fish were dead and gone, and that was that. The glass container was on its side and empty, inhabited only by a dull land snail, and a spider, and the webbed skeletons of dead leaves from the winter that was past. It was reproachful. It was finished. It was failure.

He did not tell anyone that his mother was expecting a baby, although by now Grandma and Auntie Vera had explained this to him. He was embarrassed by the knowledge. He did not want the others to make mock of his mother, who was surely too old to have another baby. Having babies was silly and smutty. He did not want them to know.

Tommy disdained and contaminated everything. But he was fascinating. And he knew a lot of things.

They spent all their days together, Sandy, Humphrey and the Kelman children. They swam, they explored, and they went fishing in the rock pools, though they never brought the fish home, as Sandy and Humphrey had done. They lowered them back into the pools at the end of the day.

Tommy was a goad. He egged them on. It was Tommy who led them back into the beach-hut café on the cliff, which was even more derelict than it had been the year before. Sandy seemed reluctant to revisit it, but Tommy insisted. Nobody had been near it for ages, or so they thought. It had been abandoned. But there, in one corner of it, was a dark brown dried mound of human excrement. It wasn't dog dirt, it was human excrement. Tommy sniggered and pointed, and Sandy laughed. They both held their noses, although the dirt was too old to stink, and they laughed and pointed. But Humphrey, fastidiously, recoiled. He backed out of the shack. He blamed Tommy for the desecration, which was unfair of him, because it clearly wasn't Tommy who had done it. It was man's business, not boy's business. Man turd, not dog turd or boy turd.

He had not known the words 'turd' or 'shit' until Tommy Kelman taught them to him. 'Number Two' was the euphemism favoured by the Clark family, and even that was mentioned as rarely as possible.

The Kelman parents did nothing much on their summer holidays. They had a dull time of it. They had a car, unlike the Cleggs and the Clarks. It was a small black Ford, but the Kelmans didn't use it much, because of the petrol. Most of the time it stood by the kerb, at the end of Turkey Bank. The Kelmans liked routine. Every day they walked from Finsterness over the bridge to the town beach, where they sat in striped deckchairs, behind a wind shelter, wrapped up in woollies, reading the newspaper and paperback detective stories and historical novels and science fiction novels by C. S. Lewis. (Mrs Kelman particularly enjoyed *Out of the Silent Planet*, and tried to get Tommy to read it, but he wouldn't.) They occasionally took photographs of one another with a box camera when the sun shone. They went for town walks along the promenade, bowed against the wind, with Monty, their arthritic West Highland terrier. The white hairs on Monty's short legs were stained yellow with age as though with nicotine, and he shivered a lot, even when it wasn't cold. Sometimes they went along the short stretch of battlements, or along the little jetty, but usually they walked along the chilly promenade, beneath the putting green and the bay windows of the Queen's Hotel. The Kelmans had mid-morning coffee in the Jenny Wren on the front, then a picnic lunch, and sometimes they had tea with scones in the Copper Kettle, in the steep cobbled High Street. They usually had fish for their high-tea-supper, cooked by Mrs Binns, with scalloped potatoes. Mrs Binns laid sprigs of parsley on the potatoes, as a refinement. She had a large pot of parsley growing on her backdoor step. The parsley was an exotic touch, rarely seen in Finsterness.

Mr and Mrs Kelman ate a lot of meals but they were not fat. They were thin. Humphrey did not find this mysterious at the time, because in those days everyone ate a lot of meals.

In the evenings, Mrs and Mrs Kelman sometimes went back over the bridge to Ornemouth to the Crescent Picture House. The Picture House was an incongruous 1930s modern structure, faced with tile-like white squares and rectangles, surmounted by a midnight-blue tiled panel inset with a thin crescent moon of silver. The silver crescent moon was surrounded by seven golden stars. The cinema was glamorous, but it did not sit easily amidst the old sandstone buildings. Humphrey had never been inside it, for his grandmother, aunt and mother never went to the pictures. Nor did the Cleggs. But the Kelmans took their children with them, when it was a suitable film, and Humphrey and Sandy were allowed to go too. The Kelmans liked to sit at the back in the more expensive seats, but children could get in for a shilling. The programme changed twice a week. They saw black-and-white American comedies which Humphrey did not understand, although he tried to laugh in the right places, and American Technicolor romances set in the Rocky Mountains or the South Seas, and films about a dog called Lassie. They saw *Blue Lagoon*, which was the film Humphrey remembered best. They saw Arthur Askey and Dorothy Lamour.

On the Pathé News they saw jungle warfare in Malaya and the Soviet troops in Berlin. They did not understand most of what they were seeing. One evening there was a short item about the effects of the H-bomb explosion on the Bikini atoll two years earlier. Humphrey knew the words Bikini and Hiroshima. He had heard the words 'fallout' and 'mushroom cloud'. He had heard his parents use these words, in hushed tones.

The next day, Tommy told them about the bombing of Hiroshima. How the eyes of the people had melted and run down their cheeks, how their skin had slipped off in huge glove-like pieces, how the patterns on their clothes was all that was left of some of them. How the people had died but the plants had grown bright green and luscious and enormous. How did Tommy know all this? He had read it in a book. His parents had hidden the book, because it was horrible, but he had found it out.

Humphrey Clark did not welcome the intrusion of Tommy and Ailsa Kelman, but he lived in fear of being left behind. He dreaded that one day he would arrive at Turkey Bank to find the others already gone, with no word left for him. Gone, with the bloater-paste sandwiches and the cold cooked sausages in their thin film of fat, with the hard-boiled eggs and their twists of salt in greaseproof paper. It hadn't happened yet, but he was afraid that it might. He anticipated rejection.

Sometimes, in the long light northern evenings, after high tea, they didn't come round to call for him. *The Fresh and Salt-Water Aquarium* was a partial substitute for their company. He read about the quarrelsome sticklebacks who could not resist a skirmish, and about newts and water beetles. He read about *Sagataria troglodytes*, the cave-dwelling anemone, which was 'chiefly remarkable for its free and roving habits'. (That sentence entranced him.) He read about the sex change of the dazzling purple cuckoo wrasse. He read about Rotifera and Infusoria and Ulva, about *Laminaria hyperborea* and *Laminaria saccharina*. He felt tragic and neglected, and he overflowed with self-pity. 'Why don't you go out and look for them?' his kind Auntie Vera would ask. But he was too proud to go looking. And then there they would be again, the next morning, wanting to enrol him, wanting to borrow Humpy's grandpa's cracked binoculars, wanting to make an expedition.

He didn't like the uncertainty, but he had to put up with it.

Mushroom clouds, babies, excrement. The cold war and the iron curtain and the nuclear threat. Those were the days.

There were moments, still, in that summer, when Humphrey thought he was about to recapture the sense of the living ocean of the earlier year, the sense of immersion, of space, of infinitude. He seemed to be on the brink of rediscovery. But then the growing sense of the ocean would ebb and leave him stranded. Disappointed, dissatisfied, and stranded. Dwindling and drying, on a stony shelf, above the water level. The water would not flow in for him. It had lost the power. He had lost its power.

But there were moments when it seemed about to return.

One day, Mr and Mrs Kelman suggested an outing. They had seen a coach trip advertised, a day trip to the little town of Durres. You could visit the weaver's croft and the specialist wool shop, and you could go to the Pool of Brochan. *See the purple heather and the rock pool*, said the painted notice on the Post Office window. *Book here. Adults 4s. 6d., children half price*. Did Humphrey and Sandy want to come too?

Humphrey was astonished. The Kelmans had seemed too set in their daily routine to propose such an unusual and extravagant diversion. He was humbly astonished that they had thought to include him. Of course he wanted to go. It was one of the things he most wanted to do in the world. He wanted to do it so much that he had never dared to mention it. He knew that a visit to the Pool of Brochan would change his life.

Auntie Vera and Grandma happily gave him the money for his ticket, and some extra pocket money to spend on the trip. They were pleased that he was included.

For once, he did not even fear that it might be disappointing. And it had not been disappointing. It had opened up to him like the navel of the earth.

Even the coach ride had been interesting. They travelled north and over the border into the foreign country of Scotland, accompanied by a modest friendly commentary from the fatherly grey-haired middle-aged driver, who was called Arthur. Humphrey and Sandy and Tommy and Ailsa did not listen to this commentary, though the unattended sound of it was reassuring, like the sound of adults talking downstairs at night. The outing was a treat for everybody, even for Arthur. After the years of warfare and self-denial, a little fun was to be permitted, and the children sensed this mood of mild relief and liberation. They sat in a row on the back seat, the four of them, and giggled and chatted and pointed. They were friends, fast friends, for the day. Auntie Vera had bought them a packet of Edinburgh Rock, because they were going to Scotland, and they chewed and sucked on its powdery pastel-shaded sticks. The pale brown ginger flavour was the best.

The town had been dull, and the wool shop of knitted goods and weaving had been duller, although the grown-ups liked it. Mrs Kelman cautiously bought a lacy hand-knitted mauve scarf. Arthur said it was a pity they couldn't go to see the place where they smoked the kippers: it had closed down during the war, but there was talk that it might open again soon. This was a disappointment to Humphrey, who would have liked to have seen a herring turn into a kipper.

But the Pool of Brochan was not a disappointment. It was at once banal and divine. Banal, in that a well-trodden Visitors' Path descended to it from the little coach park, a path so gentle in its gradient that even old folk with sticks could easily make it; divine in its archaic form and its prophetic suggestions.

For Humphrey, the earth opened. Here man and creature met and knew one another, here land and sea met and inter-penetrated. Here the species were friendly one to another, as they had been before the birth of guilt and sin and cruelty.

Or so it had seemed to the boy. Or so the man remembered that it had seemed to the boy.

Could that have been what it meant?

Professor Clark, passing by train through red-brick Retford, remembered the old crone who had fed and minded the fish, and retrieved her name.

She called herself Mother Longbone, and she was very old, like the fish. The name Longbone had not then struck the child as an oddity, for it was the family name of the largest grocer in Ornemouth, and was therefore familiar to him. It was an old name of the region. Mother Longbone was sixty, and she had been minding these fish for fifty years, or so she told them. For five-sixths of her life she had been mother to those fish. She played to her coach audience of day-trippers and to her tame fish. She affected a picturesque Scottishness, and she wore a plaid shawl pinned with a brooch shaped like a silver thistle. Her hair was iron-grey, her brown cheeks were hollow, her false teeth were small and even like pearls. The codfish were her chickens. Mother Longbone's chickens. She summoned them with a strange high-pitched crooning word-less song. And they came, and circled and swirled below her, and poked their dumb beseeching grey-lipped mouths up into the air. The green salt water seethed with their plump silver bodies. One of them was blind. She called him Blind Tom.

It was a show, it was a display, but it was powerful. It was joyful but it was disturbing. It was worth more than four shillings and sixpence for the ride.

The old woman, the rocky shore, the curving pool, the imprisoned fish.

The wind caught the strands of the old woman's grey hair, and blew them backwards from her haggard face.

The sea sucked in and out. The tide entered and withdrew. The pool had been hollowed by the endless sucking and pulling and ebbing and flowing. The adult fish remained within the hollow inlet for ever.

Humphrey, entranced, leaned on the low rusted railing and watched the fish. Ailsa Kelman was at his elbow. Her stiff copper-wire hair was wet with beads of spray. Her bony freckled elbow touched his by mistake as she leaned further over, and he withdrew his quickly from the accidental contact.

Sandy and Tommy had clambered round to the very far end of the path and were trying to scramble up the rocks. The old woman shouted at them to get down.

Mrs Kelman took a photograph of Humphrey and Ailsa leaning on the rail. She took a photograph of Mrs Longbone.

The old woman told them that the pool had been scoured into its near-perfect circle by the movement of the elements, by the incessant circular grinding of the imprisoned rocks. And the fish bred there naturally. Now they were trapped there, by a metal grid placed at the mouth of the cove, but long ago they had sought its sanctuary of their own accord. And now they no longer knew the enormous ocean with its vast horizon, although it visited them twice a day with the swell and the ebb of the tide. They were in the ocean, but they were not of it.

Humphrey was filled with pity and wonder and terror. Was the meaning of this that he too was trapped? Or was his life measureless like the fullness of the ocean?

Mrs Longbone handed out to the children little dry harsh-smelling pellets of fish food from a tin box, and told them to cast them upon the waters. Ailsa and Humphrey and an unknown and never-to-be-known girl from another family party obeyed her instructions. The fish rose and snapped and threshed and devoured the pellets.

Sandy and Tommy disdained this childish and effeminate activity. They stayed apart, at the other side of the pool, sniggering at some boys' secret of their own.

On the way back to Ornemouth, in the coach, Mr and Mrs Kelman fell asleep. Mrs Kelman snored, with her mouth open. Sandy and Tommy whispered to each other. Ailsa stared grimly and coldly out of the window at the picture-postcard purple and gold of the heather and the gorse. Humphrey sat silently, struggling with the mystery of the thing, as he sucked on a Mint Imperial. He was afraid of something, but he did not know what it was. It was a monster, a monster of the deep, but he did not know what it looked like. It was too far down for him to see. It was terrible, more terrible than a codfish. It had an open mouth, a dark and open mouth, a mouth that sucked like a maelstrom. He was afraid of it, but he needed it, and he was almost glad that it was there.

Ailsa displayed her driving licence and signed for her hire car. Her licence was not as clean as she might have wished. She had two endorsements for speeding. But she had some points to spare, and some time left, and she meant to make the most of them.

The A1 going north was what she wanted, but she was too impatient to listen to the Rent-A-Car woman's well-intentioned advice about how to find her way to it from the airport. She would just get behind the wheel of the little red two-seater and get out on the road and look for the turnings. The compass in her blood would guide her to the Great North Road and to the old spine of England.

She put her foot down, circled a few roundabouts, and hit the highway.

Her daughter Marina had never been to the old northern heartland. Well, as far as Ailsa knew, Marina had never been up here. But Marina had a life of her own now.

Marina had never known her maternal grandparents. They had died long before her birth.

Sandy Clegg and Humphrey Clark. She was on her way to see Humphrey Clark. And perhaps she would bump into Sandy Clegg strolling on the pier or on the quay or on the red ramparts. She would not know him if she saw him, after half a century. He would be old by now, as she was.

She was going back to try to find out what had happened. This is what she had said to P. B., and it had been true. It had been more seriously true than the lightness of her tone had suggested.

Whatever could have happened to Sandy Clegg? He had vanished. Unlike Humphrey Clark and her brother Tommy Kelman, he had disappeared into thin air and into a nowhere life. She had looked for his name, from time to time, but she had not found it. There were plenty of Cleggs to be found, in the old telephone directory, in public life, in *Who's Who*, on the internet, but Alistair Clegg was not one of them.

Mrs Clegg, however, had reappeared. Mrs Clegg had come back to Ailsa from the dead. Ailsa had solved the mystery of Mrs Clegg's notes and diaries. It was all too peculiar, and yet all too simple. Who would have thought it? The solution was as odd as the mystery.

Ailsa had found the real story of Mr Fell in Mrs Clegg's notebooks, deposited in the Mass Observation Archives in the University of Sussex. She had not been looking for it, but she had found it. She had been unable to decide whether it was banal or bizarre. It could, of course, like most 'true stories', be both. But the astonishing thing was that it had been recorded at all. Few of the Mass Observation archivists had been as thorough as Mrs Clegg. She had noted more than most, and more persistently. Many of the new scheme's conscripts had begun diligently, in 1937, filling in page after page of trivia for their sociologist taskmasters, but most had fallen by the wayside. Their observations had grown more and more sparse, and had then faded into silence: the struggles of daily life had overwhelmed some, and a sense of pointlessness and tedium had crushed others. The scheme itself had thinned out and foundered and been largely forgotten by the general public, though every now and then a sociologist or a historian or a journalist would rediscover it and make use of it. As Ailsa herself had done.

Most of the volunteers had soon given up their mission of observing and counting and auditing, but Mrs Clegg, occupying a useful space between housewifely struggle and housewifely tedium, had kept up her records well into the 1950s, though some of her later entries were undated, indicating that she too was at last losing interest. Ailsa had speculated that maybe Mrs Clegg was a frustrated writer, who in more auspicious circumstances might have written novels or historical romances: the unusual bulk of her contribution to the archive suggested that it had meant more to her than it had meant to most of the diarists, but her narrative style gave little ground for such an interpretation. Mrs Clegg had been told to observe, and she had observed. She had been told to note facts, and she had noted facts. She had also been encouraged to record overheard conversation, but she had not much cared for this part of the assignment, and had no gift for dialogue. She never got much further than *Overheard in grocer. "She says she saw a banana in Berwick." "I haven't seen a banana since 1942, except those dried ones John sent from Italy in a food parcel." "What were they like?" "They were very black. But what do you expect, coming from Italy?"'*

Ailsa sympathized. She wasn't very good at dialogue herself. She'd once tried to write a play, in the old days when she would try her hand at anything, but it hadn't been very good and had never got beyond a small fringe reading on a Sunday night in a church hall. She had more developed literary and verbal skills than Mrs Clegg, and a much better education, but she wasn't much good at stage dialogue. She could write monologues, but that was another matter.

On the other hand, Mrs Clegg had some good raw material.

Mr Fell, Ailsa learned, had killed his wife in a motorbike and sidecar accident in 1937, and he had thereafter been suffering from everlasting remorse. Mrs Clegg had not used that phrase, 'everlasting remorse', but so Ailsa had read the story of his vow of silence and his drawn curtains. She remembered that Humphrey Clark, whose family lived next door, had been affected by the sight of those drawn curtains and by the bowed somnambulistic walk of Mr Fell. Humphrey, in adult life, had sometimes spoken to her of him. Would she now find a chance to tell him the story, and if so, would it bring relief or further oppression? Humphrey had been a sensitive child, too much given to suffering for others.

The name of Humphrey Clark had appeared many times in Mrs Clegg's diaries, though his history had ended abruptly, a few years before the dwindling ending of those diaries. Ailsa had studied every entry, looking not only for academic fodder for the thesis with which she was then engaged, but also for clues to a personal past, so strangely and coincidentally presented. Humphrey had made his last appearance at the end of the last summer he had spent at Finsterness, the first and only summer that the Kelmans had spent at Finsterness. (She had pointlessly and portentously lied to P. B. Wilton by implying that she and her brother had spent every summer there. They had spent but the one summer in Finsterness, that one intense, decisive summer. After that, increasing prosperity and a desire for milder weather had driven the Kelmans and their children further south, to fashionable and sun-baked Scarborough. Scarborough had been pleasanter, but much less numinous.)

Mrs Clegg had written in her diary in her spare and uninflected but exceptionally copious and diligent prose:

Herrings twopence each yesterday, they have gone up.
School shoes for Sandy, fifteen shillings and eightpence.
Wellingtons, four coupons.
Fireworks Gala Display and Cossack Riders, 2s. 6d.
Finished Margaret Irwin's book about Rupert of the Rhine.
Humphrey Clark went back to Covington today with Miss Neil.

End of episode. End of Humphrey Clark, as far as Mrs Clegg and Sandy Clegg were concerned. He'd gone back to Covington with Auntie Vera. There were no more references to Humphrey Clark. He had disappeared from the record.

Ailsa Kelman, in her incarnation as a scholarly sociologist, sat in the University of Sussex staring at the white ghostly handwriting of Mrs Clegg on the dark Microfilm, carefully preserved in the Mass Observation Archives. She shivered when she saw those words.

Humphrey Clark went back to Covington today with Miss Neil.

In her lined exercise book, Mrs Clegg had also jotted down with her newly sharpened pencil the brand names of medications, though whether this was because she was a cynic or a hypochondriac Ailsa was unable, at a remove of nearly forty years, to discover.

Shadphos tonic tablets or Phylossan for your nerves, Elliman's embrocation for your lumbago, Yeast-Vite Pick-me-Up for your headaches, Musterole Ointment for your chilly coughs, Penetrol for your influenza, Carters Little Liver Pills for your Liver Bile, Benger's Food for your digestion, Sabit for your Dandruff, Silf for Slimness, Rennies for Acidity, Vironita for more or less everything.

Karswood Pig Powders for your Pigs.

Ailsa had been to Colindale Newspaper Library and looked up the advertisements for some of these products. She had used them as illustrations for her mass-readership article on Mass Observation, published in a colour supplement. She had provided a hard feminist gloss on female illnesses and hypochondria.

And now here Ailsa Kelman was, driving back to the source of memories, and leaving well behind her the Durham coalfields and the wretched, filthy little town of Bonsett. She'd seen them from the air, and that was quite enough. Unlike the famous Fairy Folk of Finsterness, they did not draw her back. After her mother's death, she had stayed well clear of Bonsett.

Some, in attempting to explain the extraordinary upward trajectory of Tommy and Ailsa Kelman, had ascribed it to the influence of Bonsett. Bonnie Bonsett, as some of its residents still call it, with savage but protective irony. What fish would not attempt to leap from such a tank? Ailsa herself had some-times suggested that Bonsett had much to answer for. J. B. Priestley, in his *English Journey* of the 1930s, had described it as the pit of hell, as a town of slagheaps, ashes, pitheads, filthy air, lung diseases, stunted adult gnomes, dirty rat-faced children taunting him from the rubble. 'Feral children', we would now call them, thought Ailsa, but that politically risky phrase had not yet been coined. Priestley, in principle and by temperament tolerant of the industrial north, had disliked the north-east, and Bonsett had been its symbol, the archetypal disaster town, a smoking, poisonous urban dump set amidst a harsh and scruffy rural wasteland.

Ailsa's analyst and confessor had not bought the environmental diagnosis. Ailsa's analyst had thought it a red herring. She had preferred to talk about Ailsa's father, who did indeed offer some grist to the twice-weekly mill, but who was not, in Ailsa's view, sufficient cause. He was odd, his habits had been odd, and his death had been melodramatic, but Ailsa claimed that she had not thought much about these oddities in her formative years. His oddities had lacked glamour. They had been embarrassing and parochial and penurious rather than interesting. She had taken him and his anal collections of jam jars full of copper coins for granted. Everyone collected coppers, Ailsa had patiently explained to her quizzical listener, and on holiday he had been quite generous: almost, by his own standards and the standards of the day, a spendthrift.

Indeed, she had argued, how could her development have been profoundly affected by her father's admittedly dreadful death, as this death did not occur until she was at university, when her psyche, as well as her body, was fully formed? Nor had the manner of his death been foreseeable. The fact that it had hit the local headlines was sheer chance, sheer mischance. It was what philosophers call 'moral bad luck'. He'd been in the wrong place at the wrong time. A minor negligence had unforeseeably sparked a major conflagration. That's all that had happened. Ailsa Kelman would still have been Ailsa Kelman had he died in his bed of pneumonia and old age.

Her analyst did not set much store by chance.

Her analyst, reflected Ailsa as she overtook a Eurotruck on the dual carriageway, was a sophisticated urban Brazilian from

Rio, who had little experience of the English landscape. Her analyst accepted the concept of environment, but only in so far as it concerned parents and siblings. The environment of the leathery womb she was prepared to consider, but rocks and stones and trees were nothing to her, and neither were slagheaps and creosote and coal tar. Ailsa suspected that her analyst had never read Wordsworth or J. B. Priestley.

Ailsa's father was not a father to boast about, or to waste much time upon. Ailsa had tried to explain this to her analyst, but her analyst had correctly pointed out that Ailsa's memories of her father's social dullness and domestic penny-pinching were hardly relevant. They were superficial. The true plot had been developing beneath the level of Ailsa's perception.

Ailsa had correctly returned that the environment and nature of her father's death had been both intimately and dramatically connected. Creosote had been the key to her father's life, to her father's living, and to her father's death. Creosote had killed him. He had died in a factory fire. It had not been a noble death. But creosote would have killed him in the long run anyway. He had been ill and wasting when he died.

Creosote had recently become a forbidden substance in Britain and the European Union. In 2003 it was put on the blacklist. Paradoxically, you could continue to own it, but you couldn't use it. But back then, back in the 1940s and 1950s, there had been good money in creosote. It had been classified as a preserver, not a destroyer.

Humphrey Clark, years later, had said to Ailsa that he loved the tarry masculine seafaring smell of creosote. The deathly smell of formaldehyde he hated, but creosote had been as a life-giving perfume and an aphrodisiac to him.

Ailsa and Tommy Kelman's father had been an industrial

chemist. Their mother had once been in service at the big bleak mock-Palladian house up the ravaged valley. Ailsa and Tommy had received mixed messages from this mixed parentage.

Their mother had known how to lay a table. Ailsa and Tommy knew how to manage their cutlery and how to hold a glass. In adult life Tommy had become increasingly enamoured of dukes and duchesses, of princes and princesses, of merchant bankers and the super-rich, so this expertise had stood him in good stead. Ailsa had found it less valuable, but she too had deployed it to her advantage.

Ailsa, trying to tune in the hire car radio for some Radio 3 musak, remembered the tame codfish in the Pool of Brochan. They had come trustingly to the hand to feed. And she remembered Humphrey Clark. Oh yes, she remembered Humphrey Clark. She had tried to scissor him out of her life, as he had tried to scissor her out of his, but she had failed. And now she was boldly on her way to look him in the eye. If he hadn't chickened out of the enterprise. But he wouldn't dare do that, would he?

He wasn't a coward. He'd never been a coward. He'd taken his defeats like a man.

Humpy knew they would do it, and they did. A few days after the outing to the Pool of Brochan, Tommy and Sandy did it.

They went off without him, the two of them, as he had known that one day they would. When he got to Turkey Bank, he found they had gone. Sandy and Tommy had gone and left him. They'd set off early, and gone. No, they didn't say where they were going. They'd just said they'd be back for their tea.

Mrs Clegg did not seem to recognize the scale of the disaster. It was just another day to her, not the end of an era.

Humphrey was relieved that she did not see how much he minded. He preferred to conceal his hurt.

She volunteered, however, that Ailsa Kelman was feeling poorly, and had stayed at home. Maybe she was going to go down to the town beach with her parents later, she wasn't sure. He could go next door and ask.

She didn't realize that it was impossible for him to go next door and ask.

Humphrey had his pride. He had nothing but his pride. Rejected, jilted, spurned and friendless. Expelled.

Expulsion. That was the word. He had been expelled.

Fish spit out the bits of food they don't want, the bits they swallow in by mistake. They expel them. They spit out grains of sand, in little clouds, from their ever-working lips. Little strings and threads of excrement dangle from one end of a fish, and cloudy spews of grit puff out from the other.

There is a fish which goes by the name of stone biter. It sucks in stones and spews them out again. He had read about it in his book.

A boy at school had been expelled. The word was heavy with disgrace. The boy had been a thief, or so the rumour went. But Humphrey was not a thief. So what had he done wrong, to be left behind in disgrace? He turned his mind over the day before, over all the days and weeks before. It hadn't been his fault. Nothing had been his fault. It had been Tommy's fault.

Tommy Kelman was a thief. He had stolen Sandy Clegg. And when he had finished with him, he would spew him out. Humphrey knew this. He didn't know how he knew it, but he knew it.

Humphrey was devoured by jealousy and envy. He suspected they had set off early to go to find the waterfall and the ring in the rock, because that was the most exciting place that he and Sandy had ever found. They had talked about the possibility of this adventure, and now they had gone off without him.

He sat on the low wall at the end of the row of cottages, and looked down across the bay. There was rain, far out to the north-east, a low purple-grey misty bank of it. Was it coming his way? He licked his finger and stuck it into the air, but he couldn't feel much of a breeze from any direction. He picked at a scab on his ankle. The intensity of his sorrow was at once painful and numbing. It filled him with a noxious deadening ache. He knew that it was not just for today. It was permanent, this nauseous sorrow. It would never pass. He was marked for life. He was chained for ever to his rock, with a vulture gnawing at his liver.

He'd read about that in *The Children's Encyclopedia*, in a section called 'The Myths of Ancient Greece'.

Humphrey had made the scab on his ankle bleed. He dabbed at the wound with a dirty handkerchief.

He was about to set off alone, to the pool in the lee of St Cuthbert's Rock, when he heard his name being called. It was Ailsa, at an upstairs window, calling from Mrs Binns's. He could see her, framed in the open lower half of the sash window.

'Hump!' she called, leaning out towards him. 'Humpy!'

She sounded pleased, excited.

He waved at her. She beckoned him over.

The cottages were small, the ceilings low. She wasn't very high above him. It was a strange angle. He could see the pale underside of her chin and her throat. He stood there, looking up at her.

'I've been sick,' she announced. 'Mummy says I've been swallowing too much seawater. I had a sore throat, and I felt as though I'd swallowed a hard-boiled egg, whole. And then

I was sick. But I'm better now. I got it all up. I'm coming down, as soon as I'm dressed. Will you wait for me?'

She seemed proud of having been sick. Not embarrassed, or ashamed, as he would have been.

Yes, he would wait for her.

She was down in a matter of minutes. She had not brushed her hair properly. He asked her if she would like to go to St Cuthbert's Rock, and she said yes, so they sauntered off together, conspicuously careless. The tide was right for St Cuthbert's Rock.

'Where did you learn to swim?' he asked, after they had spent some time crouching on the verge and peering busily and silently into the cracks and crevices. They had picked up a net and his old canvas bucket from Burnside Avenue, but they hadn't tried to catch anything yet.

'At the public baths,' she said. 'With my friend Gloria and her mother. Gloria's mother taught me. But it's more fun in the sea.'

'You're a good swimmer,' he said. It was only half true, and he didn't know why he said it.

'You're a *very* good swimmer,' she said.

He felt guilty when she said this, although it was true. Maybe he had been fishing for a compliment?

She stared down at the brilliant sunlit underwater green of the sea lettuce, with its lucent oxygenated glow.

Could it have been true that the flowers and foliage of Hiroshima flourished and blossomed after the explosion that killed so many? 'Fresh, vivid and lush,' Tommy had said, smacking his thin lips. 'Lush and luscious.' Those were the very words in the book, said Tommy, with an unpleasant pleasure.

'My mother says the public baths are dirty and they give you diseases,' Ailsa continued. 'And it's true, I got impetigo, all over my legs, and they painted me with gentian violet. I looked a real freak.'

(*We have had the first case of infantile paralysis in the neighbourhood*, Mrs Clegg would shortly record, carefully, with her lead pencil. *We have been told that children should avoid public swimming pools and cinemas*.)

'Impetigo,' repeated Ailsa with satisfaction. And she laughed, as though looking like a freak with purple legs was nothing to her. She brazened it out. She didn't mind having a freak name. She didn't mind being called after a rocky crag off the West Coast of Scotland. Humphrey hated being called Humphrey. He was glad he wasn't called Clegg, which was a silly ugly name with a low meaning. Nobody could want to be called Clegg, anyone would want to get rid of a name like Clegg, but Clegg was a surname, and you're stuck for life with a surname, unless you're a girl. Whereas his parents had chosen to call him Humphrey. He would have preferred an ordinary name, like John, or David, or Thomas, or Alan. These were ordinary, meaningless names, but Humphrey was a fancy stuck-up name, a name that invited ridicule.

'Mummy wanted me to bring Monty,' she said, 'but he's too slow.'

'Yes,' said Humphrey.

Half a day he spent alone with Ailsa Kelman, left behind, remaindered. They talked, in a desultory manner, about nothing much. They caught some blennies, and let them go again. They ate their sandwiches, in silence, and fed some crumbs to the anemones. Ailsa squatted by the rock pool as they watched the anemones waving their fleshly fronds.

'I think they're plumose anemones,' Humphrey said. He knew it was wrong to say it, but he couldn't help saying it. The pedagogue that crouched in him spoke out. Ailsa said nothing. She stared at the nearest dark jellied blob intently, squatting, knees bent. She gazed into its pulsing red Medusa valve, its pulsing female valve. She said nothing. Her legs were bare and brown, and he could see the white nubbed triangle of her knickers as she squatted there with her arms around her knees.

'They're quite common,' he said, discouraged.

Ailsa Kelman crouched, saying nothing, waiting in the nub of herself.

The anemone waved, and Ailsa advanced her finger with its bitten nail, with its nail bitten to the quick. The exploring fronds withdrew, and it closed itself up.

Her wrists were thin and bony.

She looked across at him, and smiled, with menace rather than mirth.

Why couldn't he talk about anemones, if Tommy could talk about Hiroshima and the atom bomb?

He tried not to stare at her blunt exposed female nub. Could it put out tentacles? The changing shape of his own genitals was a worry to him. A pleasure, of a sort, but a guilty pleasure, and a worry.

'You had your tonsils out last summer,' said Ailsa suddenly, in a much friendlier and more collaborative tone.

'Yes,' he agreed, surprised that this personal event should have been of any interest to her, or that anybody should have bothered to tell her about it.

'So did I,' she said. 'It hurt a lot. Did yours hurt a lot?'

He nodded.

'Horrible,' he agreed.

'I've got mine, pickled in a jar,' said Ailsa. 'I keep them in my bedroom. Next to my luminous lamb.'

'What do they look like?'

'Nasty,' she said, with relish. 'Really nasty.'

'They said I could keep mine,' said Humphrey, 'but they forgot. They threw them away.'

She laughed, but without ill will. Their tonsils had bonded them.

'I could show you mine, if I had them here,' she said. 'But I left them at home. I wanted to bring them, but they said I couldn't. They let me bring my lamb, but they wouldn't let me bring the tonsils.'

'I'd like to see them,' said Humphrey.

'I'd like to show them to you,' said Ailsa.

This was a very kind thing that she said. He remembered it.

Then they had compared throats. He had peered down her throat, and she had peered down his. They had looked for scar tissue, and they thought they found it.

'I can't yodel nearly as well without my tonsils,' said Ailsa. 'I used to be able to make the most frightening noise, but I can't do it any more. I was famous for it, but I can't do it now.'

'Maybe it will come back,' said Humphrey.

'No, I don't think so,' said Ailsa gravely. 'No, I think I've lost the knack.'

They had become momentarily friendly, Ailsa and Humphrey, on this long afternoon, forging a conspiratorial alliance with which to confront Sandy and Tommy on their return. They had got on so well that Humphrey had asked Ailsa to come back to his grandmother's house with him when it started to rain, and she had agreed. He had wanted to show her his aquarium book, and she now seemed willing to let him play the tutor. She examined the books in the glass-fronted bookcase in the front room, and told him that back home in Bonsett she had her own new school-prize copy of *Twenty Thousand Leagues Under the Sea* with pictures of the giant squid and the submarine forest and of gallant Captain Nemo and the *Nautilus*. Then she'd curled up in the rocking chair and gazed at the Reverend Twigg's illustrations and listened patiently to Humphrey's little speech about the habits of hermit crabs and jellyfish and pipefish.

He did not tell her about last year's aquarium in Sandy's backyard and the fish that had leaped to its death. The fish death had become unmentionable.

She'd left him at teatime, to go back to Mrs Binns and the family meal. He had felt proud of himself, and strangely grown-up for having had the nerve to ask her into his grandmother's house. He had salvaged his day and had shown some independence of spirit.

Next day, he heard the story of Sandy and Tommy's day out. They hadn't gone to the cave and the waterfall, they'd gone the other way, south beyond Ornemouth, to the cement landings where tanks had done exercises in the early days of the war. They'd met up with another gang, and time had flown, and then it began to rain, and they'd taken shelter in a lookout post, and in short they came back very late for their tea. Mr and Mrs Kelman and Mrs Binns were extremely angry with Sandy and Tommy. Sandy and Tommy got it in the neck. The grown-ups said they were angry because they were worried, but Sandy and Tommy knew better. That was just an excuse. They were angry because they were angry, because they enjoyed being angry.

Mr Kelman made Tommy stay alone in his bedroom for the whole evening.

Ailsa had been openly delighted by the anger visited upon her brother. She came across as very smug, for twenty-four hours.

Humphrey had kept well out of it.

Mrs Clegg had noted with a bleak impotence, *Sandy very late back, those children do run a bit wild.*

★

Professor Clark, brushing the crumbs of baguette from his lapel, remembered Ailsa Kelman's tonsils and her white knickers very clearly. He had good reason to remember them. Ailsa, Ailsa, brave and brazen. Ailsa Kelman, her own worst enemy. She had made her mark on him, and on the times she lived in. She had written her name in the sand at the water's edge, with a big flat blue stone, and then she had written it in lights and in printer's ink and on the airwaves and on the screen. She had stored it in libraries, and she had colonized the internet. Her name had spread like an infestation of algae.

Ailsa and Tommy Kelman. They had walked into his life as strangers, and taken possession of it.

He had been successfully avoiding Ailsa Kelman for more than half his life.

He wondered if they would ever meet again.

Sandy and Tommy did not say much to Humphrey about where they had been, or why. They did not admit to guilt or shame but they had been alarmed by the degree of adult wrath that their absence had provoked. They resumed their safe old formation, as part of a defensive foursome, the young against the old. But Humphrey did not feel safe any more. Something had shifted. Something had gone wrong.

The August weather had broken, and rain spattered and pocked the sands, so they spent a lot of time indoors playing Monopoly. Tommy liked to be banker and Ailsa always said he was cheating. She would glower at his heaps of counterfeit paper money with suspicious resentment. Humphrey didn't notice that anything was wrong, and thought she was just being spiteful, though he wouldn't have put it past Tommy to try to cheat.

Rich man, poor man, beggar man, thief.

His special relationship with Ailsa did not last long. She

reneged on their brief alliance, and went her own dissident female way.

There was just one more short spell of fine weather before the end of the holidays. They went to see the cave and the waterfall and the ring in the rock. All four of them went, all four of them did it, all four of them saw it, all four of them would remember it. It would have been a failure if they hadn't dared to go. This time they were careful to be back on time for their tea.

Two days later, the Kelmans drove away in their temperamental black Ford car with their suitcase roped on top. The next day Humphrey and Auntie Vera went by train to Covington, and the summer was over, and the autumn began.

Again, he and Sandy did not say goodbye to each other. Perhaps they both thought there might be another summer, in which they could make good the things that had gone bad. They did not know what the uncontrollable future might inflict upon them.

Mrs Clegg wrote in her notebook: *Humphrey Clark went back to Covington today with Miss Neil.*

Soon after his return his mother gave birth to a baby, a new girl baby which she called Diana. Humphrey did not much like this name, but he did not say so. He felt that he was too old to have a baby sister. Lizzie played menacing games with the baby, fondling it and taunting it, but Humphrey tried to keep out of its way.

Not long after Christmas his grandmother died, without warning, and the house in Finsterness was sold, with almost all its contents, and Auntie Vera moved south to live with a woman they called Auntie Madge, although she wasn't really an auntie. Auntie Madge was headmistress of a school in a village near Beaconsfield. Auntie Vera had found a post at a neighbouring school in Beaconsfield. All of this happened very suddenly. Auntie Madge and Auntie Vera lived happily together in Buckinghamshire, sharing a 1930s semi. Auntie Vera now claimed that she had always dreaded the cold winters, the wind, the damp, the dark nights of the north. She did not miss the North Sea at all, she asserted. Humphrey could not believe that she could mean what she said. How could anybody prefer the inland life? But she stuck to her story.

So Humphrey never went back to Finsterness. They had cut off his retreat, his lifeline. He knew he would never see Sandy and Tommy again. Ailsa Kelman, fair-weather friend and for one day an intimate, Ailsa with her copper hair and her brazen cheek and her tantrums, would vanish like a summer midge. Or so he thought, through the long years of his adolescence and apprenticeship. He had thought all that was over, like a pointless interlude. Slammed shut, like a closed and childish book that has been outgrown. So he put away childish things, and he tried hard to grow up.

He thought Ailsa had disappeared, and when she re-appeared, he didn't recognize her. When she reappeared and reintroduced herself into his life, he didn't know whether she was another interlude, or part of the main plot.

And he was still, of this, uncertain.

For over a decade, he made himself forget about Sandy and Tommy and Ailsa, about the good summer followed by the bad summer. He did not like its paradigm. He had made himself forget both friendship and betrayal. He had deliberately repressed his knowledge of both. He shut the lid. He screwed it down. He rolled the stone.

Latency, denial, refusal, repression, struggle, combat, maturity, acceptance. The life cycle of the marine biologist.

The Orator, following the story, following the outline of the story, trying to find the thread through the story, perceives that at this point there could yet have been many outcomes. Up to this point in the journey, no irrevocable decisions have been made, no fatal mistakes embedded. Humphrey Clark is still an innocent. His heart is still pure.

From this point on, chance and choice each play a part. If the story were unravelled to this point, to this knot, and then rewoven, it could be rewoven in many patterns. But we have to follow the facts. We cannot unweave, and remake. For chance and choice happen. They coincide, they coalesce, they mix, and then their joint outcome grows as hard and as fixed as cement. Like a fossil in stone, it hardens, in its own indissoluble, immutable shape.

How can old Professor Clark, sitting there in his railway carriage, nearly half-way up the spine of England, sitting there with his old face, and his old skin, and his old heart, and his old brain, and his wrinkled knuckles, and his spotted hands, and his thickening arteries, and his sore throat, and his expensively crowned teeth – how can he think for one moment that he has a hope, a chance, a possibility of redemption? It is done and he is damned. He must know this. It is over, the game is over, and he must face the knowledge of the way he played it. He is a child, to think that anything can be redeemed or recovered.

There is no point in this return, and no hope in it. The sea will reject him and the town will reject him, for the hiding places of his power are closed to him. He must learn to face the silence of the ending. The bell tower condemns him. The bell tower mocks him. The invitation mocks him. The honour mocks him.

It is hard, it is hard.

Is this the story that the Orator must tell?

If this is the story, then it must be told, for there is some honour left in the honest telling.

Is there a hope of another ending?

The Orator turns a page, and adjusts his glasses. It is a long struggle, and full of pain and disappointed hopes. The Orator is detached, but he can recognize and witness pain, although he suspects that he himself may no longer be able to feel it.

Ailsa Kelman and Humphrey Clark were to meet again this very night. She already knew this, and it was in her nature to assume that he must know it too. This was a reasonable assumption on her part, for she had no means of knowing the paranoid extent of his avoidances. She assumed that he must know of their imminent convergence, and had accepted it, for in her vanity she believed that everything she did was known and observed and blazoned all over the land. Therefore it was clear to her that her imminent re-entry into his life must be known to Humphrey Clark who was, as it were, in on and part of the act. It is true that P. B. Wilton, a good gauge of information diffusion, had been both ignorant of and unimpressed by her Ornemouth honour, and indeed had seemed uncertain where Ornemouth was. But maybe Peter had been pretending. He always liked to belittle and dissemble.

Yes, Humphrey would have been informed. He would have been sent the magazine with her picture in it, and his picture, their two miniatures married upon the page. The University of Ornemouth probably didn't know what it was doing, but Humphrey surely did.

It was a lark, a spree, a gamble, a game.

Humphrey Clark knew Ornemouth. It was in his blood.

Ailsa Kelman drove north towards Ornemouth in the little red two-seater and she sang as she drove.

'Ye banks and braes o' bonny Doon,' she sang merrily, at the top of her voice. *'How can ye bloom sae fresh and fair?'*

Once she had owned a folly car with the number plate AILSA. That had been in her days of vanity and glory, which she had now put so far behind her. She was a mature and adult female of her species at last, and she was rejoicing in her maturity.

> 'Thou'll break my heart, thou warbling bird
> That wantons through the flowery thorn,
> Thou minds me of departed joys
> Departed never to return . . .'

sang Ailsa, triumphant, on her way back to the pensioners' fish teas and crab sandwiches and antiquarian bookshops and tapestry kits and tattoo parlours and charity shops of Ornemouth. She is a pensioner herself now, an Old Age Pensioner, a Senior Citizen, and she tells herself bravely that she has never felt stronger in her life.

Her voice is not as good or as pure as Dame Mary McTaggart's, but she can still fill her lungs and produce a startling volume of sound.

Ailsa Kelman tells herself that she had accepted this invitation because she now considers herself ready for the challenge. Her Brazilian confessor, her lady from Rio, had encouraged her to accept it.

Ailsa has made efforts to deal with her past, with her pain. She moves in circles where such efforts are acceptable, even fashionable. Women are better than men at these explorations and these confrontations, or so Ailsa believes.

Ailsa, in what she stubbornly thinks of as her prime, still experiences moments of triumph and of joy. She can still sing loudly, and speak clearly, and stand up straight, and put on a good face.

Posture, Ailsa, posture.

But the fragility of the triumph is terrible, the psychic cost enormous. She wears little flat shoes now, but like the Little Mermaid she remembers the pain of the knives. It has not been easy, this metamorphosis.

She is brave, is Ailsa. She needs to believe in her own courage. And so she sings, against the rising tide.

She is also getting hungry. She hasn't had much to eat today. There will be a big dinner, but she hasn't had much lunch, and she could do with some tea.

She remembers the fish teas of Mrs Binns, with their brave little flags of parsley. Mrs Binns, widowed by the stormy seas of peacetime, making ends meet.

She remembers what P. B. had said two nights ago about the fluctuating fatness of Mary McTaggart. Dame Mary, like many opera singers, was famous for being fat. Ailsa no longer worries about her weight. She had worried about it, intermittently, in her forties and fifties, but then one day she had decided she didn't care if she got fat. She was getting old, and she might as well get fat too. Solidity was admirable, weight was desirable. She hadn't coined the memorable phrase 'Fat is a feminist issue' but she had decided to endorse it. And so liberating had that decision been that since then her weight had stabilized. Now she ate what she liked when she liked and it seemed to make no difference. She was a little overweight, but so what?

No wonder she thinks that by an effort of the will she can arrest time. What will happen to her when time catches up with her?

She could do with a sandwich. A crab sandwich, and a cup of tea.

So schoolboy Humphrey Clark never went back to Finsterness. Time stood still, in Finsterness, but he moved on, through puberty, into adolescence. His oceanic encyclopedic childish dreams dispersed and dissolved. He busied himself, like the normal boy he was trying to become, with schoolwork, and examinations, and university entrance. His only attempt to establish a specimen fish tank in his bedroom in Covington did not last long. Aquarium fish need a lot of attention, and die of disappointing fungal diseases, so he abandoned the project. Nor did he train to become a surgeon or a specialist in songbirds. He did not pursue a desire to become a coastguard or a lifeboat man or a lifesaver, although he swam for his school and was later to swim for his college.

He nudged himself in vain against the glass wall of mathematics, and eventually he had to give up. He found he could get so far, but always, at a certain distance, there was this glass against his nose. He mastered the riddle of Diophantus well before he went to Grammar School, and he learned geometry, and algebra, and logarithms, and achieved good grades at Ordinary Level, and then again two years later at Advanced Level. He was always top, or near the top, of the class, and his maths teacher assured him he could do it. He could read mathematics at university if he wanted, said Mr Hodges. But Humphrey Clark knew better. He knew he was not good enough. He knew that he would never hear the music of the prime numbers, he would never penetrate the thrilling mysteries of the higher orders of mathematics and physics. Numbers continued to fascinate him, but he knew that they were not for him. He read about Fermat's last theorem, then unsolved, and the Riemann hypothesis, as yet unsolved, and the Fermi paradox, still awaiting a solution from the seemingly eternal silences of space. Who was out there in all the other galaxies, Fermi had asked, but as yet there had been no reply. The planets remained silent.

Humphrey could understand the nature of the mathematical and cosmological questions, but he knew he would never find the answers, and would probably be unable to comprehend them even when others discovered them. They were too big for him. Mathematics and theoretical physics were both too big and too small for him.

He did better with zoology and biology.

Therefore he elected to study natural sciences at university, and when, in the later years of his public success, after the hiatus and hesitations of his failure, people were to ask him why, he would come up with the conventional answers – his difficulties with pure mathematics, his curiosity about the outdoor natural world, the charisma of his biology teacher at King Edward's.

Every budding natural scientist has a charismatic biology teacher, he was in the habit of saying. *It's part of the plot of the life of every zoologist, every ethologist, every marine biologist. Mr Summerscale was brilliant, I owe him a lot. He was a great romantic, Mr Summerscale.*

Ken Summerscale had died at the age of forty-eight climbing a small mountain in the Pyrenees. He had not lived to enjoy his prize pupil's success.

Mr Summerscale made me into a romantic, Humphrey Clark used to say. *He taught me to respect animals and the natural world. He taught me that we murder to dissect. He taught me that if you have to dissect, you must do it with respect. We were obliged to dissect, it was part of the syllabus, but he taught us that we must waste not a particle, not a cell. Nothing should die in vain, Mr Summerscale used to say. Not even a regulation school-issue rat or a dogfish. We should observe, that's what he told us. We should observe the living, we should observe the ways of life. You can't learn everything in the laboratory, that's what he used to say. The whole is more than the sum of its parts, he told us. The whole behaves differently from the parts, and has different properties. That's what he taught us, and he was right. It's out of fashion to say that these days, when we spend our time scrutinizing the interactions of eukaryotic microbes, but it's true, nevertheless. It's still true.*

And Humphrey, then, would mention the heroes of his apprenticeship: Sir Alister Hardy, Sir Frederick Russell, Konrad Lorenz, Niko Tinbergen.

He sometimes mentioned his grandmother, and his Aunt Vera, and his formative childhood years by the northern sea. He often spoke fondly of the sea squirt and St Cuthbert's beads.

He never mentioned Ailsa and Tommy Kelman. He never mentioned Sandy Clegg. They had been banished from the record.

St Cuthbert's beads, as he had learned at school from Mr Summerscale, were the fossils of the stems of crinoids, otherwise known as sea lilies. They were abundant on the shores of Finsterness. Crinoids were so successful in the Palaeozoic seas that their fossils had accumulated to form great layers of limestone. Humphrey had taken some specimens of fossilized Northumbrian sea lilies to school, in his mother's abandoned shell-encrusted shoebox, and Mr Summerscale had identified them for him.

The pleasure of identification had been intense and full of hope.

By the time he went to university, Humphrey Clark had become another person, of another species. Nobody would have predicted the nature of the transformation. The diffident studious delicate little boy had become healthy, physically confident, almost assured. At eighteen, he had been just too young for National Service, which was then in the process of being phased out, and some adults had told him this was a pity, as National Service makes a man of you. But Humphrey had found the Sixth Form at King Edward's full of its own rites of passage. He grew over four inches in eighteen months, or so the school doctor's rickety wooden gibbet-like measuring apparatus told him. He flourished. The virtues of the wholesome state-controlled wartime diet manifested themselves in his physique. He grew taller and broader than his father, who was in these years growing ever thinner and smaller. He made new friends, he sang loudly in the school choir with his well-broken baritone voice, he stopped saying his prayers, he drank beer and cheap wine, he smoked surreptitiously, and although he remained a little shy he joked fairly easily with the Sixth Form girls who came over the road from the Girls' Grammar for their biology lessons with Mr Summerscale. The brother of two pretty sisters, he was accustomed to girls.

He had survived the shames of puberty and adolescence, and, unlike the cuckoo wrasse and the marine shrimp, he had felt little temptation to change sex. He had become a good-looking young man, and his sisters Lizzie and Di valued him as an escort, and as a procurer of acceptable boyfriends.

Nor had he lazily, under the influence of beer and companionship, abandoned his notochord and his ambitions. He had not slumped into colonized stasis or invertebrate inertia. He was a hard worker, a diligent student. He passed without too much difficulty his Latin O-Level, then a requirement for entrance to some of the older universities and a stumbling block to many aspiring scientists. He won the Bebb-Whistler Prize for his collection of the larval cases of caddis flies. (Who was Bebb-Whistler? Humphrey had never thought to ask. Some long-dead and long-forgotten amateur, he would have guessed, if asked, but as nobody asked him he did not even bother to guess. If the benevolent Bebb-Whistler had hoped for immortality or even for thanks from his beneficiaries, he had been disappointed. Unlike Alfred Russel Wallace, he wasn't even remembered for being forgotten. He had just disappeared from the record. Humphrey wonders now, sometimes, if he should undertake some pious compensatory research into the obscure life of the obscure Bebb-Whistler. But of course he hasn't got round to it yet.)

Humphrey was appointed Head Boy, and he was popular in this apprentice managerial role. His school reports commented with what he took to be approval that he was 'always ready to accept responsibility'.

His parents were proud of him. 'Our son's at Cambridge, he got a minor scholarship,' they would say, even when they were not asked. And they were not often asked. They did not enjoy an extended social life in Covington. They were quiet people.

His mother liked to say, 'He takes after my father. My father was a grand swimmer.'

Where was that little misery, that little naked piping boy, that child who had snivelled over a dead fish and a false friend? Was he cast off for ever, or was he dormant, awaiting a miserable watery rebirth?

Humphrey Clark, tall, easy-going, presentable and well-liked, got a good but not an outlandishly good degree, and was encouraged to embark on postgraduate research on the optics of fish.

He had by this time returned with a dedicated passion to his earlier loves. In his Cambridge years he had joined a diving club, and had taken up diving and fish-watching in the long vacations. He swam with fish, and he studied fish behaviour, and once more he began to dream of fish. (Once he dreamed that the sky was full of shining fish, swimming through the bare boughs of silver-barked forest trees.) Ethology was the discipline to which he aspired, and it was in those days a respected discipline that attracted research funding, grants, honour, places on expeditions, public admiration. Fieldwork was in fashion, and its practitioners were revered. He and his fellow-students and his teachers and their colleagues were largely unaware that their ways of learning and observing and thinking were about to be phased out and displaced by molecular biology and laboratory-based neurology and physiology, and by the computerized mathematical crunching of the fossil record.

Crinoids were graceful creatures, as were their surviving descendants. Fish were graceful. Underwater life was full of movement and of grace. This is one of the reasons why it attracted him.

The computer and the DNA revolution were both in their infancy when Humphrey Clark embarked on postgraduate research. The vast fortunes and commercial wars of the patented genome lay in the future. It was still possible, at that time, to be a serious scientist and to adopt a quasi-mystical approach to the natural world. It was still possible to regard the sea as a sea of faith. Not perhaps as a sea of old-fashioned religious faith, but as a sea of faith in the glory and diversity of creation. The old traditions of respect and wonder flourished, in direct descent from those venerable Victorian collectors of snails and butterflies, those Bebb-Whistlers who had marked out the terrain and filled their cabinets and built the great museums. Those collectors of beetles and bones and the larval cases of caddis flies were his ancestors.

And some of the heavyweights of marine biology professed themselves to be devout. They believed in the Divine Flame. Marine biologist Sir Alister Hardy had delivered the Gifford Lectures on the theme of the Divine Flame, in Aberdeen in 1964. Hardy had been deeply interested in religious experience. Even the agnostics and atheists in the profession were not such confident proselytizers for their secular molecular creed as their descendants were shortly to become. Darwin and Huxley were in the right, of course, and the entrenched bishops of the nineteenth century had been in the wrong. The Edwardian imperialist religious and political agenda of the scientific articles in Arthur Mee's *Children's Encyclopedia* had long been abandoned. But nevertheless, nevertheless . . . doubt was honoured, dissent was permitted, faith was respected, and the observation of the behaviour of whole and living organisms was considered central to zoological research.

It was a tolerant time, in the days when Humphrey was an apprentice. A form of anthropomorphism was acceptable, for the human model, despite the Second World War and its revelations, despite Bergen-Belsen and Bikini, was still seen in a benign light. The great Austrian ethologist Konrad Lorenz had spoken of geese 'falling in love', and he had not been much mocked for this. He had spoken of cichlid 'marriage' and of rat 'families' and of the 'friendships' of fish. These metaphors had not yet been contemptuously deconstructed, nor had the word 'Austrian' yet become an automatic invitation to unthinking and ignorant racist assumption and innuendo.

Humphrey Clark was to watch the evolution of his faith with dismay.

The whole field of biological and zoological knowledge was about to be transformed, creating new paradigms, providing new battlefields for new theories, but postgraduate Humphrey Clark had not yet been aware of this. And if he had been aware, he would not have changed course. He was full of confidence in fish and in the saving freedom of fish. Later, he was to waver in allegiance: but not then.

The bitterness of the wars was to take him by surprise. He

had been so sure that he was on the side of the angels. But his angels went out of fashion. His angels were too large to dance invisibly upon the end of a pin, or to be captured through the lens of the electronic microscope. They were graceful, but they were gross.

The greylag goose and the stickleback were superseded by the fruit fly and the nematode worm and the laboratory mouse, and they in turn by the eukaryotic microbe and the selfish gene and the spiteful gene. Humphrey had been caught in the conflict. He survived, but at a cost.

We reduce and reduce and reduce, but the habits of anthropomorphism and metaphor are hard to kill.

Professor Clark, sitting on a train travelling northwards, turned these matters over in his mind. The folder lay closed upon his table, and he was lost for words, lost for words for his thoughts. He was on his way back to the wellspring: would he recover them there?

Maybe everybody's career, with hindsight, displays evidence of lacunae, jagged edges, fault-lines, false tributaries. So he reassures himself.

He often thinks of his palaeontologist acquaintance Stuart Troughton, who had so mistakenly convinced himself that his work on fossil distribution had uncovered significant new evidence about the early evolution of sexual reproduction. He had got his numbers and his dates badly wrong, as Darwin had done a century earlier when he had tried to estimate the age of the Earth. Troughton, like Darwin, was only a few million years out, but his theory had foundered. Troughton had been obliged to live, bitterly, with this error. Unlike Darwin, he never recovered his ground.

Barking up the wrong tree
Backing the wrong horse

Taking the wrong turning
Going up a blind alley
Digging your own grave
Meeting a dead end

Humphrey often thinks of his friend Harry Field, who had euphorically mistaken a cellular organelle for a molecule, and had published prematurely, to the ridicule and satisfaction of his rivals. And of Barry Armstrong, who had waited too long, and yet not quite long enough. Barry Armstrong had devoted twenty unproductive years to the study of the digestive tracts of colonial ascidians, and then had stopped, impatiently, just one step short of the significant discovery that had won his successor the prize. And, at the other end of the scale, he often thinks of his one-time diving companion Jack Stringer, who had drowned off the coast of Australia while investigating the suicidal impulses of beaching whales.

With all these he has sympathy.

His own career had been more successful. His mistakes had been concealed. He had been lucky.

The train stopped for a long time just outside Doncaster and engine trouble was reported over the loudspeaker.

Nothing was over. Nothing is ever over.

As the train began to stall, he began – oh, slowly, not in a wave of sudden recognition – he began slowly to realize that he had been 'out of his mind' to accept the invitation to receive an honorary degree in the new university at Ornemouth. What folly, what vanity, what complacency had seduced him into this journey? The sinews and valves of his memory would be prised open, slowly, painfully, with each mile he travelled, like the stiff hinges of a shellfish.

The scalped memory would lie open to the sky.

Folly and vanity. He struggled with these notions. He had

nourished such high hopes. Surely there had been at least a promise of restoration in his hopes?

There was a period in his life when he had been tempted to abandon any pretence of hard science, to abandon the jungle warfare of academic competition, to retire from the race, and to become a historian of science rather than a practising scientist. He had seriously thought of becoming a historian of marine biology. It was a good subject, and the funding had been adequate. He had been offered a fellowship and a publishing contract for this harmless project, and he had started work on it, but then had been lured back from this peaceful backwater into the 'real world' by flattery, big money, commerce, and glory, treacherously disguised as education and the public good. He had been seduced by the grandiose Greenwich project, by the Green Grotto. It had almost undone him.

He still continued to teach a course on the history of marine biology. It was an indulgence, a vanity, a frivolous option. His students loved it.

He looked out at the inland railway sidings, where purple and yellow weeds flourished abundantly between the tracks. Would the lost land of his innocence materialize, as he travelled towards it? The ache in his speechless throat was like an ache in an amputated limb, in a missing organ. He thought of the incoming tide, and of the ebb and flow of schools and disciplines and reputations. He was old now, and he had seen them come and go. He had heard the complaints at High Table. The resisted rise of sociobiology, the waning of belles-lettres and of literary criticism, the rise of deconstruction, the rise of literary theory, the decline of the Germanic languages, the spread of the Hispanic languages, the death of easel art, the fad for installations, the rise of women's studies, the rise of media studies, and of business studies, and of sports science, and of political correctness, and of academic servitude. He had been witness to the snapping and the sniping, the gossip and the grievances. He had seen it all, he had followed it all.

He had noted the exclusion, and then the sanctification, of Rosalind Franklin, for long the unsung heroine of crystallography and DNA, and now the icon of women's success in hard science. He had noted the recovery of the forgotten work of Cecilia Payne, famous for hydrogen and helium, and of Henrietta Leavitt of Harvard, who had discovered those dying giant yellow stars. He had watched the gender game.

The excavations, the rehabilitations, the posthumous awards. The rearguard attacks of the creationists, the intemperate responses of the geneticists, the bitter debates on heritability and race, on biological determinism, on animal experimentation, on the patenting of genes. The struggles for funding, the shifting of paradigms, the intemperate raging in the pages of academic journals.

Buckets of water had been thrown at professors on platforms, and death threats issued against heads of departments.

Professor Clark sighed.

The papers for the ceremony lay in their dark pink folder upon his table, on top of the new life of Darwin which he was attempting to read. Somewhere in the same folder lay the prospectus for a new volume of brief lives of Great Scientists of the Sea (not a selling title, they'd have to think of something better than that) for which he had been asked to write an introduction. He doubted if he would do so, for the proposal was beneath his dignity, but he had agreed to look. The volume was intended as a popular read, with a TV tie-in for one of the rapidly proliferating new digital educational channels. There were the usual characters, with one or two wild cards. There was a plan to include a chapter on Elaine Morgan's Aquatic Ape hypothesis, that farfetched and implausible evolutionary fantasy which nevertheless lent itself to fine footage of water births and water babies. Elaine Morgan had developed her thesis from Sir Alister Hardy's crazy guesses that hominids had once been water-dwelling animals, and she had elaborated it over the years with an admirable and on the whole increasingly polite and persuasive persistence.

Humphrey Clark had always valued politeness. He had been dragged into controversy reluctantly. He yearned for the polite and imaginary innocence of the early world.

Elaine Morgan's hypothesis was almost certainly (though not demonstrably) wrong, and it was dangerous to flirt with her views, attractive though they were. Her theory of the Descent of Woman had attracted the wrong kind of attention, and her feminist disciples were more fanatical than she was. They were not as fanatical as the creationists, for feminism is a more tenable position than creationism. Feminism, as he knew too well, was a dangerous bedfellow.

But Elaine Morgan was right in her view that we are drawn towards the waters and the sea, and her hypothesis seemed to be gathering respectability.

He wondered if Paul Burden's prize-winning book about hermaphrodites and the sex changes of fish had a metaphysical thesis. Hermaphroditism seemed an unlikely topic to inspire a mystic, but he had some vague notional memory that Burden, as Plato had done before him, had ventured into speculative waters in his discussion on intersexuality and the historic origins of sex.

Plato hops into Professor Clark's thought unbidden, from long ago. Plato and Ovid and sex.

The brutality and the reductionism of the microbiological victory had not destroyed all speculation. Ethology and ethologists had been savaged, but they had not perished.

Humphrey Clark did not like to think about the bitterness of the conflict, the betrayals, the mistakes he had made, the enmities he had incurred, the jealousy he had suffered, the deaths for which he had considered himself responsible. He had known the day's agony, the night's remorse.

The old town of Ornemouth and its people had been steeped in archaic biblical notions of innocence and guilt and honesty, and these had filtered into his growing self, into his bones and his brain. They were a part of him that he could not shed. He did not like the selfish gene, the spiteful gene, the inevitability of what he, in his old-fashioned way, could still call wickedness. He yearned still for the possibility of the generous gene, the sacrificial gene.

The train dawdled and delayed. Now was the time to profit from this delay by studying the papers prepared for him by Mrs Hornby. He knew he should try to memorize the names of his fellow-honorary graduands and of the dignitaries of Ornemouth: the Vice Chancellor, the Public Orator, and the billionaire Canadian-born owner of the now-thriving salmon farms and the experimental cod nurseries. It would be polite to try to weave some of them into his words of thanks at the ceremony tomorrow. But some premonitory inhibition restrained him. He was superstitiously afraid to open the folder. A technique of avoidance had become part of his nature. He knew by now that there were names in that folder that he did not wish to see.

The Public Orator knows that the name of Ailsa Kelman waits for Humphrey Clark. He planted it there.

Ailsa Kelman's name lies there, dormant, waiting. Humphrey will find it soon.

Ailsa is waiting to confront him and entrap him, as she had waited as an angry barefoot child on the seawall.

Their first adult encounter had also taken place by the sea, but on a different coastline, five hundred miles from Finsterness. On the borders of Somerset and Devon they met, overlooking the Bristol Channel.

They met, but they did not immediately, at first or at second sight, recognize and identify each other.

She was selling programmes for a show. She was a humble programme seller. She was standing there, at the makeshift entrance to the open-air theatre, with a sheaf of amateur Xeroxed leaflets in her hand. She was inspecting tickets and selling programmes, and he was waiting to buy one from her. He gave her a shilling, and she gave him a programme with a cast list for the play. It was a simple interchange.

Neither of them recognized, at that important moment, that this announced the next act of the drama of their lives.

Humphrey Clark handed the programme to his girlfriend, Sonia Easton, for it was his girlfriend Sonia who had wished to see this performance. He had tagged along with her amiably, as was his way. He had no objection to seeing a touring production of *The Tempest*, for he enjoyed the theatre, and there was not much to do of an evening in this old-style seaside town in the West Country. The small travelling repertory company, according to Sonia, had a good reputation. It was avant-garde, said Sonia, who knew about such things. Its pioneering work, said Sonia, was a showcase for some of the recently graduated names of the university circuit. They lived in caravans, and shared their wages, said Sonia. They were a sort of commune, said Sonia. She knew somebody who had worked for them during their last season who was now resident dramatist at the Royal Court. This is what Sonia, not without some complacency, had told him.

Humphrey was happy to obey Sonia, and to listen to Shakespeare, in this open-air auditorium, on a summer evening. If his mind wandered, he could think of the fish amongst whom he had swum during the day, or look out to sea, beyond the bandstand and the mild grassy knoll, towards the horizon. He could see the winking of a lighthouse across the water on the far Welsh shore. Sonia had been patient about the diving, and it was no hardship to accommodate her wish to see a play.

But usherette Ailsa, although unrecognized, had not gone unnoticed. Humphrey had registered her, for she had projected herself, even during this brief and basic commercial exchange, as a woman suffering from extreme dissatisfaction. Anger and discontent were banked up and glowing in her and their heat flowed out from her. He noticed this, and therefore he noticed her. The disdainful and flamboyantly downtrodden manner in which she held out her wares, the scorn with which she received his silver coin, the contempt with which she pointed towards the row in which he and Sonia were to sit – all these displayed a disproportionate emotion which surely exceeded any just cause that could relate either to her role as programme seller or to his as customer. True, he might have said to himself, as he settled on to his uncomfortable wooden chair, the job of the usherette is not of the highest dignity, but neither is it demeaning. The young woman was clearly not a professional usherette, for this was not a fully fledged professional troupe of players, and such services would have been beyond its means: she must be a summer volunteer, working for the love of the group, or an actress filling in for part of the season. Had the love turned to hatred? Did she feel herself to be underparted?

It says much for the powers of projection of the young and as yet unidentified Ailsa that these possibilities reached Humphrey Clark as he waited for the drama to begin, and gave him food for thought. He glanced round, covertly, past the high white well-bred profile of Sonia, to the smouldering young woman who, with indiscriminately bad grace, was continuing to tear tickets savagely in half and to sell her tedious wares.

Did she look familiar? It cannot be certain that he suspected that he recognized her at this point. Her hair was still the same thick copper-brown, but the wide-angled shape of her face had altered, very much for the better, and her body was now fully adult. She had a body which protested spontaneously and almost audibly against its subjugation, a body not so much of beauty as of bravado. She was dressed in a parody of servility, in an ill-made little black dress that would have suited a waitress, had not its neck been scooped so low. Even if part of Humphrey's brain had not been searching for a spark of a memory link, he would have noticed those breasts. Sonia Easton's attractive bosom, in or out of its standard Marks and Spencer 34B brassiere, was familiar to him, but this unfamiliar bosom was a statement, a challenge. The legs of this woman – he lowered his gaze, visibly peering, by now, through the rows of chairs and the seated and incoming audience – were muscular and powerful. They were clad in fishnet stockings, and they looked as though they could kick. The ankles were fine yet sturdy, and the heels of the black patent open-toed shoes were painfully high. No professional waitress, no usherette would have sported those punitive shoes.

Yes, thought Humphrey, as he sat back and heard the opening words of the play make their way through the light breeze, yes, there is a woman who thinks she deserves better, a woman who is angry with her lot.

It says much for Humphrey's perceptions that even then, at that early stage, he recognized that there was something impersonal, something generic, about that anger. The young woman who shortly turned out to be Ailsa Kelman was not simply herself, she was a portent. Her message was directed towards every man within her reach, but Humphrey was perhaps the only one to receive its full blast, and he received it because he remembered her from long ago, and was searching and searching for her name, her place, her meaning.

Humphrey did not go to the theatre very often, but he went often enough to recognize, as the production unfolded, that he was watching something as unusual, in its way, as the programme seller was in hers. This was not a tired and elderly classical turn in shabby, well-worn costumes, dragged around from village hall to school hall to community centre to disused cinema, such as he used to see (and to see happily, to see gratefully) at King Edward's in Covington. It was a dark production with a sharp and sinister focus, which owed something to the films of Ingmar Bergman, then much in vogue. Sonia had been right in her high expectations. Prospero was powerfully portrayed as an arrogant and sadistic Svengali/Mephistopheles figure, more wedded to power and to destruction than to peace, poetry and reconciliation. His relish in the tempest he called forth was alarming, his tormenting of Ariel and Caliban and indeed of his own pale daughter was merciless.

The edges of the production were a bit rough, and some of the exits and entrances somewhat embarrassing, owing to the lack of wings and proper backstage cover, but the overall spirit of the piece was impressive.

Prospero was the star, and, despite the professed communal aspirations of the troupe, he imposed himself forcefully as a star. His clipped diction was eccentric but not unpleasing: it had an old-fashioned, upper-class, public-school ring to it, interestingly at odds with the innovative mood and means of the production. His face was chalk-white (but was that natural?) and he wore a small, trim, very black continental beard. His was a name to remember, and an easy name at that. He was called Martin Pope. (The Miranda and the Ferdinand were, frankly, substandard: you could hardly hear a word Miranda said.) Humphrey, consulting the programme in the interval while Sonia went off to the pebble-dashed building that housed the coin-operated ladies' toilets, discovered that Prospero was the director as well as the principal player. He stored the name of Martin Pope away.

And there, in the programme, he found the name of Ailsa Kelman. The name jumped up at him from the page, just as Sonia returned to his side.

Ailsa's name was listed as a member of the company. There was a brief biography of each member, in alphabetical order. Ailsa Kelman, in the travelling repertory, appeared as Marina in *Pericles, Prince of Tyre*, and as the Mermaid Princess in an adaptation of Hans Andersen's *The Little Mermaid*, a work advertised as 'not suitable for young children'.

So the Princess had to sell programmes, from time to time, and she made it clear to all that she did not like it much.

As the second half of the performance began, Humphrey was unable to continue to pay attention to Shakespeare. He was transported back to the summer of the rock pool and the codfish, to the white knickers and the games of Monopoly. So here was Ailsa Kelman, Tommy Kelman's little sister, grown up. Tommy Kelman, who had poisoned the summer with his stories of Hiroshima and his sniggerings about sex and his theft of Sandy Clegg. Would she remember him, as he remembered her? Surely she would not. He was ashamed to remember her and her brother so well. He was ashamed that they had had the power to make him suffer. He had tried to stifle his memory of them, to put it behind him. How best, he wondered, to survive this chance encounter? Should he pretend to himself that it had not happened? Or should he confront her, after the show, with his grown and armoured self? He could introduce her to his girlfriend Sonia, and ask her to join them for a drink. That would be a sophisticated thing to do. He could impress her with the optics and the cleaning symbioses of fish, and with the renown of his underwater expertise. He could exorcize rejection and dependence and loneliness, and show his new colours and prove himself a man.

Sonia Easton seemed pleased to make the acquaintance of the fish-netted Ailsa Kelman. Sonia was a mild-mannered, eccentric, upper-crust Bohemian, a student of algae and lichen, but not, as she emphatically insisted, a diver: she did not, she told Ailsa, with her curious high-pitched nervous neighing laugh, she did *not* like *getting her hair wet*, she found diving suits *claustrophobic*, she was frightened of *sharks*, and, in short, she preferred to *keep her head above water*. I leave all that underwater lark to Humphrey, she confided, over her glass of cheap white Spanish wine in the smoky bar of the Sandpiper Inn by the harbour steps.

The authentically sixteenth-century bar was bedecked with unconvincing and largely twentieth-century marine paraphernalia. Coarse fishing nets hung from the ceiling, ornamented with highly coloured plastic crabs and lobsters of scarlet and salmon-pink and orange and navy-blue. Glass globes pretending to be buoys and thick bottles of dark green and poisonous purple dangled from outsize hooks, and anchors and oars were stuck haphazardly about the distempered walls and over the boarded fireplace. Incongruous horse brasses were nailed to low nicotine-blackened beams. A large brown smooth varnished spotted fish in a glass case sneered down at them from above the lintel. The barman wore a Guernsey sweater, and sported a nautical beard, a sprouting untidy red beard very unlike that of Martin Pope, who was sitting at the far end of the bar, still unnaturally white of face and black of hair, surrounded by admirers.

Ailsa, for her part, protested that she was not and would never be a professional actress. This was a one-off for her, she said, perched on her bar stool, her skirt riding high over her knees, sucking hard on a stylish menthol cigarette. This one summer on the road, and then she was off and out. They had begged her to stay, but it had been a disaster, she said loudly, and in earshot of her fellow thespians: the takings for *The Little Mermaid* had been dismal, the so-called communal company spirit was a fake and a fraud, actors were monsters of egotism, she was sick of sleeping in a bunk, and Martin was a tyrant.

He's good, though, said Sonia, who had enjoyed the production.

Oh yes, he's *good*, said Ailsa dismissively, as though that had nothing to do with anything.

The two women ignored Humphrey. He bought them another round, and listened politely as they nattered on, competitively, making their pitches not at him, but at each other. It was an interesting display of redirected behaviour, and he was not quite sure what it meant, but he was happy to remain an observer. Sonia described her doctoral thesis, and drew a little picture on the back of the programme, of her favourite lichen. Ailsa confided that she too had been writing a dissertation, when the roles of Marina and the Princess had beckoned her: she would return to it, she asserted, as soon as the season was over, and as soon as she could re-organize her funding. And what had been her subject, enquired Sonia, with a very slight tone of patronage. Expressionist drama in France and Belgium, retorted Ailsa with panache. With special reference to the work of Eloise van Dieman.

Humphrey wanted Sonia to say, 'Who?', but she lacked the

guts, and so did he, so the esoteric name of Eloise van Dieman had to join that of Martin Pope in the memory bank, for future reference and examination.

A third round followed, this time boldly purchased by Ailsa, who made short work of capturing the barman's attention. This round revealed that Ailsa had studied modern languages at Edinburgh, and had then spent a year or so of further post-graduate study in Paris, attached to the Institut des Arts Dramatiques, where she had unfortunately made the acquaintance of Martin Pope. (She said this very loudly indeed, but by now Mr Pope appeared to have left.) So now, said Ailsa, she was rethinking her strategies. Very wise, said Sonia, in a voice of submission and agreement that implied nothing about the stability or fragility of the nature of her relationship with Humphrey Clark. Or if it did, Humphrey failed to detect what it was, and he had been listening attentively. He himself often wondered what their relationship was, and what Sonia expected of him, or he of her. Some of his university friends were married already, to wives who had opted for domesticity: one or two of them even had children. He did not know what Sonia expected, if she expected anything. He knew he seemed to have become responsible for her, but he did not know why.

The specialist topics of algae and Expressionism being temporarily exhausted, the two women fell silent for a moment, and then, suddenly, Ailsa Kelman looked up from her heaped ashtray and looked accusingly at Humphrey Clark and said, 'So how are things in Finsterness? I suppose it's changed a lot?'

She professed herself astonished when he said he had never been back. She stared at him for an unguarded instant of surprise, before she continued her approach.

'But I imagined you were there every summer?' she wailed

interrogatively, with a mock indignation which concealed, he was sure, a different emotion, though what emotion it was he could not divine. 'I thought it was sort of your home? I thought it was where you *lived*? It was where your family lived, wasn't it?'

He shook his head, and gallantly extended his gunmetal lighter towards her appealing cigarette. Her wrist, unlike her ankles, was very thin. Her nails were bitten and painted, but her wrist was surprisingly small-boned and delicate. It was encircled by a little bracelet of woven red and white thread, which looked not unlike a hospital tag. The pale skin of her arm was lightly freckled, as it had been when she was a child.

'My grandmother died,' he said in explanation.

'But you had an auntie?' she persisted. 'I remember an auntie, who took an interest in your fish?'

'Auntie Vera,' he said. 'I'm surprised you remember.'

'Oh,' she said, back in a teasing mode, a flirtatious mode. 'I remember everything about that summer. Everything.'

Sonia was not so happy with this exclusive interchange, and was showing signs of restlessness. She shifted on her bar stool, and yawned.

'My Auntie Vera moved to Beaconsfield,' said Humphrey, in a tone that closed the topic of Finsterness for the evening. Ailsa let it go.

When they stepped out into the summer darkness, Humphrey pointed out the boat at anchor, the *Sally Jane*, the boat which would take him and his Marine Society-sponsored colleagues out in the morning on the fish watch. He nearly said, 'Would you like to come too?' but he thought that Sonia would not like it if he said this, even in play. And also he feared that Ailsa might have said yes. Ailsa had been a bold child. She had walked along the wall of that northern harbour at high tide, and climbed down the metal rungs over the slippery weed and barnacles to the landing stage, a steep descent that Humphrey found frightening. She had danced barefoot on the ribbed beach, her hair in rats' tails, taunting Sandy and Humphrey and Tommy, and singing a naughty song. Once for a dare she had eaten a raw shrimp.

She might want to learn to dive with him. He did not want the responsibility, the embarrassment.

The three of them walked up the beer-smelling uneven cobbled back street together. Humphrey offered each woman an arm, and they hooked together, a threesome, their arms through his elbows, warm against his body in the summer night.

Come unto these yellow sands, and then take hands . . .

So the imprisoned Ariel had sung, in her bizarre and unflattering white feathered space-suit.

Ailsa Kelman, rescued from the past. He had forgotten to ask her about her brother Tommy. Neither of them had mentioned Sandy Clegg.

Sonia and Humphrey walked Ailsa back to her gypsy encampment in the grassy upper car park, on the green turf of the promontory near the bandstand. It looked ramshackle but not unromantic, with twinkling lights shining from the caravan windows. Tomorrow Ilfracombe, said Ailsa. Don't drown, Humphrey, said Ailsa, as she reached up to kiss his cheek. Goodbye, Sonia, said Ailsa. Good luck with the hunting and gathering. They said goodbye beneath the stars, and said they would keep in touch. Then Humphrey and Sonia walked back down the hill to the boarding house, where they occupied adjacent rooms.

In those days, in the early years of the sixties, it was not so easy for an unmarried couple to share a hotel room without hostile comment or unpleasant innuendo. This was a relief to Humphrey, and he suspected it was a relief to Sonia, although he could not be certain of this. She seemed to welcome his advances, but she also seemed content when he returned, after non-penetrative mutual orgasm, to sleep in his own room.

The orgasms were non-penetrative because the contraceptive pill was not yet widely available to unmarried women, who lived in well-founded horror of unwanted pregnancy, and Sonia and Humphrey had agreed, without ever discussing the matter, that condoms and Dutch caps were repulsive as well as unreliable.

Sonia had once had penetrative sex in a tent with a condom-wearing botanist, an act which had given her an appalling allergic vaginal reaction. It had been her first sexual experience, and it had been horrifying. She had been so sore and so inflamed and so ashamed for so long that she had gone off the whole business. She had not dared to visit a doctor, and had daubed herself, guiltily, with Savlon and Nivea cream, which had made matters worse. She had thought, for a while, that the botanist had given her a sexually transmitted disease, but eventually the raging inner rash and gross swellings of the labia had subsided, and had not recurred. Her accommodation with handsome Humphrey suited her well, and she could not afford to worry too much about whether or not it suited him. She did not tell Humphrey the details of this deterrent experience, but she told him enough about it to let him guess at the causes of her sensitivity. That's how things were, in those days.

Humphrey, post-orgasm, lay on his narrow lumpy bed and stared at the stained ceiling and thought about Ailsa and Martin Pope. So the caravan of players would move on along the coast to Ilfracombe the next day, and perform *The Little Mermaid* there under cover in the little theatre. He knew Ilfracombe. Philip Gosse, the devout father of marine biology and the inventor of the aquarium, had explored the seas near Ilfracombe, and to this day it maintained a modest little town aquarium with an interesting selection of specimens from the local waters. And there was a Victorian natural rock bathing pool at Ilfracombe, a tidal pool not unlike the saltwater pool at Ornemouth which had been inexplicably out of bounds because of the war. He had accepted this prohibition meekly as a boy, but now he wondered: why on earth had they been forbidden the pool? Was it just general anti-child meanness, or was there some more plausible reason? Ailsa had once tried to climb over the fence, but they'd caught her at it and stopped her.

He wondered if he would ever see Ailsa Kelman again. It had been interesting to bump into her again, so unexpectedly, but he would not pursue her along the coast. He was glad that he had not been expected to see a performance of *The Little Mermaid*. He did not want to see Ailsa Kelman making a fool of herself on stage. She did not seem content with her lot, but it was not clear whether her anger arose from her unsatisfactorily subordinate relationship with her Svengali, or whether it sprang from a deeper career indecision. She evidently considered herself wasted on selling programmes, and that was surely right. He had been unable to follow her description of her interest in Expressionism, and indeed he hardly knew what Expressionism was, but she had made it plain – she had been anxious to make it plain – that her university had awarded her an excellent degree and a choice of research options. She had displayed all the symptoms of driving ambition. These were no surprise to him. But what would be the object of this ambition?

His own ambitions, in contrast, were at this period in his life well defined, and well funded. He knew where his ship was sailing. Next year, he hoped, the Damascene Islands in the Indian Ocean. He was a lucky man, and full of confidence.

> 'For my false lover broke my heart
> And ah, he left the thorn wi' me.'

So sang Ailsa, heartlessly, as a pageant of false and discarded lovers paraded through her memory, rising like spectres from the high green fields of the sheep-dotted borders, from the windswept hedgerows, from the deep fast brown treacherous waters of the tree-shaded ravine of the salmon-sporting river Orne. How beautiful is the summer landscape, thought Ailsa, how heartlessly, how patiently it has waited for us, through all these years, with its unimaginable message!

The debacle with Humphrey Clark had been her fault, for the next time she and Humphrey met was not by chance, but at her initiative. 'I was the criminal,' insisted Ailsa, decades later, to her analyst, who remained silent. 'All right,' said Ailsa, 'I suppose you think I *want* to think I had control over it, even if that makes me out to be a criminal. But I *did* have control over it. If I hadn't sent him that card, that invitation, he might never have seen me again. He might have married that nice lichen woman. Or he might have married Beattie Lovelace.' (The unlikely thought of his marrying a woman called Beattie Lovelace made Ailsa laugh, even though she was a self-confessed unhappy, guilty, tormented criminal.) 'He might have settled down in San Diego or in Woody Bay or Woody Hole or whatever that marine biology place in Massachusetts was called. He might have won the Nobel Prize.'

The analyst remained silent. She had her own version of this story, and was waiting to see if Ailsa Kelman would stumble upon it as she wandered helplessly round the minefield of accusation and counter-accusation.

The Public Orator is trying to work out yet another story, and is both frustrated and encouraged by the lack of an ending, and by what appears (can it be?) to be the free will of the protagonists.

'Yes,' repeated Ailsa with an air of guilty but proud conviction, 'if I hadn't got in the way, he would certainly have won the Nobel Prize.'

Ailsa Kelman sent a printed card to Humphrey Clark, advertising herself in her new manifestation. Nearly two years had passed since their chance encounter near the border between North Somerset and North Devon, and she was not sure if her card would reach him at the Marine Institute in Lowestoft, to which the laboratory in Cambridge said he had been temporarily posted. Lowestoft did not sound like a good address to Ailsa, despite the subversive success of pirate station Radio Caroline, but she was willing to believe that this secondment was a staging post to higher things in the marine life, and that Humphrey's career was prospering. Hers certainly was. That was why she was trying to get in touch with him. She wanted him to know that she was no longer a programme seller. Maybe he knew already, but maybe, in Lowestoft, he didn't watch much television or read the right newspapers. His frame of cultural reference had seemed fairly broad, for a natural scientist, but she had enough realism left to recognize that her fame, although from her own perspective resounding and indeed irreversibly accelerating, might not yet have reached him. Not everybody watched *Late Night Line Up*, not everybody saw the *Evening Standard*, not everybody knew the chic alternative nightspots of Soho.

'I mean, I know I was self-centred, I know I expected to be able to force things to revolve round me, I know I have this problem with perception, but I do have *some* sense of proportion,' Ailsa said from time to time to her analyst, as she looked back over these giddy years of relentless and successful self-absorption and self-promotion.

On the blank back of the printed card, she had given her address and telephone number (the exchange was, quaintly, called Museum) and had written in black ink, 'Do come one night, if you can. I could get you a ticket and we could have dinner after the show. Tommy says he would love to see you too. Did you get to the Damascene Islands? You never sent me a postcard, or if you did, I didn't get it. You said you would. I went to see that darling little museum in Ilfracombe that you recommended. Do you remember the Pool of Brochan? How are you enjoying Lowestoft? I have never been to Lowestoft. Yours ever, Ailsa.'

Humphrey studied this message carefully and subjected it to close textual analysis. It was an invitation, and a come-on of a sort, no doubt about that. The printed side of the card advertised an event that it described, in large gold letters against a maroon ground, as a Candid Cabaret, which took place nightly in a cellar off Shaftesbury Avenue called the Tinder Box. A design of little golden flames licked around its borders. The card gave a box-office number, times, and the names of the cast, including that of Ailsa Kelman and one or two Scottish-sounding personages. (He looked for the name of Martin Pope, but it was not there.) Whatever was she up to now? He was sure it must be embarrassing. She had pledged herself to foreswear theatrical enterprises and devote herself to straight scholarship, but here she was kicking her high heels in some kind of a nightclub. He did not know what to make of this, but noted that the card was professionally printed, smartly designed, and felt expensive to the touch. And he knew enough of the geography of London to know that the location was central. The Candid Cabaret must be a fringe event, but it was not out in the sticks. It was in the square mile where things happened. Perhaps (he did not welcome this suspicion) it was indeed a Happening? But no, the card was too orthodox for a Happening. Perhaps the Candid Cabaret was what an earlier generation had described as a revue?

When he turned his attention to her personal message, he encountered further perplexity. He had never seen her adult hand before, and he took in her clear, decisive, well-formed female script. So far, so good. But her proposition was obscure. Was she suggesting that he, she and Tommy should meet and dine together? Why had she mentioned her brother at all, if this was not her intention? The phrase 'dinner after the show' struck him as very adult, almost comically so, but he could see that to her it might be nothing out of the way. Maybe she had dinner with a different admirer every night, 'after the show'. But why did she want him to see the show at all? And why had she mentioned the aquarium in Ilfracombe and the Pool of Brochan? He had no recollection of having told her to go to look at the aquarium, nor did he remember mentioning the Damascene Islands, or offering to send her a postcard from them. The epithets 'darling little' as applied to the aquarium (she had got that wrong, it was an aquarium, not a museum) seemed inappropriate, and rang deliberately false. Actressy, affected, unconvincing. They had not used words like 'darling' up in Ornemouth or in Bonsett.

She was dangling her hook: but why? What was in it for her?

He remembered her strong ankles and her plaintive little wrist.

Should he write back to her saying that he would love to see her and Tommy again, and asking if he could bring his fiancée Beattie too? Should he ignore the message, and pretend he had never received it? Should he send a card saying not now, he was very busy, and had to spend all his spare time visiting his ill father, who was in and out of hospital in the Midlands, but that he hoped they might meet again another time one day before too long?

He put the card on the mantelpiece of his chaste and spartan room in the Institute, along with a sparse and comfortless array of invitations to lectures and seminars and sherry parties. It glowed at him with a steady subversive allure.

It was that phrase 'dinner after the show' that did for him. It was irresistible. Nobody had ever invited him, in so many words, to 'dinner after the show' – nobody, let alone a West End actress.

It was true that his father was ill, terminally ill, and it was true that he himself was, after a manner, engaged. He was not engaged to Sonia Easton, who had left him to his indecision and gone off to look at lichens in Northern Australia: she had been obliged to choose between them and him, and she had chosen them. They had parted without recrimination, but a quasi-fiancée called Beattie had swiftly moved into the place Sonia had vacated, and she and Humphrey seemed to be drifting, at least in public perception, towards a public betrothal. Beattie Lovelace was a very clever woman, and in many ways a suitable fiancée, and Humphrey was frightened of her. But did he want to marry her? Probably not. Did she intend to marry him? Possibly. That was how things stood, when Humphrey Clark received Ailsa Kelman's proposal.

It was to be a very long time before anybody dared to ask Humphrey Clark why he was attracted by clever women, and why he let them bully him. When asked, he did not have a ready answer.

Ailsa sent him a single ticket and his notional club membership for a Saturday evening. She made no further mention of her brother Tommy. Humphrey intended to take the last late train or the early milk train back to his old digs in Cambridge. It would be a long night, and he would never get back to Lowestoft.

During the fortnight that elapsed before their meeting, he wondered if he ought to try to find out more about the Candid Cabaret and the Tinder Box. The names of one or two of the cast were familiar to him from his undergraduate days, for they had been associated with the Cambridge Footlights: Humphrey had been briefly involved with helping with the lighting of one of their shows. Other names meant nothing to him. Were they perhaps some of her Edinburgh connections? The Tinder Box was not listed in the major broadsheets, and he did not know where else to look for it. It would be by way of a blind date.

This was the age of satire and of stage nudity and of improvisation; this was the last ditch before the final overthrow of censorship and the Lord Chamberlain. Humphrey Clark, marine ethologist and happiest underwater, suspected that he was about to enter an alarming and possibly dangerous new environment. As he walked from Leicester Square tube station, through Soho, past the beckoning neon-lit brothels of Greek Street, on his way to meet his fate (*on his way to take the bait*), he reassured himself that he was a grown man, who had survived three months on an island in the Indian Ocean, and swum with sharks and devilfish, and bore a handsome three-inch jagged scar on his knee to prove it. (He had swum into a rock while mesmerized by the seductive weaving movements of his zebra shark, but nobody needed to know this.) He had endured freezing conditions on a trawler in the North Sea, and explored the plankton and the sewage of the Dogger Bank. He had braved the wildness of the elements, and fish tagged by his own hands were even now coursing the globe. He had slept, on several not wholly enjoyable but necessary and memorable occasions, with a Damascene Islander. He could surely cope with Ailsa Kelman in a nightclub.

The Tinder Box was in a basement in theatreland. Dickensian steps led down from the side street, beneath an old-fashioned gaslight. It was a popular spot: a queue was waiting to descend into the dark and smoky crowded white-tiled cellarage. Everybody was smoking, including the healthy hero Humphrey, who bought himself a pint from the bar at the back of the cavernous room and settled himself down, a little self-consciously, as far from the rickety little stage as possible. The air was so thick that it was hard to say if there was an underlay of cannabis beneath the smell of continental Gauloises, of beer, of spilt wine. The very floorboards were impregnated with decades of drinking, and worse than drinking. The audience, he noted, was predominantly young, as one would expect, though there were one or two suave and suspect-looking silver-haired older men: spies, talent-spotters, perverts, pimps, stage-door johnnies, theatre critics? Humphrey was out of his depth and had no idea what was happening, or why he was here. In Cambridge, this kind of show had been a joke, a prank, a bit of harmless undergraduate fun. This all seemed more serious, more professional, and at once more overt and more oblique. Humphrey was sure that Ailsa was about to make an exhibition of herself, and wondered what he would find to say to her about it afterwards. He was already nervously planning his escape.

The performance, when it launched itself, was satiric, and to his relief it was scripted, not improvised. The targets were soft and random – the public-school system, advertising, the British Board of Film Censors, and a cluster of Scottish themes: Scottish food, the Edinburgh Tattoo, Scottish clans, the royals at Balmoral. The tone varied from the broadly comic to the uncomfortably abusive. It was all very clever, but where was Ailsa? The actors, to this point, had all been male, which had not surprised Humphrey, as the stand-up female comedian was a phenomenon of the future, but he knew that she must be about to put in an appearance soon, or she would not justify her equal billing, or the overture she had made to him in distant Lowestoft.

Her appearance, when she finally arrived at the end of the first half, was shocking. She had made them wait, but she was worth the waiting. She had gone through yet another metamorphosis, from sulky servant to disgraceful diva and provocative *diseuse*. It was clear that at least in this confined space she was a recognized attraction, for she was greeted by wolf whistles and friendly cries from her admirers. She deserved these, in Humphrey's view, for the bravura of her gear alone, which was glitteringly manifest before the nature of her act declared itself: she was wearing two stuck-on silver metallic breast-plates that concealed her nipples but little else of her powerful bosom, and a clinging skirt of a thin purple-red fabric beneath which one could clearly discern, through a flimsy cache-sex, her more or less knickerless condition and the sprouting of what looked like a bush of maroon pubic hair, of wine-red valiant hair.

The hidden Medusa, the sea anemone in the cleft.

This was the time of the miniskirt, but her long infernal clinging garment was as revealing as and more suggestive than a miniskirt. She gave her all.

What was she going to do, in this outlandish rig-out? Good God, she was going to dance – to dance, as she had danced as a thin white freckled child upon the sands. And she was going to sing. He was mesmerized by her courage and her effrontery. So he sat up a little more erectly on his cheap hard bentwood chair to face the music, which began to play loudly and rhythmically from two large speakers precariously rigged up over the stage. (The whole place was a health hazard: he could see wisps of bluish smoke snaking up from the spotlights.) She danced, a strange, weaving, sexual dance, not quite a belly dance, but rudely, crudely and suggestively Oriental. He watched, in a mildly erotic daze, as his eyes fixed themselves to the vibration and undulation of those vulgarly out-thrust silver nipples, that swelling mound of hair. Humphrey knew that his sexual organs would wither before such intense and public inspection: privately, they responded to encouragement, but he had never been tempted to expose them to group admiration. Ailsa's, in contrast, seemed to delight in this massed attention, this concentrated gaze. Fascinated, horrified, delighted, he gazed.

And then, as the music faded, she began to chant. She chanted a monologue about menstrual blood and the phases of the moon. He could not hear all the words, but he got the gist of it. Ovulation, insemination, conception, gestation, the birth canals, the waters of birth, the breaking of the waters of the womb. Her voice was insidiously penetrating, with a strange lilting accented lisp to it that had been absent from her normal speaking voice. What she did was not singing: it was more of an incantatory recitation, almost a calypso. Was it meant to be comic? Some of the audience laughed, but he could not see why.

Humphrey was appalled, but at the same time he was proud to know her. She had certainly changed from the angry girl who had lost her temper so uncontrollably as she complained that most of the top edge of Mrs Binns's jigsaw of Constable's *The Hay Wain* was missing.

The transformed Ailsa bowed and took her exit to excited applause. She was a sensation.

During the interval, Humphrey drank a large and solitary Scotch.

Either the second half was less alarming, or his ear had become attuned. This was not so bad after all. He began to look forward to his 'dinner after the show'. He had a moment of misgiving when he wondered if she might have expected him to book a table, but he put it to the back of his mind: this was her patch, it had been her suggestion, and anyway they were surrounded by restaurants at all prices and from all known cuisines. They could not go hungry here.

She had booked a table. She emerged from the darkness, after her last duet and the final curtain, to tell him so. She kissed him, ostentatiously and possessively, on the mouth, and embraced him, and rubbed herself against his trousers. She had become very physical. She ordered him to buy her a drink while she got changed: she was very thirsty, she would have half a pint of stout, please, and then they would move on to the Dolphin in Frith Street.

He was relieved to hear that she was to change, but unsure whether a dinner à deux was, after all, what she had planned. There was something inclusive in her gesture and manner, and she made a point of introducing him, before her disappearance backstage, to various hangers-on and fellow-artistes: maybe they were all expected to move on, in a shoal, to a communal celebration? Was that what people did, in the West End? Obligingly, he bought a glass of stout for her and another whisky for himself and a glass of red wine for a friendly stranger, and chatted to the stranger until she came back to reclaim him. There was a lot of laughter on her return, and many show-business jokes which he did not follow, but he noted that she referred to him generously in a protective and proprietorial manner as her 'long-lost friend' and her 'childhood sweetheart'. Neither description seemed to be in any degree accurate, but they made him feel welcome, which was perhaps more important.

A slight moustache of froth settled on Ailsa's upper lip, and, sensing it, she tried to lick it off with her reaching tongue, and then attacked it more efficiently with the back of her hand. He saw her pink tongue.

The childhood sweethearts, now in the prime of their twenties, eventually set off together towards the promised Dolphin, as part of a general exodus. She slipped her arm through his, as she had done two years before on the Devon coast, but this time there was no Sonia to attach herself to his other elbow, and she pressed against him with a more intimate insinuation. The busy street was flowing with people, and he wondered, again, if he were on his way to a long table and a gaudy night. But when they arrived at the restaurant, they were ushered to a table for two in a lovers' alcove, for a tête-à-tête.

Ailsa was well known in the restaurant. She was a regular. The plump and dimpled middle-aged manageress greeted her warmly, and smiled her smooth approval at Ailsa's fresh, well-made, well-weathered catch. The manageress lit their candle with a taper from her own hand, and shook the soft pale green-and-white napkins from their folds, and placed them in a motherly manner upon their knees. The napkins and the tablecloth were embroidered with a dolphin emblem, executed in reassuringly old-fashioned and slightly irregular white chain stitch.

She brought them a bottle of white wine, recommended the *moules marinières*, and discreetly withdrew.

By this time, in the 1960s, the people of England were eating mussels and garlic, and drinking rather a lot of wine. They had eschewed mussels during the war, when they were on short rations and mussels were plentiful, and they had queued long hours for cod and herring. Few of them had ever seen a bulb of garlic. But now the people of England were bolder, and were willing to try strange foods. Herrings were out, mussels were in.

The brazen public Ailsa had fallen abruptly silent. She took a tentative sip of her wine and looked down, modestly. He feared that she would ask what he had thought of the show, and tried to think of some topic that would pre-empt that query, but he too was overcome with sudden shyness. The strangeness of the moment lingered and deepened. Neither of them spoke, but when Ailsa looked up, their eyes met. They stared at each other, eye to eye, with an interlocking and questioning gaze, and then, unthinking, unpremeditating, instinctive, he stretched out his hand across the table towards her. She took his hand in hers.

So, it was done. Their hands remained joined, in a pledge that they did not begin to comprehend.

The prim children were swept over the sluice.

The silence lasted, as time unrolled behind them. They were young yet, they had travelled less than a third of their way through their expected span, but already the time behind them was enormous, archaic, Precambrian. Vast tracts and deserts of it already lay behind them, charged with the irredeemable, the unchangeable, marked by prints that would never be erased. Now they must move forward, through the feature-less wastes ahead, without a map, without a compass, over the dunes and up the foothills and towards the journey's unseen end. Could they make it? They sat as though in a trance, their hands gripped together in fear and in hope over the pale green cloth. They were willing to try, but they were ignorant and helpless and they did not know what lay before them. And it was too late to retreat.

Ailsa spoke first. She cleared her throat, and released his hand, and leaned back, and sat upright, and spoke. She spoke obliquely, but she knew that he would understand her. Their understanding had sunk beneath the level of words. Decisions were being made for them that had nothing to do with words. Choices, mistakes, wrong turnings, in an empty and unformed terrain. An untrodden track was winding its way onward through brightness and through obscurity, the weather was clearing and darkening and pulsing, and on they went and on they would be compelled to go.

Ailsa spoke first, and tried an ameliorating social smile, to calm the silent tumult.

'I told you I was giving up the theatre, last time we met,' she said. 'And now I'm saying it to you again. This really is my last season.'

'So, what next?' he asked.

'No,' she said, as though he had contradicted her assertion. 'That's it. It's bad for me, this show-biz lark. It's exhibitionism. It's bad for my character. Let's not talk about it. What next for you? Are you still spending most of your time underwater?'

So he talked to her, as they ate their mussels, about the underwater life, about the blue lagoon, about the familiar graceful zebra shark in the cave, about the habits of fishes, about the Indian Ocean, about career choices, about marine laboratories, about fish stocks, about the eyes of the ray and the mating habits of the dragonfish. He told her that he was good at swimming, but bad at slicing. He was no technician. He envied those who had dexterity and patience. He was bad, physically bad, clumsily bad, at slicing and photographing eyes, though he knew about optics, and could read and interpret the results of tedious experiments. He was good outdoors and underwater, but he needed support in the laboratory.

He delivered his credo, his faith in naturalistic observation and field study and the primary significance of movement. He aired his doubts about experimental techniques in the laboratory and the study of captive or dead animals. He tried to tell her why he thought that the whole was different from the parts, why instinct did not reside in a cell. She listened patiently, intelligently. He could tell that she had never heard of any of his mentors. She had hardly heard of the discovery of DNA. But she listened. She lived on the far side of the gap between the two cultures, but she listened.

He, for his part, had not heard of most of her points of reference. He remembered the name of Martin Pope, the tyrant of *The Tempest*, but he had not heard that Pope had become a resident director at Stratford-upon-Avon, or that he had married a film star. (He had, however, heard of the film star.) He had never seen the late-night television programme on which Ailsa claimed to have appeared so often. He had never been to the Arts Laboratory, and had never seen a copy of the notorious literary magazine which was even then going through the courts on a charge of obscenity.

'Don't you *ever* watch TV?' she asked with a good-natured impatience, as he admitted to yet another large area of ignorance. 'Television is the future, you can't just ignore it. You must surely have seen it sometimes. What about Jacques Cousteau?'

'I think he's a dangerous example,' said Humphrey. 'I don't want to end up like Jacques Cousteau. It's an underwater circus. It's all done for the camera.'

He sounded priggish, even to himself.

'You're very high-minded,' she said.

'Nothing wrong with that,' said Humphrey.

'Good boy Humphrey,' she said, teasing, lifting a slate-blue shell and swallowing down the sea liquor. 'You always were a good boy. You were a very nice, well-behaved, good boy. I bet you were Head Boy at school.'

In answer, he poured the last drop of wine from the bottle into her glass, and silently conceded her point.

'I knew it,' she said. 'You were always very good. Except that time you and Tommy and Sandy tied me up in the cave. *That* wasn't very good.'

'I don't remember that,' said Humphrey, but he was blushing, beneath his permanent seafaring tan.

'That was *very* naughty,' said Ailsa.

Perhaps he didn't remember? How could he forget? Maybe he hadn't been there after all? Maybe it had been Tommy and that other boy called Sandy? If he didn't remember, why did he blush?

'You were good,' said Ailsa, exhaling a heavy sigh as she laid down her heavy, slightly pitted pre-war silver spoon. 'And I was always very bad. I was always a bad girl. I was a wicked girl.'

He didn't know whether to contradict her, or whether she was proud of her bad-girl status. He looked at her again, trying to recapture her gaze, which had been distracted by the complicated diversionary performance of eating mussels. She met his eyes steadily. Yes, there she was.

'I didn't like tagging along,' she said in explanation. 'I was always tagging along. It was hard, being a girl, with you boys. It was hard, being Tommy's little sister. I had to fight for survival.'

'So do we all,' he said.

'Tommy is bad, too,' said Ailsa. 'But Tommy enjoys being bad. I don't.'

Her brother Tommy, she explained, was in television. He had his fingers stuck deep in the rich commercial pie, and he also presented – surely Humphrey *must* have seen it? – a current affairs magazine programme on Tuesday and Thursday evenings. He was doing well. Very well.

And Humphrey's baby sister, asked bad girl Ailsa politely, in turn: she must be grown up too by now?

He explained his sister, he explained both his sisters, he told her that his father was slowly but surely dying. He told her that in his view his father was dying of nuclear fallout from his time in the Pacific, but that the Navy would never admit responsibility. His older sister Lizzie was married to a schoolteacher in the Cotswolds, his younger sister Diana was studying chemistry at Birmingham.

She told him of her father's death in the creosote factory fire.

They ordered a slice of lemon tart and a crème brûlée.

'Do you remember Tommy telling us about Hiroshima?' he asked her.

She shook her head.

'He'd read John Hersey. God knows how he got his hands on that, at his age. It gave me nightmares for years. Don't you remember?'

No, she did not remember.

They commanded, on her recommendation, two glasses of Calvados, a liqueur then unknown to him. This order struck him, as she had intended it should, as very suave.

He caught the milk train to Cambridge, and woke on Sunday morning with a hangover.

Ailsa, sitting in an old ladies' tearoom in Ornemouth with a cup of stewed and acrid tea, stiff with tannin, believed that she could recall almost verbatim that long-ago conversation about goodness and badness. Such a puzzling evening, with such a strange outcome. Had she intended to seduce him? Poor Humphrey, poor good Humphrey. Even his name was virtuous. A comfortable, old-fashioned, virtuous name. Whereas Ailsa was sharp and rocky and washed with icy spume. Ailsa was a weatherbeaten sail, putting out to sea. Ailsa Kelman, Ailsa Craig.

The tea was the colour of red Devonian mud, and as thick as poster paint. She shuddered as she sipped.

Was this the tearoom that had once been the Copper Kettle, where her parents had sometimes taken tea and scones? It had relabelled itself the Periwinkle, but was not otherwise much altered, and the familiar façade of Longbone and Son, Grocers, still occupied a large stretch of the frontage across the road.

She had not seduced him that night, nor he her. Instead, they had 'fallen in love'. This was not what had been intended.

The courtship had proceeded along conventional lines to its unconventional denouement. She had taken more of the initiative than was usual for women at that period, but that was because her status as *grisette* and woman about town justified it, indeed in a manner dictated it. Her boldness, in those early days, was only body deep, and in herself, deep in herself, as she later tried to explain to her analyst, she had been frightened. 'I was such a mixture of cowardice and confidence. I would hype myself up and psych myself up and perform, and then I would go home and cry. I had to *throw* myself at things,' said Ailsa, 'or I couldn't do it at all.'

Like the salmon going up the falls.

And so she had thrown herself at Humphrey Clark.

Ailsa stared at her undrinkable tea, and at the common pattern of the cheap pale green teashop crockery. *Eau de Nil*, was that the name of that unpleasing colour? Jacques Cousteau had made a film about the sources of the Nile. She had watched it, long ago, with Humphrey.

Tears rose to her eyes, and the waters threatened to break and spill over.

Prince Rupert's tears, St Cuthbert's beads.

So hard, so fragile, so old, so indissolubly frail.

*

She had thrown herself at Humphrey, as though hoping that he could save her from herself. And he was bewitched by her. She was powerful, irresistible. And he had no wish to resist. Why should he? She was glamorous, attractive, exciting and she seemed to want him. He gave himself up to her. He had not been formally engaged to zoologist Beattie Lovelace, had he, and these were the Swinging Sixties. Many months, indeed whole years had passed since sexual intercourse began. Everybody was doing it, or so he told himself.

She introduced him to her world and poured forth her secrets. She sucked him into her whirlpool. He learned her frame of reference, and she made some attempt to acquaint herself with his: she quickly grasped enough of it to be able to introduce him effectively, and to make the most of his deep-sea enterprises. 'Here's Captain Clark, Cambridge's answer to Captain Cousteau.' 'Here's the Darwin of the Damascene Islands.' 'Here's the zebra shark man.' 'Here's the new Thor Heyerdahl.' He became the recognized escort of Ailsa Kelman, as well as her night-time lover. She took him about on his London visits, and showed him off, and showed herself off. She took him to pubs and to clubs, to restaurants and to parties, she introduced him to painters and actors, to broadcasters and poets, to set-designers and artistic entrepreneurs, to comedians and singers. He was a novelty: he was the bridge between the two cultures.

He soon learned that in her circles the name of Martin Pope was a talisman, a key that opened many doors, though the villainously and trimly bearded Martin Pope himself did not in person reappear. He was safely installed in Stratford-upon-Avon, married to his film star, and directing a bloody production of *Titus Andronicus* in which the star was to appear as Lavinia.

The film star's attempts at verse-speaking would not be well received.

Humphrey was content to be in thrall. He did not neglect his studies, for he remained, by nature, irredeemably conscientious, but at every opportunity he was on the London train, first from Lowestoft and then from Cambridge. Through the spring, and into the beginning of the long vacation of the summer, he paid court.

He sat through her act many times, and learned to measure the audience's responses to minute variations in the routine. He watched her as she danced and denounced: Ailsa, the stormy petrel with red feathers. He watched the smoke from the footlights, and became familiar with the hot and risky smell of the red and purple gel, with the theatrical and pungent odours of glue and white spirit and lanolin and cosmetics. He got to know the cast, who accepted him as a hanger-on, and seemed quite pleased to welcome a man from such a different world of expertise, a man who had no desire to tread the boards in competition. His exploits in the Damascene Islands improved slightly with the telling. Zebra sharks were smart.

The zebra sharks, he explained to them, are spotted, not striped. They are striped when they are young, but as adults they become leopard sharks. They change their stripes and their name and their spots. But they remain graceful. The grace of the sharks had been remarkable. He had tried to map their movements, but the pattern had continued to elude him. They were full of pretty tricks and habits.

These were the free-and-easy sixties days of open doors and informality, of experimentation and fun, of flower power and of making friends and love with strangers. Humphrey would sit obediently in the hospitality suite at the BBC Television Centre at Wood Lane, drinking free-flowing alcohol and watching Ailsa on a monitor as she discussed Expressionist theatre and abortion law reform with a fresh-faced young interviewer: God knows what the links were between these subjects, but she made them. She liked an audience, on screen, in the studio, backstage, the larger the better. He watched her talking about under-appreciated women painters, about Artemesia Gentileschi and Gwen John and Laura Knight and Eloise van Dieman, about van Dieman's ground-breaking sets for *The Blue Bird of Happiness*. She talked well. She played to the camera, she talked beyond the camera. She was brave, she would take on any subject, she spoke fiercely. Sometimes she was inconsistent, but nobody but Humphrey seemed to notice her contradictions. He would sit proudly watching her, thinking of the moment when he would have this lavishly broadcast and much duplicated and refracted woman to himself, in the flesh, alone.

He enjoyed his enslavement.

Once he even sat in a hairdressing salon in Mayfair, waiting for her, and watching as her hair was teased and moulded into the high back-combed beehive of the day. This hour of his life remained forever vivid in his memory. The subjugation of his attendance gave him a thrill of sexual satisfaction.

Everything about her gave him sexual satisfaction.

She reintroduced him to her brother Tommy, who appeared one night at the Tinder Box with the queen's little sister in tow, and took them both on after the show to a noisy party given (as it later emerged) by a film producer in a big wild Victorian family house on a village green in Wandsworth. The party was crammed with stoned film stars and small children shrieking in nightclothes. The queen's little sister left after half an hour, but during that half-hour Humphrey had plenty of time to notice the extraordinary obsequiousness with which Tommy tended his royal catch: he listened intently to every word she said, laughed dutifully, contorted his features into expressions of loyal attention and approval, and looked around ostentatiously to widen the circle of admiration that naturally surrounded her. He brayed and whinnied and nodded like a donkey, and lurched forward with his cigarette lighter and his shoulders like a flunkey. The queen's little sister did not seem to register surprise at this bizarre behaviour. She must, thought Humphrey, be used to it.

When the princess departed with her chauffeur, Tommy briefly turned his attention on Humphrey.

'So you've popped up again,' said Tommy, slapping him on the back, with the loud relief of one who has just survived a testing social ordeal. 'Little Humpy Clark, like a bad penny. I always knew you would.'

'I'm amazed that either of you remembered me,' said Humphrey warily.

'Oh yes, we remembered you all right,' said Tommy. 'How could we forget?'

And Tommy laughed, with a mirthless laugh full of unpleasant innuendo.

Humphrey was embarrassed by this, and made an excuse to back away. What had Tommy been trying to insinuate? He did not want to know. Would he dare to ask Ailsa when they got back to the Room? He thought not. He was afraid he might not like the answer.

The public life of the coupled Humphrey Clark and Ailsa Kelman took place in a heady variety of unfamiliar locations, amidst a swimming haze of alcohol and nicotine and glitter and display. The queen's little sister was in her element in these colourful shallows, and so was a whole host of nibbling little client fishes. Cameras snapped, gossip columnists made notes. Cameras snapped, occasionally, at modest but photogenic Humphrey Clark, mistaking him for a famous person.

(*Do cleaner fish prefer to eat ectoparasites or client flesh?* This was the question posed by a paper that came before Professor

184

Humphrey Clark for peer review with a view to its publication in the periodical *Marine Undertakings*, 2003. He had once written a paper on the cleaning symbioses of fish, and he knew a lot about this kind of behaviour. The sinister and suggestive phrase 'client flesh' took him by surprise. His surprise had reminded him that he was losing his touch.)

Ailsa's social life was more interesting than Humphrey's, and took precedence: that went without saying. The arts were more fun than the sciences. He met her crowd, but she did not meet his. She went to Cambridge once, on her insistence, and he showed her round the laboratory and the aquarium, and she admired the wavy smooth blue-grey-green thin plush tentacles of *Anemonia viridis*, the snakelocks anemone. She found this creature exotic, and was astonished to learn that the specimens she admired came not from the Damescene Islands but from Worthing pier. Her responses, he noted, were primarily aesthetic, which was only to be expected from a woman.

He did not show her the experiments and the dissections. He did not attempt to introduce her to the head of his department, a brilliant and eccentric misogynist whose ground-breaking work on male submarine aggression was even in those early days considered provocative by his women students.

This was their public life.

The private life of Humphrey Clark and Ailsa Kelman took place in the Room.

His first experience of the Room was a shock to the fastidious Humphrey, but, in overcoming his initial recoil from it, he overcame many other inhibitions.

She had led him there, by the hand, by the nose, after the second long evening they had spent together, and it was there that their pre-pubertal seaside romance was consummated.

The Room was a bedsit in Bloomsbury. It was not, she had explained, her primary place of residence: she also shared a large and airy apartment with an old college friend across the river in salubrious Dulwich, to which he was not to be invited. The Room was her private place.

She told him this as she walked him towards it from the Tinder Box, through Soho, northwards, through the porn-bright streets and past the open doorways of brothels and sex shops, with their crude and colourful solicitations, with their winking breasts and sizzling bubbling neon cocktail glasses. Past the nipples and sperm and spume she took him, through sombre back streets, through cobbled yards and alleys, beneath old lanterns and arches, along the protected footpaths and rights of way of old London. He was lost. He did not know where they were going, or what to expect.

They soon came to the junction of various broader commercial thoroughfares, which he vaguely identified as Holborn, and then plunged off again along a shabby narrow one-way street of tall and austere early-nineteenth-century terraced houses, which gave straight on to the pavement. She stopped and fumbled in her bag and opened a door with a Yale key, and let him into a dark and pokey hallway. This was a multiple-occupation dwelling, for he could see a row of named pigeonholes for letters, like the pigeonholes in the Porter's Lodge of his college. She pressed a meanly timed light switch, which briefly irradiated a steep uncarpeted wooden staircase, and shabby walls decorated with a variety of wires, antique disconnected gas pipes, and amateur telephone leads stuck about with tape. This was, he guessed, London bedsit territory. Were they near the university? Was this where the glamorous and sophisticated Ailsa had her dwelling?

He followed her up the bleak stairs and into her domain

on the first-floor back. It had a high ceiling, too high for the single room's width: it had been partitioned off from a larger drawing room. But it was large enough to contain a low collapsible bed on metal struts, a small sofa, an old armchair, a small rolltop desk, a home-made bookcase made of bricks and planks. In a corner, behind a screen covered in shiny Victorian scraps, was a washbowl. Posters adorned the walls, and on a once-handsome Georgian mantelpiece stood an untidy array of cards, invitations, news cuttings, photographs, puppets, shells, jars, bottles, glass balls.

She switched on a small light with a red shade. The room glowed with a louche theatrical intimacy.

The lavatory, she told him, was in the courtyard below, but she was off to visit it first.

This practical information, so instantly offered, was a relief to him. He was modest about enquiring about such matters.

He took advantage of her brief absence to examine her habitat more closely.

The surface of the mantel was thick with dust. A pickling jar on the mantel contained what might have been her tonsils. She had once offered to let him see them, and, true to her childhood pledge, here they were. Next to them stood another childhood relic: her tallow one-time-radioactive luminous lamb. He noted also a large red glass ashtray, filled with little long-tailed tadpoles of glass of different colours: he recognized them as Prince Rupert's tears, those strange and magic droplets of glass that can withstand a heavy hammer blow, but by the cunning may be made to shatter into a thousand grains.

Most of the posters, pinned and pasted inexpertly and haphazardly to the flaking and irregular walls, portrayed theatrical-looking ladies in historical costume, perhaps café performers, probably of the late nineteenth and early twentieth century. He thought he recognized some of the artists but he did not know enough about art to identify any of them. Like Ailsa, these divas displayed a penchant for silver and gilt glitter and for metallic surfaces – a penchant which, as he was soon to discover, was an enduring component of Ailsa's presentational psyche, perhaps even of her innermost being. The only poster-painting which bore a title and the name of its artist was in a slightly different genre, though it too showed an exhibitionistic woman, or at least her head and naked torso, swooning as though at the power of her own image in a mirror, in pale and naked and faintly despairing self-admiration. It was called *Conception*, and it was by Edvard Munch, hitherto known to Humphrey only as the creator of the notorious *Scream*. In the bottom left-hand corner of the image's framing surround crouched a threatening and malevolent homunculus-embryo, and the pattern of the frame itself was composed of a stream of swimming sperm.

Ailsa had already informed him that she was taking the pill, so he didn't have to worry about that aspect of the night's events. The technology of contraception had improved rapidly since his inconclusive summer vacation affair with the apprehensive lichenologist.

A little tree grew in the centre of the courtyard. Outdoors, beneath the London stars, there was an unexpected outdoor country smell of leaf and earth.

That night the bed creaked and threatened to collapse. It was not built for such activity, but they managed to ignore its protests. Ailsa shuddered and slithered, she groaned and leaped beneath him. She gaped for him. She went at it and at him, with an intensity to which he was unaccustomed. Her thighs ran slippery with sweat, and he drank the brine from her body. A thin salt flow burst from her, smelling and tasting of weed and salt and sea, of soft oyster and hard bone.

He hammered at the cuttlefish bone of her. They were both heaving with exertion, until they both crashed, together, from the peak of the wave. He slumped down on to her, heavily. He was a heavy man. She told him that she felt safe at last beneath the heavy weight of him. Under a weight like this, she said, into his damp shoulder, a woman can rest.

It was very good, for both of them, that first time. After it they both slept, profoundly.

In the light of morning, the state of the Room appeared even more shocking, but by then he had entered it and made it his own. He was over the threshold, and there was no withdrawing now from these stained sheets, these limp yet lumpy yellowed pillows, this cheaply, deeply, uncomfortably studded mattress with its painful buttons. The sash windows were smeared with city grime, and grey net curtains hung limply from lengths of plastic-coated wire. The old cream gloss paint of the walls ran with sweat from the kettle. The horror and squalor of it entrapped him, enslaved him. Her beautiful body shone, opalescent, like a pearl in its unworthy case.

They lay there, in each other's arms, in the light of the morning, and slowly, deliberately re-enacted the first coming. Then he got up, at her request, and made her a mug of instant coffee: she kept the milk in a bottle outside on the window sill, and to his taste it was slightly off but she did not seem to notice. The tea towel was stiff as cardboard with usage, and could no longer be used to dry a mug or a spoon.

The sheets of the bed were stiff with semen.

And so they remained, through the weeks and the months. He came to love the very smell of the Room. He insisted on fixing the legs of the bed, so that it did not make so much noise or threaten to break beneath them, but he did not suggest a visit to the launderette.

The objects in the Room became fetishes: the dark green

face flannel, the dirty towels, the thin enduring amber sliver of Pears soap, the tonsils in the jar.

The tea towel had a design of robins and holly. Ailsa, in her later incarnation as a feminist sociologist, was to write a monograph on the iconography of tea towels.

In *The Children's Encyclopedia* in Finsterness, there had been an unsuitable illustration of an unsuitable story about a shipwrecked woman who had gashed her bosom with a knife in order to conceal within her breast a ruby. The blood had spurted out from her, clouding the water, tempting the sharks, but she had kept her treasure. As a boy, he had been aroused by this drawing. And now Ailsa was his prey, and he sank into her again and again, in search of the ruby. He plunged into her through water and brine and mucus and sperm and menstrual blood. Fastidious Humphrey, all inhibitions washed away, swimming hard upstream.

She rented the Room, she told him, for £6 a week. She had seen it advertised in the *New Statesman*, as 'close to the British Museum, and suitable for a student', and she had snapped it up. Her landlady was a quiet old lady who lived in Kent.

Ailsa Kelman, in the tearoom in Ornemouth, inspected the bill for her cup of tea and her buttered teacake. (She had restrained herself, at the last moment, from ordering a crab sandwich.) She counted out the coins. Life was still cheap in the north. London was one of the most expensive cities in the world. A bottle of water in London cost you far more than a pot of tea with a teacake up here.

The waitress had seen her on television, although her expression indicated that she couldn't place her, and probably thought she was somebody quite different. Ailsa could spot the familiar look of puzzled recognition.

Should she drive, now, to Finsterness, and gaze across the

sands to St Cuthbert's Rock in the summer light of the afternoon? Was there time, or would she be late?

She thought of the Room and of its shameless secrets and satisfactions. Humphrey had been good at it. He had been good at it and at her. He understood her body, and he could make it dissolve and flow for him like a fountain. She had been surprised by how good he was at it. He was strong and tireless and he was even inventive. He was more gifted and better equipped than Martin Pope, who, like a true man of the theatre, had relied on mesmerism and manipulation for most of his effects. Humphrey seemed to do it all by instinct, though she did accuse him, one night, of having learned a trick or two in the Damascene Islands. He had laughed, flattered, but had protested. No, no, he had sworn to her, I learned nothing there but how to get rid of the crabs. This is all for you, and it is love itself that teaches me.

They had used the word 'love', lavishly, recklessly, generously, unwisely. They had poured love forth, they had let it spill out all around them, as though it could never be spent, as though it would renew itself for ever. They were willing victims of the romantic fallacy.

'I love you for ever.' They had said it. She had written the words on a white wall in an experimental art gallery in Long Acre, for which the proprietor was soliciting comments and quotations and cartoons. 'You'll not forget me, ever, ever, ever?' she had added, in her flowing hand, with thick blue poster paint.

The proprietor of the gallery had watched, and laughed, a cynical admiring laugh. Humphrey had watched, but he had not laughed.

It was a quote from Robert Graves, but she didn't tell either of them that.

Humphrey was obsessed by her firm and fleshly body, by

her solid opaline throat and breasts and thighs, by her mackerel movements. He could not get enough of her, nor she of him. Their flesh was perpetually inflamed, weeping with the wounds of love. His body hair was golden and thick, and she ploughed her fingers through it and sucked at it and spat its little golden curls out from her mouth. It was a mutual exploration, a voyage of shocking delight. These were the liberated sixties, when fantasies were not only permitted but obligatory, and these two shivering puny children of the north-eastern shore made their adult best of what was offered to them by the spirit of the age.

There were private desires she had not mentioned or introduced, liberated though she was. And maybe he too had had his.

She would never know now what he had wanted, what she had failed to think to deliver. She had failed him. And now it was too late, too late, too late.

She thought of this now, in the tearoom in Ornemouth.

Sometimes, even today, in her sixties, she dreamed that she was still paying rent for the Room, that she had forgotten to cancel her standing order, that she could go back to the little street in Bloomsbury any day she chose and that it would be there, empty, untouched, waiting for her to let herself in with her Yale key. Perhaps the dust would have grown a little thicker on the mantelshelf, but it would be otherwise unchanged. This was a very vivid dream, and one that she never told her analyst, because it was too transparent and too embarrassing and needed no interpretation. And she had, in fact, kept the Room on, unused, long after she needed it, years longer, long after she married the many-mansioned Martin Pope. She had given it up only when her landlady died, when she received a note from the niece who had inherited it. By then, the dust had indeed been thick. She had not returned the key, because the niece said the locks would be changed, and not to bother.

The key was still in her desk in London.

Humphrey had said he had forgotten the last day of summer, and the rusty ring in the rock in the cave in Finsterness. Perhaps she had dreamed of that too: a fantasy dream of bondage, of mounting death, of the rising tide, of her face pressed against the streaked wet grey and iron minerals of the cliff, of the slow drip of the waterfall, of her back exposed to the eyes of the boys. Andromeda, Angelica. Perhaps, after all, he had not even been there? Perhaps it had been that other boy, the boy called Sandy, who had touched her there, from behind, so slyly, so shyly?

Tommy had made the boy lift her skirt from behind and touch her, through her wet white salt-sprayed cotton knickers. Then they had told her they would leave her there to drown, if she did not let them pull her knickers down.

Did Tommy remember any of this bad play?

Tommy was a bad boy.

Humphrey had repressed the game in the cave, but he had not forgotten the codfish in the Pool of Brochan. He had reminded her of them, in one of their quieter and more sober moments, as they sat in the back row of the Academy Cinema in Oxford Street waiting to see a Fellini movie. He told her that he had been dismayed when he had learned, years later, that the Pool of Brochan was a Victorian larder of living fish. 'I didn't realize they *ate* them,' Humphrey had said. 'That old crone didn't *say* they *ate* them, did she? I mean, she had *names* for some of them. I thought they were – I thought they were . . .'

'Pets?' she had suggested, as he groped for a word.

'No, no, not pets,' he had insisted. 'Something more important. Something more sacred than pets.'

'The sacred codfish,' she had echoed. But he had not found it funny.

'Yes,' he had said. 'The sacred cod.'

She had not told him then, she had never told him, that the photograph of Ailsa Kelman and Humphrey Clark, standing together by the iron railing with Mother Longbone, above the suck and pull of the tide, had become a Kelman family joke. In so far as the Kelman family recognized the concept of a joke, this photograph had been a joke: not a kindly joke, not a funny joke, but a joke. It had been labelled carefully, in blue Quink fountain-pen ink, with their names, *Ailsa Kelman and Humphrey Clark at the cod pool*, with the date. And so it was that the name of Humphrey had survived, fortuitously, in the communal Kelman memory. Photographs were quite rare in those distant days, and this one had become a legend and a mockery.

Ailsa had once, stupidly, told Tommy that Humphrey had showed her his tonsils, or rather his absence of tonsils. Humphrey, she boasted, had let her look down his gullet by St Cuthbert's Rock, and she had looked down his. Never one to miss a trick, even when he was not sure what the trick was, Tommy had pounced on this disclosure, and for years after he would taunt her: 'Anyone shown you their tonsils lately?' Or he would refer knowingly, meaningfully, meaninglessly, to 'Humpy Clark, that boy who showed you his tonsils'.

It was a dirty joke. It hurt her pride. It infuriated her, but she knew better than to let Tommy see her rage.

Humphrey Clark's name became, for a while, a synonym for teasing and humiliation, for bullying and ridicule.

She had hated her brother Tommy.

She had wanted to conceal the details of her affair with Humphrey from Tommy, but at the same time she had wanted to boast about it. She had wanted to vindicate the past, to

194

切除

prove that she had shed its miseries, and yet she wanted to forget it altogether. Excision, exorcism. It was a dilemma. You couldn't choose both, could you?

Humphrey and Tommy had become friends, of a sort, in later adult life, in the worldly middle years of their success. They became fair-weather friends, bumping into each other at pompous public events, and greeting each other warily at fund-raising functions. Tommy was ubiquitous. He put himself about. You could never be sure that he would not be there. And you always had to pretend to be pleased to see him. It was not safe to be displeased by Tommy. Omnipresent

Humphrey, clearly, could not have wanted to see him. After the severance, he must have dreaded his frequent reappearances. But Tommy was everywhere, at everyone's elbow, whether you wanted him or not. Tommy was always in the know.

Ailsa over the years had watched her brother's technique with appalled curiosity. It was like a parody of her own ascent: or was hers a parody of his? Tommy worked his contacts. He knew how to work a crowded room. He had a nose and a mouth. He hung on, he attached himself, he sucked at the glass, he made himself useful, he made use of others. Occasionally he ran the risk of being named as a toady, but for the most part he got away with it. And the longer you got away with that kind of thing, the fewer people distrusted you, the less they wished to name you. You became part of them, and they did not like to name themselves. The conspiracy spread its nets. They forgot that Tommy Kelman was making use of them, and they thought that they were making use of Tommy Kelman. It was a useful symbiosis. After twenty years, nobody could tell which was the client flesh and which the parasite.

Tommy, in the 1960s, assembled a shoal of fair-weather

辞(2)

acquaintances whose names were often in the press. He knew pop stars and film stars and hairdressers and princesses. (Hairdressers held a curiously high status at this volatile and transformative period: Ailsa in her forties and the century's eighties would make a television programme trying to explain this phenomenon in sociological terms, but although the pictures would be good, she would remain dissatisfied with her commentary and analysis. She would continue to set herself high standards, and to worry away at problems she had set herself and failed to solve.) Tommy knew editors and drama critics and comedians and designers and television interviewers and crime writers who lived in the West Indies. He claimed to know the Beatles. He knew a few politicians. He deployed his cutlery deftly and held his glass correctly. He could eat and drink without spilling anything, and make small talk at the same time. He was an increasingly useful bachelor.

She had suspected, in those early days, that Tommy used her as a front for his sparse and uninteresting sex life. He was not, physically, sexually, an attractive man. She had transformed herself into an attractive woman, but he had remained somehow unfinished, pasty-complexioned, under-chinned, large-eared. He was socially bold, but physically timid. He needed an escort, so he took her to places. Sometimes she went along with this.

Ailsa and Tommy Kelman had taken to the new medium of television like fish to water. Both of them had been quick to grasp its potential, although he had been quicker than she. Long, long ago, when they were uncorrupted schoolchildren, they had watched the queen's coronation together, in a crowded, smoke-filled front room in a neighbour's house in Bonsett. The pretty young queen, in grainy flickering black-and-white, had been projected forcefully into the heart of her nation. Ailsa had been hypnotized by the black swollen mulberry lips, the wide white brow, the deeply shadowed eye sockets, the death-in-life of the pale skull of the pretty young queen, flickering beneath her stately sparkling crown. The jewels of the crown sprouted out of its dark and fleshly velvet mound. Ailsa Kelman, pre-pubertal ugly duckling, drunk on a thimbleful of dark-brown sweet sherry, crouching on a pouffe, had dreamed of exposure. Should she model herself on the pretty young queen, fully robed as she paraded slowly before the eyes of the nation, or on Jean Simmons in a scanty dress in a blue lagoon?

Ailsa had taken a small sweet sip that had tasted deadly. It tasted of addiction. Tommy had drunk more deeply from the same phial. The sister had dreamed, girlishly, of clothes and nudity and enslaved attention: the brother had dreamed of profit and exploitation.

And now Tommy had ceased to be a sucker, a parasite, a hanger-on, and he had become a power in the land. He had ceased to be a cautiously neutral voyeur. He had married, twice, though he had produced no children. His current wife, a fair-skinned woman of very small but strong opinions, was the granddaughter of an archbishop, the daughter of a marquis, and the ex-wife of a merchant banker. Tommy had risen from the downstairs world of his mother, whom he had treated, in her lonely later years, with cowardly neglect.

This neglect had allowed Ailsa, improbably, to cast herself as a dutiful daughter. She had salvaged some sense of old-fashioned virtue by being kind and attentive during her widowed mother's last years in Bonsett.

Sometimes Ailsa thought that she was not wicked, at heart, at all.

Ailsa's ambitions had not been social. Nor had they been

financial. They had been grander and purer and more original. They had been ideological.

Tommy's flourishing progress had soon taken on a tinge of the lush and the lurid. In the early years, he had applied himself and worked hard. He had gained a respectable university degree, a second-class Cambridge degree in History, but he had never had a settled intent of pursuing a respectable profession. He had wanted a career, but not a profession. At university, he had discreetly sniffed around for those with money and contacts, for prototypes foreshadowing the shape of things to come. While still at school he had rejected the law, medicine, academe, the Civil Service, the Foreign Office – these were dusty paths that led but to the grave. He had never been attracted to any form of hard science: the life and death of creosote were not for him. Tommy had known that there would be softer money, big money, pots and pots of money, which would be there for the taking. All he had to do was to learn where to dig for it. He was willing to dig hard, if he could find the right place.

Tommy Kelman's detractors, and there would be many, were to accuse him of imitation, of plagiarism, even of theft. They suggested and indeed believed that he always took the easy, secondary option, and followed trails hacked out by others. This was not wholly true. Tommy Kelman worked. He served his apprenticeship. As a new graduate, he worked for a whole dull ill-paid year in cinema management in outlying London regions, in Acton and Ealing and Southgate, employed by the movie mogul father of a college friend. This grim but useful year taught him that the cinema was dead. So he moved from the rows of empty seats and the pensioners' matinees and the deserted gloomy between-war Bingo-designated edifices of the suburban past to television, which was alive. The monstrous baby of television was growing at an extraordinary, an <u>exponential</u> speed, and Tommy Kelman grew along with it.

Tommy Kelman put himself in the right places at the right times. He developed an instinct for the expanding business of the small screen. In those early days, he would have a go at anything. Presenter, writer, producer, director – he tried it all. He watched and he watched, and he was always there at the moment when one programme dwindled and died, and another was trying to grow out of its decaying compost. He knew how to develop the ideas of others, the ideas that he saw struggling to take root. He watched the slower progress of more gifted friends who had set their ambitions or maybe even their hearts on a single pure trajectory – as film director, as actor, as playwright, as journalist, as <u>orator</u> or Member of Parliament – and he sensed that the odds were that he could get ahead better and faster and maybe even further by diversifying. He would become a jack-of-all-trades. He did not want to be a professor or a prime minister. He wanted to do it all another way. He was not yet sure what way that would be, but he knew he would find it.

In the sixties, all things seemed possible.

Tommy had worried Ailsa in her youth. She had recognized him as a <u>portent,</u> but she was not sure what he portended. How long would this bubble last? Some of his cronies were clearly doomed to oblivion. Those Beatles, whose intimate friendship he claimed, whose irritating names he so tirelessly dropped – their vogue would never last. They would surely sink forgotten beneath the froth. (*foam*)

But she hadn't been able wholly to resist Tommy's version of events, his plot for the future. He was her brother, and he exerted a peculiar power over her. He tempted her from her highbrow academic ambitions with his visions of cheap and worldly success. Tommy persuaded her that he held the key to a glamorous television career, and that prospect had frightened Ailsa. Ailsa was so deeply mesmerized by the new medium of television that she found herself dreaming about it. It was intoxicating. She loved it and she hated it. She had thought she could ride the wave.

Tommy had made millions out of commercial television. He owned companies worldwide. He had made a fortune, and become a philanthropist. His financial reputation was dubious, but he had bought impunity and respect.

Tommy had skated very near the edge with that insider trading business, reflected Ailsa in Ornemouth, as she handed her dull yellowish and copper coins over to the still-puzzled waitress. The profile of the queen's not-so-young but nobly idealized head adorned the coins.

Tommy, although a personal friend of the queen's little sister, had nearly spent time inside at Her Majesty's Pleasure because of shares in a new satellite television station serving the Middle and Far East. It had been an unpleasant few months. At least half of Ailsa had wanted him to end up in jail, despite the spill-over and contamination of family shame, but he'd wriggled out of it all. He was as clever as a weasel.

Tommy Kelman had come a long way since the days of the codfish.

The sign for Longbone and Son across the road was reassuring, and the shop front was not much altered. The Longbone family business had not changed its name, and that was a comfort. Not everything had changed. And the Pool of Brochan was still there, just up the coast, as one would expect. She had looked it up last week on its website. Old Mother Longbone was long dead, but the rock was sempiternal, and the restless sea still entered and withdrew at the moon's command. (That tautologous word, sempiternal, had enchanted her as a child, and it resurfaced now in her memory

↳ eternal

200

with a glimmer of its ancient incantatory magic.) It cost you £3.50 now to visit and feed the fish. The website claimed that generation after generation of holidaymakers returned to the pool to feed the fish, drawn back compulsively to revisit Mother Longbone and Blind Tom. (The website did not use the word 'compulsively': this adverb was suggested by the lady from Rio, who had enjoyed the story of the Pool of Brochan.) The pool claimed all who saw it. Grandparents, parents, grandchildren had returned again and again to the source.

Ailsa wondered if Blind Tom had outlived Mother Longbone. Blind Tom had surely been inedible. *uneatable*

She and Humphrey Clark had been happy together. Together, they had known extreme happiness, and they had destroyed their happiness. It was a common story, a dull story, a sixties platitude, an eternal platitude with a sixties gloss. Love, passionate love, obsessive and consuming love had turned to resentment, jealousy, anger, desertion, and the sudden parting of the ways.

Ailsa picked up her bag and wandered, somnambulant, entranced, into the cobbled street, thinking of that lost happiness, of doomed attempts to rediscover the quality of that happiness, of satisfied ambitions and ideological justification and diversionary goals. Of lingering slower later years of regret, remorse and self-reproach.

Her analyst had said, intending comfort, *You were both young, these things happen, you were too young to handle it, Eros is a dangerous god.*

Yes, said Ailsa, head bent, her nose running, her eyes weeping, histrionically clutching her paper tissue, *but it was my fault, I betrayed him. I couldn't resist the temptation. I betrayed him, I abandoned him.*

It wasn't as simple as that, said her analyst.

We should never have done it, repeated Ailsa.

It takes two to do a thing like that, said her analyst patiently.

But I knew, I knew, I was always more knowing than he was. He was an innocent. I knew it was foolish. I knew it would be a disaster. So why did I do it? Why did I let him do it?

Look, said her analyst, *these things happen. The tide of events was pulling very strongly at that time. You can look back now, more than a quarter of a century later, and you can surely see the currents. It wasn't you that made them.*

Oh, but it was, said Ailsa. *It was me. I made them.*

You didn't do it single-handed.

You want to make me feel powerless, said Ailsa.

It is sometimes better to feel powerless than to feel omnipotent.

Ailsa had not liked that comment.

'*It is sometimes better to feel powerless than to feel omnipotent.*'

No, it is never better. It is always better to keep the initiative. It is always better to drive than to be driven.

The hire car had been a good notion. She'd nearly chickened out of it, but it had worked out well.

And the problem is, thought Ailsa, as she stared unseeing at the strangely assembled clutter of objects in a Help the Aged charity shop window in Ornemouth High Street, the problem is that I *was* powerful. I believed that I was then, and I believe that I am now. I cannot rid myself of the illusion. So how can I ever be cured? I am locked into the madness. I am mad. I still believe that I have the power.

Staying her eye on the glass, her elderly self looked back at her. She was in her sixties now, and she was older than the ancient sunken-cheeked Mother Longbone had been all those summers ago. She was ashen-grey, and at times she looked her age. The power was ebbing and seeping and leaking away, and at times she was afraid.

She sighed, and blinked, and stared herself out, and straightened her spine, and pulled in her chin, and summoned up her forces. She straightened herself, in the way that Martin Pope had taught her when she was still very young. When she was playing the Shakespearean virgin in the brothel in *Pericles*, so badly, all those years ago, he had put one pale long-nailed manicured hand on the back of the base of her skull, and the other in the small of her back. He had pushed her skull upwards and forwards, and her shoulders down and back, as though he were pressing her from a primitive humble hominid posture into that of a more evolved life form. *Posture, Ailsa, posture*, he had said. His touch was powerful. It was not sexually arousing, or physically comforting, but it was powerful. From him an electric current flowed, an inhuman gift. It flowed from his hand, through her head and her shoulders and down her spine to her feet.

She had seen others dance to his tune, and straighten themselves at the end of his strings. Dame Mary McTaggart herself had felt the force. Dame Mary had once sung to the tunes of Martin Pope.

It is better to feel powerless.

She would go back to the hotel now, and look through her folder, and check the details of what was to be expected of her this night, and then again in the morning, and on the day's parade. It was not as though she could avoid the hotel for ever. She could not avoid for ever the night's events.

She had packed her silver dress. Suitable or unsuitable, she had packed her silver dress, and her soft little metal purse, and her golden slippers.

And she had packed her bathing suit. She rarely travelled overnight without her bathing suit, because she was supple and she liked to swim. She enjoyed swimming more and more as she grew older. The weightlessness and the defiance of gravity seemed to roll back time. Paul Burden's book had claimed that the North Sea was getting warmer, but she wasn't sure if she believed him. None but the mad swim in the North Sea. The hotel might have a pool, for the town was now a city, recognized by the ageing queen herself, and the shabby old Queen's Hotel overlooking the bay might by now, in the third millennium, have acquired a pool and a gym. She had swum in stranger places than Ornemouth in the last three decades.

The train began to move, slowly, with more apologies for signal failure and delay. The next stop was York. Although the delay had seemed lengthy, the train was running less than an hour late. He would still be in time, if there were no further hitch, to take a little walk before dinner. He had at one point, earlier in the journey, thought that he might cross the bridge, to Finsterness and to Turkey Bank, to the quaint homes of the Cleggs and of Mrs Binns. But that had been an unrealistic plan, a young man's plan. He knew by now, well in advance of the possibility, that he would not have the energy. He would be better off taking a siesta, and having a rest before the evening's festivities. Maybe tomorrow he would make his way to Finsterness, after the procession and after the recessional and after the luncheon.

The movement of the carriage and the flow of the landscape rocked him forward, and released him from his inertia. He reached for the pink folder, with its names and its lists. By now, he had reconciled himself to the knowledge that something bad lay in there waiting for him, lurking in its cave, and he had been brave enough or foolish enough to try to imagine what it might be. This had involved running through a whole backlog of professional disasters, failures and resentments, but that did not deter him: he pressed on the bad tooth, he picked at the scab, he probed for the splinter, he swallowed with his tender throat. For there had been something, surely, in Mrs Hornby's demeanour that had alerted him to danger. There was something in his notes that she had been unable to remove or disguise. He had read a warning in her face. A Medusa name lay in there, a name with poisoned tentacles, a name which had already struck him dumb, and would now turn him to stone.

It could not, he reflected, be the name of his second wife Dorothy, for she was now settled far away in distant Harvard where she shone like the star she had so improbably become. She was not likely to be tempted out of her orbit by an invitation to a small place like Ornemouth. She was in the big time, in the big country: she had won the waiting game, and she had shed him like an old sock. There might, he supposed, be some reference to her, somewhere in the vicinity of one of the citations, or lurking spitefully in the shadows behind the eulogy of the Public Orator, but nobody would be tactless enough to bring her name too directly into play. Their differences, their parting, had been too public, too abrupt, for her to be invoked on so formal an occasion. Humphrey Clark and Dorothy Portal Clark, now Dorothy Portal Herzog, had made it plain to their colleagues and to the press that they never wished to be associated with each other again, either professionally or personally, and on the whole this wish had been respected. He had not seen her in years, and had not wished to do so. He hoped he would never see her again. She was welcome to the brilliant Herzog, and he to her. She would not come anywhere near his patch, of that he was sure. They had skilfully negotiated the problem of their joint parenthood of their only child, to the advantage of both women, with a guilty understanding of the need for distance. It was only accidental conjunctions or allusions that he had to fear from her direction, from her claque and her supporters.

It could not be said that Dorothy Portal, his one-time

student and lab assistant, and later his wife, had blushed unseen and wasted her sweetness on the desert air. No unsung Rosalind Franklin or overlooked Cecilia Payne was she. The ironies of his professional and marital relationship with Dorothy were multiple, and he hoped that only he was aware of all of them. Portal, Dorothy (Mrs Conrad Herzog), R.S., b. 9 May 1950, daughter of Eric and Enid Portal, m. 1st 1975 Humphrey Clark q.v. (marr. diss. 1980), one d., 2nd, 1982, Conrad Herzog q.v. Educ. Lady Bannister's Sch., Loughborough, Downing Coll., Cambridge, Imperial Coll., London . . . and so on, through her citations and honours and publications, to her recreations: bird-watching, walking, cooking.

Cooking.

She had not been a good cook, he spitefully recalled. What concept of political appeasement or rebellion had led her to claim that she was interested in cooking?

The spiteful gene.

He resented the spite that had been grafted on to his good nature.

He had married on the rebound, for comfort, for kindness, and he had married his nemesis. It was like a Greek tragedy.

No, it would not be the irritations and inflammations from the sealed but still infected sore of the Dorothy Portal connection that would leak out when he began to read the papers in the folder. The possibility of finding a reference to his ex-colleague and rival Arnold Moule had occurred to him as much more likely. Habitual civility coupled with professional self-interest had obliged him to conceal his loathing and distrust of Arnold Moule. Moule's name and indeed his person continued to present themselves to Humphrey with uncanny frequency, no matter how hard the discreet and sympathetic Mrs Hornby worked to avoid such collisions. Humphrey Clark loathed Moule, and loathed himself for loathing him, but the world believed that they liked each other, and continued to seat them side by side at dinners, to mention them in the same paragraphs, to couple their names in academic papers, to invite them to introduce each other at conferences. Moule's promotion had dismayed him, but he had hidden his dismay, perhaps too well, and had listened patiently and silently when Moule was praised for Humphrey's successes and when Moule appropriated initiatives for which Humphrey should have been credited. This was the way of the world and the way of academic life, and there was nothing to be done about it. Nevertheless, he deeply hoped that he was not being asked to sit on a platform and share an honour with vainglorious, overlauded, mean-spirited little microbiologist Arnold Moule, the successful scholar of very small things.

These thoughts were paltry, ignominious, piffling, trumpery, dishonourable, and he strove against them. But they lurked, fathoms deep. He told himself, from time to time, that it was the disappointment of a lost collaboration that he mourned. They had once been friendly, he and Arnold, although they had not been friends, and Humphrey Clark had valued the decency of their good manners to each other. But, in truth, he knew that he now hated Arnold Moule, and that he hated him largely because he had got ahead. He had not got ahead as spectacularly as the patient Dr Portal, once his wife, but Moule, like Portal, had, through patience and determination, achieved priority, and Humphrey found it hard to forgive him for this. Portal and Moule had stuck it out, and Humphrey had caved in. He had failed, in the long haul. It was a comparative failure, but a failure. He had been tempted away from the long slow tedious dedicated watch, he had stepped aside for good reasons and for bad, he had accepted incompatible appointments and responsibilities and promotions, and Portal and Moule had moved ahead. He had been promoted, but they had moved ahead.

The riddle of the shifting meanings and allocations of time, the riddle of Diophantus.

At least, he told himself, he had not become a semi-popular television scientist with diminishing credibility and a diminishing market value. He had swum dangerously near that reef, but he had not been wrecked upon it.

It occurred to him, subliminally, hardly consciously, that perhaps it was the name of the ubiquitously destructive Tommy Kelman that lay in the pink folder. But no, surely not, it could not be. It was Arnold Moule whom he had most to fear.

He did not want to be forced to be pleasant to Moule, even for twenty-four hours, and anyone connected with the later fiasco of the Green Grotto of Greenwich would also be unwelcome. The Grotto, for which he had worked so hard, had failed on so many levels that it was hard to know which failure had been the most wounding. It had proved to be neither fish, flesh nor fowl. In Humphrey's view it had failed financially, intellectually and aesthetically. It had failed as a research institution, it had failed as an educational resource, it had failed as an ecological project dedicated to the renewal of marine life. It had wasted its lottery grant, its cement had been cancerous, and its tanks had leaked. Nevertheless, it was now accounted a great success. After much tampering and tinkering, the accountants were happy. The bottom line was secure, and the tanks had stopped leaking. It was an icon, not a disaster.

Everything about it disgusted its first advisory director, who had given it his influential blessing: its stupid name, its ill-written and ugly advertisements, its misleading gobbets of information, its vulgar branded merchandise, its horrible shop full of soft toys and inflatable frogs and sea shells and jellyfish and tea towels and rubber sharks, its plopping blobbing screeching interactive website.

The Green Grotto had been turned into everything that Humphrey despised in modern education and popular culture, and therefore it thrived. He had tried so hard and for so long to preserve its integrity, but he had been defeated and outwitted. The spirit of the age had been against him. Shortly after its official opening Humphrey had been, in effect, constructively dismissed, and the venture had begun to prosper as the accountants and the salesmen and the PR women moved in. It was not widely known that he had left under a cloud of his own making, and therefore his name was linked with its prosperity, and he frequently had to face congratulations for a project which he would have preferred to disown. He had schooled himself to accept these congratulations meekly and without protest, but it was hard for him to do so. One day, he feared, he would hear himself speaking out.

He dreaded that one day he might speak out about the disgraceful death of the three humphead wrasse. They had been ill caught, ill packed, ill transported. These beautiful, imperial and valuable fish had died needlessly in the hold of an aeroplane standing at Gatwick airport. They had died in their shark coffins, an unfortunate and in this instance too-apt nickname for these containers. They had been murdered, and he had been guilty of their death, for he should never have permitted their capture, and, having condoned it, he should have supervised their transit with more care.

He had set up an Ethics Committee at the Grotto, but it had been too late for the wrasse.

The humphead wrasse, also known as the Napoleon wrasse (*Cheilinus undulatus*), of the Labridae, were denizens of the coastal waters and coral reefs of the Indo-Pacific oceans, and were all too often to be found on the dinner plates of the Japanese. This species of fish was now on the CITES protected list, but that would not profit those three poor specimens who had ended up, partly through his negligence, in formalin.

Better to be eaten than to die in transit.

No, he hoped he would not have to stand up on a platform and smirk by the side of one of those ignorant and merciless traders in the flesh of fish. He would not even wish to shake a hand of one of them. They had despised him, and he despised them. They had debased their remit.

He had been dismayed by his most recent visit, incognito, to the Grotto, and now, remembering it, his anger and his humiliation returned to him. He had taken with him his solemn sallow boot-polish-black-haired American grandson, his daughter's son, a child whom he hardly knew, and, for the child's sake, he had had to pretend to enjoy himself.

Humphrey had done his grandfatherly duty. He had bought two tickets, one Senior Citizen's and one child's, and they had done the tour. First they had been to the as yet inoffensive and unspoilt Rescue Room, where they watched the play of some diminutive freshwater Mexican fishes, pale and agile fishes of subtle mottled gold and silver and blue and pink, fishes of a species now extinct in its native land. The grandson had read the label respectfully, respecting his grandfather and the fish, and together they had watched the small survivors of a lost tribe as they darted and displayed themselves and turned and wheeled about and scattered and re-formed themselves in tiny shoals. These little ones would never know their natural home. They would die if they were to be released into it. So they could not be counted as unhappy: they lived a false life, but there was no other life that they could have led. The delicate colours and habits of these ignorant little creatures were pleasing, soothing.

But coloured fish were two a penny these days, and the American child from the land of Disney would want to see something more dramatic.

They wandered on, these tentative blood strangers, through a dark corridor walled with larger tanks of dogfish. The dogfish were subdued to their element. They turned and cruised, and cruised and turned, in sleek dull blue-grey boredom. They had become psychotic. They were too large for their tank. The Ethics Committee was supposed to report on aberrant and distressed behaviour, but the circling and cycling of these fish had been overlooked. It is true that they were common fish, easy to replace. Humphrey had wanted to say to the child, *They should not be here*, but he had said nothing, like a false apostle or a careless father. He had denied them.

He would have preferred to pause by a small corridor tank containing a hunched and lonely cuttlefish, and to point out the little tallow colony of waving semi-translucent sea squirts that kept it company, but he did not think he could communicate his enthusiasm for these strange but simple organisms. He did not take the risk. He followed the easier route.

The sea squirts looked like little graceful waving condoms. Would the child recognize a condom, if he saw one? Condoms and tampons had been washed up on the beach at Finsterness, and at first he and Sandy had not known what they were. Tommy Kelman had always known.

Blinking green arrows on the walls and a track of glowing yellow Man Friday naked footprints on the floor led them onwards, through the darkness, towards the Blue Lagoon. Humphrey had fought hard against the Blue Lagoon, and lost. He had never seen it in its kitsch and crude vulgarity. It was the one of the Grotto's most distinctive and widely promoted attractions. It appeared on all the adverts.

The Blue Lagoon looked like an oval blue plastic hotel

swimming pool, and it occupied a large arched hall. It was surrounded by palm trees, some of which were fake and some of which were real. In the middle of the water was a small atoll-shaped island, on which a life-size mermaid lolled, her tail dangling into the water. She was supported on one elbow, and a comb and a glass lay by her on the white sand. Her head moved sinuously, electronically, from side to side, and her eyelashes fluttered. She was wearing a diamanté turquoise bikini, and her full curved lips were very red. The silver scales of her tail glittered, and her golden hair was artificially lifted and fanned by an invisible breeze. In the shallow waters around her inexpensive little fish played, and small fountains spurted, and miniature wavelets lapped. A wretched turtle cruised sadly and aimlessly about, and crabs and clams studded the carefully positioned rocks. Visitors were invited to touch panels and press buttons for information about coral-reef fish, about coral formation, about pollution and environmental hazards. 'Don't let Miranda the Mermaid Die!' exhorted one aspiring notice. 'Do not throw coins in water!' declared another, more reasonably. 'Durty water kills!' said a third.

Durty? Yes, *durty*. Humphrey glanced at his grandson to see if he had noticed the spelling error, but the child was staring intently at a starfish. Was the starfish real or was it a fake? It moved, but that did not mean it was real. The child did not seem very interested in the mermaid. He was too young to be interested by ladies in bikinis, even if their brown breasts rose and fell with the simulated and seductive breath of life.

Humphrey wondered if he should put some anonymous suggestions in the suggestion box. Perhaps the Grotto ought to set up a piously informative and politically correct panel about Bikini Island, nuclear fallout, and the long-lasting effects of low-level radiation? Maybe there already was one somewhere on the premises? All that stuff was common know-ledge now, although recognition had been so slow to come, and so stubbornly resisted. Everybody knew now that nuclear fallout was bad for you, and that you should never have put your feet into those glowing green X-ray machines to check your shoe size when you were a child. It had been fun, one of the more fun things of being a child forcibly taken shop-ping, but like most fun things, it was bad for you.

Professor Clark's mind flitted like a bat's wing to Barbed Wire Island, and Anthrax Island, and Tommy Kelman's tasty nuggets of bad news from John Hersey's *Hiroshima*. His mind flitted to the remote island in the Pacific where his research plane, fifteen years ago, had been forced to put down briefly because of engine trouble: the island belonged to the American military, and was used for the Army's chemical weapon storage and destruction programme, administered by the euphemistically entitled US Defense Threat Reduction Agency. The whole area was highly toxic, and a cloud of reddish smoke hung over the island's cluster of sinister instal-lations. Faceless men wearing helmets and silver protective suits had emerged from these installations to fix the plane, and then had silently disappeared again, as in an episode from an H. G. Wells novella. Rumoured to be one of the most toxic places on earth, the island also claimed to be a Wildlife Refuge. This dual role, of chemical weapons base and wildlife refuge, had puzzled him then, and it puzzled him still, but then he had still retained a hope of understanding the mysteries of global power, and of decoding superpower doublespeak. Now he knew that he would never understand.

The Damascene Islands, so 'unspoilt' on his first Marine Society visit, were now a much-visited tourist resort. It had been years before he had fully taken in the knowledge that his expedition had been sponsored by an American property company, which had subsequently developed the islands and made them accessible to cheaply run airlines and rich travellers. He had not thought that he had been part of such a programme.

Toxicity or tourism: that was the choice. Tourism was the better choice of the two. Most conservation programmes are sponsored by oil companies and mineral rights conglomerates. That's the way it is. Shell and BP and the miners of zinc befriend corals and barnacles and sea lilies. They welcome little fishes in, with gently smiling jaws.

This American child's English great-grandfather had died of radiation sickness, years before his grandparents had met and so unwisely married. The child would have no knowledge of this. The child would know nothing of his Great-grandpa Philip Clark, who had served in the Far East in World War Two, and died a wasted skeleton in Covington Hospital.

Every twenty minutes Miranda the Mermaid went for a swim. Humphrey and the child watched as she slithered mechanically off her stretch of sand and set off round her island. The poor distressed and living turtle got out of her way and skulked till she had passed. It was used to this routine performance. Its sad face was carved with decades of boredom and despair.

'Can you swim?' asked Humphrey nervously of his grandson, as they left the lagoon and made their way towards the Coral Reef Tank. (Was the child bored out of his mind? At least he was quiet and polite, this little half-Japanese grandson, as English children used to be. That was good. But Humphrey hoped that he was not too bored.)

'Oh yes,' said the carefully self-contained child, with composure. 'Yes, I like to swim. But I can't dive yet.'

Then the child hesitated, and took a very small leap. He

looked obliquely up at his grandfather from beneath his long black eyelashes, and said, 'My mom says you are a great diver.'

The grandfather was childishly pleased by this compliment. He had hardly dared to expect that his name was ever mentioned, let alone favourably, in that other larger world across the pond.

'I *was* a great diver,' he admitted, feeling more cheerful as they made their way along a subterranean corridor towards the great high wall of fish and coral that was the Grotto's most expensive treasure. 'But I don't go down much these days. You should learn to dive, when you're a bit bigger. It's easy. And it's great fun. Look, imagine, you can swim amongst fish like these.'

The show tank, he had to admit, was impressive. It was well designed and well stocked and well lit. Its improbable and beautiful and graceful inhabitants grouped and circled and lurked and darted as though they were unobserved, and its hundreds of thousands of litres of water were clear and bright and gave an illusion of limitless space. The illusion was a clever simulation of freedom. The exhibit had attracted a crowd of admirers, who were watching the display with something approaching the awe that it deserved. Tangs and triggers, damsels and butterflies, hawks and humbugs, eels and angels, clowns and cowfish, the spotted and the striped, mingled and wove and flaunted themselves. The child stared intently. As they stared together, side by side, a large thick-lipped square-tailed humphead wrasse appeared in the middle distance and swam towards them, conspicuous in a dazzling livery of electric green shading into purples and blues.

'What's that one called?' enquired a stout middle-aged woman of the uniformed attendant, pointing at the noble wrasse.

'He's called Elvis,' said the attendant with a snigger, to a dutiful but half-hearted simulation of general mirth. 'And look, there's his friend, Mick Jagger, coming round the corner.'

The woman disapproved, as did Humphrey.

'I meant, what *sort* of fish is it?' she said crossly.

The attendant took offence. 'There's a chart over there, with their names, and an interactive console,' he said ungraciously.

A slight discomfort spread through the mildly offended gathering, as the indifferent fish continued their watery weaving dance. Bad customer relations, noted Humphrey with malicious satisfaction, as he consulted the identification chart.

The information about the wrasse was not, he had to admit, too bad. It did not of course mention the disastrously premature death of those first acquisitions, those Gatwick murders for which Humphrey still held himself responsible, nor did it indulge in jokes about fat lips and pop stars. It emphasized the endangered status of the species, and described the wrasse's diet of molluscs and worms and crustaceans, and its ability to digest poisonous marine animals such as the sea hare, the crown-of-thorns starfish and the box jellyfish. It managed to describe the unstable sexuality of the hermaphrodite wrasse without vulgar innuendo or facile explanation, and it admitted that 'nothing was known' about the mortality of the species.

'We do not know how long these fish may live in their natural habitat.'

Humphrey noted that it was now politically necessary to claim that protected species had not been captured and introduced from the wild, but had been bred in captivity or offloaded from other aquaria. Some of the more dubious fish in the Green Grotto were from Ellesmere Port, some from Plymouth.

He remembered the magnificent and well-curated display

in Monterey. We can't afford to build like that in England. He had tried, he had made plans and suggestions, but he had been outmanoeuvred.

When he was the age of this child, he had been entranced by phrases like 'little is known'. They had recurred frequently in his old-fashioned childhood reading about marine species, and had given him a little sensuous mystic thrill. He had thought he would be able to answer all the questions.

'I have not the remotest idea what can be the use of these remarkable appendages . . .' 'Inside the canopy of mouth and nose, I find some peculiar little white bodies. I have no notion of the meaning of all this . . .' 'The hog fish, known in Flamborough as the Devourer, has not yet been traced to its breeding ground . . .'

These phrases, in old Victorian books of natural history, had delighted him.

Would the child be interested in these mysteries, as Humphrey had been at his age? He could not begin to guess, and did not wish to inflict his tedious schoolmasterly tendency upon his grandson. The child was watching, intently, the sporting of the little shoals, and the mesmeric weaving of the stocking body of the black-and-white eel, peering from its hiding place on the floor of the tank.

The child was still engrossed in the display when Humphrey saw, approaching the six-inch-thick crystal wall, a small delegation of visiting foreign dignitaries, led by a man whom he recognized from the old days as one of his more obsequious, ambitious and duplicitous young employees. Would they see him, here in the aqueous half-light? If they were to see him, would they recognize him? No, they would not. They passed him by, talking importantly in pompous public self-congratulatory tones. They paid no attention to the small child with his nose glued to the glass, nor to the modest old man with his dutifully purchased Senior Citizen's ticket, lurking guiltily in the shadows like a paedophile by the chart of the simplified story of the life cycle of the handsome endangered purple fish.

Professor Clark, if he had had the choice, would have preferred to remove the details of his involvement with the Green Grotto from *Who's Who* and his curriculum vitae. But he had not had that choice. They were part of his history. He had made a bad career move, late in the day, and he would have to stick with the consequences. Nevertheless, he hoped that he would not have to listen, or not for too long, to the praises of the Green Grotto during the ceremony at Ornemouth in the morning. Perhaps he would marginally prefer Arnold Moule to the Green Grotto. At least Moule was a serious scientist.

Indeed, that was just about all that Moule was.

This train of thought, these meanly articulated sentiments, were not very pleasing to a man who prided himself on high thoughts and fair play and generosity and good humour.

Paltry, ignominious, piffling, trumpery, dishonourable.

These were the hard words that Darwin had used of himself. But Humphrey knew that he had not earned this comparison.

Too much super-ego, that had been one of Ailsa's taunts, during the bitter time of the dissolution.

He had not thought of his retort for twenty years: *'That's good, coming from you,'* he should have said.

The Green Grotto could not be removed from the official story of his life, but the name of Ailsa Kelman had not been allowed to enter it. She belonged to a buried Precambrian layer before these records began. She could not be excised, because she had not been admitted.

As the train pulled northwards out of York station, Humphrey saw the Minster, which had been struck during his agnostic lifetime by the lightning of God. The numinous sight of the cathedral fortified him to gather his waning courage, and he opened the pink folder. And there, of course, as he had divined and denied, lay the name of Ailsa Kelman: the name of Ailsa Kelman, with whom he had once known Perfect Happiness. Ailsa Kelman, who, although human, had been as beautiful to him as a zebra shark. He was on his way towards her, and it was too late to turn back. He was not a coward, and he would not turn back now. He could not jump ship and deny her now.

The Public Orator pauses here, relieved that at last both of the principals have recognized the necessary shape of the plot. It is a story of convergence, but it is not yet clear whether the story will end in recognition, reconciliation, refusal or rejection. The Orator does not know the end of the story, but has come to see that, defiantly ageing though those two be, enfeebled by age though they be, alternately rash and cowardly though they be, over-reaching, over-extending, over-ambitious, over-weening and intermittently defeated though they be, they may yet, even at this late stage in the game, find in themselves enough strength to push on towards their own resolution. Technically, the Orator is a recorder, a reporter, and not a fashioner. The Orator cannot even be described as a witness, for the events to which he will bear witness have not yet occurred. The Orator is certainly not a precipitator, for that is not a legitimate role for one in his position. So the Orator cannot forge the ending. It must arise, it must ensue, it must not be forced. The Orator will be present, and will comment, and will possibly even dare to prompt, but the powers of the Orator are limited. They have been limited to the forethought, to the planning, to the invitation, to the setting of the stage, to the choice of the venue, to the public confrontation. After that, the actors have this terrible freedom. They can write their own script. The Orator's formal script is already written, but they can write their own informal interchanges, as they meet in a crowded room, and as they climb the painful cobbled steps. This is risky, this is terrible.

Perfect Happiness

Nessun maggior dolore che ricordarsi del tempo felice nella miseria

Dante, *Inferno*, Canto V

Can anyone say with certainty that he was happy at a particular moment of time? Remembering the moment makes him happy because he realizes how happy he could have been, but at the actual moment when the alleged happiness was occurring did he feel happiness? He was like a man owning a piece of ground in which, unknown to himself, a treasure lay buried. You would not call such a man rich, neither would I call a man happy who is so without realizing it . . .

Delacroix, *Journals*, 28 April 1854

Humphrey Clark and Ailsa Kelman have known Perfect Happiness. They have known it and named it. It has a place, and the place has a name. It is a memorable name. Their lives will flow outwards and onwards, bearing them helplessly away from this place and from each other, but here they are together, in this place and in this moment, and they lie calm and still, with the peace that comes from satisfied desire.

They lie flat on their backs beneath the blue sky on the warm wooden deck of a large boat that rocks gently on the infantile blue waters. They listen to the slap and cluck of the small ripples of the sea. The movement soothes and assuages, like a cradle, or like the movement of the waters of the womb.

They are not entirely naked, for the boat has unseen and senior occupants to whom they owe respect, but their handsome young bodies are well exposed to the rays of the afternoon sun. They are both tanned, and he is golden. They are in their sexual prime, and they know that they are beautiful. They are beautiful to each other and to any observing human eye. The gods smile on them. They are a fine couple. Natural selection and Eros have done their best for them, and here they lie, paying tribute to the processes that have brought them together to this Aegean paradise.

It is primarily his place, and she is here as his guest. He has priority here, and the balance is here in his favour. This makes them equal, as they lie becalmed.

He has tried to teach her to dive with him over the last two days, and she has made sporting attempts to learn, but she is still nervous about the unplumbed depths of emerald and indigo. This hesitation adds to his power, but she is so contented here with him that she concedes his advantage without grudge. She finds the contraptions of the diving apparatus cumbersome and knows she does not look her best as she struggles with them. Nor does she look attractive when she has at last managed to squeeze and buckle herself into them. She prefers to swim prettily and lightly clad in the surface of the waters, wearing not goggles or a mask but fashionable starlet sunglasses. She plunges and turns and floats in the safe swell of the small translucent waves, amongst the pale green and turquoise bubbles, where she can admire her own body, and his. He tempts her with stories of the fish and the coral of the world below, but she vows that she is happy in the shallows. She will leave the depths to the men. Tomorrow, perhaps, if there is a tomorrow in this timeless world, she will subject herself to another lesson.

They have agreed that swimming here is very different from swimming in the North Sea, that grey surge which they had braved together in their immature livery of white and childish puckered gooseflesh.

She is smoking a cigarette, wilfully defiling the pure air with a thin plume of blue smoke. The smell of nicotine mingles amorously with the smell of salt and garlic and Ambre Solaire. An occasional sun-warmed breath of citrus and of pine, of oregano and of thyme, wafts towards them from the shore of the island.

Two books lie by her side on the whitened plank of the deck. One of them is an Everyman copy of Darwin's *On the Origin of Species*, for she has been taking lazy lessons from her incurably pedagogic lover on the subject of evolutionary biology. The other is a luridly jacketed and battered paperback copy of Henry de Vere Stacpoole's *Blue Lagoon*, showing a bronzed blond naked couple frolicking on a rock on a coral island. Its jacket says it costs 2s. 6d., but they had picked it up for a few drachmas at a shabby quayside bookstore at Piraeus on the mainland.

They have been discussing the Jean Simmons movie of *Blue Lagoon*, and whether they could have seen it together all those years ago in the quaint little white Crescent Picture House in Ornemouth, with its crescent moon and its seven stars. Both have seen it, but they cannot remember where and when, and are not sure if the dates would fit an Ornemouth viewing en famille with Tommy and Mr and Mrs Kelman and that other boy called – was it? – Sandy Clegg. Ailsa thinks she may be confusing some of its images with frames from the colourful *South Pacific*, which she knows she has also seen, but which she thinks was of a later date. They cannot check, for there are no reference books (or not of that nature) on board the *Bride of Abydos*, but they do not argue about it. They are happy with the uncertain fusion of their past forgettings and rememberings.

The text of *Blue Lagoon* has, like Darwin, provided them with themes for enlightening discourse. The fairy-tale story tells of shipwrecked cousins, Dick and Emmeline, who grow innocently and ignorantly from pre-pubertal childhood into sexual maturity on their idyllic desert island. There, to their astonishment, they produce a baby which survives their attempts to feed it on bananas and green coconut juice. Inexplicably, they call the child Hannah, although it is a boy, and the child turns out to be 'a most virile and engaging baby'. The author claims that Dick and Emmeline chose this name because it was the only name they could remember, but Ailsa divines in it a deeper if unconscious purpose. All three members of this primal family meet an ambiguous fate as they drift, unconscious, out to sea in their little dinghy, having consumed (whether fatally or not is not made clear) the crimson berries of the never-wake tree. Ailsa has compared this fantasy, to her own satisfaction if not to Humphrey's, with the plot of George Eliot's *The Mill on the Floss*, where the estranged brother and sister are reunited in death as the flood of unconsummated incestuous passion bears them away on a tide of all-conquering, all-punishing super-ego.

She is very pleased with this theory, but as Humphrey has not read *The Mill on the Floss* he is unable to appreciate its ingenuity. He does know that George Eliot is not a man but a woman, but he has never read any of her novels. He comes back with a commentary on de Vere Stacpoole's censorious views on the nature and behaviour of coral. Coral is not, Stacpoole tells the reader, what the reader might expect. The creature which constructs the coral reefs is not an industrious insect, as you might suppose, busily building its gorgeous underwater palaces year after year, with the patience of Job and the genius of Brunel, but a sluggish and gelatinous worm, leading an idle and useless life, and producing its beautiful structures by chance, not by design. Humphrey finds this attitude as curious and as unexpected, in a work of that date and that genre, as Ailsa had found the moving and mythic irresolution of the final voyage of the childhood lovers, and it inspires him to bring up memories of the moral tone of *The Children's Encyclopedia*, and the evolution of the primitive notochord, and the laziness of sea squirts, and the sexual behaviour of angler fish, and other zoological oddities.

The female angler fish, says Humphrey, consumes the body of the male, and reduces it, within her body, to a sperm bag.

Whereas, according to Darwin's Glossary, the male of the cochineal is a small winged insect, and the female is a motionless berry-like mass.

They both laugh, easily, at these monstrous quirks of nature, confident that the human form is divine, and assured of their place in the divine plan.

He tells her about the hermaphrodite wrasse, and the sexual instability of the crayfish.

So when, asks Ailsa, did sex begin?

In the Precambrian age, says Humphrey with ignorant and sunny confidence. A couple of billion years ago, he hazards. That's when it all began. When cells first developed a nucleus.

Why did they develop a nucleus? asks Ailsa.

God knows, says Humphrey.

And what, asks Ailsa at random, as she flicks through the pages of Darwin, is morphology?

Morphology is dead rabbits in formalin, says Humphrey, and he tells her about the charismatic Mr Summerscale and biology lessons at King Edward's and why he has stopped eating meat. He explains to her why it is so important to learn to tag fish underwater.

If you tag them in air, they tend to die, says Humphrey.

He quotes Mr Summerscale's Wordsworthian motto, *We*

murder to dissect. He describes his dislike of gratuitous animal experimentation. Rats made to swim in circles until they drowned, rabbits tormented with cosmetic eye drops, pigeons left with half a brain. He speaks of his hero Niko Tinbergen and the classic stickleback.

She responds with memories of her glamorous misfit drama teacher at school, Mrs Lesley, Bonnie Lesley of Bonnie Bonsett, who had been in thrall to the love songs of Burns and of Byron, and who had made Ailsa learn them by heart. She tells him about her course in theatre design at the Institut des Arts Dramatiques, and the Gallic instructor who had seduced her so easily and so cheaply and so merrily.

Supine on the deck they lie, talking, falling silent, now and then reaching out a hand for each other, smiling at each other, lighting a cigarette, sharing their schooldays, pooling their speculations, effortlessly crossing the barriers that divide them. Their thoughts permeate, interpenetrate, drift and spiral, with the random freedom of the certainty of love. The sun beats down upon them, on their closed eyelids. The future glitters before them, and they know that all they have to do is to wait for it to happen to them. They are secure in the present, and their future is also secured. They have their plans, their prospects. They believe, as lovers do, that they are complementary, that they are halves of the same whole, that everything that is in them will fit into the pattern, that one day everything in them will be known to the other, and that by this knowledge they will be redeemed and completed and saved from eternal solitude. All will be for the best.

She tells him about Plato's speculations about hermaphrodites and the origins of sexuality, as expressed by Aristophanes in *The Symposium*. This evolutionary myth, of the symmetrically divided self which seeks union with its lost half, is unfamiliar to him, but it is instantly attractive to him.

So we have been seeking one another since the first separation, he says.

I don't know how his theory fits in with geological time, he says, *and with what went on or didn't go on in the Precambrian, but it seems a good enough explanation to me.*

They wonder what Darwin thought about Plato's morphology, but they have no reference book aboard that can tell them. They agree that Darwin must have read Plato. In those days, they concur, before the two cultures divided, gentlemen had to read everything. Women weren't allowed to read much, but gentlemen were forced to read the classics. They had to read Latin and Greek.

Women, says Ailsa, were not allowed to take part in a symposium. They had to sit in a back room with the servants and the flute players.

She has forgotten that Plato puts the principal speech of *The Symposium* into the mouth of a woman, Diotima, and as Humphrey has never read *The Symposium*, he cannot provoke her by reminding her of this. And when, years later, she recalls this conversation on board the *Bride of Abydos*, she will nevertheless conclude that she was correct in the sense of her forgetting. For Diotima was a hollow personification, an abstraction, not a woman.

Ailsa tries to tell him some more of the story of *The Mill on the Floss*, and of its heroine's thirst for a classical education, but she stops when he says he will read it himself one day if she doesn't spoil the plot.

They discover they had both done Latin O-Level, for the same exam board. Humphrey says he had found it difficult, but Ailsa claims to have sailed through.

They talk, they make love, they swim, they uncover, discover, and educate each other. She too has a strong pedagogic streak, and she teaches him lines of poetry and speaks to him of Sappho and Eloise van Dieman, of Burns and Byron and of Caroline Lamb. 'Roll on, thou deep and dark blue ocean, roll,' she commands the passive Aegean, and it continues, indifferently, to do as she commands.

Humphrey has by now been made familiar with the career of Ailsa's heroine, Eloise van Dieman (d. Bruges 1929), and with Ailsa's determination to pursue her abandoned doctoral thesis: he has heard all about her earlier difficulties with funding, her struggles with archaic institutions and supervisors whom she knew to be her intellectual inferiors, her certainty that she was on to a winner and that one day the world would know it. Ailsa swears that she, like Eloise in her day, is ahead of her time, but the world will catch up with her, as it will with Eloise. As yet ill-recognized female cultural figures will have their turn, she informs him. She will abandon, she earnestly insists, the not-so-easy pickings of cabaret and the siren calls of vanity and television, and devote herself seriously to what is not yet securely established either in name or in practice as feminist scholarship and Women's Studies.

He in turn teaches her about theories of species and speciation and speaks to her of the causes of phosphorescence and of the peculiarities of plankton and of the parathyroid hormone in the gills of fish. She listens, as Desdemona listened to Othello: he listens, as Adam listened to Eve. It does not occur to her to rebel, it does not occur to him to suspect or to doubt. It is peaceful, it is heavenly. They complement each other. Science and Art lie side by side: together, they cover (or at least illustrate) the spectrum of knowledge. (She cannot understand what the spectrum is, however often he explains it to her, however often he shows her the prism and the rainbow and the colours of the sea spray, but, here, suspended for a while, this does not seem to be important.) They are happy with their lot, with their identities, with their perfect bodies, with their present incarnation. They do not, under this hot annealing sun, dispute territory, or display the cruel spines and colours of aggression. Like Dick and Emmeline by the blue lagoon, they are self-sufficient, even though they are in the company of a crew of at times rowdy and hard-drinking marine biologists. They see themselves easily, lazily, fantastically, as archetypes, as heroes, as glamorous characters in a nouvelle vague Italian movie.

They are peacefully at anchor off the island of Chios, the island of massacres.

They do not mention the massacres.

Male and female created He them, at some point in the Precambrian or shortly thereafter, and He allows these two this moment of equilibrium, of sexual symmetry. How are they to know that it cannot last? They do know, because they are not stupid, but they do not know that they know.

Time is suspended.

He dives into the water, and she jumps after him, and they swim together, away from the boat. Treading water, they embrace. Bubbles of air are trapped in the golden hair of his chest and thighs, but she is smooth and slippery like a fish. Their solid bodies meet, weightlessly, supported by the thick salt water. He feels her saline breasts against him, she feels his hot thighs through cool water. Their hard bodies press against one another. They defy gravity. There is no effort in it. They are free. They kiss.

This is the perfect happiness. It is for ever, it is archetypal, it is sempiternal. Time has ceased.

Eternity did not last long. Time reasserted itself unpleasantly and uncomfortably, stage by stage, on the long hot dusty journey back, towards the town, towards the ferry, towards Athens airport and the aeroplane, towards England, towards inevitable and foreseen divergence. Humphrey and Ailsa parted from their chorus of complaisant companions, and they journeyed onwards, together and alone, and, as they journeyed, doubts about the future surfaced, one after another. Apart, together, they had doubts, doubts that gathered strength, doubts compounded by the minor and mundane irritations and uncertainties of travel, by unconfirmed tickets and ill-considered connections, by the absence of Tampax and of soap and of paper tissues.

He looked to the future, guiltily, and wondered whether he had been right to accept the imminent posting to distant California. Should one not be willing to sacrifice one's career for love, for such a love? Should he not have stayed in England, to be with his love?

She looked to the future, anxiously, and wondered whether she had been right to reject the lucrative though unsecured offer from the BBC, whether she would have the guts and perseverance to return to academe and to finish the book that she had promised herself and her prospective publishers that she would write. Had she overestimated her sticking power, she wondered? Had she overestimated her intellectual weight? Had she guessed wrong about the future, her future? Did she need an agent? Tommy said she needed an agent. Tommy had offered to find her an agent. Tommy was a crook, but Tommy was canny.

Their prospects were incompatible. There they were, high on well-consummated sexual passion, jogging along side by side in a dusty jeep driven by a crazy Chiot, protesting their undying love and enduring union, and yet they were about to part. Of course they knew they would never stay faithful to each other. It wasn't on the cards. This was the end of the romance.

They spent, as they had planned, a day and a night in the

town on the island. They thought they had been looking forward to some privacy and a proper bed, but as they checked into the bald-faced shabby Hotel Actaeon in the late morning their spirits sank yet further. The bedroom was small and dark, and though the bed was wide it was hard and low with concealed and vicious metal corners. It was far worse than the bed in the Room in Holborn, whose tricks they knew, and which they had subdued and tamed to their familiar demands. Within five minutes, as she unpacked her small bag, Ailsa had barked her shin. She yelped and bled. He too shortly bled, from her over-enthusiastic attempts to probe the weathered heel of his foot with a flame-blackened sterilized needle. She was trying to extract the embedded spine of a sea urchin, but her search verged on sadism, and he told her, quite sharply, to stop. They sat together on the hard low mattress, and laughed at their injuries, but there was a forced note to their laughter, for the ambience of the room was lowering. The long thin bolster-pillow was scratchy, the mosquitoes were active, the washbasin had only a trickle of water and no plug, the handle of the plywood wardrobe was broken, the lavatory down the corridor lacked paper and was blocked. The Hotel Actaeon was a disappointment. They had been expecting a more attractive, a more romantic departure from Cythera and Perfect Happiness.

Maybe, said Ailsa, looking at the blood and the mosquitoes, we should have had a tetanus injection.

He forbore to admit that his injections were all up to date. He knew he should have warned her, but he had forgotten.

They both wanted to explore the town, and discussed their itinerary over a miserable lunch of leathery rings of squid and roughly hewed tomato and onion salad. She had wanted to go to the town's museum, because that was the kind of thing she always wanted to do. He resisted, she insisted. They quarrelled pettily, like a married couple, or like lovers who are tired of each other and are looking for release. They knew this quarrel was a warning, but they ignored the warning. What else could they do?

The future, over the long wait for the meal, had begun to oppress them. They talked about it, but it had lost its confident shine. They talked about their research grants. His, thanks to some long-deceased and long-forgotten zoologist called Vickery, was munificent. Hers was meagre. Was this discrimination, and if so, of what nature? The plan had been – what had it been? To write love letters, to ring long distance, to keep in touch, over their year of separation. It would be a trial, but their love would surely survive a trial, would perhaps thrive on an endurance test. It would prove them, and they would triumph over it. Anyway, there would be visits and vacations.

What does one do about love, at that age? How does one trap it and tag it and clip its wings?

She had won the argument about the museum. He had wanted to loaf and to idle by the quay and to drink his last glass of the island's speciality ouzo as he watched the fishing boats and the ferries, but she marched him in the heat of the late afternoon to look at incomprehensible prehistoric shards and vessels, at vases and broken pottery, at copper fish hooks and bones and shells, at amber and faience and marble dagger pommels and obsidian blades and old maps and Venetian coins. She forced him to admire the exploits of the British women archaeologists who had led the excavations on Chios between the World Wars. He could see that her insistence on female accomplishment, which had amused him on board the *Bride of Abydos*, might irritate him if she insisted on overplaying it on dry land. He did not want to know any more about those old spinsters, Miss Edith Eccles and Miss Winifred

Lamb and the Honourable Mercy Money-Coutts. He was bored by findings from the tombs in the Valley of the Sacred Milk, and he did not see why Ailsa found the milk so significant. He had a headache, and the labelling in the museum was unhelpful, although she would not admit it.

She was on terra firma now, and she was letting him know about it, though she herself was not quite sure of what it was that she was letting him know. Her programme was forming itself there, dimly, assembling its shapes, as she paced by his side across the marble floors. It was not yet articulate. It was in its prehistory, but it was evolving, even there, as they stared together at the ruins of the ancient cultures of the island of Chios. Over the past two or three years she had lunged at this programme, wildly, with little jabs and large assertions that sometimes joined and sometimes missed and sometimes hit an unexpected and unintended mark. She had previewed it and foreshadowed it, and now it was beginning to take shape.

It had no place in it for this man.

In the largest room in the museum hung a copy of the most famous painting inspired by the history of the island. It was called *The Massacre at Chios*, and it was by Eugène Delacroix, who had never visited Chios (or Scio, as it was alternatively labelled in French). Painted in 1824, it recorded the massacre of the Greeks by the Turks in 1822. The artist had worked on it for many months.

Together, they paused and stood in front of this vast and terrible and overwhelming canvas. Even in reproduction, it overwhelmed. They stood, and they stared.

Ailsa, in her role as semi-trained art historian, had already spoken to Humphrey of this masterpiece of Eros and of Death, and had sought it out here to show it to him. She had come to the museum to inspect it. And now, confronting it, confronted by it, he remembered that he had seen it before, somewhere – who knows, perhaps in the section on 'Famous Paintings of the World', in *The Children's Encyclopedia* in distant Finsterness? (There were many improbable works reproduced in that fatal compendium.) There it was, *The Massacre*, in all its macabre glory, in all the extravagance of its beauty and cruelty.

He could see, years later, as he looked back over this passage, over this moment, that the painting already stood as an emblem, as a paradigm, of two of the great intellectual and aesthetic causes of the last four decades of the twentieth century, but he had not known it for what it was, and even Ailsa, quick though she was, had not known quite what she was seeing.

Feminism and Orientalism had been conjoined before their eyes.

Alisa had known a half of it, and she had sensed the rest. She was a conduit, a conductor, a receiver. She picked it up before it was officially transmitted, and she would wait her time to process the message and to name it and to pass it on.

She was more than a conduit. She was a pioneer. She was the message itself.

She had fallen silent by his side, as they gazed at the eerily silent and stoic scene of butchery. It was the beauty that appalled. To the right of the painting, the curving torso of a young Greek woman was voluptuously displayed as she was twisted backwards against the prancing horse of her Turkish conqueror. Her figure was conventionally beautiful, beautiful in the manner of conventional sado-masochistic fantasies: her upstretched arms and manacles of bondage, her swooning head, her bared breasts, her rapture, her imminent rape and her enslavement to her turbaned ravisher were designed to arouse the viewer, and not with pity. But the naked Parisian model was but one motif, rearing herself up to one side of the large and crowded canvas. Who had posed for the dark-haired, heavy-lidded dead woman in the foreground with the fair-haired child clinging to her lower body? Who had posed for the strangely indolent reclining dying man with the staring knowing eyes? Who had posed for the handsome chiselled old woman to the right of the centre of the pyramid of death, with her bared and wrinkled chest and her transfixing prophetic Sibylline gaze? It was wrong to admire, and yet the work was wonderful. Its wonder was shaming.

Staring at it, Humphrey was ashamed, and when he turned to look at Ailsa, he saw moving through her expressive face an eddy of impressionistic emotions, like the clouds scudding over a stormy sky: anger, desire, envy, indignation, apprehension, intent. A deep ripple moved through the dark current of sea and sky and swelled up and sank again. A mouth in the water opened, and closed. She tried to speak, and failed. He remembered her suddenly, three years before, on the Devon coast, in her little programme seller's black dress: her insubordination, her violent energy, her assertion. But it was not herself that she asserted. Something welled up, and she received it. The dead women, the enslaved virgin, the delicate, vulnerable little spine of the orphaned or slaughtered boy, the abused models, the enraptured and dedicated painter of romantic death and romantic love: she took them in, and they became not her, but the process of which she was part, the tide on which she was carried. He would never be able to withstand its force and its drag.

They were subdued and silent over their glass of ouzo on the quay. They spoke little over their dinner of charred and martyred skewers of fish and lamb. A mood of despondency possessed them: this was the end of the road, the end of his working vacation, the end of the affair. They knew that this would be their last night together. He poured her a last beaker of retsina, and watched as she sombrely drank it down. She stared into the dregs, and looked back at him, and smiled mournfully, her face suffused with sorrow and regret.

'Creosote,' she said.

Each knew more than a little, now, of the family history of the other. They had their own shorthand. It would be a pity to waste it. It would be a pity to waste so much of their conjoined past. They had known each other for a long time now. For most of their lives, they had known of and known each other.

Her father had died of creosote, and his of nuclear fallout. These untimely deaths hung around in the lower air, in the shifting haze of the biting insects of the evening. A swathe of little insects lifted and sank and hummed around them, light on the small breeze. The cheerful fairy lights of the boats bobbed mindlessly over the harbour, yellow and red and green and blue.

That night, they made love as though it were a parting, although they spoke no words of parting. Their lovemaking was not satisfactory. The god had left them. And in the wake of the god's departure, the mosquitoes came in for the kill. They hovered and whined and bit. Ailsa tied herself up in the shroud of thin hot sheet and groaned, while Humphrey attacked the mosquitoes with the sole of his sandal when they settled to digest their human prey upon the plaster walls. Splats of fresh commingled blood joined the darker stains of the dried blood of earlier guests. She laughed at his antics and his poor aim, and they regained a little good humour as they settled themselves, itching, scratching, inflamed, for an attempt at sleep.

They slept badly, but dreamed much. They dreamed of swimming in a shrinking sea.

It was on the bus from the ferry, a long day's journey later, that he declared himself. It was a jolting, uncomfortable metallic local bus, lacking upholstery and air-conditioning, and Ailsa insisted on changing her seat to avoid the sight and the proximity of wads of old chewing gum stuck in the ashtray on the back of the seat in front of her. She moved to the seat behind and sat alone by the window, gazing fiercely and angrily out at the passing landscape of the mainland. The bus had a noisy mechanical problem, the clanking of a detaching exhaust, and eventually it broke down, as Humphrey had said it would. So they sat there, stationary, by the roadside, with a view of a sloping rubbish tip of pale scarred cabbage stalks and fruit rinds and old cans and thin scavenging cats and bald yellow dogs.

It was there, as they waited in the heat, that he suggested that they should get married. The idea came to him like a sudden inspiration, like a challenge. How else could they be redeemed from decay and defeat, how else could they trap the intensity of timelessness that they had known, how else could they make a bid to remain beautiful, pure, free, weightless, aspiring, and all of those things that they had for the past ten days felt themselves to be? Why should they descend, feebly, unprotesting, into the rubbish heap of decay?

He turned round to look back at her, with his shocking proposal, his arm along the back of the seat. She leaned forward towards him, surprised. Had she heard him correctly?

'Why not?' he said, as he gallantly repeated his suggestion.

The metal rim and the ripped plastic of the back of the seat divided them and their bodies, but their heads were close as they leaned intently towards each other. Their eyes met and interlocked and searched and challenged. A flare of wild hope seemed to ignite between them. Why should they not be together for ever, and be obliged to keep faith with the best that they had been? Why should they not be the exception to the rule?

It would be an act of faith.

'Why not?' he said again.

Her eyes held his, and then she rashly, inexplicably, abruptly agreed. She accepted him. He had hardly dared to fear or to hope that she would, but she did. The flame between them burned, very brightly, for a few seconds. And yet, within a few more seconds, as they continued to stare at each other, it began to fail, for they knew that it was impossible and wrong. The words that pledged them had barely left their lips before they knew that it was wrong, and that it would end badly. All this knowledge crowded into them and surged through them as they sat there, apart yet together, by the rubbish tip. Time slowed down, time stood still, to allow them to receive this inassimilable knowledge. It was too late to seal their faith, and yet, stubbornly, foolishly, they pressed on. For it was also too late to undo the words that had been spoken. They would have to live slowly through the process of fading and dying, through the ebbing and the emptying. The pool would drain dry, the flame would flicker and die, the embers would blacken into darkness. That would be how it would be, but there would be no turning back now from the choice they had made, from the leap into the unknown known.

But they would be obliged to suspend knowledge of this moment of mutual despair, in order to live through the process that held them in thrall.

The proposal of marriage (for such it was), once made and once accepted, gathered a momentum of its own. Afterwards, they could never remember in detail how it had all come about, though they remembered well the hard seats of that dreadful bus and the horseshoe scars on the thick stumps of cabbage. They forgot the quality of the moment of hope and fear and knowledge, as one forgets the moment of impact of the near-fatal crash. They submitted themselves to their rash decision, and invested it, for a while, with a kind of last-ditch romantic heroism. They forged ahead stubbornly, against all their doubts and better wisdom, against every practical difficulty that presented itself. They tied, for better and for worse, the Gordian knot. It was an old-fashioned mistake, but they committed it, and they committed themselves to it.

In Athens, to celebrate their engagement, he bought her three cheap silver bangles from a little shop by the side of the Agora, a shop overflowing with beads and bracelets and necklaces and rings. They were her choice. She said she wanted the silver slave bangles, she said she loved them. He offered her gold or turquoise, but she chose the silver. She tried them on, and they glittered on her slim brown arm, above her deceitfully fragile little wrist.

He wanted to buy her a ring, but she refused a ring.

'I like these best,' she repeated, stubbornly. 'I like these best.'

The bracelets were made of a thin soft pliable silver wire, woven into a repeating Grecian pattern of coils and swirls.

'I'll buy you a proper ring when we get home,' he said.

She shook her head, declining the offer, but still she smiled.

She turned and twisted her bangles, and made them glint as they caught the slanting Athenian sun. They imprisoned her wrist, her arm.

They agreed to marry quietly, and to tell nobody. They knew that if they told, they would be talked out of it. Their lunatic engagement would not bear the light of common day. If they told their friends or their families, the folly of their choice would be taken from them, and they would be robbed of the full-scale disaster that they had promised themselves.

In those days, marriage had not gone out of fashion. It was still a widely chosen option, even for those who did not 'believe' in it. But its status was uncertain. It was neither a safe refuge nor a liberation nor an act of rebellion. It was a statement, but nobody knew any more what the statement meant. Ailsa Kelman was, in years to come, to speak and write much about the meaning of marriage: its bondage of women, its inequity, its appropriation of property, its legal trickeries, its false promises, its slow and grudging evolution.

But she kept her own first marriage very quiet.

Two witnesses attended the marriage in the discreet register office in Rosebery Avenue opposite Sadlers Wells in the borough of Holborn. One of them was Tommy Kelman. How he first got to know about their intentions was a mystery to both bride and groom. Each accused the other of telling, and each denied guilt, but there Tommy was, in on the act, in at the kill, and it was just as well that he was there, because he had thought to bring with him a borrowed wedding ring, without which the pedantic registrar refused to marry them.

The other witness was a taciturn and monastic entomologist who worked on the unpleasant and cruel life cycle of the Ichneumonidae of the Soviet Union. Harold Blake was a man who asked no questions and told no lies.

It was a stupid time to marry, just as Humphrey was about to fly off alone as the Vickery Fellow to a marine laboratory in the New World. Why not wait till he got back?

Because they both knew that if they waited, they would lose each other. Probably they had lost each other already, in the Hotel Actaeon in Chios, or somewhere on the dusty road to Athens, but there was a chance, a very small chance, that if they signed the register, they would keep whatever it was that they so feared to lose.

And if they didn't keep it, they could always get divorced. Divorce was becoming easier every year. By now, they knew plenty of people who had been divorced. The day of the no-fault divorce had not yet arrived, but it was on its way.

Getting married, said Ailsa over the wedding breakfast, *is like throwing yourself out of a high window or off a high tower, to see if you can fly.*   說得多好.

Tommy laughed. The <u>entomologist</u> appeared not to hear her. Humphrey loved her for her bravado, although she made his heart stand still with fear.

Foolhardily, for old times' sake, they took their wedding breakfast, with their two witnesses, at the Dolphin Restaurant in Frith Street. They ordered a festive oval silver platter of oysters perched upon a rocky shore of cracked ice and dark green decorative seaweed, and they drank too much Chablis. The smooth and dimpled and matronly manageress watched anxiously from the wings. She had seen everything in her time, but Ailsa was her protégée, and she did not like the way this luncheon was going. The auguries were not good. This couple was not suited for the long haul, and she had always known it. There was a wild look in Ailsa's eye, and her familiar brother Tommy was never good news. The manageress feared a scene, and tried to ration the wine. She did not want them to start their quarrelling here, in her house. She did not want to be a witness. She did not want to have to say, I told you so. She watched as Ailsa pulled off her borrowed wedding ring and handed it ostentatiously back to her brother. Tommy put it in his breast pocket, 'for', as he said 'the next time round'.

Ailsa and Humphrey Clark had already had their honeymoon, more or less for free, on board the *Bride of Abydos*. He had chivalrously proposed to her a celebratory wedding night in the Savoy, or in the Ritz, but she had declined the gesture. She had pledged herself to be an inexpensive, self-supporting, hard-working wife, a New Model Wife, and she invited him to spend the night with her, for old times' sake, in the Room. And there, in the Room, they tried to invoke the passion that they knew they had felt for each other, the passion that they willed themselves to perpetuate. They hoped that the Room itself, the scene of so many ecstatic consummations and impregnated with so much past desire, would come to their assistance. But it left them thrashing and gasping like fish on stones in a withdrawing tide.

Professor Clark, gazing at the notorious name of his first wife, Ailsa Kelman, emblazoned there in his pink folder, rapidly relived his entire life with her, like a drowning man. He saw her on the harbour wall with her thin bare legs dangling, he saw her crouching by St Cuthbert's Rock, he saw her dancing rudely on the sands, he saw her selling programmes in her little black maid's dress, he saw her chanting her gynae-cological calypso in the Tinder Box, he saw her lying naked beneath him on the stained mattress, he saw her lying flattened in her sunglasses and bikini on the whitened deck, he saw her buoyant in the waters of the Aegean, he saw her in the museum of Chios as her face furrowed with the hard intensity of giving birth to thought.

He saw her swallowing a living oyster on her wedding day. He saw her as she walked away from him at the airport terminal at Heathrow, without a backward glance. He saw her as she walked towards him at the airport terminal at Los Angeles, a month later, her face set with the determination of rejection. She was walking towards the first brief disastrous reunion of their brief married life.

He saw their afterlife. He saw the divorce papers, he saw the bills for the divorce, he saw the lawyer's cheques he signed. (She had demanded no maintenance: on that front at least, she had been true to her word. She had proved a cheap ex-wife.) He saw the headlines of her ascendant career, he saw the press photographs of her wedding to Martin Pope, he saw an announcement of the birth of her daughter Marina, he saw the second-hand news coverage of her rapidly following divorce from Martin Pope. Her second marriage was nearly as brief as her first, and the divorce had not required fabricated grounds. He saw her on television, he heard her on the radio, he read articles about her and articles by her in *The Times* and the *Guardian* and the *Daily Mail* and *New Society* and the *New York Review of Books*. He even, God help them both, saw her name in *Nature* and in the *New Scientist*. She had put herself on the agenda of the age. He looked at her books, surreptitiously, secretly, in libraries and bookshops. He bought a copy of her glossy first publication, on the rediscovery of the art of Eloise van Dieman, and gazed at its lavish illustrations in envious wonder, remembering that Ailsa Kelman had once been his bride.

He had hidden the book in a drawer, as the Kelman parents had vainly hidden John Hersey's account of the bombing of Hiroshima, but he had it still. After that, he bought no more of her publications, although he kept track of them.

In this her afterlife, it was as though their aberrant early marriage had never been. Never did she mention him, in any interview, in any discourse. She had blotted him out. No first husband ever appeared in any news item associated with her name. The first Mrs Humphrey Clark had never existed. And she stuck with her maiden name, even after her monstrous marriage to Mr Pope.

Marriage had not suited her.

He had married the second Mrs Humphrey Clark for a quiet, safe and unostentatious life, a life without risk. That had been a worse mistake. At least he and Ailsa had been young and foolish, not nearing middle age and foolish. The second Mrs Clark, now Professor Dorothy Portal Herzog, had been more demanding about the terms of the divorce. And worse than that, she had stolen his only daughter, and taken her across the Atlantic. He does not like to think about this loss, and the supine way in which he had submitted to it.

Old Professor Clark in his first-class railway carriage wonders if he is man enough to face the shame of the turbulence and failure of his first love. Ailsa Kelman has made such an exhibition of herself over the years. She has shown the worst of bad taste. She has been vulgar, strident, disgraceful. She has histrionically and hysterically bared herself in public, and boasted both of her abortions and of her androgynous amours. She has worn an aborted foetus on a chain around her neck, and submitted to a cervical examination on television. The viewing public has looked right up her vagina. She has risked imprisonment, not, like her brother Tommy, for conventional financial offences like minor fraud or insider dealing, but for what have now become known as Women's Reproductive Rights. She has appeared in court for assault, and been sued for libel. She has appeared in court as a witness in defence of oral sex, risqué art galleries, sodomy and sin.

But never, in all this wash of vulgarity and publicity and suicidal altruism, has she mentioned the name of Humphrey Clark. She has both disowned and protected him. She has left him to his dull scientific respectability, to his dishonourable ambition and his honourable research. She has never suggested, in any text or subtext of any statement she has ever issued that he has ever seen (and there was a time when he looked closely), that her hysteria has been in any way prompted by the failure of her marriage to a semi-eminent marine biologist called Humphrey Clark. She had hurled enough abuse at him during their brief marriage, but since their divorce she has never in print or on screen or as far as he knows in private accused him of being a vile man, a man of the old patriarchy, a male chauvinist, a prick or a prig. She has accused most of the other men with whom she has ever been associated of these and other offences, but she has left his name out of it. Their secret has remained a secret.

There had been a time when he had thought that Tommy might shop them. Tommy could have sold them to the *Evening Standard* for a few quid and a laugh, but he didn't. Maybe he didn't need the money. Maybe Ailsa had blackmailed him into silence: she must have known more about Tommy than Tommy could have wanted anybody to know. One way or another, Tommy had kept his mouth shut, and by now the secret was probably past its sell-by date. Ailsa was still newsworthy, but maybe not for so much longer.

The other witness to the marriage, the man called Blake, was last heard of in a psychiatric hospital in Surrey, driven mad, in Humphrey's view, by the behaviour of his Ichneumonidae. These were the creatures whose unnatural and destructive instincts had confirmed Darwin's suspicions that there was no God, and that evolution condoned all cruelties, all crimes. Blake would never have betrayed a secret, and if he were to speak now, who would believe him?

Darwin had not liked the way cats play with mice. God, in Darwin's view, would not have endorsed such behaviour.

Humphrey sighed at these memories, but then his spirits rose a little. Blake might have gone off the rails, but Ailsa was still in fighting form. And her form has not been entirely vulgar. At times, she has been splendid. Indeed, at times, she has been little short of sublime.

The Hall of the Muses

It is a classically formidable venue. Standing in the wings, she sees the platform and the podium and the screen and the carousel of slides. She can hear the undifferentiated murmuring of the audience, which is already seated in the dim, expectant hall. The lofty Palladian dome of the historic ceiling soars, and the high walls are rich with the dull gleam of the heavy gold-framed oil paintings of antique muses and eighteenth-century worthies. This audience is hard to please. It is scholarly and patrician and discriminating. It is hardened against charm and brilliance alike. It does not suffer fools gladly. The anticipatory murmur may be hostile, for the audience enjoys the spectacle of the failure of others. It has patronized events in this hall for two centuries, and it has disdained some of those who have addressed it. It does not throw eggs, or knit stockings, for it is too well-mannered for such plebeian displays of hostility or indifference. But it knows how to spurn.

Some of its members object to the very word 'venue'. But it is a useful word, and so the Committee has at last begun to employ it. The Committee moves, slowly, with the times.

The innovative young Director, standing by her side, is nervous, though he cannot yet know precisely what he has to be nervous about. Ailsa Kelman is a wild card, but she is also a fine catch, and she brings in the crowds. Not that they need 'crowds' here, but they do need to broaden their appeal, or so the Scottish Arts Council has told them. The traditional audience this evening has been augmented by the presence of some younger people, which must be thought to be a good thing. There are even said to be some students out there tonight. Students do not often bother to come to the McIveagh Memorial Lecture, although it is free for all.

The Director is nervous about Ailsa Kelman's performance, and he is also nervous about the discreet presence of television cameras. It is only the second time that they have been admitted into this venerable room, and the insurance problems have been complex. Television is a fire risk and a theft risk. Nothing will go out 'live' to the nation, of course not, but there will eventually be an edited version for public distribution showing highlights from the exhibition and clips from the lecture and close-ups of some of the more distinguished patrons. (It is interesting that the patrons, even the titled ones, seem to like to see their faces on television. They are as childish about this as those teenagers whose ambition is to appear in the audience of *Top of the Pops*, although naturally they do not admit it. They pretend to be coy, but they manage to find themselves standing at a helpful angle in front of the camera just the same.)

Ailsa has already been filmed and interviewed on a prerecorded tour of the exhibition, which is based on the theme of Byron and the liberation of Greece. This is not a very Scottish theme, but Byron was a Scot, and the ingenious Curator has managed to assemble an impressive and curious array of what may later be called Scottish Orientalism, although the word 'Orientalism' in its modern pejorative sense has not yet come into common usage – Edward Said's book on this subject had not yet been published. But the ideas of Said are blowing in the wind, and have reached Curator James McClintock and the Academy, and are now embodied in the Waverley Gallery in his eclectic display of landscapes and maidens, boats and marines, portraits and tableaux.

Ailsa Kelman had been full of admiration for the exhibition, for these ideas had also reached her and inspired her, and she had been working on them in her own free-style restless random way. Ailsa Kelman lacks method, but what she lacks in method she makes up for in energy and originality and output and panache. She has pursued Delacroix from Chios to the Louvre, and she has written and lectured on Lord Byron and Lady Caroline Lamb and the significance of fancy dress in the Regency period. She has written a pioneering study of one of Delacroix's models, a study so avant-garde that nobody, not even she, its author, realized what it signified. She has made a television series about European women who fell in love with and in the desert, a series with the (borrowed) title of *The Wilder Shores of Love*. She has skipped from the desert to the Pacific to study the sexual fantasies inspired by blue lagoons and coral atolls, for her imagination is fertile and her curiosity, though often short-lived, is insatiable. And now she is back where she started, with Byron, in the Isles of Greece. She is, at this point in her career, an admirer, though not an uncritical admirer, of Lord Byron.

Byron and Burns, those faithless lovers and shameless womanizers, have long been recognized as problematic figures by female critics. Nearly two centuries ago, Jane Austen was sharp about both of them. Ailsa Kelman takes her own line on Byron. She has not as yet addressed herself to Burns, although she knows many of his poems by heart from her schooldays and the indoctrination of Bonnie Mrs Lesley of Bonsett.

The Devil has the best tunes, says Ailsa, and the libertines write the best love songs.

The Director of the Caledonian Academy is pale of skin and has dark flowing 1970s hair. His hair is longer than Ailsa Kelman's and Lord Byron's.

Ailsa is the first woman ever to deliver the McIveagh Memorial Lecture, and both she and the Director are highly conscious of this novel aspect of the evening's proceedings. She has somehow achieved a high level of academic respectability, in a manner that evades definition and arouses considerable distrust, envy and resentment.

One would not readily divine her academic status from her dress.

One may distrust Ailsa Kelman's academic qualifications, but one can trust her to dress with deliberation. For this occasion, she has chosen to become a Muse. She has selected a flowing full-length low-bosomed pale cream dress with a silver thread woven into its fabric: her arms are encircled by bangles of silver wire, and her dark red hair is caught back in a white silk snood embellished with a few fragile little silver coins which will quiver fetchingly as she speaks. The softly draped back of the dress is cut even lower than the frontage: when she turns her back upon the audience to point at her slides, as she does frequently, she is nude to the waist, and the cleavage of her buttocks is suggestively indicated. Her shoulder blades are in full view, and so is the curve of her spine. Her eyes are heavily accented with black liner, and her lashes are theatrically enhanced. The effect of the whole is hybrid: there is a touch of the classical, a touch of the Oriental, and more than a touch of the hippie in her presentation. As she steps forward on to the rostrum, hooded old eyes open wider to appraise her effrontery. The age of opera glasses and lorgnettes is over, but spectacles are taken out of cases and polished on spotted cotton handkerchiefs and venerable scraps of chamois leather to aid a better viewing of her fine bosom and her round arms.

The miniskirt is passé, which is a relief to Ailsa, who has decided that her legs are too muscular to display to advantage.

Posture, Ailsa, posture, says Ailsa to herself, as she straightens her spine to address her task.

The lecture is mesmeric, the slides sensational. At first Dr Kelman speaks knowledgeably and solemnly and respectfully of landscapes and seascapes, of Byron and Goethe, of Sir Walter Scott and Saladin, of the Celtic and the Germanic yearning for the soft south. She contrasts images of bleakness and opulence, of shade and sun. She allows the audience to settle into her voice and her rhythm. (She has entirely lost the strangely depressed and elongated diphthongs of the Durham coalfields, and the American overlay with which she had once tried to disguise them: her voice in this middle period of her career is confidently cultured, melodious, Third Programme.) The audience, although puzzled by the contrast between speech and speaker, relaxes and decides to enjoy itself: this is a good deal less boring than that old chap from the Fitzwilliam who harangued them for fifty minutes about Poussin last year.

The audience relaxes, and Ailsa, sensing its lowered guard, goes in for the kill. She summons up to the screen a shocking image of rape and slaughter, and embarks on her proto-feminist analysis of the massively cruel canvas of Delacroix's *Death of Sardanapalus*. Detail follows detail, of breast and thigh, of buttock and throat, of knife and nostril. This is not a picture for easy communal viewing, and Ailsa's commentary and her choice of slides spare them nothing. The dying bodies writhe, the old gentlemen in the audience cough and rustle, some of the old ladies shut their eyes and try to shut their ears. It appears that Dr Kelman is mounting a pedantic defence of Byron's verse tragedy, which is said to have inspired the pornographic and sadistic vision of Eugène Delacroix. She is trying to tell them that in Byron's poem, only two people, a mere two people, die. Only Sardanapalus and his beloved Ionian slave Myrrha die, as it were on stage, and they die in fiery ecstasy by their own hands after the notional curtain falls. This vast oil painting, this tasteless and offensive spectacle of despotic torture and mass murder and female sacrifice, watched by a gloating Assyrian monarch, cannot be laid to the charge of their countryman Byron. No, the Frenchman Delacroix is the offender. Byron, the noble Scot, is innocent. And so, incidentally, for what it's worth, is Syria.

She reads to them from Byron's poem, she reads to them from unnecessarily graphic contemporary accounts of the massacres at Chios, she reads to them from the journals of Delacroix. She mentions rapes and genitals and eviscerations and disembowellings. It is very strong stuff, X-Certificate stuff. The Director is not sure whether it is a triumph or a disaster or both, but he is gripped by it. It is like nothing he has ever heard before. Here is a woman who lacks all sense of decorum, talking passionately about the lack of decorum of two great men.

He is fairly sure that nobody in the Hall of the Muses will ever have read Byron's *Sardanapalus*, though many of them will know the painting. *The Assyrian came down like a wolf on the fold*, maybe they may know that one, because it is in every anthology, but they will not know *Sardanapalus*, or even the *Giaour*. He cannot be sure if her account of Byron's poem is fair, for he has not read it himself. She compels them to listen to the obscure, the unfashionable, the unknown. It is brave. She has strayed far from her brief, and she has upstaged the Curator, but who cares? The Director does not care if his job is on the line, so full of admiration does he find himself. He is enslaved. He would drink champagne out of her slipper, as the oil-rig workers drink these days from the shoes of the whores in the pubs of Aberdeen.

Her conclusion is theatrical and superb. Having berated

poor Delacroix at length and with a display of overpowering erudition for sadism, eroticism and pornography, for abuse of models and of women and of Turks and of Greeks and of Jews and of gin, she draws to a climax by bringing up a slide of a drawing of a naked woman, seen from behind. The model is naked except for a little slipper that falls seductively from her heel. This is, as Ailsa tells them, a pastel sketch for the larger canvas, red chalk on paper. It is delicate, beautiful, fragile. She informs them that it has recently come up for sale, in a small gallery in Paris. She informs them of the high price that had been asked and indeed received. She lets the image linger on the screen.

'We must ask ourselves,' she says, 'what we feel when we look at this image. We must ask ourselves about art, anger, beauty and cruelty. Ask ourselves about the nature of Eros, and why we are attracted to these images. And we should consider the attractive title that the dealers saw fit to bestow upon this image. They sold it as "Female nude, killed from behind".'

She delivers these last five words with conviction and contempt and a tempting, collusive allure.

'Killed from behind,' she repeats. 'A high art image, by one of the greatest painters of the nineteenth century, of a naked woman, killed from behind, sketched here for our arousal and for our delight.'

And then, in a rapid swirl from her carousel, she silently projects upon the screen a shotgun, stroboscopic, barely visible sequence of slides, culled it would seem from mid-twentieth-century medium-core SM pornographic magazines, of breasts and backs and female orifices, of knives and whips and thongs, of penetrations and bodily invasions, intercut with flashes of Andromeda and Angelica in bondage culled from more orthodox sources. The involuntary response of the gathering is palpable, audible, as these violently erotic images flash almost imperceptibly by: it expresses itself in heavings and low rustlings and swellings and shiftings and indignant mutterings, but before any protest has time to formulate itself, she returns to linger on a final, frozen, haunting, arresting detail from *The Massacre at Chios*.

The beautiful dead child lies on the breast of the beautiful dead woman.

'So how can it be,' asks Ailsa rhetorically, 'that I am so much in love with the genius of Delacroix? With the *very great genius* of Delacroix?'

And Dr Kelman closes her notes, and bows, and turns her aggressively, seductively naked back and curved buttocks upon her audience, and then walks rapidly off into the wings.

The applause begins tentatively, but grows and grows, to an immense and flattering crescendo. They want her back on stage, they want to take another look at her, to see if they can believe their eyes. She returns to the platform, the lights go up, and she takes her bow.

The Director steps forward and thanks her for an historic evening, a landmark lecture, an unforgettable event. She bows, and smiles. She is a star. The applause follows her backstage.

As the Director told her much later that night, as he congratulated her more intimately in her hotel room over a rapidly emptying bottle of Macallan's malt, she had wowed them all, even the Chair of the Board.

'For e'en the ranks of Tuscany', he said, as he slid his hand beneath her firm but compliant breast, 'could scarce forbear to cheer.'

Humphrey Clark had watched on his television set, alone, the heavily edited but nevertheless sensational version of that evening's spectacle in the Caledonian Hall of the Muses. He had seized the thread of her lecture, and he had traced it back to the old museum on the island of Chios. (There is a new museum there now, called the Homerion, but he has not seen it.) He had remembered the Hotel Actaeon, and the assault of the mosquitoes, and her peculiarly insistent probing of his heel with a needle, and the proposal by the rubbish tip. He had noted that she was wearing the silver bangles that he had bought in Athens to mark their betrothal. So she had them still, she wore them still, although she was, by this stage, twice married, twice divorced. Would she know that he would watch her? Had she thought of him as she clipped the bracelets around her arms? Did she even remember who gave them to her? Did she think of him, ever, ever, ever? Did she think of the many times that he had made love to her, and of the fantasies they had enacted, the games they had played? He was the only man alive who knew that section of her history, and he had kept his knowledge to himself. A part of her lived on in him, in his body, in his consciousness, and nowhere else.

Yes, when she was young she had been, at times, sublime.

> When we two parted
> In silence and tears
> Half broken-hearted
> To sever for years . . .

Martin Pope presumably knew some other sections of her history, but Martin Pope was a cold fish, and did not understand what he knew. He knew without knowing. He had no right knowing, no bodily knowing. Of this Humphrey was convinced. He had seen Martin Pope in the flesh once, and once only, but he had seen enough.

> They know not I knew thee
> Who knew thee too well
> Long, long shall I rue thee . . .

Humphrey had followed Ailsa's career over the years from a distance, secretly. Nobody spoke of her to him, not even her brother Tommy Kelman. Once or twice, over the years, late at night or in forlorn anonymous hotels, Humphrey had thought of ringing her. He had this notion that she would answer him, and that they would be able to speak to each other, and that no harm would be done, and that the harm that had been done would be undone. But he had no number and no voice and his words stalled before they began to shape. The current was dammed.

His second wife Dorothy knew the bald facts and dates of his brief first marriage (shamingly, he had been obliged to provide his divorce papers and his decree absolute in order to marry again) but she had been more than happy to enter the Ailsa-denying conspiracy of silence. Stout, dull, clever, plodding lab assistant Dorothy had been happy enough to snap up Humphrey Clark, and to obliterate the catastrophe of Ailsa. She had jumped at his proposal. Now, looking back, he realized that she had angled for it. Her career prospects were at that time poor, and his were good. He was a good match, a good catch. At that time, he had thought he was being adult in marrying the subordinate Dorothy. Mature, adult, responsible. Not immature, impulsive, romantic. He would look no more for Eros and Perfect Happiness. He would settle for a supportive, secondary, faithful, caring, capable wife.

It hadn't worked out quite like that. Nor had he deserved that it should.

Ailsa Kelman had not invented feminism or Women's Studies or Orientalism single-handed, but she had been there as they gestated, she had been there as they were being born, she had played her part in their history.

And so, through her, had he.

He had seen her thinking. He had seen her struggle, and then he had seen her thoughts dart free from her, like silver minnows. Her thoughts were free and fast and fluid, and found their own way into the current of the mainstream.

Her lecture on Byron and Delacroix had been a first draft for what was soon to follow. She had moved on, to the theme of Gender, Art and Anger, and then she had tired of that, and had taken up sociology and the iconography of domesticity and Mass Observation. She had written a book about Mass Observation techniques and the inter-war and post-war life of the housewife. He had never read it, but he had read about it. She had edited a book (with funding from the Wellcome Trust) on the history of hypochondria and patent remedies and the once-fashionable and predominantly female afflictions of neuritis and neuralgia and 'nerves', now subsumed, according to her, under the equally imprecise label of 'depression'. (Her essay entitled 'And then her health broke down' was greeted as a landmark, though its claims have since been hotly disputed.) She had made programmes about house and home in the 1930s. For a brief period she had perversely and provocatively sung the success of suburbia, and she had narrated the history of the vacuum cleaner. She had a knack of dramatizing the familiar, of making it appear weird and strange. Humphrey, covertly watching her demonstrating on screen both the practical capacities and metaphorical significance of the Hoover and the Electrolux, had remembered the undusted unswept filthy glamorous squalor of the Room.

At times, in his forties, in his fifties, he dreamed vividly of the Room. Most of these dreams were unpleasant dreams of exposure and shame, in which a wall of the Room would dissolve or fall, and he and she would be discovered in bed, entangled, in flagrante, lying naked to the gaze of his parents, or of cameras, or of colleagues, or of students, or of strangers. Occasionally, a benign dream came to him, in which she lay by his side with her head on his broad shoulder, breathing peacefully, breathing in unison, sharing the rhythm of his rest.

Which were the true dreams, and which the false?

All were false, for she was gone, and the past was dead, and they had denied one another.

Bored with the Hoover and the lower middle classes, she had then ascended the social scale to examine the lives of late-nineteenth-century nouveau riche wives who were afraid of and dominated by their own superior professional domestic staff. She had found some good diaries to illustrate her thesis, but he had found these excursions less interesting, and had not bothered to try to follow them.

During their brief marriage, he had not been allowed to meet her mother, that genteel one-time lady's maid. But he remembered Mrs Kelman from his childhood, sleeping in her deckchair, sitting in the Crescent Picture House, walking poor old quivering Monty along the prom.

And now, in his sixties, he was on his way northwards, towards the reunion he had been avoiding for so many decades.

His most frequently recurring dream now is that he is standing on a sandy shore, or on the bank of a river, and is about to immerse himself joyfully, and to swim deeper into the clear water: but in his dream he never reaches the water, for at his approach it recedes, or dries up, or vanishes, and leaves him dry and beached and stranded.

This dream does not require much interpretation.

He looks at the pink folder, and the name that lies there, and swallows hard, and forces himself, with much foreboding, to read the brief biography that accompanies her name and her shrunken passport-sized publicity photograph.

Ailsa Kelman, scholar and feminist, is celebrated for her pioneering studies of gender and for her gift for lucid and dramatic exposition. Born in Bonsett, County Durham, she is renowned around the world for her courageous explorations of women's achievements, ambitions and limitations. Her classic works include her ground-breaking study of the artist Eloise van Dieman and her analysis of the Bohemian space occupied by the artist's model (both male and female) in fact and in fiction, but she is known to a much wider public for her television presentations of the paradoxes and mixed messages of everyday domestic life and sexual deviance. The University of Ornemouth is proud to recognize her unique achievements as a cultural historian in an area that she has made her own, but into which she has welcomed many of her admirers.

Professor Humphrey Clark reads this short summary of the past forty years of Ailsa's eventful life with admiration and a mute surprise. It is remarkable both for its discretion and its literacy. He could not have put it better himself. He could not have put it as well. He could never have encompassed Ailsa's career with this precise and generous clarity. Whoever wrote this knew who its subject was and what she had done. Whether the author knows the subject personally is not manifest, but the encomium has authority. It avoids the word 'celebrity', which in the context of Ailsa's biography has become almost unavoidable, and it refrains from mentioning any detail of her private life. There is nothing here carried mindlessly and lazily over from old press files, and there is no mention of the scandalous and tired story of the foetus-on-a-chain. There is no allusion either to Martin Pope or to Tommy Kelman. There are no misspelled words, no grammatical errors, no solecisms.

The restraint is unusual, the tone encouraging. 'Lucid and dramatic exposition' is a felicitous and, one might say, a forgiving phrase.

Professor Clark looks out of the window, and then he looks down at his large-faced waterproof watch. Ornemouth is less than two hours away, if there are no more delays or unscheduled stops.

The old LNER train used to take seven hours, from Coventry to Ornemouth.

The waterproof watch was given to him by his parents for his twenty-first birthday. It has kept good time, even underwater, amongst the fishes. It had been the last word in its day, and it is still a faithful timepiece.

No, there is no mention of her second husband Martin Pope. Pope too is still a 'celebrity', although his name is less fashionable, less current, more arcane than Ailsa's. Martin Pope had more or less abandoned the theatre for opera, and Humphrey does not follow opera. He goes to concerts occasionally, alone, but not to the opera or to the ballet, except when he is invited for public occasions, to make up a party. The programme for special occasions consists usually of mainstream work. Martin Pope's productions have become mannered, minimalist, some say mad.

Humphrey had recently met a young woman whom he took to be the daughter of Martin Pope and Ailsa Kelman, although he had not during their brief encounter worked out her identity and parentage. It had come to him later, as he was walking home from Burlington House through illustrious night-time Mayfair towards Portland Place and Regent's Park. The child had had a look of her mother, and had been indicatively named. Marina Pope was employed by a learned society, and had been delegated to look after him at a gathering in honour of a Fellow of his old college. He had half-recognized her name because she had pinned it helpfully to her bosom, though he had not at first taken in its message.

They had chatted, agreeably: she was well briefed, and had asked him about the Green Grotto, as people did, but her manner had been so unassuming and so lacking in innuendo that he had been able to respond pleasantly, without displaying the prickling spines of resentment. She had told him that her seven-year-old son Sam liked fish, and that she had taken him to the South Bank Aquarium, where he had stroked the flounders in the Touch Tank. She had never been to the Green Grotto: should she take Samuel there too? And did the fish enjoy being petted, or was it cruel to touch them? Sam longed to go for a Sleepover in the Green Grotto, and to sleep on an inflatable mattress amongst the illuminated fish tanks. Should she encourage him? Would it be a fun thing to do?

Of course, of course, said Humphrey.

The Sleepover was one of the better initiatives of the Grotto.

'I'd have loved to have been able to do that, when I was a boy,' said Professor Clark. 'I thought of taking my grandson, when he was over from Boston, but I'm too old for that kind of caper now.'

Marina Pope was pretty, tentative, gentle of speech, and somewhat sad and diminished of demeanour. She looked tired. Working late hours, if you have small children, is tiring. Even he knew that.

At least she had not ended up as a foetus in a necklace, or as an advertisement for abortion law reform.

Was it his fault, wondered Humphrey, walking home, that the child had looked so pale? Was it his fault that Ailsa had gone back to Martin Pope, like a dog to its vomit, and married him? Damage has no limitations.

'*Always ready to accept responsibility . . .*' his school reports had said.

Of course it was not his fault.

He knew that whatever had happened to Ailsa's daughter was nothing to do with him, but he could not prevent his mind from moving along the old tracks.

When he had reached home that night, sitting in his large and solitary apartment, listening to the howls of the wolves of the Zoo, he had been unable to resist consulting the dangerous red-bound gold-lettered reference book, and had, by cross-checking, established that both Ailsa Kelman and Martin Pope laid claim to *one daughter* as issue of their cross-referred but long defunct marriage.

So that had indeed been Marina Pope, who was, after a manner of speaking, his stepdaughter. His secret stepdaughter.

He wondered if Marina knew who was the father of the half-brother or half-sister who had dangled on a chain around her mother's neck.

Ailsa was a brute.

So, he and Ailsa Kelman had but one child each, one daughter each. There was a symmetry in that. He had lost his daughter to America, but maybe Ailsa had maintained better contact with hers.

Maybe he would ask her. Maybe when he saw her he would be able to risk saying to her something trivial, something friendly, like, 'Ailsa, how good to see you again, after all these years, I met your lovely daughter recently at Burlington House, did she tell you?'

Is that how it could be resolved? In simple-hearted social friendliness? Human beings are very good at triviality. They can adapt to almost any level of social intercourse. They can live better, perhaps, in the shallows than in the depths. It had been his mistake to try to descend too far.

The press release describing Ailsa is so unexpectedly acceptable that, fortified, he turns the pages of the leaflet to find the entry on his own life and work, hoping that maybe it will restore his confidence in himself and tell him who he is and why he is here. His paranoia over the last few years has become intense, at times disabling, although, like many paranoids, he has made a good job of concealing it.

Paranoia has made him a lonely man. A lonely public man. There are many of these, but he has the rare distinction of knowing what he is.

He dreads the cursory dismissal, the patronizing compliment. But why should he find them here, when it is honour to him that is intended?

Hic labor, hoc opus est.

What he finds is acceptable to him. His curriculum vitae has more of the ring of an obituary than Ailsa's, but that is not surprising, for she is now more in the public eye than he. He reads that he was born in Covington, but had spent '*formative boyhood years in Ornemouth, which contributed to his love of marine life*'. His innovative work on the underwater tagging of wrasse, his study of habitat preference and population growth, his successful directorship of the laboratory, his early election to the Royal Society and his skills as an administrator are all accorded a brief space. There is no mention of Portal or of Moule or, more surprisingly, of the Green Grotto. Nor is there an account of his dead-end study of the structure of the parathyroid hormone, a study so devastatingly and successfully completed by Portal and Herzog. That section of his life is as though it had never been: it has been excised as neatly as though the protective Mrs Hornby herself had dictated the terms.

(Maybe she had?)

The mini-essay ends,

Professor Clark will be remembered not only for his scientific achievements but also for his ability to convey the complexity of the myriad interdependent but individual lives that make up the marine environment. In an age of increasing specialization, his most widely read work, *The Immortal Shore*, is a reminder that, though we may see eternity in a grain of sand, we may not discover it so easily in a laboratory.

He reads these last sentences over and over again, looking for the hidden barb. Does it imply that he has wrenched success out of failure? Is he being dismissed as a second-rate scientist, as a popularizer, as a soft-bellied and sentimental ecologist, as a waffler of codswallop? He recognizes the quotation from Blake, for it is a quotation much used by scientists and science journalists, but it seems to be used here with an unusual if enigmatic care.

He wonders who is responsible for the wording of these brief eulogia, and whether the Public Orator will be up to the mark. He thinks that maybe he should have spent more time preparing a proper speech for his address the next day. He has his notes, but maybe they will not be adequate. The Ornemouth standard, he now belatedly discovers, is unexpectedly high. It was wrong of him to have thought he could mumble and ad lib his way through, on the lazy and patronizing grounds that Ornemouth is a small, new, provincial university in a small border town. To Oxford or Cambridge or St Andrews, to Chicago or San Diego, he would have paid more respect.

It is true that he had spent '*formative boyhood years in Ornemouth*', although this aspect of his intellectual history is not always invoked. He has not kept it secret, and indeed he had assumed that there was a link between the invitation, the honour and his sojourn in Finsterness. But it is surprising to find it thus singled out for mention, when so much else of his career has been mercifully omitted.

The programme for the degree ceremony displays coloured photographs of the university campus and of some of its halls and buildings. The campus covers a green-field site, a mile or two inland from the little port and the Old Town, but it is centred on Hawick Old Hall, an old mansion that has been rescued by academe from neglect and death duties. During the war, it had been commissioned as a girls' boarding school, and after standing empty for some years had passed into a transitional phase as a Field Study Centre.

Humphrey cannot remember anything of the Old Hall's history. He is not sure that he has ever seen it. It had not been part of his boyhood map. Had it been too far away, or out of bounds, or merely uninteresting to small boys? He remembers vividly the beach-hut café, and the mound of dried excrement, and Sandy and Tommy's escapade to the cement runways. He can remember the Crescent Picture House. He can remember St Cuthbert's Rock and Barbed Wire Island. But Hawick Old Hall is a blank.

How small their world had been, and yet how illimitably vast.

He looks again, hardened now to memories, at Ailsa's paragraph. The only topographical reference there is to her place of birth, which also has a contextual significance, for it marks her out as a child of the north. Universities tend towards the distribution of regional favours. Bonsett is less than a hundred miles from Ornemouth, and thus is well within its sparsely populated catchment area. Ornemouth can lay legitimate claim to the Kelmans. He wonders if Ailsa Kelman has received honorary degrees from the more ancient universities of her past and her heritage, from Durham, or from Edinburgh, or from Newcastle. He had not thought to look for these distinctions, when he had guiltily and furtively opened the perilous paranoid red book in search of the pedigree of Marina Pope.

He thinks of his mother's collection of St Cuthbert's beads, so carefully gathered on the shore at Finsterness. They had survived for many millions of years, and they had survived the return to Covington: where were they now? He thinks of St Cuthbert, and of the Venerable Bede, and of the plump and friendly mild-faced seals that swam companionably in the shallows round Holy Island, like illustrations of Elaine Morgan's aquatic hypothesis.

His mother would have been proud of his worldly success, but she had not been very pleased when she had discovered that he had once been married to the notorious Ailsa Kelman. He had told her, during her last illness, at her bedside, thinking it right to confess before she died, but she had pretended not to hear, and she had never again alluded to his youthful indiscretion. He did not know whether or not she had passed the information on to her daughters. If she had, they too had kept their mouths shut. Denial is an easy English route.

His mother had thought that his wife Dorothy Portal was a nice girl. He had not disabused her. She had lived to see her granddaughter, but she had not lived to witness the divorce.

He sighs, and resigns himself to the task of looking through the rest of his pink folder of paperwork. Now is the time to memorize the names of the Vice Chancellor and the Public Orator, of the other fellow-graduands, of the senior professors. He is acquainted with the head of the Department of Marine Biology, a St Andrews man called Jimmy Ruthven, but other members of the department are unfamiliar to him. And he must get to grips with the timetable. There is a reception, this evening, at the Queen's Hotel, to be followed by a dinner, and in the morning there will be an assembly at the bell tower, a procession through the town, a motorcade to the university, the degree ceremony, the speeches, the recessional, the luncheon at Hawick Hall. He need not fear to look, for he has surely seen the worst that the folder can hold.

It will be a day of instant new traditions. The famous old boat of the year of the great flood, the *Damsel*, has been restored, and she will be wheeled through the streets as part of the procession.

The great flood was well before Humphrey's time. He had never seen the *Damsel*, and is surprised to discover, from these notes, that this story of this vessel's intrepid rescues had long been considered one of the most celebrated episodes in the town's history. He had never heard of the *Damsel*, as a boy, although he had known all about Grace Darling. Perhaps the *Damsel* is a fake heritage item, invented for the occasion.

The Chancellor, he learns, is Lord Lanark of Lanark, the Public Orator is Dr Alistair Macfarlane, and the Vice Chancellor is Professor Helen Sinclair. These are all good northern names. Maybe they are all local names, from the Borders. But he cannot discover much from the names alone. By this evening, these names will have become flesh, but for now they are words on paper. *Lanark, Macfarlane, Sinclair*, he repeats to himself, not very confidently. L. M. S.

LMS, LNER, LMS.

He depends much on mnemonics these days, but they do not always do the trick.

Dolerite and whinstone, granite and sandstone.

These words of the earth are not a mnemonic, they are more of a lullaby. He has been reciting them for months now to lull himself to sleep in the small hours.

When he was a child, he hadn't realized that dolerite and whinstone were different names for the same stone. He'd thought they were two different substances. But they are the same, under different names. Like zebras and leopard sharks. *Stegostoma fasciatum.* Some of the happiest weeks of his life had been spent with the sharks in the clear and warm and weightless waters of the Indian Ocean.

Lanark, Macfarlane, Sinclair. He should have checked all these names out earlier, discovered their hobbies, their marital status, their publications, the numbers of their children and grandchildren.

There will be more colour added to the names of the fellow-guests.

He turns the page, and inspects the tiny photograph of a well-known soprano, showing a bare-throated round-faced young-middle-aged woman with a great deal of bouffant curly hair. She is captioned as Dame Mary McTaggart, a name which seems almost ridiculously familiar to him, although he cannot think that he has ever met or seen its owner. He must have heard her on the radio, seen her name many times subliminally in the press. He applies himself to the print, and is told that although Scottish by descent, she was born in Canada. She has sung around the world (famous venues, directors and co-stars are mentioned) but has also in recent years been *highly praised for her roles nearer home with the Winter Palace Company. She is as distinguished for her interpretations of traditional Scottish folk song as she is for her work with some of the more innovative groups in Britain. Her pure and soaring siren voice bears us with its disembodied magic to dangerously enchanted realms.*

So here is another northerner, receiving honour both for herself and for her ancestry. Her Scottishness must be part of the deal. Again, he recognizes the literary allusion, for one of the very few records possessed by his aunt and grandmother in Finsterness had been a scratchy but enthralling rendering of some famous singer pouring forth various popular

Victorian parlour arias, of which Mendelssohn's most famous piece had been one:

> On wings of song I'll bear thee
> Enchanted realms to see
> Come O my love prepare thee
> In dreamland to wander with me.
> By the banks of the Ganges we'll wander . . .

These words come back to him from the past, from the Sunday evenings of childhood, along with a sense of the melancholy, boundless intensity of yearning, the oceanic desires and aspirations, the certainty of an ever-extending future. To his embarrassment he feels his eyes fill with tears. He tells himself, sharply, that he has become a sentimental old fool. A foolish old curmudgeon, and an old fool to boot.

He looks back at his own citation, searching once more for ambiguities and insults, and then, again, he re-reads the praise of Ailsa. He thinks of the shifting sands, the quick and shifting sands of reputation. He thinks of the sands of life and of time, and of the old wooden egg timer that hung on the kitchen wall at Burnside Avenue.

The Bebb-Whistler Prize, the Vickery Fellowship, the Chancellor Medal, the Fellowship of the Royal Society, the Gomme-Hardy Chair . . .

The programme says that the soprano will sing for them this evening, after the dinner: there will be no after-dinner speeches, but, in their place, a 'short recital' by Dame Mary. It does not say whether her choice of song will be traditional or innovative.

On wings of song I'll bear thee . . .

The high notes whine and keen in his head from the grooves of the brittle old black recording, and as he listens to them, a short but large woman passes conspicuously towards him through the compartment, clutching in her hand a square brown paper buffet bag which smells strongly of bacon burger. As she draws nearly level with him, the train gives a sudden lurch, and she grabs the back of the empty seat opposite, then straightens herself, murmuring a diffuse and unnecessary apology. Their eyes meet, at an uncomfortably close proximity, and he knows that she identifies him. He knows that canny look of recognition. He can see that she considers speaking to him, and then thinks better of the impulse, for, having regained her balance, she goes on her way, with comic dignity, proceeding past him towards the adjoining compartment. The doors open themselves for her, and she disappears through them to her retreat with her shameful <u>booty.</u>

It is Dame Mary. He has summoned up this apparition by his reading of the programme notes.

He hopes that Ailsa is not on the same train. He knows that Ailsa is not on the same train. He would have felt her pulsing and rustling and pumping through his valves, and forcing her way through his veins and his <u>arteries.</u>

Dame Mary does not look very much like her miniature publicity photograph, although she is surrounded by an unmistakably operatic aura. Her hair, in the thumbnail image <u>copious</u> and dark and conventionally well-coiffed, is now cropped defiantly short and trim and tight about her skull, and it is dyed an unnatural apricot-orange. It sprouts like stubble. He has had time to take in that she has a considerable double chin (he strokes the folds of his own throat) and that she is dressed colourfully, in a shapeless mid-calf gown of brilliant blue, of the vaguely ethnic style often favoured by fat but fearless ladies. Her bosom is looped with a triple string of bright green beads. She is a spectacle, and her face has a jolly determination, a set chuckle.

After her stumble she had recovered herself, and walked off stoutly. If she had not been about to <u>munch</u> her way through a gross bacon burger, she would have stopped to introduce herself.

But soon, on the platform of the bright, quaint geranium-and-lobelia-tubbed Victorian station at Ornemouth, beneath the pretty fretted white-painted wooden canopy, they will meet. A car will be waiting for them, to take them to the Queen's Hotel.

He gazes out of the window, and waits for the great arches to appear.

Ailsa Kelman has already settled into the hotel. She has parked her little red hire car, and checked in, and she is sitting perched in the armchair in the window bay of her first-floor bedroom, leaning forward and looking out towards the sea and the promenade. The hotel is on the lowest terrace of the sloping hillside rising inland to the south of the town, and it commands a good view. Below lies the <u>levelled</u> terrace of the putting green, bordered by orderly municipal flowerbeds of red, white and blue: to the left, the harbour and the cobbles and the steep narrow wynds of the Old Town, and beyond that, round the promontory and to the north, invisible Finsterness. It is late afternoon, and she is possessed by a near-overwhelming sense of fatigue. Her buoyancy has deserted her, and she feels her age, and worse. She cannot face Humphrey Clark, and she is frightened of imminent death. If she sits back, or lies down on her bed, she will die. Energy is draining out of her like water out of a basin. She has kept going all day, but now she is tempted to give up, and to give in.

In the hotel car park, she had found a space with a sign saying 'Reserved for Lady Drivers Only'. She had occupied it gratefully, too tired to worry about whether its message was very modern or very old-fashioned. It was a space, and it was easy of access, and she had taken it.

She tells herself that it is not surprising that she is tired, for during the day she has travelled many hundreds of miles, and journeyed backwards through many decades. She has had a busy week, and she has been up since dawn, and she will be late to bed this night. The day has been exhausting, and its memories full of accusation. But she is incapable of admitting the concept of exhaustion. Exhaustion is for lesser spirits, for the old, for the weak, for the failing. And she will never join their ranks. She is immortal, for she was born into the confident baby-boom generation of the high-earning, high-spending, fearless, untiring immortals. So she sits there, to attention, leaning forward towards the distant mirror of the sea. The air is still, the silvery-blue water smooth like glass. She cannot see, from here, the little curls of the small waves as they break.

Along that modest little promenade she had walked with her mother and her father and her brother Tommy and that long-dead dog, in an agony of premature resentment, impatience and self-pity. Tommy, Humphrey, and that other boy called Sandy Clegg. In one of their more ludicrous quarrels in that dreadful semester in California, she had accused her poor husband Humphrey of having been enamoured of the boy called Sandy, and then of having had a yen for his handsome Greek diving colleague Iannis. She had accused poor Humphrey of being 'queer', for that was the word they used in those days. This had been a ridiculous, a random accusation. He was a 'straight' chap, whatever one might mean by that term, and moreover a decent chap, and she had used him horribly. She had got in his way. And on the rebound from the disaster of their affair and brief marriage he had stupidly married that plain woman who had won the Nobel or married the Nobel or whatever it was that she had done. Humphrey had married another clever woman, who had ditched him. And it had all been Ailsa Kelman's fault. Without her, Humphrey Clark could have been a happy man, happily married to some suitable woman, and in command of honour, love, obedience, troops of friends. She had set him off course.

It was she herself, as she had later discovered, who could lay a more legitimate claim to bisexual leanings. But maybe those leanings had been merely a fashionable phase of feminism, a rite of passage through which all women of the 1960s and 1970s were obliged to make their way? She liked women, she had made friends with women, but she had much preferred sexual intercourse with men.

After Humphrey, she had slept with many men, as was the vogue, and she had stopped counting. But she had married only once more, and that once had been a grave error, committed through vanity, greed and ambition. She had married Martin Pope because he was rich, and powerful, and cunning, and well placed: because he had not been born in Bonsett or Covington but in the London Clinic: because he had been to Eton and King's. She had married him because he had asked her to marry him, and because she had wanted to usurp the bed place of a film star. She had married him because he had surprised and flattered her by asking her to do so.

She had married him, in a fit of weakness, for security.

She had lived to regret this mistake.

Now she lived and slept alone, and here she sat, alone in a hotel room, tense with expectation.

She believed that Humphrey lived and slept alone, in an old-world bachelor apartment overlooking Regent's Park.

Sometimes she had thought of giving him a ring, out of the blue, but had restrained herself. She'd done him enough damage already.

She had never met Dorothy Portal, but she had seen her picture in the papers. Dorothy Portal might be a clever woman, and she might have won half a Nobel Prize for parathyroid hormones, but she does not photograph well.

What was I so cross *about*, Ailsa asks herself, when I was a child? She remembered her mother's unpleasing refrain, 'If you don't stop yelling, I'll give you something to yell about.' But her mother hadn't dared, or not very often. Her mother had been frightened of her. Once, or perhaps more than once, Ailsa had been handed over to her timid father, who had beaten her ritually on the bottom with the back of a black varnished Pearson Mason hairbrush as she lay face down screaming with fury on her little bed. She'd tried hard to recover any erotic elements of this incident during her talking cure, elements that could have influenced her later sexual predilections, but was not convinced that she had succeeded. Her father was not suitable material for that kind of fantasy. All right, she knew that wasn't the *point* of a fantasy, but truly, her *father*, if you had *seen* him . . .

And the hard bristles of the hairbrush had been disgustingly matted with her mother's wiry grey hairs. The bristles sprouted fiercely out of a repulsively convex pink fleshly oval dome.

No, what she remembered was not sex but rage. She remembered indignation, self-importance, a refusal to submit to subjugation, either by person or tribe or race or gender, or by the filthy little town into which she had happened to have been born.

She could see, from the hotel's slight elevation, the people strolling along the promenade below, taking their sober evening walk as they had done for a century and more. Once, on that summer holiday, the Kelmans had repaired to this hotel, the best hotel in town, for their tea. It was a treat, to celebrate her parents' wedding anniversary. She had eaten a slice of chocolate cake with a cake fork. The cake had been filled with a deliciously sweet pale pinkish-brown artificial cream. There had been shocking-pink iced cochineal fancies, on a cake stand, and she had eaten one of those as well.

Then they had gone back to Mrs Binns for plaice and scalloped potatoes, and she had not been able to finish her portion. 'Your eyes were bigger than your tummy,' Mrs Binns had said to her, more as a joke than as a reproof, as she removed the plate with its distressed fillet of uneaten fish. Ailsa had found this phrase extraordinarily offensive and humiliating. She hadn't asked for the plate full of plaice. She didn't want to eat its wet white flesh and its orange spotted skin, cunningly concealed beneath the vinegary yellow batter. And her eyes weren't bigger than her tummy. Her eyes were a normal size. She wasn't a sea monster.

One evening in Burnside Avenue Humphrey Clark had shown her his pictures of the monsters of the deep. He had shown her the vampire squid, and the hideous female angler, which she had much admired. But she had not liked the drawing of the fish with a grotesquely extended external stomach, a stomach into which it had engorged a whole fish larger than its own body. The big-bellied fish had frightened her, and she had never forgotten it. She had not admitted to fear, but she had been afraid. ~~sad~~

She hears the plaintive, angry cry of the gulls.

One summer, from Scarborough, in a fit of boredom, she had written a soppy and obsequious little letter to Uncle Mac on *Children's Hour* on the radio about kittiwakes, and puffins, and about Ailsa Craig, her namesake rock, the breeding ground and home of the gannet, a seafowl also known as the Solon goose. The common plants on Ailsa Craig grow strangely large, she had helpfully informed Uncle Mac, because of all the guano. On Ailsa's rock the red campion, the white dead nettle and the wild hyacinth had flourished, and seals had thrived in the Mermaid's Cave. She had been trying to impress Uncle Mac with her precocious learning, which she had gleaned from a couple of pamphlets. She had never been to her namesake rock. She has still not been to her namesake rock. All her life, she has been trying to impress the world with her learning. She had been in love with learning. She is still in love with learning. Knowledge is sadism, said Sigmund Freud. Once, she had been innocent and had not known what Freud meant, but now she knows.

The people stroll, up and down, dying slowly as they walk.

She longs to lie on her bed, to put her feet up, to rest, but she is afraid that if she lies down and shuts her eyes, she will die. Her lady from Rio has tried to help her to overcome this fear, and she sleeps better at night now in her sixties than she had slept in her haunted, hag-ridden and panic-stricken fifties, but still she dreads the horror of the sleep in the afternoon, the horror of the waking from the little death.

So she stays awake, on duty.

Her parents had slept, side by side, in their striped deckchairs, of an afternoon, in Ornemouth, in Scarborough, facing the sea. Even in the bitter wind, they had dozed, stoically, fearlessly, indifferently, her mother's head tied up in a scarf, her father's covered with a cloth cap.

In the old days, there had been a machine in the little amusements arcade on the front, which told your fortune. You put a copper penny into the slot in the hand of the Robot King, and pressed the red Impulse Button on his stomach, and then he whirred and his eyes flashed and his head wagged, and when the whirring stopped a card with your fortune printed on it was excreted from beneath his feet into a little bronze metal cup.

Tommy said it was a waste of a penny. He liked the machine with a spring lever and little balls that whizzed round and rolled until they dropped noisily into Win-or-Lose slots. If you were clever you could win your money back, and sometimes more. It was more skill than luck, said Tommy. If you leaned hard on the machine from the left and joggled it a bit, the ball was more likely to go into the Win hole. He'd tried it lots of times, and he knew.

Ailsa's little printed fortunes had always been <u>propitious</u>. The Robot King unfailingly promised her fame and riches. The Robot King had been on her side, and his prophecies had been fulfilled. But by now she had forgotten how to identify herring gulls and gannets and kittiwakes. She had forgotten many of the things she had once known.

These circling birds were common gulls. They were not even black-backed gulls.

In Helsinki once (or perhaps it was in Oslo) her hotel room looking over the port had been furnished with a heavy pair of binoculars, chained by a handsome nautical fake-antique chain to a brass ring set in the ledge of the window seat. (It must have been Oslo, because of Edvard Munch, of whom she was then fleetingly in pursuit.)

The Queen's Hotel is a little smarter than it had been in the bleak post-war austerity years, but it still has a nostalgic and old-fashioned feel to it. The bathroom is large, and the deep claw-footed bath and its verdigris-stained silver taps are original. The spacious bedroom has not yet been cut up into ill-proportioned box compartments, though it may be, in time, for the population of Ornemouth has been growing steadily since the foundation of the new university, and demand for hotel accommodation is on the increase. The fishing industry has declined, the academic industry has expanded.

Knowledge is sadism, said Freud.

There are no luxury binoculars here to amuse her, but there is a bowl of deep red roses, and a smooth glass decanter of sherry, accompanied by a couple of very small glasses. It is years since she saw a decanter filled with amber sherry. This is so old-fashioned that she can almost believe it is avant-garde.

The sherry is the colour of the amber sliver of Pears soap.

The Public Orator, from his hidden vantage point, trains his binoculars on Ailsa Kelman's window. He knows which room is hers, for he had made sure of it in person. Will she advance towards the window, and wrestle with the double glazing, and pull up the old-fashioned sash, and lean out, and expose herself to his view? He cannot see her. She may be in there, for he knows that she has checked into the hotel, and parked in the Lady's Parking Space, but she is not yet in his sights. Maybe she is changing for the reception and the dinner.

> O Ailsa, at thy window be,
> It is the true, the trysted hour . . .

He is already dressed for the occasion, in the dinner jacket specified by the gilt-edged invitation.

He scans the promenade, looking for Professor Humphrey Clark or for Dame Mary. They may be taking a turn, taking the sea air, together or separately, before the evening's programme begins. They have travelled, as he knows, on the same train. They will by now have been introduced to each other. Their interaction, for better or worse, has begun.

He cannot see either of them.

The Public Orator knows exactly what to expect from the current physical manifestation of Ailsa Kelman, for he had watched her live, a couple of nights ago, on television, as she presented the Plunkett Prize to Paul Burden for the book called *Hermaphrodite*. He had seen the cones of her iron-clad breasts in their casing of chain mail. He suspects that she is planning to wear the same armour tonight. She will have thought it not inappropriate.

He had searched the television audience for a glimpse of Humphrey Clark, but had not been able to spot anybody who could plausibly have been him. He had feared that the Plunkett Prize ceremony might pre-empt and upstage his own little drama, but a telephone call on the following morning to his chief spy had reassured him that Professor Clark had declined an invitation to the Plunkett Prize and the Marine Hall, and had spent at least part of the evening talking university politics with Professors Roberts and Freeman at the Athenaeum.

To Ornemouth, as the Public Orator had planned, would belong the honour and the confrontation.

The Public Orator takes a small and cautious sip from his preparatory glass of whisky. He must take it easy, for it will be a long night.

He lifts his binoculars again, and focuses once more on the bedroom window of Ailsa Kelman. And, as he watches, he sees her emerge from the shadowy depths of the room. He can see that she is wearing the white hotel towelling bathrobe. She advances towards the window and stands there, overlooking the hotel terrace and the geranium-planted urns and the flowerbeds and the putting green. Then, slowly, deliberately, she takes hold of either edge of the robe, one lapel in each hand, and pulls it open, to expose her naked breasts. She stands there, like a figurehead, defiantly holding her robe wide open, and breasting the swell of the seafront and the sea air and the penetration of his unseen but surely imagined gaze.

The reception is building up its volume of chatter and clatter, as it recovers from the respectful feudal lull that had accompanied the unexpectedly early arrival of the young duke. The late father was always late, as dukes are expected to be, but his son, young Gerry, does not seem yet to have caught on to the proprieties, and had arrived when the Neptune Suite was still embarrassingly under-peopled. His chauffeur had dropped him off early, and ruthlessly abandoned him for the evening. The dutiful Vice Chancellor had been there ready and waiting to greet him, to be sure, and so had the omnipresent and omniscient Public Orator, but others of the more distinguished guests were yet to show. Luckily, Dame Mary appeared in full fig only a couple of minutes after the duke and saved their bacon. Full of fizzle and bubble and pop she had been: *Gerry darling, Mary darling, Oh you naughty thing, why didn't you come to stay at the castle, I told you, Gerry darling, I need my beauty sleep, I am Cinderella these days, I need to be in my bed by midnight, and the castle is so haunted and so creaky, and last time I stayed a little mouse ran under my bed, now Mary don't tell tales, I swear to you, Gerry, a little grey mouseling, with whiskers . . .*

Dame Mary in her voluminous shiny royal-blue satin and jewels was a mercy, she makes enough noise to fill any gap, she's the kind of good sport who would always make things go with a swing, her hair's a strange cut and colour, people say it's cancer and chemo, but with theatre people how can you tell, and there's Lord Lanark, he's a grim-faced old stick, but people say he's a decent old boy really, but then they would say that, wouldn't they, and that's Martin Gibson, the laird of the salmon fishery, at least I think it is, or is it Professor Rickwort from Reykjavik, and that's Vice Chancellor Helen Sinclair, she's an epidemiologist, a what, an epidemiologist, she studies epidemics, at least I think that's what she is, or was, I suppose she's too busy running things to do any real work now, it's been a good thing for the town, don't you think, well, it's nice having some young people about for a change, not many young people here tonight, are there, well, you wouldn't expect them tonight, would you, this is for the top brass, for the likes of you and me.

White, please. Thank you. She's going to sing, later. That'll be nice. Well, maybe. Do you remember that *Beggar's Opera* they did last year? Don't remind me, what a night, I thought I'd die, I thought I'd never get back to my bed.

It will be a very public meeting. Humphrey had thought of sending a little note of warning round to her room, more for the sake of his own dignity than of hers, for he is sure she must have known the game and the score. But he had been unable to think of any words to express the diverse and indeed unidentifiable emotions that assailed him. It is better to meet here, in the open, surrounded by an indifferent crowd which will not know of their conjoined past. The diffusion of good manners and a habit of public behaviour will carry them through. He is a gentleman, and she is a performer. Between them, they will brazen it out. She will not cry out, or faint, or assault him, or suddenly demand forty years of back payments of alimony.

Will she?

She does, of course, love a public exhibition. Like Lady Caroline Lamb, on whom she had long ago written an interesting essay. Maybe it is she who has organized this whole event, in order to confront him. She is capable of anything.

There is no shame in having once held high hopes. Or is there?

Shame is a mystery, and a familiar.

His throat is still sore. He swallows, nervously, as he descends the wide curving shallow-stepped floral-carpeted staircase towards the open entrance of the Neptune Suite. He had hardly been able to speak to Dame Mary in the car on the short journey to the hotel. She had been professionally sympathetic to his vocal plight, and had rummaged around in her bag for her magic opera singer's lozenges, which, she said, would do the trick at least for the evening. She had been effusive in her helpfulness, and had smelt, faintly but intimately, of bacon. She knew he had seen the brown-bagged bacon burger. It was an instant bond between them.

And there she is now, waving at him like the oldest of old friends, as though she has known him for a lifetime. And there is the duke, and the magnate, and the professor, and the bishop, and the bookseller. He is drawn into their orbit, warmly, as Dame Mary enquires after his voice, explains his speechlessness, urges on him the medicinal champagne rather than the white or the red wine, and takes care and charge of him.

'Poor Humphrey,' says Dame Mary, with that extraordinary and slightly coarse giggle lurking playfully under her words, 'he can't talk, he's struck dumb with the honour, he's appointed me his spokesperson for the evening . . .' Oh, she is a comfort to him, she is his protector, this motherly woman with orange hair, he is immensely grateful to her for taking him under her wing, and she stands staunchly by his side, small but loyal, as his first wife Ailsa Kelman makes her dangerous entrance, glittering in silver sequins, sailing through the room towards him, her head held high, her carriage straight (*posture, Ailsa, posture*), with her silver-bangled Athenian arms outstretched for him.

'Humphrey!' announces Ailsa dramatically, in her lower register.

'Ailsa,' mouths Humphrey in response, as he accepts her embrace and kisses her expertly on either cheek.

It is done, it is over. Here is the woman the sight of whose name has, for years, been a trauma to him, and he has kissed her on both cheeks.

Dame Mary beams her approval, and takes her turn with the public kisses. The Public Orator watches silently, discreetly, from his corner by the board with the dinner placement pinned upon it.

Little shallow springs of small talk well up and gush and bubble and course around them, happily, plentifully, as over short green grass, as Ailsa Kelman and Humphrey Clark inspect each other with quick sideways glances, with social smiles and becks and nods. The glorious weather, the happy occasion, the auspicious signs, the year's fine results, the promising league tables . . . Ailsa is practised at such encounters, but, to her quick professional eye, dinner-jacketed Humphrey seems equally at home in this gathering, and as handsome as ever, if more than a little heavier: he is tanned and genial and clean-shaven, confident and affable, a smiling public man. Maybe this will be all that there will be: a little shallow sprinkling of good will and forgetfulness. Maybe that is all that life has left: a friendly peck on the soft cheek, and then you go your way.

It is trivial. It is without meaning. It is, perhaps, disappointing.

Their glasses are recharged, and their little group is invaded, fragmented, re-formed. Ailsa is sucked away into another eddy, and the head of the Department of Marine Biology attaches himself to Humphrey, with talk of renewable cod fisheries and of the Ministry. Humphrey listens politely, inattentively, a little restlessly, making the odd murmur of assent, and, after a minute or two, while still showing every symptom of listening, he turns his head, as people may do at parties, to scan the room, and at that moment Ailsa also disengages her gaze from her interlocutor, and their eyes meet. Each had been looking for the other, and their eyes unmistakably meet and hold the moment. So, they both acknowledge, they have not forgotten, and they will not pretend to have forgotten. They will not take the route of denial. They will accept the challenge.

Their eyes make this pledge, before they return to their social duties.

The Public Orator has been standing patiently by the chart of the dining tables, waiting to usher the guests to their seats if they become confused or lost, and wondering how soon, or if ever, he will be recognized. He is a trim, neat figure, of pale complexion and of middle height, thin and precise: his hair is now a pure and snowy white, and he wears a small close-clipped white beard. He looks simultaneously distinguished and inconspicuous, scholarly and frivolous, ironic and engaging, harmless and sinister.

The gong booms, and the guests begin to move towards him and the entrance to the Davy Jones Dining Room, some with purpose, others in the muddled, diffident way of those who do not like to seem too eager for their food. There is no High Table, and the round tables are not numbered (a practice which can cause offence) but named after local beauty spots: Ailsa Kelman is seated upon the table called Montrose, between the magnate and her first husband Humphrey Clark. The Public Orator has placed himself directly opposite the reunited couple.

A halt in the flow of diners causes Ailsa to pause in front of the Public Orator by his blackboard of names. Interrogatively, but without recognition, she extends her hand to him and introduces herself, and he in response names himself. He says he is Alistair Macfarlane, and he gives her what she will later tell him was 'a very funny look'. But, for the moment, that is all that passes between them. A similar introduction is shortly effected between Macfarlane and Clark, but this time with manly hands extended and shaken over the table. And so they settle on to their solid Edwardian hotel dining chairs, the seventy-two guests at their nine tables, and they pick up their printed menus, and they fish out their spectacles, and they inspect, some with much appreciation, others in suspicious bewilderment, the amusing list of delicacies that is about to be offered to them. It is an entertaining and slightly surreal and cunningly planned repast, of gulls' eggs with lumpfish caviar, of renewable cod on a bed of seaweed with jewels of sea urchin, of salad of sea lettuce, of Camembert *au requin*.

'We thought of roasted puffin or Solon goose,' says the Public Orator, rather loudly, to his neighbour, 'but we thought there might be an animal rights protest. And we were going to call it Captain Nemo's Banquet, but that excessively popular Disney movie about that clown fish rather spoiled our joke, and we didn't want you to think we had let our standards lapse.'

Humphrey hears this remark, as he is intended to do, and he looks sharply at Alistair Macfarlane.

Through the speckled turquoise gulls' eggs, Ailsa Kelman talks to the magnate, and Humphrey Clark talks to the headmistress on his right. Over the next course, he and Ailsa turn towards each other.

She opens the conversation by pointing at his plate of mixed vegetables.

'So you've stopped eating fish now,' she says, with a hint of accusation, as though she had seen him quite recently, as though little time had passed between them since their parting.

Their last bitter parting, in silence and tears . . .

'I prefer not to,' he whispers mildly. 'But I'm sorry to miss the sea urchin. Is it good?'

'Have a bit of mine,' she urges, this time with confident and teasing familiarity. 'Come on, do have a mouthful. They're invertebrates, you know. No nervous systems and no noto-chords. They don't feel pain. Or so I'm told. They're delicious. I had them in Japan once, a whole feast of them.'

'Well, perhaps a morsel,' he says.

She picks up an orange fragment of flesh on her fork, and deposits it on the side of his plate. He stares at it, accepts it, eats it. She watches his face as he swallows.

She does most of the talking, because of his throat. She chatters on, as she can. His throat is recovering, thanks to the lozenges, but it is still tender.

A stranger, listening, would deduce, rightly, that they had known each other for years. She makes him laugh, and she laughs herself, almost to choking, at one of her own jokes. A stranger might reasonably deduce that they are delighted to see each other.

They are laughing about her attack on his foot in the Hotel Actaeon. If they can laugh about this, they can laugh about anything.

The Public Orator, who is not a stranger, eavesdrops on their interchanges, even while maintaining a conversation with the woman on his right. He is able to hear several conver-sations at once. He has that power. He would have preferred to have other powers as well, but this is the power that remains to him. He cannot hear everything she says, but he can hear enough of it to tell that she is sailing along riskily and so far gaily on a brisk breeze of double entendres and hidden allu-sions. He is still waiting for his moment of recognition, and he senses that it is near. And it arrives before the cheese, some-what unexpectedly, with a hint of anticlimax, when one of his colleagues calls out to him from another table.

'Sandy,' calls jovial Jim Campbell from Geology, 'Sandy,

when's the singing? Is there a comfort stop coming up soon?'

So Sandy Alistair Macfarlane Clegg is named and outed. He can see suspicion begin to dawn in the eyes of Ailsa and Humphrey. Recognition and identification and possibly denunciation will soon follow.

Is it a game, is it a trick, is it a trap?

Ailsa is bold, self-trained for decades in boldness, and she leans forward as the Camembert *au requin* and the dessert of cherries and grapes are handed round in an antiquated collegiate manner. She leans forward, her bosom pressing low over the tablecloth, her cleavage proud. She beards the impish man disguised as Alistair Macfarlane, the impostor who was once a pale-skinned serious freckled boy called Sandy Clegg.

'Dr Macfarlane,' she says, 'would I be right in thinking that this is your home town?'

He inclines his head slightly, in assent.

'Would I be right in thinking,' she pursues, as he holds her interrogative gaze, 'that we have met before?'

Again he assents, with a courtly little nod.

'Well,' declares Ailsa, to the table at large, 'this *is* a surprise.' She looks around her, smiling inclusively, defiantly.

'We knew each other,' she tells the duchess and the magnate and the mayor and the headmistress and the microbiologist, 'when we were children.'

Humphrey is staring at Sandy Macfarlane Clegg with less composure than Ailsa has been able to summon. He is staring at his old friend with horror, as though he has seen Banquo's ghost at the feast. He clutches at the collar of his dinner jacket, and tugs at it, and experiences a sudden difficulty in breathing. He thinks he may be going to faint. His vision blurs, his head swims, as his childhood rises up before him in accusation. A suffocating sense of panic and defeat sweeps through his body, shaking him to the invisible core. He is speechless, and worse than speechless.

It has all gone wrong. It is too hard for him. There is no sense in it. All those years of moral effort, the struggle, the resistance, the persistence, the seeking, the stubborn search for and hope of meaning, the hope of virtue, the claims of the super-ego, all to end here, shamed and choking, tricked and shamed by Finsterness and his boyhood friend.

Hic labor, hoc opus est.

It is hard, it is hard. Goodness and generosity are required of him.

But he is not up to it. He cannot clamber back up to the light of day.

He surrenders to grief. The foreshadowed prospect and then the living and forgiving sight of Ailsa on this night had at first seemed to offer a truce, then even a reprieve and a possibility of the remission of sins: or if not so much, then at least a call to a renewed and not impossible effort. But the sight of Sandy Clegg has filled him with unutterable despair.

Is he having a stroke? Or is it merely a spasm of violent indigestion?

To admit to a hollow failure on all levels – moral, emotional, professional – that is the hardest thing. That is the bar to which Public Orator Sandy Clegg has so cruelly, and in public, summoned him.

Humphrey shuts his eyes, and submits, but when he opens them again after an eternity of horror they are all still smiling around him, unconcerned, as though they were characters in some other more pleasing drama, a drama scripted in a lighter vein. The conversation continues, now on a high note of banter, as Ailsa Kelman accuses Sandy of having changed his name in order to mislead them all.

'You trickster, you Machiavelli!' she attacks.

Oh God, how he loved and how he loves his Ailsa! Where does she find her courage? And how could he ever have been brave enough, so long ago, to board her?

'When were you going to let us know? Or were you going to sit there laughing at us?' demands Ailsa.

'I would probably have declared my hand later in the evening,' says Sandy demurely, 'if it had seemed appropriate. But I wasn't sure if you would remember me.'

Ailsa finds this remark preposterous and disingenuous. She has spent many hours poring through his mother's wartime diaries at the University of Sussex in the Mass Observation Archives at Falmer, trying to reconstitute every moment of their mutual past: she has solicited and published (though with less publicity than her work usually attracts) her comments on them and other related diaries of the period. Surely he must know this? But perhaps he does not. She is aware that a whole minefield of disclosures and denials and disclaimers may lie before the three of them, and she stalls for a second, and eats a cherry. After all, she thinks in half an instant, it is true that I might not have made a connection, it is true that I might not have known, had I been as stupid and forgetful and witless as some people are, had the names of Clark and Clegg meant less to me.

This small pause gives Humphrey time to recover an appearance of equanimity, and he turns to the headmistress and says, 'Dr Macfarlane – my old friend Sandy – and I were at school together for a while at Finsterness. But it is a long time ago.'

His voice sounds unnaturally low and hollow and pompous, like a bell. Its pained timbre is, perhaps, further distorted by Dame Mary's pastilles.

Sandy, who is watching Humphrey intently, expands on this statement.

'It is a lifetime ago. It is fifty years ago, since we last saw each other.'

'Let us not count the days and the years,' disclaims Ailsa, with an attempt at a conventional but inapposite feminine disclaimer.

'But surely you may rejoice in them, and be proud of them,' says Sandy, with a mocking gravity. 'After all, we are here to celebrate those years, and the achievements of those years.'

How much does he know, this enigmatic name-changed aged Orator? Does he know of the hidden marriage? She can tell from his smug and contained demeanour that he does. Are there other secrets he knows, as yet unknown to her and to Humphrey, the gullible and innocent victims of this elaborate party trick? Secrets otherwise known only to God?

Inspired, she pounces on Sandy Clegg.

'You remember my brother Tommy? My brother Tommy Kelman?'

'Of course,' says Sandy, suavely. 'How could I forget? I learned half of what I know from Tommy.'

'Ah!' says Ailsa.

'Yes,' says Sandy, thoughtfully, 'I've seen Tommy from time to time, over the years. We've kept in touch, after a fashion.'

The notorious name of Tommy Kelman fragments and disperses the conversation, as others round the table rashly rush in to lay claim to his dubious acquaintance. Tommy, says the duchess, is an old chum of the duke's, and has often been to stay at the castle: Tommy's wife is one of her best friends, they were at school together, they had played tennis together, they had flunked their A-Levels together . . .

Ailsa and Humphrey fall silent, separately, as they dwell on the implications of Sandy's associations. Who is Sandy, and what has he become? Their shared but dissimulated confusion gives them a comradely and palpable sense of collusion, and Humphrey begins to feel a little better, and almost to sense a kind of grim amusement rising in him as he hears Sandy explaining to the duchess that the university had thought of honouring Tommy and Ailsa Kelman in the same ceremony, as a rarely distinguished brother-and-sister duo, but had thought better of it: Tommy would have to wait for another year, and let his little sister take precedence for once.

Ailsa's expression, as she listens to this bit of plot, is a study. She grabs another cherry, eats it, spits out the stone into the cup of her palm, then spears a bit of rotten cheese on the point of her knife, then puts it down again. Then she lays her left hand on top of Humphrey's, and squeezes it. He looks down at her defenceless little wrist, and her ringed and wrinkled fingers, and is filled with tenderness and regret. He can feel the slump of her energy, and the effort of will with which she tries to regain it. The touch of her is at once strange and familiar. Nobody touches him now, and yet she has dared to reach out for him. She has laid claim to him, for all the world to see.

These bracelets cannot be the bracelets that he bought her in Athens, for how could such cheap and trumpery little trinkets have survived the battering of the years, even had she cared to cherish them? She had worn his bangles in the Hall of the Muses, to praise Byron and to denounce and reclaim Delacroix, but that had been decades ago.

She has simply bought more of the same, as people do. Faithfully, she affects the same style, of silver, of sequins, of scales, and of guanine and essence of Orient.

They sit there, side by side, in a kind of stupor, as the feast unravels and reshapes itself, as guests begin to depart to and return from the cloakrooms. There is no new seating plan for the end of the evening: Ailsa, when she returns from refurbishing herself, finds Humphrey still in his place in a trance, behind his honest name card which tells him who he is. Whatever ill may ail him, she deduces, it is not a weak bladder. Side by side, with a good view of the platform, they sink into the stunned passivity of spectators, to watch the fat lady sing. Tommy Kelman, in either of their places, would have been bustling forward, asserting himself, getting in on the act, making sure that everybody knew who he was (and who *was* he?), but they sit in shock, waiting for the music, as they try to process the evening's events and the significance, if any, of the sudden reappearance in their lives of Sandy Macfarlane Clegg.

Dame Mary is stout of body and spirit. She gives a jolly little preamble, about her Scottish ancestry and her family connections and her delight at being back in the very special little town of Ornemouth, of which she has such happy memories. And then she sings. Her singing voice is unearthly and seems to issue from a different personality and from a different order of being. Her speaking voice is friendly, embodied, double-chinned and full of chuckles: her singing voice is inhuman in its beauty.

She gives them an air from the Orkneys and a modernist snatch from an eminent Scottish composer. She sings an unfamiliar setting of Wordsworth's 'Highland Lass', single in the field. Then, with apologies, she gives them 'the unavoidable, the inevitable, the incomparable' Robert Burns.

She sings.

> O, my love's like a red, red rose
> That's newly sprung in June:
> O my love's like the melodie,
> That's sweetly play'd in tune.
>
> As fair art thou, my bonnie lass,
> So deep in love am I,

And I will love thee still, my Dear,
Till a' the seas gang dry.

Till a' the seas gang dry, my Dear,
And the rocks melt wi' the sun:
I will love thee still, my Dear,
While the sands o' life shall run.

And fare thee well, my only love,
And fare thee well a while!
And I will come again, my love,
Tho' it were ten thousand mile!

It is a wicked trick. There is hardly a dry eye in the house.
Ailsa's eyes are red and bloodshot like the eyes of an old dead
fish on the slab.

Humphrey sighs, a heavy sigh of mortality, and then he
squares his shoulders, like a man, and sits upright. He feels a
new resolve rising in him. He will have it out with Sandy
Clegg. He will not take this assault upon his emotions without protest. The shock could have killed him, at his age. He
hasn't been feeling well all day. He will expect an account of
this prank.

The Symposium

When the guests have departed, to their castles and their cottages and their university lodgings, the three honorary graduands and the Public Orator meet in the cosy Edwardian Heather Lounge for a nightcap. Sandy has it all arranged, and they follow him, docile, like dogs, and settle down at his bidding. The armchairs are deep and comfortable, and a full bottle of Macallan's ten-year-old single malt whisky and a bucket of ice and a glass jug of tap water and a green plastic bottle of sparkling Highland Spring stand waiting for them on a homely round wooden table, scarred with many a stain and a circle. Sandy does the honours, and pours for each one of them a generous tumbler. None of them thinks to demur or decline. They accept their whisky and their fate. They raise their glasses to one another, silently, and take their first sip.

They look historic, anachronistic, in their evening dress. They seem to inhabit a nineteenth-century oil painting of uncertain genre: not quite a salon or a conversazione piece, but something along those lines.

Ailsa is the first to speak.

'You are an evil man, Alistair,' she declares, with a mournful extravagance.

Then she relapses into silence.

'That's a little hard,' says Sandy reflectively, after a while.

'I suppose you think this is funny,' continues Ailsa, in a lighter tone.

'No,' says Sandy.

Dame Mary pulls towards herself a little tapestry stool, and puts her feet up on it, and cocks her head on one side, waiting. She has ascertained that these three are old friends, of a sort, and she wants to hear more. She is not sure where she comes into the story, if at all, but she senses entertaining gossip, and is happy, for the moment, to sit back and listen. She knows she has met Sandy Macfarlane before, somewhere surprising, somewhere incongruous, in slightly risqué company, probably at a party in Earls Court, and wonders whether this has any relevance to her honorary degree or to this small gathering. All things considered, she is in good spirits. She has done her bit. The relief of having successfully sung for her supper is still warm in her belly, like a mulled posset, though behind the glow in her gut she is beginning to feel just a tiny bit hungry. It's hard to enjoy your food, when you have to perform later, and the meal, though fancy, had not been very filling. She had only picked at it.

'So why did you change your name?' persists Ailsa to Sandy. 'Why the disguise?'

'Why not?' says Sandy. 'Women change their names. Why shouldn't I?'

'*I* didn't,' says Ailsa.

'Nor did I,' echoes Dame Mary.

'Times have changed,' says Sandy.

Humphrey and Ailsa stare at Sandy uneasily, a little apprehensively. Sandy looks from the one to the other, as though he has no answer to offer, as though the mystery will remain a riddle without an answer.

And then he relents.

'I changed my name for two reasons. Do you want to know them?'

Humphrey and Ailsa exchange glances, and then they nod, with an encouraging eagerness. Yes, they want to hear his account of himself. They are willing to be a receptive audience.

'I changed my name,' says Sandy, 'because Sandy Clegg is an unfortunate name. It's not a pretty name. It's a heavy name, an ugly name. An inferior-form-of-life sort of name. Do you know what a cleg is?'

Humphrey nods, but Dame Mary and Ailsa shake their heads. Sandy bows towards Humphrey, who is obliged, as so often, to take the role of schoolmaster.

'A cleg is a horsefly,' he whispers hoarsely. 'Cleg-flies are bloodsuckers. Well, the females are. The female is more dangerous than the male.'

'I think that's more than we need to know,' says Dame Mary, with a mock and girlish giggle.

'Well, I never liked the name of Clegg,' continues Sandy. 'In fact, I hated it. And Macfarlane is my middle name, and always has been. I've a right to it. It's a more attractive name. It's more distinguished. Don't you think?'

They do not judge this apologia worthy of an answer, so he continues.

'So I changed my name. I began to use Alistair Macfarlane as my nom de plume. And then I began to use it professionally, and now it is my name.'

This is a clever move. Nobody dares to ask him what he has published, under this nom de plume. They ought to know, but they do not know, and they are not sure how to ask. Maybe he will tell them?

'That's only *one* reason,' says Dame Mary, overriding this small obstacle. 'Come on, out with the other.'

'The other reason is that at first I did not want my family to know my identity. I was a criminal, in the eyes of the law, and I do not think my parents would have liked that.'

The high-minded Humphrey is bemused by this remark, and Ailsa's thoughts flit disbelievingly to her wicked brother's insider dealings with television network shares, but Dame

Mary is quicker off the mark, and guesses the explanation in one. She was right, she must have met him at one of those parties in Earls Court.

'You mean you were gay,' she says. 'Well, *anyone* can see that. Your parents must have known.'

Sandy looks slightly deflated by the pre-emptive speed of this remark, but he concedes at once.

'I suppose they did,' he says, 'but we didn't want to have to talk about it. And they wouldn't have liked the poems. Or, later, and even less, the memoir. And they wouldn't have liked my partner. And he wouldn't have liked them.'

'Now you've given more than two reasons,' says Dame Mary. 'So you might as well tell us everything.'

As she says this, the grandfather clock in the corner of the Heather Lounge strikes the quarter with an indeterminate high single silvery note.

'Well, *nearly* everything,' amends Dame Mary. 'Give us an outline. Give us a plot summary. We don't want to be up all night.'

So Sandy Clegg tells his tale.

Sandy's Story (abridged version)

Once upon a time, says Sandy, there was a little boy called Sandy, who lived in a picturesque little fisherman's cottage, in a village at the end of the world. He was a happy little boy, and he played happily on the sands, in his kingdom by the sea. When he was a child, he played like a child, and he went to the village school with all the other village children. And then he grew up and put away childish things and went to the big old school of stone across the bridge. There Sandy fell in love with words and with language and became very unhappy, and the classics master fell in love with Sandy and became very unhappy. And then Sandy went off to Oxford to read Greats.

And at Oxford Sandy Clegg began to write poetry, and he co-edited a university magazine with a poet who has subsequently become (for a poet) well known, and the little magazine published Sandy Clegg's poems under the name of Alistair Clegg.

('Copies of that magazine are collectors' items now,' says Sandy dryly, in parenthesis, 'but not because of my poems.')

And after Oxford the young man drifted miserably, sick at heart and down at heel, guilty and miserable, trying to scratch a living as a journalist and a poet and an extra-mural lecturer, and then he went to Paris, as such young men do, and got in with the wrong set, and started to write homoerotic pornography for the Olympia Press.

This unexplained jump in the narrative momentarily jolts his listeners out of their inert Listen-with-Mother mode: Humphrey reaches for the whisky and refills his glass in a devil-may-care, in-for-a-penny-in-for-a-pound manner; Dame Mary's mind leaps involuntarily to the exotically metal perforated leather-dressers of the Earls Court party and the diversionary relief of a ham sandwich, and Ailsa emits a small squawk of surprised admiration.

A period of happiness and fulfilment ensued (Sandy does not give much detail) and Sandy Macfarlane (also known as Max Angelo) exchanged neurotic celibacy for a multiplicity of partners (the use of the phrase 'wrong set' had, as his listeners now realize, been ironic) and, eventually, he had found true love with a handsome continental intellectual.

'Are we still in Paris?' prompts Ailsa, who is wondering if her sojourn in that city had overlapped with his, and if so, whether they had ever unknowingly bumped into each other, in a café on a boulevard, in a gallery, in a bookstore, or crossing a bridge over the Seine.

'Yes,' confirms Sandy, 'it began in Paris, though we were soon to move to the West Coast and all it had to offer.'

'Beach Boys?' suggests Dame Mary eagerly, who seems by now to be well in tune with this part of the tale, and Sandy nods in agreement.

'Great days, great days,' says Dame Mary to herself.

But it had not been great for long. In California, Sandy continues, the lover falls ill, and the story takes a dark turning. This is not an AIDS story, for at that period AIDS had not yet begun to terrorize the gay world, and indeed had not even been identified. This is a good old-fashioned drugs story, with a bad ending, says Sandy.

In short, the lover died, and that was the end of that.

Sandy does not seem to wish to describe this denouement more vividly. He discloses that he has described it already, to the best of his limited ability, in a volume called *The Queen of Clubs*. Although he says it himself, this work is recognized as a minor classic, and it has never been out of print on either side of the Atlantic. It has been translated into several languages, including Japanese.

'I suppose it's what you'd call a cult book,' says Sandy modestly.

Dame Mary and Ailsa nod knowingly, as though they are pretending to have heard of it, and Ailsa thinks she may even have read it, or at least looked at it, though she does not say so. If she remembers rightly (and she may not), the nameless lover had been world famous. But she has forgotten who he was, and Sandy has not identified him. So she had better keep her mouth shut, and keep her ignorance to herself.

Humphrey does not even pretend to have heard of it. He does not need to. He is finding it impossible to believe in this version of Sandy's career. It is simply not possible, and yet it must, he supposes, be true. Why should Sandy invent it? Humphrey has taken Speed and smoked cannabis and eaten home-cooked cannabis cake, in his time, and he has inhaled a lot of high-tar nicotine, but he has never knowingly been in a room with hard drugs or with serious drug abusers. The Sandy Macfarlane Clegg whom Humpy Clark had known had not been a candidate for this kind of consequence. He had belonged to an era of Cherryade and Mint Imperials, and had seemed set to stay put in it. Humphrey backtracks, fast, but he cannot join the dots. He cannot even see the dots.

A long pause follows, from which Humphrey eventually speaks, in a somewhat aggressive voice, which, although still thick, seems to be regaining its power.

'So what brought you back here?' he says, getting to the heart of the matter.

Sandy's face is as pale and delicate as ivory, and his hair is as white and as soft and as fine as thistledown. He sits there, precisely, and raises his thin freckled yellowish hands, and joins his palms and the tips of his fingers together as though in meditation or in prayer.

'I came back here because I yearned for Finsterness,' he says, with a pedantic simplicity. 'The place haunted me, and so I came back. I was born here, and I was in exile and home-sick for years, and so I came back. I suffered from nostalgia for my native heath. Like poor Emily Brontë. And when the opportunity to return arose, I accepted it.'

This explanation is at once implausible and convincing. Humphrey Clark feels a shudder run down his spine. This small old man alarms him. Perhaps he is not Sandy Clegg at all, perhaps he is a real impostor? There is nothing here to recognize, after all these years. This is a shell, a husk, a shadow of a man. Yet why would anyone tell such lies? Why would anyone wish to impersonate Sandy Clegg and steal his name and story?

Sandy explains briefly that after the death of his lover in San Francisco he had returned to London to a life of voluntary celibacy and extra-mural teaching and semi-respectable literary journalism. He had given up writing poetry ('the Muse abandoned me', is how he quaintly put it) but he had studied for a doctorate, published an opaque novel with the help of an Arts Council grant, and had found full-time employment in a red-brick university, as a beneficiary of the expansion of Higher Education and a burgeoning interest in gender studies.

And in due course a post had been advertised in the new University of Ornemouth, and he had applied for it. It had seemed to be designed for him.

'And here I am,' says Sandy, smiling, 'for gender studies and the slender reputation of *The Queen of Clubs* have reached even the backwater of quiet little Ornemouth. Oh yes, I have owned up to my past now. My parents are long dead, and I am thought to be mildly if eccentrically distinguished. Our department is not as prosperous and as well funded as Marine Biology' (here he bows his head in deference towards his old friend Humphrey) 'but we get by well enough. I teach a little, I give a few lectures. Life is still quite inexpensive in this neighbourhood. One can live well on a doctoral salary here.'

Ailsa nods, in worldly endorsement. She had noted this herself, in the prices on the modest menu of the namechanged Copper Kettle, now reborn as the Periwinkle.

And Sandy bows his head courteously in turn to Ailsa, and says, 'You were very good, the other night on TV, on the subject of the intersexuality of fish. On the study of the changing gender of fish. Gender studies, feminism, the Plunkett Prize. You marry all the disciplines.'

'Thank you,' says Ailsa, for whom any unexpected compliment, however ironic, however unconvincing, is welcome, so deep is her well-hidden insecurity.

Humphrey does not follow this allusion fully, though he had caught up with some of the details of Ailsa's recent exploits over dinner. He feels excluded, and attempts retaliation.

'So,' says Humphrey, with more than a hint of aggression now, 'you brought us all this way, just to listen to your story?'

'No,' says Sandy. 'That was only a part of it. I wanted to hear your stories too. I wanted to fill in the gaps. I wanted to see you again, before we all die. I wanted to read the next chapter. So I thought, why not? There isn't time to wait for another fifty years.'

There is no reason why he should not have implied that they would all be dead in fifty years, but nevertheless Ailsa is not pleased with his blunt turn of phrase.

'So you arranged it?' challenges Humphrey.

'Your names came up,' says Sandy. 'You were on a list. You didn't have to accept.'

'Who brought them up?' insists Humphrey.

Sandy shakes his head, disclaiming responsibility.

'Maybe,' says Humphrey, 'others are not so willing to tell their stories. And maybe there is no next chapter.'

Sandy takes time to consider this point, with a considered expression of academic detachment on his donnish features; as though he were conducting a seminar, and Humphrey were a not unpromising pupil.

'It's not that I want a tidy ending,' Sandy offers eventually. 'It's not as though our story were a detective story, with a list of suspects and a revelation and a summing up. It's not a question of forensics or of exegesis. It's not that kind of story. It's not in that genre. But it needs some kind of –' he hesitates, for some lingering meditative time – 'some kind of resolution. Or do I mean reparation? Or maybe, after all, I do mean exegesis. Anyway, I want to know what happens next.'

They all sit and think about this.

'I think Sandy's story is a good story, with a lot of plot,' says Ailsa after a while, in a puzzled and palliative but nevertheless brisker tone, playing for time. 'It's just that we're a bit shocked, to hear it all so suddenly, and in such a condensed version. We're a bit shocked to see you again at all, frankly, after all these years, Dr Macfarlane. And what was that other name you had? Max Angelo? That's a good one, Sandy, that's really good. However did you come up with that? And *The Queen of Clubs*, that's very good too. You *have* done well.'

Ailsa is feeling suddenly pleased with herself, because she thinks she has remembered the name of Sandy's lover. She has been fishing around for it in the little creeks of her memory, and she thinks she's got it. Sandy's lover had been an Algerian, like so many French intellectuals of the period. She is almost sure she has got his identity right. She is pleased with herself not only because the name retrieval confirms that she is not yet suffering from degenerative memory loss, but also because the lover had been a scholar of some fame and reputation. Ailsa is comfortable in the company of those who are famous, and Sandy's reflected glory pleases and fortifies her. She has a little rush of relief, of regained and reassuring selfhood.

Dame Mary is less satisfied.

'I don't see the *meaning* of Sandy's story,' she says.

'Does a story have to have meaning?' asks Sandy.

'Of course,' says Dame Mary.

'Only the vulgar crave for meaning,' says Sandy.

'I *am* very vulgar,' says Dame Mary.

'You might as well ask, does a meaning have to have a story?'

'I'll ask that as well, then,' says Dame Mary staunchly. 'It's a good question. Does a meaning have to have a story?'

The four of them look at one another, as though they are playing a parlour game, and waiting for someone else to come in from the dark to lay down the rules.

'The problem, as I see it,' says Sandy, after a pause for thought, and resuming his doctoral role, 'is to do with teleology. We were all brought up in a teleological universe. We were brought up to believe that stories have meanings and that meanings have stories and that journeys have ends. We were brought up to believe that there would be an ending, that there would be completion. For each and every life, for each and every organism. But now we know that that's not true. It was true, once, but it's true no longer. We have passed the point in time and in history where that truth applies. The universe has shed the teleological fallacy. So now we have to work out what can take its place. We have to tell and shape our stories in another space, in another concept of space.'

'I dispute that,' says Ailsa.

'I don't know what teleology is,' says Dame Mary, defiantly accepting her role as prompt and stooge.

Sandy bows, with mock courtesy, towards the singer.

'Then perhaps,' he says, 'you are exempt from its demands. You are a child of nature and of instinct.'

It is not clear that this is a compliment, and Dame Mary makes a snorting noise of dismissal.

'And I don't know what exegesis is, either,' she adds, in a muttered throwaway that receives no acknowledgement.

'Do you mean to say,' says Ailsa indignantly, at Sandy, starting off in another direction, on another and baser level of counter-attack, 'that for all these years you have been spying on us, like a little sneak, and planning your revenge?'

'And what do you think you were doing, reading my mother's diaries in the University of Sussex?'

'That was a coincidence,' says Ailsa. 'I didn't know they were there, when I started on that project. I wasn't looking for them, in particular. It was Mass Observation that I was working on, not the Cleggs of Turkey Bank. I was astonished to come across them. I wasn't being intrusive. And I wasn't looking for you, if that's what you think. I'd forgotten all about you. I hadn't forgotten Humphrey, it's true, but I'd forgotten you. It was an accident. I wasn't even looking for me. And anyway, your mother's diaries weren't very interesting. They weren't very personal, you know. She'd deposited them in the public interest, but they weren't very interesting. It wasn't me that was the spy.'

'I didn't need to spy on you,' says Sandy. 'You didn't exactly court obscurity, did you? You were hard to miss. You nailed your knickers to the mast.'

Ailsa takes this camp and unexpected coarseness tolerably well, and turns in appeal to Dame Mary.

'This rude and naughty man,' she says, 'is playing games with us. He has brought us all together on purpose. I don't believe it happened by accident. There *are* accidents, but this little gathering isn't one of them. I don't know where you come into it, Mary, but I bet you do. You said you'd been to Ornemouth before, didn't you? When was that, I wonder? Don't tell us that you too were at school with Sandy? No, you can't have been, you're too young. And anyway, you're Canadian, aren't you? Did you meet him in Paris, in his belle époque, at a transvestite ball? Don't tell us you're an impostor too. Maybe you are Humphrey's long-lost cousin? Or mine? Come on, tell us what it is with Ornemouth for you. What are you doing here? Tell us your story.'

'Dame Mary,' says Sandy, reprovingly, 'came here because

she was invited by the Vice Chancellor, who is a great fan. As am I. Dame Mary came here to sing to us. Which she has done, very beautifully. Dame Mary is very welcome here. The Burns song was unforgettable, and if I may say so very moving. Very appropriate, very moving. She came ten thousand mile.'

Dame Mary shakes her round stubble head, shaking away this not very convincing compliment.

'Not quite,' she says. 'I came from St Vincent's Wharf. I've got a nice apartment there. Not quite a penthouse, but very nice, very modern. I've got a lovely concierge, and a very nice river view. I'm glad you liked the song. It's a bit of an old chestnut, but Sandy put in a request for it, and I thought, why not? Sandy and I met at a party in Earls Court once, but I think he's forgotten about it. It was a bit of a *wild* party.'

'The Devil has all the best tunes,' says Ailsa, 'and the libertines write the best lyrics.'

'Yes,' says Humphrey, listening to an echo.

'Tell us your story,' repeats Ailsa.

And the Dame, with good humour, obliges.

Dame Mary's Story

Dame Mary discloses that her connection with Ornemouth is tenuous and superficial. She had been there once, for a day, as a tourist, but of course she'd tried to make it sound a bit more intimate than that, in her little speech before her after-dinner singsong. She'd wanted to flatter the local populace. Well, you have to, don't you? It's part of the job.

A few years ago, she can't remember how many, she'd been on tour with the Winter Palace company, and they'd been playing the Royal at Newcastle, and she'd stayed with the duke at the castle. Gerry's father was still alive then, but only just.

And Gerry had taken her for a spin, to show off his future fiefdom. He'd driven her round and about, and shown her salmon rivers and grouse moors and some old churches and all that kind of feudal thing, but what she remembered best were the three bridges over the Orne at Ornemouth, and the codfish in the Pool of Brochan. Had any of them seen the codfish of Brochan? Gerry was mighty proud of those fish, he said they'd been in his mother's family for centuries.

'Once seen, never forgotten,' murmurs Ailsa.

'But I don't suppose,' says Dame Mary, 'that me being given an honorary degree has much to do with Gerry or with those fish.'

Ailsa agrees that Gerry and the fish are a distraction. There is more to it than that, and, after a little probing, and with some embarrassment and fluffing of lines, Dame Mary admits to a closer connection with Ailsa Kelman. She knows her brother Tommy, of course, but then everybody knows Tommy, there's nothing very special about knowing Tommy. But, more particularly, she had worked, surely they must all know, for a short (but significant and she has to confess productive) period of her life with Ailsa's ex-husband. 'You know, you remember him, you remember your ex,' says Dame Mary, intercepting Ailsa's sideways glance towards the now morosely hunched and silenced and thoughtful Humphrey.

Dame Mary reveals that, like Ailsa, she had once been in thrall to that dreaded martinet, Martin Pope. Martin was a horrible man, a monster, a tyrant, a bully and a genius. The Infallible Pope, as they used to call him in the business. He had tortured her. She would never work with him again. But he had got good work out of her, she had to admit it. He'd made her do things she didn't know she could do. She'd sung roles for him that she'd thought beyond her range. And she'd lost three stone for Martin Pope. He'd threatened her with a stomach clamp, so she'd gone on a diet, and she'd lost three stone.

'He's ill and he's mad,' says Dame Mary. 'He is really mad. I'm ill, but I'm not mad.'

Martin Pope, claims Mary McTaggart, is still obsessed by his second wife Ailsa Kelman. He does not talk about her, but his gruesome fifth-floor Deco apartment in the Adelphi off the Strand is a shrine to her memory. It is full of photographs of her, stuck all over the place. It is ghoulish. There is no sign of his first film-star wife, or of his third secretary wife, or of his fourth Greek actress wife, but the image of his second wife Ailsa is everywhere.

Ailsa says that this is news to her, and that she does not believe it.

'It's like a shrine,' repeats Dame Mary with some relish, 'with candles and picture lights. It's ghoulish.'

Sandy laughs, a small and private and defensive laugh.

'I didn't know that chapter of the story,' admits Sandy.

'There's a lot you don't know,' says Ailsa defiantly, hoping that this is true. She is shocked by the shrine, and does not know what to make of it. She had thought she had dropped out of Martin Pope's memory as she had from his life. She cannot believe Dame Mary's story. She must have made it up.

There were photographs of Ailsa, continues Dame Mary relentlessly, and shelves of her books, and posters of her shows, and videos of her television programmes, and a whacking great oil painting of her, a really *terrible* likeness, stuck over the mantelpiece. And all along the corridor there were pictures of Ailsa with her baby on her knee. Taken by Lord Snowdon, if she remembers rightly.

Ailsa stares at Dame Mary blankly, as if mesmerized by this surreal vision of her ex-husband's mania, by this glimpse into a forgotten passage.

'You did *have* a baby, didn't you?' asks Dame Mary.

The Dame sings tragedy, but she talks comedy.

Ailsa does not seem to take in this query. She shakes her head, in response to it.

'You've got a daughter called Marina,' Dame Mary informs Ailsa. 'I met her once. She came to a rehearsal. She seemed to me to be a very nice girl, a nice ordinary kind of girl. I don't think she sees much of her father, though she tries to keep in touch with him. But he is a difficult man. Well, I don't need to tell *you* that, do I?'

'But Martin *hated* me,' offers Ailsa, with a tremor of doubt now wavering in her voice. 'He can't have stuck me all over his apartment.'

'Love, hate, it's all the same,' says Dame Mary.

'Is it?' says the unhappy Ailsa.

'How long did you stay married to him?' asks Dame Mary, in a more cajoling tone.

'Oh, I can't remember,' says Ailsa, resigning herself to an explanation of the inexplicable. 'We didn't really live together much. I wasn't very good at being married. It wasn't my thing. I'm no good at living with people. I should never have accepted him. It was a very bad move on my part. Were *you* ever married, Mary? I can't remember if you ever went in for marriage?'

Dame Mary is embarrassed by this diversionary but direct enquiry and she deflects attention from it by saying that she could really do with a ham sandwich. Nobody listens to her. They are too engrossed in decoding and re-encoding what has already been said, what has long ago happened, what might be on the verge of happening. They pursue their elaborate thoughts, while Dame Mary thinks about her ham sandwich.

Appetite and nausea are finely balanced in the struggle for Dame Mary's body, and at the moment appetite dominates, through force of habit and a long history of triumph. Appetite is on the side of life, and will overcome.

At this point, Humphrey emerges from his brooding to remark that he thinks he too has met Ailsa's daughter, Marina.

He describes his brief encounter with Marina Pope in Burlington House.

'Did she know who you were?' asks Ailsa.

Humphrey shakes his head.

'How could she?' he says. 'I worked out who she was, because she was wearing a label, but how could she know who I was?'

'That's a fair point,' says Ailsa.

'And who *are* you?' asks Dame Mary, turning to Humphrey with an air of accusation, demanding clarification. 'You've all got me in a right muddle now. Who *are* you?'

'I'm Sandy Clegg's old playmate and classmate,' says Humphrey, 'and I'm Ailsa Kelman's first husband, and Tommy Kelman was my brother-in-law.'

Dame Mary looks bewildered, and scratches at her scalp through her short apricot curls.

'Is that a conundrum? Is it a mind game? It's too late at night for games. Is it one of those "This man's father is my father's son" riddles? I don't get it. I don't like being teased.'

'Everyone,' says Sandy Macfarlane, who has had time to recover his composure and to replan his strategy, 'is related to everybody else, and at very few removes. It's something to do with six degrees of separation. I used to be fascinated by networks and synchronicity. Have you ever played that game where you find out how many people round the table or in the class share the same birthday? It's always more than you think. It's uncanny, but it nearly always works.'

'Your *brother-in-law*?' echoes Dame Mary to Humphrey, ignoring this frivolous intellectual interjection and seizing the issue before it is lost in casuistry. 'Did you say Tommy Kelman was your *brother-in-law*? Does that mean that Ailsa was your *wife*?'

'Yes,' says Humphrey. 'That's what I just said. Ailsa and I were married, long long ago, in another lifetime, as Sandy has clearly discovered. But unlike Mr Pope, who was also at one point Tommy's brother-in-law, I don't boast about my marriage. I don't keep photos on my mantelpiece. I keep it quiet. I haven't got many mementoes. I've a few, but I keep them hidden away. It wasn't a very public marriage. Was it, Ailsa? Tommy was there, at the wedding, but it wasn't very public. No cameras, no journalists. No paparazzi. It was all very informal, very low-key. Wasn't it, Ailsa?'

Dame Mary looks from one to the other, in mock or real bewilderment, and then at Sandy Clegg, who is nodding in affirmation.

'I don't think they called them paparazzi, in those days,' says Ailsa.

'So you and Humphrey were *married*?' demands Dame Mary, who wants to make sure she has got it right.

Ailsa nods. Humphrey nods.

He does not disown her, or not in public.

'We haven't met for more than thirty years,' says Ailsa plaintively, and with an unwonted meekness. 'And I'm not sure it was such a good idea to meet now. I wasn't certain, but my lady from Rio told me I should give it a go. She said it might be time to try. I don't know, maybe it's all a big mistake. I don't know why I accepted. It's all got a bit out of hand. I'd braced myself for Humphrey, and Ornemouth, and Finsterness, and memory lane, but I hadn't reckoned with Sandy and his schoolboy tricks.'

'I didn't know you were going to be here,' says Humphrey

to Ailsa, as though there were nobody else in the room. 'Nobody warned me. I never read the small print. I didn't know you were going to be here until I reached Darlington. When I got on the train this morning at King's Cross, I was an innocent. I'd no idea. I swear to God, I'd no idea. It's been a long day. God knows why I accepted this tomfool stupid invitation. I knew it would be a disaster. First you, then Sandy. It's been too much.'

'Poor Hump,' says Ailsa. 'What a shock. I think you rose to the occasion very well. So why *did* you accept? I know why I did, but why did you?'

'It's the place,' says Sandy. 'I told you. It draws you'.

'Yes,' says Humphrey, 'it draws you.'

'Is this rigmarole *all* true?' insists Dame Mary.

'Yes,' say Ailsa and Humphrey, with one voice.

'The place casts its spell,' says Sandy, with authority. 'You have to return to the place, to find the explanation. The place is written on the tablets of the heart.'

And at this prompting, Ailsa intones, as she had done as a child, the incantatory rhymes to which she had once danced upon the beach.

> 'I stood upon the Ornemouth Fort
> And guess ye what I saw
> Brochan Bay and Broomside
> Fairhouses and Cocklaw,
> The Fairy Folk of Finsterness
> And the Witches of Edincraw.'

A graveyard shiver passes through Humphrey Clark as he listens.

'Tell more, tell more,' says Dame Mary.

The clock strikes the half hour.

'But make it quick,' says Dame Mary, 'because I've not got long to live.'

There was no twenty-four-hour Room Service in the old Queen's Hotel at Ornemouth. You could ring till dawn, and nobody would answer. But canny Sandy Macfarlane knew where to find the key to the pantry, and he returned, after a brief sortie, with a reassuring blue-and-white willow pattern plateful of ham sandwiches and a jar of English mustard and a slab of Cheddar cheese and some cream crackers. That would see them through, he said. Though through to what, precisely, was still unclear.

Dame Mary had greeted the tray with gratitude and pleasure.

'I'm such a greedy pig,' she had said, as she munched with relief.

Two hours later, all the sandwiches were gone and the level in the bottle of Macallan's was very low.

'Macallan's was always Steven Runciman's favourite malt,' Sandy had confided, impressively, summoning up a world of closeted aristocratic old border queens and towers, as he once more refilled their glasses. 'Sir Steven swore by it. Sir Steven had this beautiful little castle, just over the border.'

('Name-dropper,' Ailsa had murmured, under her breath.)

The whisky level was low, and some of the gaps in the story had been filled. Names had been retrieved from the lower depths: Ailsa found she had guessed right about Sandy's famous French-Algerian lover, and Sandy had provided both the name and fate of the girl called Heather Robinson, whose family had preceded the Kelmans as lodgers at Mrs Binns's.

On the sandwich level, Humphrey was feeling fine. His throat was much better, his voice was stronger. On the levels of shame, remorse and paranoia he was faring less well.

He had coped adequately with the story of Heather Robinson, the lonely stubborn little hopscotch artist whom he and Sandy had spurned, the child whose loneliness had set the seal on their boyhood friendship. Her life had not been marked by worldly success, but the blame for this could hardly have been laid at the door of schoolboy Humphrey Clark. Not even he could hold himself responsible for so tangential and brief a connection.

Heather Robinson had not been eligible for an honorary degree in Ornemouth, said Sandy. Had she been, he would have made sure she would be invited. He has influence, as they have guessed, on the Honours Committee. But she would not have been eligible, and anyway, she was dead. She had lived and died in obscurity, unmarried. No pomp and circumstance for her. No honour, love, obedience, troops of friends. She had lived most of her uneventful adult life with her widowed mother in Sunderland, and had died less than two years after her mother, at the age of forty-eight, of a respiratory disorder.

Humphrey found himself swallowing painfully with useless sorrow, useless and misplaced remorse.

Sandy told them that he knew these facts because he had found Heather's address in Mrs Binns's Visitors' Book, and in his role as archivist and auditor of the summers he had been to London to look up Heather Robinson's death certificate.

('Necrophiliac,' muttered Ailsa, to herself: then recalled, instantly, guiltily, her own satisfaction at having discovered in distant southern Sussex the nature of the affliction of widowed Mr Fell.)

'Your names were in the Visitors' Book too,' said Sandy to Ailsa. 'Yours and Tommy's. You all signed, all four of you. And in the Comments column, your mother wrote, "A very nice holiday and lots of sunshine. A real break." But you and Tommy just signed your names.'

Humphrey could cope with that information, just as he

could cope with the news that Tommy Kelman and Sandy Clegg had tried a bit of hanky-panky in the bracken on the day they'd disappeared together. He'd half-guessed at something like that. Boys will be boys, he'd worked that out, over the years. Nobody cared about that kind of thing these days, and it hadn't been very unusual, even then.

'You were always so high-minded, such a good boy, Humpy,' said Sandy, in explanation, in demi-apology.

But Humphrey had not guessed at the story of Jock in the garage.

'He had skin like hide,' said Sandy. 'His skin was dark and hard as hide. We did it in the back of the garage. I suppose I liked it, or I wouldn't have kept on going back for more, would I?'

Humphrey was repelled by this disclosure, and looked at Sandy in prim disbelief, thus reinforcing Sandy's censorious view of his high and narrow mind.

Sandy had liked Jock. Jock had done Sandy no harm.

The aquarium had been of solid, thick, moulded glass. It had been beyond price. They had bought it from Jock for a shilling.

Dame Mary, who had been snoring intermittently, surfaced at this point to contribute a dubious sexual reminiscence, involving a groping priest and the fat leather apron of a church door. This story (which disquietingly introduced the words 'hymen' and 'membrane') was met with initial mirth, then a lull of silence.

'I'm sorry,' she said, into the silence. 'I think I've lowered the tone. It's time I went to bed.'

But she did not move. She shut her eyes, but she did not move.

Humphrey also shut his eyes, and leaned back in his chair. Although exhausted, he was deep in what was still some kind of thought. Both the tone and the content of all these huddling hustling revelations were perplexing to him. He was finding it hard to absorb, in the space of two hours, the compressed narrative of lives that had taken fifty years to develop to this point: lives compact with successes, failures, adventures, loves, deaths, finalities: lives of which, until so recently, until this evening, he had known next to nothing. His sense of the shifting intensities and variable measurements of time was making him feel giddy, as though he were looking through too many lenses, and none of them in focus. How could it be that two or three unimportant years of his childhood had altered the flow of the course of his future? Who was answerable for this error, this arrest, this misdirection, this strange shift of the landscape, this brick dropped casually to dam and divert the stream?

The riddle of Diophantus came back to him, with its retrospective calculations, its portions and proportions, its message of failure and of limitation and of immortal reputation.

Call no man happy until he is dead. That is what the ancients had said.

Heather Robinson, poor late-born child. What was she to him, that he should remember her so well?

It had seemed, at one point, early in the evening, hours ago, at the reception, that the whole melodramatic Ailsa business (their childhood meeting, their accidental encounter, their love, their days of perfect happiness, their foolish and impetuous sixties marriage, their ridiculous quarrels, their rushed divorce, their long-drawn-out silence) could be turned off with an adult smile and an unspoken mutual agreement between the two of them, with a social contract of polite acceptance and disclaimer: and, looking back, he did not think that he and Ailsa had failed each other or their witnesses on this superficial level. They had greeted each other bravely, they had saluted and acknowledged each other with courtesy, and they had kept up a good front for the duke and the duchess and the magnate and the professor and the head of the department and the headmistress and the bishop and the bookseller. They had bitten on the bullet, and the social structure of the new University of Ornemouth had supported them. But now they were being driven into deeper waters by the late night and this small séance. It was a dangerous game that Sandy was playing. Should Humphrey cling to the plank and try to keep afloat, or should he let himself drift free and drown?

Ailsa and Sandy were now engrossed in the pursuit of trivial recollections. They were talking about the ice-cream man and the Robot King and St Cuthbert's Rock and Mrs Binns and her jigsaws and her jar of pearly beads and the games of Monopoly and Tommy's attempts at cheating. Ailsa's tone was nostalgic, affectionate, forgiving. She was behaving well, this grown and ageing woman whose reappearance he had dreaded for so many decades, the sight of whose name in print had made him flinch with guilty failure and remorse. She was neither the temptress nor the vulgarian nor the avenging fury that he had imagined her to have become. She did not seem to be in any way angry with him. She had not been nursing her anger for decades, as he had fancied. So she was not a Bad Girl, after all. Tommy had been bad, but Ailsa had nobly over the years resisted the bad Kelman gene. She had endured and weathered and come through the other side to somewhere better, somewhere more peaceful. She had grown up, in the thirty years and more of their separation. He should not have been surprised by this, but he was.

'I was such a bad sport,' he heard Ailsa say to Sandy, in mocking wonder, of her angry childhood self. 'Do you remember how I used to scream and yell when I thought I was losing? I was a horror.'

Yes, she had grown up.

And then he heard himself say, unprompted, without caution or forethought: 'And you, Sandy, do you still write?'

He knew enough of writers to know that this was not a question to ask lightly. Ailsa in her silver gear went very still. Her sequins froze.

'No,' said Sandy. 'As I told you, the Muse abandoned me.'

'But that was your poetic Muse,' pursued Humphrey cruelly, 'the Muse of your poetry. What about your prose? I gather you are now best known for your prose?'

'That gift too,' said Sandy, 'departed'.

He sighed, a cold little sigh.

'It's amazing to me now,' said Sandy, 'that I ever managed to believe I could write. It was all a confidence trick. I tricked myself into believing I could do it. But it was all derivation, it was all imitation. Unlike you, Ailsa, I had no originality. I was trapped in the styles of others.'

Ailsa wanted to know what models he had followed, whom he had imitated, what styles he had affected. Sandy, meekly, came up with a list. His poetry had been after the manner of Auden, his pornography after the manner of de Sade and Genet and Apollinaire, and his Arts Council nouveau roman was a Robbe-Grillet crossed with a Butor set in Stoke-on-Trent.

And the memoir, pressed Ailsa. Had he found his true 'voice' in the memoir, she wanted to know.

'They're very keen on "voice" these days,' said Sandy evasively. 'They talk about it a lot in Creative Writing courses. Or so I'm told. I've never been to one, of course. Nor have I ever taught one. I know my limitations.'

Well, repeated Ailsa, had he found his voice?

'I found *somebody's* voice,' admitted Sandy. 'But I don't know if it was mine. And whoever it belonged to, I lost it.'

During the lengthening pause that followed this admission,

Dame Mary stirred, surfaced, rummaged around her, collected her little pearl-embroidered evening bag from the depths of the coarse crumb-filled pocket of the arm of the chair, searched in her bag for her weighty room key, jangled it indicatively at them, heaved herself up from the sagging depths, tugged and straightened the stoutly creased and crumpled bodice and skirt of her blue satin gown, and made gestures of farewell. The men politely tried to rouse themselves to see her out, but she flagged them back down into their seats, and they unresistingly relapsed.

'I'm off for my beauty sleep,' she said, her hand on the brass doorknob of the Heather Lounge. 'It's above my head, all this book talk, all this talk about voices. I've got to look after mine, I've got to give it a rest. And you should go to bed too, Humphrey, or you'll be speechless in the morning. Goodnight, my sweets. I'll see you all tomorrow, for the grand recessional.'

She made a large gesture that suggested the swelling music, she hummed a phrase, she kissed her fingers at them, and she departed.

'So *The Queen of Clubs* was the last book you published?' resumed Ailsa, as soon as the door closed. She had not quite finished with the revenge of interrogation. 'Fifteen years ago, was it? Or maybe even more?'

'I've published papers,' said Sandy, 'academic papers. You may have seen my name in the *TLS*?' (They shook their heads.) 'But I've published nothing very substantial. Well, I was quite proud of my contribution on Beaumont and Fletcher and cross-dressing. It was called *Salmacis and Hermaphrodite*. Beaumont's version of Salmacis is quite interesting.'

(They looked blank.)

'Salmacis was the nymph of the fountain,' said Sandy. 'The water lady. Any man who bathed in her fountain turned into a woman.'

'Just like Paul Burden's book,' said Ailsa.

'That's right,' said Sandy. 'That's probably why I remembered it. It's a few years ago, now, that piece in the *TLS*.'

'Sometimes,' he said, his face pinched and pale, 'I sit there, in the window of my room over the bay, and I try to write. Words, you know, words. I think that if I sit there and put the words down on the paper, it may happen. Who knows what meaning may spurt and spring, even so late, so late in the day? But I don't even think of myself as a writer now.' He pauses, then finishes.

'Irony is the enemy of small talent,' he says. 'It kills.'

Humphrey was silent with shame, for he had not meant to initiate this miserable confession. He was thinking of his own failures, his own dead ends. The abandoned parathyroid hormone, the dead wrasse. He was thinking of the Green Grotto, that simulacrum and sepulchre of science, into which so much good work had been poured and parodied, where so many creatures had met a confined and miserable death, where the turtle swam round and round in its prison lagoon and the bejewelled mermaid brushed her fibreglass hair. He was thinking of the sham of the Ethics Committee on which he had served, from which he had too late resigned. He wondered if Sandy remembered the death leap of their fish, and if he had dared to use this shameful private knowledge in his wretched nouveau roman.

Ailsa also was still brooding on style. She was not yet ready to relinquish the subject.

'Your mother wasn't much of a stylist,' she informed Sandy aggressively. 'Plain stuff, plain stuff.'

'That was all that was asked of her,' said Sandy. 'And maybe I should have asked less of myself.'

'My style has been the ruin of me,' said Ailsa. 'I used to try to think things through, but now I think I can solve everything with a cheap joke. I think I can jump across any gap with a sound bite or a stunt. That's what the culture had done to me. No, I take that back, that's what I've done to myself.

'Or maybe that's what I've done to the culture. I used to be a serious person, once. I had a serious agenda, before I learned to play the media. Before the media learned to play me. Humphrey, you must try to remember me at my best. In the old days, I had ideas. And we had some good times. Do you remember the *Bride of Abydos*? Do you remember Plato and Darwin and the Blue Lagoon?'

'Forgive and be friends. Forget and forgive,' said Humphrey. 'We are old now. What's done is done. We tried. We all tried, all three of us. We did our best.'

Humphrey saw, as he spoke, a subliminal flash of salmon after mating and spawning: gaunt, crimson, gape-jawed, dying, cartilaginous, scaly, exhausted, upriver, in the stony shallows. The eggs are in the burrows of the pebbles. The adult fish are dying.

The fish return to their spawning ground. They die at the source.

Sandy's face was white and drawn with age and fatigue and thought and effort, but at Humphrey's words he summoned up a spark, and a sudden smile of great encompassing and unexpected sweetness. Humphrey had shown himself to be pure of heart, and therefore Sandy smiled.

'Tomorrow,' said Sandy, 'I can show you the unborn souls as they come leaping and splashing on the incoming tide. I can show you the free souls jumping and splashing. If you come with me, we shall all be born again on the rising tide. It is a miracle. It happens daily. You will have the time, I promise you. I am in charge of the arrangements, and I know the timetable, and I know the tides, and I will be your guide.'

Recessional

In his unfamiliar hotel bed, Humphrey dreamed his familiar dream. He was standing on the beach of a bay, beneath a summer sky, stripped, gazing at the water. He could feel the hard ridges of the rippled sand beneath the arches of his bare feet. The bright illimitable sea lay before him. He walked towards the water, longing and yearning to immerse himself in it, but knowing in his dream that it would recede and drain away as he approached.

But for the first time in his dream life, the water did not retreat from him. He stepped into the waves, disbelieving, and then waded to thigh depth, and then began to swim. But as he began to swim, the frame changed, the time shifted, the air darkened, the water darkened to a steely grey, and a dim fog thickened and smoked upwards from the surface of the water. He was swimming now, freely, in deep water, but there was no longer any shore in sight. He swam round in circles, looking for a sign, but there was no sign, no shore. There was nothing but this circular horizon of greyness and fog, below and above, extending for ever in every direction. He knew that he would swim until he drowned, and that this was the end, and that there was no meaning in it. There was nothing but the unlimited greyness of ocean, and he did not know where land lay. He had lost all sight and hope of land. He would swim in diminishing circles until death. This dream would be his death, and in his sleep he would die.

Along the corridor, Ailsa, in her unfamiliar bed, dreamed an unbidden and unfamiliar dream, a new dream. She dreamed that she was climbing up the exposed outer wall of the bell tower, towards the belfry, on a crumbling and ever-extending and ever-steepening and ever-narrowing stone staircase. Ahead of her and above her climbed another figure, a shrouded female form. She could not identify the figure. Maybe it was her daughter Marina, maybe it was the poor princess, maybe it was the poor princess's aged and ugly big sister, maybe it was Eloise van Dieman. This figure laboured upwards, and Ailsa followed, until the figure came to a projecting overhang, and gripped it from beneath and tried to pull herself over it and up again towards the summit. Ailsa below, hanging on to the crumbling stonework, cried out to her, 'No!' and as she cried out the woman lost her grip, and let go, and began to fall, and Ailsa saw her falling, and saw the fragile skirts of her gown held in a spiralling wind. The figure was suspended for a bloodless crystal instant, and then began to fall like shattering glass, transparent in the air as she plummeted downwards, and a fraction of a second before she was about to spill in fragments upon the earth beneath Ailsa knew that she herself must let go and fall and die, because she could not bear to see and witness the impact and the blood of human death. But she could not force herself to let go, her fingers clung to the stone and to survival, her body wished to clamber on, and by an immense effort of the sleeping will she woke sharply in horror, as dawn came sweeping towards her in a low light over the North Sea. Waking saved her from the impact, and condemned her to live on, a little while.

The Public Orator did not dream and he did not sleep. He worked in the night.

Sandy Clegg slept, for a few brief hours in his narrow bed, but while he slept his shadow self was keeping watch by his bedside. The cowled form of the Public Orator was process-ing the day's events, and anticipating the rising tide of the day.

The first day had been satisfactory. The anachronistically heterosexual couple had played their parts better than had been anticipated. They had not backed away and rejected each other. They had shown a sense of occasion. Dame Mary, their siren muse, had sung them into sentiment, and Ailsa Kelman had wept. (He had seen her tears.) They had accepted the scenario and their allotted roles within it, but they had played it in their different, distinctive styles and come up freely with their own lines. They had touched each other, of their own free will. (He had seen them kiss, he had seen them clasp hands.) And they had accepted Sandy Clegg, and had acknowledged him. They had not forgotten him. They had listened intently to his story.

Sandy Clegg, the writer without words, turned restlessly in his sleep, his hair white on the white pillow, his cheeks sunken, his frail teeth clenched in the rigour of sleep.

The Public Orator watched and waited. Sandy Clegg was not in good health. He was not as robust as his old friend Humphrey.

Ailsa and Humphrey Clark had come up to scratch. So far, they had acquitted themselves with some honour.

The Public Orator had been watching over this couple from a distance as they performed the scripts of their severed lives.

He had followed the trajectory of Humphrey Clark's conventional masculine career, with its appointments and its disappointments, with its leaps and its falls, with its snakes and its ladders. He had watched as Humphrey failed to cope with the challenges, first of dissection, then of microbiology: as he failed to accept the intellectual and financial supremacy of the research institutions of the United States of America. He had watched Humphrey recoil from the larger scene, and resign himself to the smaller tank, the second rank.

(Humphrey had enjoyed the seas off San Diego, but, some years later, he had been deeply depressed and unhappy in the Institute in Massachusetts.) He had witnessed Humphrey's struggles with envy, bitterness, ignominy, paranoia. He had seen Humphrey rub his nose against the smeared glass, and gallantly attempt to preserve his good nature. He had watched the fiasco of Greenwich, the expulsion from Greenwich.

The Public Orator had been a spectator at the colourfully staged tableaux of the career of Ailsa Kelman. He had watched over her vanity, her fallibility, her inconsistency, her relentless restlessness, her vainglorious triumphs, her sensational blunders, her cleverness, her stupidity, her courage, her thoughtlessness, her late-onset humility, her attempts at a truce with herself. He had eavesdropped on her night thoughts, and detected from afar the concealed hurt in the face of her daughter Marina.

What will they do now, these two ageing ill-matched lovers?

They have not been good spouses or good parents. Ailsa has on principle denied the maternal instinct, and Humphrey has weakly allowed his only child to drift away across the ocean. They should have had a child together, but they failed to stick at it. They were genetically well matched, and sexually attracted, but they had ignored the Darwinian imperative.

They had not lived out their marriage, and they had not lived out their parting. Ailsa had behaved both too badly and too well, following the whim of an emergent ideology, and Humphrey had failed to be man enough to resent her vanishing as he should have done. There had been no true ending. They had not succeeded in playing to the full the role of embittered divorcees. They had frozen rather than killed off their connection. They had arrested it. It was in storage. It had been silted up.

This is what makes it fun for the Devil to try to play games with them.

The Public Orator has toyed with the ideas of endings.

Could he ratchet the plot onwards one more notch, by one more turn of the screw? He could ring Tommy Kelman, or P. B. Wilton, or the misogynist daily newspaper which loathes Ailsa Kelman most intensely, and which defames her regularly to within an inch of the law. (When she writes for it, it pays her very well.) He could summon the paparazzi, to inspire Ailsa Kelman to a final spectacle. There is still some mileage left in Ailsa Kelman. Professor Clark is no longer very newsworthy, he is too respectable and too passé, but there are some out there who remember the diving exploits of his youth, when he had swum with sharks. The two of them together would make some kind of a story.

The Devil buys up the stories.

Secret marriage revealed.
Childhood sweethearts reunited.
Celebrity scandal: was the famous foetus Professor Clark's baby?

Words, words. The Public Orator plays with words.

They could remarry, and settle down together as Darby and Joan in the apartment in Regent's Park, or in a little cottage near the river in Chiswick, pooling their resources. They would have a lot to talk about.

> Jack shall have Jill
> Nought shall go ill
> The man shall have his mare again
> And all shall be well.

Sandy Clegg stirs in his sleep. His glasses lie neatly folded on his bedside table, on top of his bedside book. He has been re-reading an old copy of Ballantyne's *The Lifeboat*, which he had bought this spring in the marine section of the antiquarian bookshop in Ornemouth. He and Humphrey Clark had read it fifty years ago, and this may well be the very copy that they had read, the copy that had once belonged to famous swimmer Grandpa Neil of the Merchant Navy. Sandy returns more and more to the books he had read as a boy, as ageing men do. He is looking for something that he cannot find. He had been anxious to re-read the Royal Humane Society's rules for the recovery 'of those who are apparently drowned'. He and Humpy had been enthralled by this dull book. He had hoped to rediscover the secret of its enchantment, but it has fled. It is a very dull book.

The three honorary graduands do not meet for breakfast in the hotel dining room. They are too exhausted. They breakfast alone in their rooms, and meet in the foyer. Dame Mary is thickly layered with theatrical cosmetics, and Ailsa has also done her best to conceal the ravages, but Humphrey is ashen-faced and red-eyed and sagging with lack of sleep. They are all too old for late nights. They look at one another for some moments, unspeaking, appalled, before they pull themselves together and force a social smile of greeting.

A car will pick them up to take them to the robing room in the Town Hall beside the campanile of the medieval bell tower. There they will be dressed in borrowed robes, the scarlet, the green and the black, and foolish dunce-scholar hats will be perched upon their heads.

Humphrey has Mrs Hornby's notes in his breast pocket.

Ailsa is wearing a decorous mid-calf black dress and a silvery necklace of cheap, dull and sullen tin.

Dame Mary is wearing dark glasses with bright purple-pink fuchsia plastic frames. They look jolly with her bristling orange hair.

They are ushered into a black limousine.

Humphrey stands in the cold stone antechamber, lifting his arms obediently like a child so that they can fit him into his gown. He feels Mrs Hornby's fingers pressing on his windpipe, he feels the sore throat of the infirmary bed, he sees the old men in their threadbare pyjamas, he sees his Auntie Vera walking towards him with her anxious smile and her shopping bag. His dream of death is heavy on him.

When he first woke, he thought he had died in the night. He had looked round his hotel room, and had been disappointed with death. A bedside table, a digital clock, a pink folder, a life of Darwin, a coffee tray, a television set, a wardrobe, an empty suit upon a hanger, and some trousers in the trouser press. Death was not up to much. Sandy Clegg was right: Humphrey had clung, like a child, like a coward, to a belief in purpose and meaning. He had clung to a teleological fantasy of a glorious destination, towards which, though with many a wrong turning, he had been slowly treading all his life. But it was not to be so.

They are to file in slow procession up the rising cobbled street, two by two in a crocodile, like schoolchildren on their way to church, or monks from a seminary on a pilgrimage to a shrine. Humphrey is near the front of the line, behind the Visitor and the Vice Chancellor, with Dame Mary at his side: Ailsa and Sandy are to follow. They make their way from the cool shade into the bright sunlight, shuffling and joking and blinking, twitching and hitching at their unfamiliar garments, patting at their precarious and ridiculous headgear. An attempt has been made to remove Dame Mary's sunglasses, which clash violently with the scarlet of her hood, but she has successfully resisted it. She has laughed, protested, used colourful language, and won her point. Humphrey admires her guts.

Dame Mary's chumminess and cheeriness would get you down in the long run, but this isn't the long run. It's shorter than you think.

They set off. Cameras flash. The local press is with them.

As they approach the windows of the Periwinkle Tea Rooms, Dame Mary mutters sotto voce to her escort, 'Are you feeling all right? Bit of an ordeal, last night, don't you think? How's the voice?'

'Better,' grunts Humphrey. 'But the rest of me is worse.'

'I feel like death,' returns Dame Mary gamely. '"Like death warmed up". That's what we used to say at school, when we felt ghastly. This whole charade is a bit like school, isn't it? Our headmistress in Calgary used to wear a gown. She thought she was the bee's knees.'

'I had a dream about death last night,' says Humphrey. 'It was a premonition so strong that when I woke up I thought I'd died for real. I thought I'd died and gone to a very boring place.'

'Well, this bit isn't much fun, but it's better than death, and I'm told there's a very nice lunch waiting.'

'Will you sing at my funeral?' asks Humphrey.

'No, my sweet,' says Dame Mary. 'I shall predecease you. But I'm going to sing at my own. I've got it all arranged and pre-recorded.'

Humphrey laughs, obligingly.

'I'm not joking,' says Dame Mary. 'I sang on my own *Desert Island Discs* and I intend to sing at my own death. And on, and on, for ever. They'll never be able to shut me up. I'm on the hard disc of time. They've sent my voice to Titan. Do I mean Titan? One of those moons.'

'What will you be singing at your funeral?'

'Oh, various heart-rending laments. I haven't quite made the final selection. *"Never weatherbeaten sail more willing bent* to shore". It's a madrigal. Do you know it? *"Never tired pilgrim's soul affected slumber more . . ."* It's very affecting.'

It is so affecting, even when delivered in this spirit, that Humphrey's foolish old dog's eyes fill with tears.

'Come on, old boy,' says Dame Mary. 'Nearly there. These cobbles are hell. I should have worn flatties, like Ailsa.'

As she speaks, she slips, and stumbles. Humphrey grabs at her, and she hangs on to his arm.

'Shit,' she says. 'I've turned my fucking ankle.'

She hops, and lurches, and giggles, and regains her balance. He has to support her up the rest of the hill. She clings to him. He finds this comforting.

'So your friend Sandy,' she says, when she has recovered herself, 'is going to deliver the orations. I thought he said quite enough last night. He can't have much more up his sleeve, can he?'

She glances behind her, as she speaks, but Sandy, in his deeply sleeved and pocketed purple and lilac doctoral gown, is deep in conversation with Ailsa Kelman.

'I met your friend Sandy,' says Dame Mary, 'at this gay soirée in Earls Court. Do you want to hear about it?'

Humphrey shakes his head, but she tells him just the same.

Ahead of them, the Vice Chancellor and the Visitor are talking about university top-up fees and foreign student intake.

Behind them, Sandy and Ailsa are talking in erudite but impassioned tones about Beaumont and Fletcher and gender and sexuality during the Renaissance. They are talking nineteen to the dozen. Ailsa can hardly believe that she has wasted so much time not knowing Sandy Macfarlane Clegg, and reproaches him for his many years of delay in reintroducing himself to her. To think of the programmes they might have made together, the sparkling flow of books on which they might have collaborated! Mass Observation, gender studies,

Eloise van Dieman and the Theatre of Cruelty, feminism and the Liberation Movement in Algeria, *Last Year in Marienbad* and the seaside resorts of the north-east coast . . . the leaps, the conjunctions, the discoveries!

'I didn't think you'd want to hear from me,' says Sandy coyly. 'You're a star, you're a celebrity. I didn't think you would want to hear from a nonentity like me.'

Ailsa groans.

'Don't talk crap,' she says scornfully, in the tones of the old Ailsa.

Dame Mary, ahead of them, is limping. Sandy and Ailsa moderate their pace.

'You kept in touch with Tommy,' says Ailsa. 'Why did you keep in touch with him? He's the celebrity, not me.'

As they parade slowly up the cobbled street, Sandy Clegg outlines the nature of his shady and somewhat compromising acquaintance with her brother Tommy. Ailsa's eyes pop out of her head.

'No!' she protests. 'Not really! He's supposed to be a married man.'

'Worry not,' says Sandy, in his old-fashioned parlance. 'All shall be redeemed. All shall be reborn. At the stroke of the evening bell, an hour before high tide, we shall all receive new souls.'

'I've brought my bathing suit,' says Ailsa gaily. 'I've got it in my handbag.'

And so the long hot day unfolded, the long and ghostly academic day of mumbled honours and rolled scrolls and illuminated letters and Gothic script and gowned students and Latin tags and fulsome speeches and newly minted rituals and ancient music. The students taking their first degrees looked very, very young. Ailsa, sitting primly exposed on the platform with her spine straight and her knees clamped politely and tightly together (*posture, Ailsa, posture*) watched their fresh and spotted and smooth and shining faces, their Nordic and European and Asian and African and Japanese features, and longed to be young again. Multi-ethnic were the students of Britain, even in faraway out-on-a-limb Ornemouth, and varied and modern and strangely combined and aggregated were the many modules of their degrees. Some of them, improbably, seemed to have been learning Swahili: others had been studying the science of sport. From Caledonia and the Caucasus they came, from Seoul and Yokohama, from Sri Lanka and Senegal and Suffolk, from Portpatrick and Pakistan and Peterborough. This was the new wave of gender and racial equality and equal opportunity which she had seen emerging, the coming of which she had applauded and analysed, and which would now leave her far behind as it rolled on towards an unimaginable future in which she would play no part. Up to the platform they marched, the young ones, one after another, in a roll-call of honour, to the tattered and occasionally swelling applause of parents, to the catcalls of peers and classmates, in black gowns that only partially concealed an eclectic array of dress: there were skirts of every possible length and colour, and trousers of many variegated fabrics, and a few tartan kilts, some affected by students not evidently of Scottish origin. Nobody was seen to be wearing jeans, so jeans must have been banned, but the footwear, unlike the clothes, observed a remarkable degree of uniformity, in that nearly all these new graduates and some of the postgraduates were wearing versions of the globally dominant and ubiquitous training shoe. To their owners these shoes were sharply differentiated by price and label and signification, but to the platform party they all looked much the same. Uniform, reflected the sociologist in Ailsa, reflects a deep need, and expresses itself in odd ways.

Ailsa suddenly remembered one of her fellow-judges at the Plunkett Prize, distinguished and conspicuous amongst the evening's glamorous revellers in her grey business suit and her shockingly clean white and pale blue Nike trainers. She remembered, in the same memory flash, that odd caption about the dense aggregations of solitary sea squirts, and told herself that she must ask Humphrey what this paradox meant. How can you be solitary and thickly clustered at the same time? And damn it, she must remember to text her daughter Marina about meeting for supper at the weekend. She'd forgotten yet again. She thought of writing a message to herself in ballpoint on the back of her hand, but reluctantly decided it wouldn't look good.

She hadn't been able to get to Marina's graduation ceremony. She'd been filming viewer-response to *The Massacre of Chios* in the Louvre, and couldn't get back in time. Marina had assured her it didn't matter, but maybe it had mattered.

On and on they came, the novitiates, each following each, to accept their scrolls, some stumbling, some smirking, some shy, some eager, some scornful, some with limp handshakes and some with firm, some making eye contact and some with a gaze aimed firmly at the floor. From the round world's imagined corners they came, and Sandy Clegg announced the name of each and every one of them, with an unhesitating and well-rehearsed command of the pronunciation of many languages. Each one of them was recorded in the annals, each name was inscribed in the book.

In the old days of childhood, Ornemouth had been homogenous and monochrome, its populace as undisturbed as the gene pool of the fish in the Pool of Brochan, but the presence of the university had changed all that. Currents were flowing in freshly from new directions, and the species were mixing and mingling.

At the end of the procession, Sandy in his role as Orator would pronounce the eulogia of the honorary graduands, and after that, Humphrey Clark would deliver his short speech of thanks and his words of exhortation.

Sandy betrayed no bodily sign that he had been up late, drunk deep, summoned up the ghosts of his past, and relived his entire life in a short span. His pallor was an everyday, habitual pallor, and he hid behind its mask. He was a good performer.

So was Dame Mary, who hid behind her shades and her expensive face powder and gave nothing away. Her ankle hurt, but so what? She knew how to be stoical in front of an audience. She was an old trouper, with decades of practice, accustomed to larger stages than this.

Humphrey was less successful in concealing stress. His head was sore, his throat was sore, and Dame Mary's gallantries had not dispelled his sense of premonition. But he knew he couldn't die here, in public, on a platform. He wanted to go home to die, in private, and the sooner the better. He was ready to throw in the sponge. He'd get through this ordeal, as best he could, and then he'd make his escape. Mrs Hornby could deal with the paperwork: she'd know where to find it. She knew his phobias and the contents of his pigeonholes. She knew where he'd filed his will.

He tried to sit upright and to attention, but he was conscious that he wasn't looking his best. He wished he'd written his little speech out on his laptop, and printed it out with large letters and spacing, instead of relying on the inspiration of the moment. He did not feel inspired, he felt overwhelmed. He was going to stutter and stumble. He would have liked to have been able to say something encouraging to these youngsters, and to tell them to avoid all the mistakes he'd made, but he was past it. The words would not come. And the prospect of sitting through Sandy's no doubt ironic and covertly malicious peroration of praise was humiliating.

He was feeling surreptitiously for Mrs Hornby's jottings when he became aware that Ailsa, sitting next to him on the front row of the platform, was trying to catch his attention. She had been fishing around noisily in her handbag for a pen and a scrap of paper, and now she successfully managed to pass him a note, as though they were in the back row of the classroom, not perched up here for all of Ornemouth to behold. His instinct was to stuff it into his pocket, but the expression on her face was both appealing and supportive, so he glanced down to see what she had written. Her message was banal, but it did the trick.

'Cheer up, chin up, perk up, Hump,' she had scribbled. 'We'll all do better next time round. Ever, ever, ever, Ailsa.'

Despite himself, it made him smile.

The Public Orator's appreciations of the two honorary ladies were elegant, witty and discreet. He gave away no secrets and he told no lies. Some of what he said was in Latin, so perhaps some hidden meanings lurked under the cover of an ancient tongue, but if they did, nobody spotted them. The congregation sat in docile silence, as he gave a résumé of the dazzling and triumphal careers, first of Ailsa Kelman, then of Dame Mary. Each had to stand to attention to receive the accolade, and neither flinched, though Dame Mary was seen to shift her considerable weight from foot to foot and to make the odd comical sympathy-seeking grimace.

Humphrey's citation came last, and as he stood to face it he was observed to look a little weary, quizzical, self-deprecating, perhaps even dejected.

The Public Orator stuck, for the most part, to the public domain. But in his last paragraph he paid tribute to Professor

Clark's aunt, Miss Neil, the much-loved one-time teacher at the village school of Finsterness.

'The word *Finsterness*,' said the Public Orator, in summation, 'suggests, as some of you will know, *Darkness*. In the German language, *Die Finsternis* means darkness, obscurity or gloom. And Humphrey Clark was here as a child during the darkness and gloom of the Second World War. But to the children of Finsterness, it was a place of light and learning. The children played upon the shore, in sight of the immortal sea. And to Humphrey Clark's scholarship, inspired by these early years, we owe a sense of wonder, indeed of immortality. He taught us that, though inland far we be, we may yet see the children sport upon the shore. We yet may hope to hear the mighty waters rolling evermore. We welcome him home.'

Professor Clark was visibly moved by these words, as he lurched towards the lectern to give his response.

Many of the Orator's words were borrowed from Wordsworth, and Professor Clark knew them well.

Sandy Clegg would have given his right arm to be able to write words like those. He would have sawn it off himself with a hacksaw. But to write them, you have to feel them. To write them, you have to be pure of heart. To write them, you have to believe them.

Professor Clark was looking dishevelled: his gown was hanging unevenly, his cap was lopsided. He held a scruffy little wad of handwritten notes which he deposited upon the lectern. He cleared his throat, coughed, and began to speak. As he ran through the preliminary courtesies (Your Grace, Your Eminence, lords, ladies, gentlemen, fellow-graduates and honorary graduates) one of his scraps of paper detached itself and drifted on to the floor, to land at the feet of the Vice Chancellor. Humphrey gestured helplessly after it and let it lie.

He paused, at the end of his list of titles and arcane honorifics, and coughed again, and began again. He had decided to go for it. Ailsa, watching him, gave a silent cheer.

'Ladies and gentlemen,' he repeated, 'this is a very moving experience for me. I stand here before you in the presence of my oldest friend and my first love.'

He coughed again, lost his nerve, riffled through his scrappy bits of paper, and started off at a tangent.

The audience, or those members of it who were bothering to listen at all, was confused. Some were paying little heed, absorbed in private contemplation of private matters: they had not even attempted to identify the uninteresting grey-haired old scarecrows on the podium. Some were wondering who this blundering old fool was, and why he had been asked to speak, instead of that television celebrity, Ailsa Kelman, who would have made a much better job of it. ('*He shouldn't have been allowed,*' hissed one indignant local mother to her sister, in the second-to-back row. '*Maundering on about cats and goldfish and the girl next door, what's he on about?*') Others looked nervously at their watches, and thought of their lunch. One or two listened with a keener attention, wondering how he would follow up his opening salvo.

Nobody, not even the speaker, could follow the tangled thread. Humphrey Clark was aware that he was in the grip of that recurrent nightmare of public figures: the nightmare of talking nonsense on a public stage.

Ailsa was wondering at what point she should deploy her long presentational experience to intervene and wind him up when he seemed, suddenly, to pull himself together.

'And so,' he said, with a more-than-welcome note of finality, 'in conclusion, I would like to wish to all of you young people a free, happy, and adventurous future, in your chosen professions. And on behalf of Dame Mary McTaggart, my wife Ailsa

Kelman, and myself, I would like to thank this innovative new university for the honour it has bestowed upon us. This is a numinous place, and it has been good for the spirit to return to the source.'

And he sat down, wiping his brow, pocketing his notes and adjusting his gown, to polite applause.

Most of the congregation was so relieved that the ceremony had come to an end that they did not even notice that he had claimed Ailsa Kelman as his wife. A few who did notice assumed it was bizarre wishful thinking or a slip of the tongue. Had not the unmarried Secretary of State Condoleeza Rice on a recent occasion even more strangely referred to President George W. Bush of the United States as her husband? People who talk too much in public get muddled: sometimes there's a Freudian explanation, sometimes there isn't.

Sandy Macfarlane Clegg, Mary McTaggart and Ailsa Kelman sat on their chairs like statues, smiling fixed smiles, until the music for the grand recessional began to swell forth from the orchestra in the musicians' gallery.

Then they rose to their feet, and they receded.

The Public Orator was satisfied with his grand finale.

Sandy Clegg has promised them rebirth and redemption with the incoming tide. They accompany their confessor, obediently, in the full encircling light of the early summer evening. Dame Mary has wished to be excused, pleading exhaustion and her twisted ankle, and Sandy has allowed her to retire. Her supporting role is over, and she is on her way home, on the five-forty train to King's Cross and St Vincent's Wharf and the remains of her own life.

Sandy drives Humphrey and Ailsa down to the little beach of the Victorian tidal bathing pool, to the beach that had been inexplicably forbidden during their childhood. He parks his nondescript car in a scruffy little unofficial car park on an uneven patch of dry earth surrounded by a joyously, irrepressibly springing scrub of yellow and purple wild flowers and bushes. He leads them through a little wooden wicket gate, towards the path and the steps that descend, through a tunnelled archway, to the hidden cove.

The cove is nearly empty, for it is late in the day, and most of its visitors have gone home for their tea. An elderly woman sits in a deckchair, in a severely upholstered black and white cotton floral sunsuit, with a towel on her head, her large and muscular reddish-brown shoulders naked to the sun, reading a book. A stout young couple in jeans stand arm in arm on the edge of the rocks, on a sloping shelf of seaweed-covered slate, gazing out to sea. A young mother joggles a mewing infant in a pushchair. A clutch of diehard children are gathered together on the southern bank, in their swimsuits, waiting on the brink.

It is a small communion of the few. They are all waiting for the incoming tide.

The pool is formed by an arc of rocks, which reaches across and encloses the little bay, forming an irregular circle. It is a bridge of natural rock, its breaches reinforced here and there by small artificial boulders of cement and aggregate. Notices warn children and the elderly not to venture on to the pool wall.

Another notice informs them that 129, 602 tides have flowed in and out of this bay since the archway approach was built.

It does not seem to be very many.

'What happens now?' asks Ailsa.

'We wait,' says Sandy.

They sit, in a row, on a rock, and wait.

The calm unruffled water level in the sheltered pool is low, and the barrier of the pool wall looks, from this angle, high.

Beyond the wall, the more animated surface of the sea extends to the horizon, broken here and there by the jagged peaks of rocks. The light is strong. They can measure the rise of the tide by its level as it creeps up the rocks. It seems to move imperceptibly slowly, and yet it moves. At first Ailsa and Humphrey wonder if Sandy has mistimed his miracle, and brought them here too early, but after initial moments of doubt they grow calm and peaceful and trusting as they wait, for they can see that the sea will come.

It has been a journey of purification.

After a while, the sea beyond the low and stony wall grows brighter, and is seen to flow faster and more strongly. Currents display themselves and sparkle in ripples and eddies and flurries. The three friends are watching now to see where the water will make its first leap across the wall. Sandy has said that the point of entry varies, slightly, with the direction of the wind. This is a calm evening.

The surface beyond the brink gathers and swells and rises, like mounting tears.

And then it breaks. First, a solitary little spurt of seawater bravely splashes over, in a tiny low cleft to the left, and this is followed by a trickle, which becomes a stream, and then a little waterfall. To the right, another spot is breached, and the water begins to gush more continuously, here and there, on both sides, making its way over the wall, more and more rapidly, gathering momentum, gathering power, until the whole semicircle is pouring with descending glittering threads and cascades of running rushing water. The music of the waters grows louder as the water level within the bay rises to meet and mingle with the incoming sea, and, as it rises, the little knot of waiting children darts forth, and runs along the flowing almost-underwater barrier. The little ones hurl themselves from it, one after another, into the pool. They swim, they leap out again, they run along the wall again, they plunge in again. One of them produces a small red and yellow inflatable raft, on which, breast down, he breaches the rapids. He floats, climbs out, drags out his raft, pulls it along the wall, descends again, is reborn again. He repeats, and repeats, and repeats, and will go on until the waters meet and are one and are level and there is no more waterfall.

It is a scene of hilarity, of purification, of endless fun.

The children are brave and skinny, they are the new souls, each time they leap they gain a life. They splash and jump and pipe and squeal with joy.

Ailsa cries out in delight.

'It's like the Zambesi! It's like Niagara!' she cries.

The old woman in the deckchair lays down her book, rises up, and advances slowly on the pool. She walks into the water and joins the little souls and swims amongst them with stately strokes, her head held high.

Ailsa, seeing this, cannot restrain herself. She cannot resist.

She tears off her clothes, exposing her puckered ageing thighs and her triangle of grey wire hair and her sagging breasts to the evening light, and squeezes herself clumsily into the bathing suit she has been carrying around with her all day. She sheds her garments and abandons them with Humphrey and Sandy on the rock, and she runs into the water. Only the mad swim in the North Sea, but the sea is in her blood, and her salt blood meets the salt water. She gasps, she splashes, she strikes out, she waves to shore, and she flounders. She disports herself amidst the warmer shallows, which are forever renewed by the cold wash of the incoming main.

As Humphrey watches her antics, it comes to him that forgiveness need not be maintained in time. It may come in an instant, like grace. It need not endure. One may be redeemed in an instant. Repentance needs only an instant, a measurement too small to show on the clock face. They have forgiven one another, for this instant, and that will suffice.

The Final Curtain and the Last Tableau

Dame Mary sings at her own memorial service, as she had threatened to do, and the gay world lines up to hear her and to salute her as she bids it an operatic and posthumous farewell. Her ashes will be scattered in the Thames and snapped at by disappointed fishes, but her voice lives on.

The formalities are properly observed.

Professor Humphrey Clark, in the third pew back, is wearing a dark suit with a sombre dark green Marine Society tie. Next to him stands Sandy Macfarlane Clegg, whose paler tie is striped with pink and silver.

Ailsa Kelman, in the middle of the front row, is dressed in steel-grey and charcoal. Next to her stands her brother Tommy Kelman. His expression of affected solemnity is extremely irritating to Ailsa, and as he starts to bray out the words 'Blest are the pure in heart' she digs him in the shoulder with her elbow and tells him to shut up. He never could sing in tune, and she hates this pious hymn. She can't think why Mary had wanted it. It is hardly appropriate.

Martin Pope is not there.

Marina Pope is sitting near the back, with her partner, wearing a black cloth coat and a neat black hat. Her partner's navy blue hat is broad-brimmed, and adorned with a saffron feather.

P. B. Wilton, an old hand at memorials, sits in the back row, making notes.

It is midwinter. The church is cold. It warms itself, a little, from the bodies and the blood and the breath of the people, and from the sounds that run through the veins of its stones.

Dame Mary had been planning her obsequies for many months, ever since the fatal diagnosis. She had made one or two late alterations, in the light of her late-flowering friendship with Ailsa and her daughter, both of whom had been attentive during her last months. Ailsa is scheduled to read one of the lessons.

So Humphrey Clark and Ailsa Kelman are not even sitting in the same row, notes P. B. Wilton. The reconciliation has not been a full-blooded affair. But there is still time for further developments. Not much time, but a little. P. B. is a sentimental romantic at heart, like many sadistic gossips and voyeurs, and he wishes Humphrey and Ailsa to get together again. It would be more fun for him that way.

The presence of Marina is surely promising.

P. B. Wilton does not recognize Sandy Clegg, in any of his impersonations.

The hymn draws to a sonorous conclusion. The congregation, despite its complement of professional singers, has rendered it very badly.

Ailsa, who has been waiting impatiently and nervously for her moment of glory in the public eye, rises to her feet, and strides towards the pulpit. She mounts the worn stone steps. She straightens her shoulders, and opens her text at the marker, and she begins to read.

It is a familiar text, a text for all seasons, and it ends with a dying fall. She reads it with unfeigned emotion. Her voice echoes and vibrates through the stones of the ancient nave and rises up to beat and flutter against the stained and jewelled and toughened glass of the high windows.

The words are seeking the air.

Vanity, saith the Orator, all is vanity. All the rivers run into the sea, yet the sea is not full. Unto the place whence the rivers come, thither they return again, Vanity, saith the Preacher, all is Vanity.

Remember now thy Creator in the days of thy youth, while the evil days come not, nor the years draw nigh when thou shalt say, I have no pleasure in them.

For then the keepers of the house shall tremble, and all the daughters of music shall be brought low.

Ailsa replaces the dark blue satin ribbon bookmark in its place in the Book of Ecclesiastes, and closes the thick wad of the gilt-edged Bible. She lays her hand in farewell on its womb-heavy cool leather binding. She has read the lines well, and without stumbling, but there is no applause, for this is not a theatrical performance. She looks out, over the congregation, and her gaze seeks Humphrey Clark. At first she cannot locate him, amidst the silent and attentive ranks, but there he is, looking upwards towards her. He inclines his head, very slightly, towards her, in recognition. He smiles, in support and approbation. She has done well. She begins her spiral descent from the pulpit. She treads carefully, clutching the polished brass handrail. It would not be good to slip now. Her ankles are not as reliable as they were when she was young. She feels the weakness of the many little bones, the intricate frailty of the joints. She finds it easier to walk up stairs than to walk down them. Although she has renewed herself in the waters of youth, the relentless approach of age has not been arrested.

Humphrey watches her, as she slowly picks her way down, step by step. He is thinking that he will ask her to dine with him one day soon at the Dolphin, for old times' sake. It is too late, now, to become a specialist in the songbirds of Britain. He will never solve Riemann's hypothesis, and he will not hear the music of the prime numbers. He will continue like a guilty thief to avoid any reference to the parathyroid hormones of fish. But there is still time for a comforting dinner at the Dolphin, where he had first stretched out his hand towards her, and seen a glimpse of the long journey ahead of them. The journey draws to its end, but it is not over yet.

The Public Orator watches. His role is over, his part is played. From his perch in the gallery he watches Sandy Clegg, his shadow self. Sandy's face is drawn and dry with suffering. The dry point of the needle of suffering has etched itself in lines and wrinkles into his fine pale skin. The Public Orator cannot alleviate Sandy's suffering. He is powerless. There are no more words. Sandy has freed Ailsa and Humphrey, but himself he cannot free. Sandy is not a coward, and he does not look for comfort. This is the way of it. Sandy hears the echoes of the words of the Preacher, as they spiral upwards, and waste themselves in the empty air.

Acknowledgements

I would like to thank the Royal Society for inviting me to be one of the judges of the Aventis Science Book Prize for 2003, a task which I enjoyed so much that it prompted me to attempt a novel with a man of science as its protagonist. I would also like to thank Dr Geoffrey Potts, who talked to me about marine biology and diving, and made me wish I were young enough to learn to dive myself. Elaine Morgan's books on the Aquatic Ape hypothesis have been a joy and an inspiration to me. I have taken some poetic licence with the names of fish, though in the underwater realm nothing seems impossible, and some of the strangest things are true. Any mistakes about marine biology and evolution are, of course, mine alone, and all the characters, both scientific and unscientific, are wholly fictitious.